C000130155

Spire Publishing

www.spirepublishing.com

Anne of Almondbury

Patricia Robson

Spire Publishing
www.spirepublishing.com

First published in Great Britain 2004 by Patricia Robson.
This edition first published in Canada 2007 by Spire Publishing.
Spire Publishing is a trademark of Adlibbed Ltd.

*Note to Librarians: A cataloguing record for this book is available from the Library and
Archives Canada. Visit www.collectionscanada.ca/amicus/index-e.html*

Designed in Toronto, Canada, by Adlibbed Ltd.
Set in Baskerville and Baskerville Italics.

Cover Illustration:
Portrait of Anne from an original painting by Caroline Robson.
View of Catterstones, at the foot of Castle Hill, in the nineteenth century.

Printed and bound in the US or the UK
by Lightningsource Ltd.

ISBN: 1-897312-53-9

Spire Publishing
www.spirepublishing.com

*To my husband, family and friends,
with gratitude
for their love and encouragement.*

CHAPTER ONE

With heart thudding, Anne hurried along the path to the front door. Grasping the heavy iron door-knocker, she lifted it up a little way before letting it drop. There was no response. Please, please come to the door, begged Anne silently. I can do nothing until then.

The second time she raised the knocker higher, thrusting it down firmly so that the impact sent vibrations through her arm. Pressing her face against the glass panel in the door, she could see a faint light inside. Still no-one answered. Her desperation became tinged with anger. Why didn't someone come? She had seen him only yesterday. He must be here, surely, at such a time?

Finally, she seized the knocker, now warm from her touch, and began hammering it against its striking-plate, making the door shudder at every blow. Then, above her, she heard the sound of a sash window being lifted. Backing away from the door, she looked up. An old servant-woman was leaning out, scowling at her.

"Stop that!" she shouted.

"Where is the vicar?" cried Anne. "He promised to come when it was time."

"He's not here!"

"When will he be back?" called Anne, her voice cracking with emotion.

"He didn't say. He's gone. They've all gone – vicar, wife, children, all of 'em."

"Where?"

The woman glared down at her.

"Away," she snapped.

"But the funeral must be tomorrow! It has to be!"

For answer, the woman pulled back and slammed the window shut with such force that the glass shivered in its frame.

Alone in the vicarage garden, with the light fading, Anne stood motionless, staring at the upstairs window, willing the woman to return and the vicar to appear, although she knew it was hopeless. Eventually she faced the fact that little else could be done that night and turned towards home. With all urgency gone, she realised how tired she was but trudged on, her boots scraping on the paving stones.

It was damp and chilly as spring evenings could be, with a mist coming off the river and hanging low over the rooftops. Anne pulled her shawl tighter around her. The London streets were strangely deserted. A cab rumbled past, blinds down.

Somewhere close by, Anne heard a child crying. The sound seemed to unlock something deep inside her. She stopped, feeling the grief pushing its way up through her chest until it burst out in great racking sobs that shook her violently. When the spasm had passed, she trailed on, wearier than ever.

She thought of her mother, now free of the dreadful disease, lying at peace. Anne had stripped the bed of its sheets and taken them to the bottom of the garden, dousing them in paraffin before setting them alight. All this had been done automatically, almost without feeling. Then it had flooded back over her, impelling her to find the vicar, someone who could provide the only consolation of any meaning for her.

When she came to the house, she went down the area steps carefully, holding her skirts to one side. Without taking off her bonnet and shawl, she lit the oil lamp and carried it through into the room beyond.

The shock took Anne's breath away. Her mother's body was gone. Not just removed, but snatched – the quilt was rumpled as if the body had been lifted off in haste. With an effort, pulling herself together, she extinguished the lamp and ran back up the steps as fast as she could.

The door to the basement of the adjoining house opened as she approached. The pinched, anxious face of her Irish neighbour appeared.

"They've taken her, Miss Anne. Not an hour ago."

"Who? Where? Did they say?"

"Yes, to be sure. The parish men. To Old Hackney Church. The one they don't use any more."

Anne was away immediately. She ran along the street and then, out of breath, forced herself to walk before giving way to the urge to run once again.

As she hurried along, she became more and more angry. How dare they take her mother's body in her absence? It was only hours since the doctor had called to certify cause of death. She had promised to do as he said, to bury her mother without delay. Indeed, that had been the purpose of her fruitless visit to the vicarage.

Suddenly she found herself at the gate of the old church. Her mind had been so full that she had not realised how far she had come. Nor had she noticed how the darkness had crept up on her nor how the fog had thickened. She picked her way through the nettles and dockweed, led by the sound of a spade hitting earth, to the derelict churchyard beyond.

Out of the greyness loomed figures of men, the lower part of their faces muffled with scarves and rags. Rough torches had been lit to illuminate the work; they sparked and spluttered their grease onto the exposed earth. The men moved slowly and wordlessly, carrying the flimsy shells that served as makeshift coffins. As they lowered them into a mass grave, others were digging to make more room for those still to come.

Anne stumbled forward over the rough ground, her shawl pulled up over her face. Even so, her nostrils were full of the stench of burning tar. The smell made her feel sick but it was as nothing compared to the sense of outrage within her.

"Who is in charge here?" She spoke with such vehemence that the workman blinked and said nothing. She repeated her question, this time more quietly.

The man, wrapped in dirty sacking, pointed to another who stood close by, supervising the work. Anne touched him on the elbow. He turned, the whites of his eyes startling in his grimy face. Anne made an effort to sound reasonable; she needed his co-operation.

"Pardon me, your men collected my mother's body – Emma Graham, from Victoria Park, no more than an hour ago."

The man did not respond.

"Can you find her for me, please? I wish her to have a proper Christian burial, not go to her grave without any funeral service."

The man did not reply at once. For the first time, Anne noticed a cart, standing near the stone tower.

"The curate comes every morning. He says funeral prayers for all we buried the day before." His tone declared the matter closed.

As Anne hesitated, she saw two men approach the cart and begin to unload its unhappy freight.

"Where does the curate live?" she asked. As she spoke, she pressed a shilling into the man's hand. "I would be grateful if you would tell me."

The man paused while he fingered the coin and then walked slowly over to the cart. One man raised a torch while he inspected the names chalked on the coffins. He returned.

"We've found your mother."

Anne gasped but before she could say anything, he spoke again.

"But you can't take her away. We've strict orders to bury them directly - all them that have died of the cholera."

It was the first time the word had been uttered. Anne looked round wildly. Behind them was the dark shape of Old Hackney Church, long shut up and deserted.

"Could she be taken in there?"

The man pondered. Anne judged it was time for another precious shilling.

It took two men and their crowbars to prise open the great oak doors. Inside, it was gritty underfoot and smelt of damp and dry rot. But the moon was filtering through the high windows. In the dimness, the altar could just be made out.

At Anne's direction, her mother's coffin was carried along the aisle and laid at the altar steps. Then she hurried out of the churchyard and up to the presbytery nearby.

Her ringing of the bell brought an elderly housekeeper who admitted her without question. An inner door opened and a young priest emerged – thin, serious-looking. Anne was relieved. She felt he would understand. And she had only sixpence left.

"Good evening, Father."

"Good evening, my child. What can I do for you?"

"It is my mother, sir. She has died suddenly. Our own vicar is away and I wish her to have a Church of England burial service."

"I am afraid my time for services is already reserved by mourners all this week."

"It has to be now." Anne was aware of speaking rudely but she did not care.

"Your mother has died of the cholera?"

"Yes."

"Then I am sure you will understand the sense of the arrangements made by the parish – the burial of the victims within twenty-four hours. Prayers are said, each morning, at interment."

"Yes, yes, I know. But it is not the same. Not what she expected. What is right."

The priest hesitated.

"Where is she now?"

"They have carried her into the old church."

"It is many years since that church was used."

Anne met his gaze steadily.

"But it is still a holy place."

He looked at her face. Whatever he saw there decided him.

"Very well. If you will wait while I fetch my stole and prayer-book."

He followed her out into the night. Entering the church, he picked his way carefully up the aisle. Anne stood beside her mother's coffin while he ascended the altar steps.

"I am the Resurrection and the Life, saith the Lord : he that believeth in me, though he were dead, yet shall he live : and whosoever liveth and believeth in me shall never die."

Anne, head bent, felt the tears well up in her eyes and brim over. But inside she was calm, thankful that what her mother would have wanted, and deserved, had come to pass.

The young curate's voice gained strength. He did not need light to see the prayer-book; he knew these words only too well, saying them so often this year throughout the cholera epidemic.

"Therefore my beloved brethren, be ye steadfast, unmoveable, always abounding in the work of the Lord, forasmuch as ye know that your labour is not in vain in the Lord."

He stopped. Anne raised her head.

"After this come the prayers at interment, when the body is laid to rest in the earth. I shall speak those words at dawn when your mother will lie among a company of souls. Will you trust me to see her buried in this way tomorrow?"

"Yes, thank you, Father. I am at peace now. Thank you again."

She moved forward and put the sixpence near his hand. He took it without taking his eyes from her face.

"Thank you. I will put this in the offertory and pray for her tonight."

Once outside, Anne waited until she saw her mother's coffin laid alongside the others at the far end of the churchyard. Only then did she leave and begin her walk back to Victoria Park.

It was the only place she could ever remember as her home. But for how long would it be her home now? Her mother had lived and worked there for almost twenty years as cook-housekeeper to a lawyer, Mr Pearson. At the moment, he was away at his son's house in Kent, leaving London as soon as the dreaded word "cholera" was out, like all those who could afford to.

No doubt that was the reason for the vicar's disappearance, thought Anne. A gentle, kindly man, he would not have been able to resist his domineering wife if she had decided that they, and their numerous children, should flee the capital at this time.

Anne sat for a long time in her mother's chair, as the oil in the lamp burnt low and the room grew dark. A week ago, her mother had been alive and going about her work with her usual energy. All the neighbourhood knew that the cholera was stalking only a few streets away. Anne prayed that they would escape the infection. However, she had reckoned without her mother's compassionate nature. When she heard of the suffering of a young woman in Bethnal Green who attended the same church, her mother had gone at once to give what help she could.

"Just imagine, Anne," she had said, removing her bonnet, her face drawn and pale, "the dreadful purging of the mother and the helpless children, all six of them, sent to stand at the bottom of the garden out of the way of the infection, the youngest a mere baby, the eldest no more than ten, I swear."

Early next morning, Anne and her mother had attended the woman again. In the evening, her mother had laid out the corpse while Anne searched for relatives to take the children in and avoid the workhouse.

Compassion cost them dear. Within a day or two, the fever had taken hold of her mother. Now she lay helpless as the disease raged. She had died shortly afterwards, her daughter at her side.

Grieving, Anne felt terribly alone. She had never known her father who had died before she was born. All she knew of any relatives was what her mother had told her, of the village in Yorkshire where she had grown up and where her mother's younger sister Agnes still lived with her husband and children.

"We shall go there some day," her mother had said. "A visit, in the summer when the weather is kinder. I would love to see the hills and valleys again – there's no better sight anywhere! To stand on top of Castle Hill on a sunny day with the wind taking your breath away! All your troubles vanish – your mind seems washed clean. Nothing but the wind and the great sky, and down at your feet, the green valleys."

But they had never managed to make the journey north together, two hundred miles from London. Now it was too late.

Rousing herself, Anne re-filled the lamp. In its pool of light, she forced herself to write letters to the two people who needed to be told of her mother's death – her aunt, Agnes Stott, and her mother's employer, Mr Pearson.

Her task completed, she sat gazing at the addressed envelopes. What now for her? Her temporary post at the Church School had come to an end but she had heard a rumour there was a permanent position coming up. She would see about it tomorrow.

Suddenly a great wave of exhaustion swept over her, leaving her trembling with weakness. She was grateful for it. It helped her to return to the double bed she had shared with her mother and ignore, for a moment, the emptiness by her side.

The Church School was the tallest building in the street, its brick gables poking up above the soot-grimed rooftops of the neighbouring houses. As she approached, Anne felt cheered by the sounds of children at play behind the encircling walls – a roaring, irregular noise of shouts and cries, full of life.

When she came to the head teacher's office, two boys were leaving. One spat on his red palms nonchalantly and sauntered off. Anne was distressed to see the other, near to tears, cross his arms and press his hands into his armpits in an effort to soothe them. She wanted to hug him but he dodged away, as if sensing her impulse.

The head teacher stood just inside the door, a tall, angular man, his moustache strangely sandy against his greying hair. Anne had never liked his harshness with the children. She did not like him now as he laid the cane along the front of his desk so that it was exactly parallel with the edge. It made her shiver.

"May I have a word with you, Mr Erskine?"

He nodded and indicated that Anne should sit down. He then sat down himself, elbows on the arms of his chair, resting his fingertips together.

Anne felt very uncomfortable. The man's pale-eyed, unblinking stare did not put her at her ease. There seemed to be a degree of interest in his look but it was without warmth.

"You may know – I have to tell you that my mother died yesterday."

It was not how she meant to begin.

"What I wanted to say was that I should be very grateful if you felt you could recommend me to the Governors for a permanent teaching position here."

The words came out too fast. She felt her cheeks go pink with confusion. She wanted so much to sound mature and in control of herself.

Erskine said nothing but simply stared at her. She tried again.

"I hope you were satisfied with my work. You may remember I was a pupil teacher with Mr Smith and took the Infants' class when Miss Jones was ill."

"You said your mother had died?"

"Yes."

"Will you continue to live in the house where she was employed, I believe, as housekeeper?"

What had that to do with anything? Anne was puzzled. Anyone else, surely, would have first offered their condolences on the death of her mother?

"The rooms will be taken over by the new housekeeper, I imagine. At present Mr Pearson is away in the country and unlikely to return until the epidemic is over."

Erskine's eyes flickered. Anne found it hard to fathom what was going through his mind. Was he perhaps thinking she had been too lenient with her infant pupils? She had certainly never sent any of them to him to be caned. Nor would she. Ever. But he said nothing, merely kept looking at her, his eyes dropping from her face to her body, right down to her ankles. She did not like the feeling it gave her, of being intruded upon.

Finally he spoke.

"It is not my decision, of course. It is, as you say, a matter for the Governors. But still, my recommendation will carry considerable weight."

His face altered. Anne realised he was attempting a smile. It did not suit him. She stood up and smoothed the front of her skirt. Erskine's pale eyes slid downwards again.

"Thank you, Mr Erskine. If you could recommend me, I should be most grateful. If possible, before very long."

As she moved away, Erskine uncoiled his considerable height and was suddenly beside her.

"Good day, Miss Graham. And my condolences, of course." He had her hand in his. The feeling was not pleasant and she freed herself as soon as politeness allowed.

Back home, she visited her next-door neighbour and told them of her mother's burial. The Irish woman, a Catholic, approved Anne's conduct.

"Ye did a grand job, getting the priest. Just pity the poor souls dying every day! Don't forget. Any time ye need a bit o' company. Or help. Just bang on the chimney back and Dooley will be round directly."

She cocked her head towards her husband, a big man more often out of work than in, who nodded and continued sucking on his pipe.

It seemed to have grown dark very quickly. Anne drew the curtains. During the day, she liked seeing the feet and legs of passers-by from the basement room. It was chilly so she lit a fire, now uncomfortably aware that she must be careful not to use too much coal.

Lifting out the drawer where her mother had kept all her correspondence, she began sorting through it. A wave of grieving love swept over her as she touched the papers; the memory of her mother sitting at the table writing was painfully vivid. Among the few letters were two from Agnes in Yorkshire, announcing the births of her children, Ned and Sarah. Anne kept looking and reading. Amongst the notes and bills, there was no sign of what Anne really wanted to find – information about her father, Arthur Graham. No postcard, letter, keepsake, nothing. There was not even a marriage certificate.

Anne's curiosity was aroused. Why was there nothing, nothing at all? It was as if he had never existed. She remembered that her mother had always seemed reluctant to talk about her late husband. Apparently, he had been a military bandsman who had died less than a year after their marriage. Beyond that, she would say nothing. Anne had always supposed that his untimely death was too painful a subject to revisit. She had never pressed her mother further, out of concern for her feelings.

But that did not stop her wondering. She looked in the glass now, over the mantelpiece. How did she resemble him? Her wavy auburn hair and pale skin could be traced to her mother but her eyes were blue, unlike her mother's hazel brown. Was it from him she inherited her wide forehead? If only there was a likeness of him!

The fire had almost gone out. Seizing the poker, she prised it between the coals, sending a fresh spurt of flame up the chimney. Watching it, she did not see the man coming down the area steps and approaching the door. The knock made her jump.

Opening the door cautiously, she was surprised to see her visitor.

"Mr Erskine!"

"Forgive the late hour, Miss Graham."

Without waiting to be invited, the head teacher, a tall, thin figure in his black coat, pushed past her and walked in. Anne was nonplussed. Could it be good news about the teaching post, so soon after her meeting with him? Seeming strangely excited, he said nothing but gave her his odd, unfamiliar smile. Anne fought down the first sensations of alarm.

"What is it, Mr Erskine? Have you some news for me?"

"News? News? Oh yes, news," he muttered.

To her horror, Anne realised he had been drinking. He swayed slightly and as he came closer, she smelt the spirits on his breath. Before she could move away, he leant forward and grasped her shoulders with a grip that was unexpectedly, frighteningly strong. Terrified, she gave a cry and pulled away, desperate to get the table between them.

"What is the matter, Miss Graham? Or can I call you Anne? Don't you know I'm your friend?" He moved round the table. So did Anne, her heart starting to thud with terror. She could hardly believe this was happening.

"Don't move away, Anne. I've always liked you. Don't you know I've always liked you?"

A foolish smile spread across the man's face and he hiccuped slightly. If I can only keep him talking, thought Anne, calm him down, get him to the door. But her heart was racing by now and she could feel the sweat breaking out on her body.

"Yes, Mr Erskine. Thank you," she said, speaking as calmly as she could. "Have you come to tell me something? Can it wait until tomorrow when I can come to the school again?"

Perhaps the reference to school would bring him to his senses. But he appeared not to have heard her. He rubbed the back of his hand across his mouth, leaving his lips slack beneath the wet, sandy moustache.

"Always liked you, Anne. Always liked you," he mumbled, fixing her with a look that was supposedly affectionate.

Anne found him both ridiculous and repulsive. Speaking as sternly as she could and holding onto the edge of the table in order to still her trembling, she said loudly, "Mr Erskine! I must ask you to go! Please leave now!"

"What? What?"

Unfortunately, her words seemed to have the opposite effect. Glaring at her, he suddenly lunged forward and with a force that took her completely by surprise, he flung the table on its side and threw himself on her so that they fell heavily to the floor. Frantic now, Anne struggled beneath the weight of his body, twisting and turning with all her might to get out from under him. Thrashing about with her arms, her right hand fell on the smooth, warm handle of the poker which still protruded from the fire. Fighting away from him, she managed to scramble to her feet, dragging the poker out of the fire as she did so.

"Get out! Get out!" she screamed.

Undeterred, he came on. As he raised his arm, Anne, without quite knowing what she did, struck his coat sleeve with the red, glowing end of the poker and held it there. The black cloth shrivelled instantly, baring the white cotton lining inside and filling the room with the acrid smell of burning.

Anne stared at the burn, transfixed with shock. Erskine too was stunned. But she was the first to recover. Leaping to the fireplace, she faced him, brandishing the poker again.

"Get out or I'll call my neighbour. He'll do more than singe your coat!"

She was amazed to hear the strength of her voice. Inside she was quivering violently. Cursing, not meeting her eyes, Erskine left, throwing the door open so roughly that it slammed against the wall.

Anne locked and bolted the door with trembling fingers and made sure all the windows were secure. She made herself some weak tea but could not settle to drink it until she had got up and checked all the locks and bolts again. She wondered whether to go round to her neighbours and tell them what had happened but decided against it. For one thing, she would have to unlock the door and then return to an empty house. She would have to learn how to stand on her own feet, be strong, whatever happened. She put her cup back on its saucer and was pleased to note it had stopped rattling. See, she was calm now.

Feeling herself cold, she fetched the eiderdown from her bed and wrapped herself in it as she sat by the fire. She was not quite ready to get undressed for bed yet. She would just sit for a while. Just for a while.

"How old are you?"

"Eighteen."

"And no experience of being a governess?"

The narrow-eyed woman in the dusty black dress spoke sneeringly. As if I am nothing, thought Anne. But I will not be humiliated. I know I can do this if I am given the chance.

"No," she admitted, "but I have taught young children. In the local Church School."

Before she could continue, the woman lifted her head and sniffed.

"No experience with people of quality then."

Anne felt herself go hot. She wanted to defend her young pupils, but perhaps this was not the moment. With an effort, she held her tongue.

For all its high-sounding title, the Sackville Agency for Educational Employment was nothing but a poky office above a pie-and-eel shop in the Kingsland Road. As Anne opened the door from the street and began to mount the worn stairs, the reek of fish was unmistakable. Her hopefulness wilted.

"You have references, I assume?"

"No, not yet. But I am awaiting one from the Church School Governors."

"Anyone else? Vicar?"

"No. My vicar and his family are away at present. But when –"

The woman curled her lip.

"No experience and no references. I don't know what you expect."

Anne drew herself up, her face flaming.

"I will return when I have a reference."

The woman made no attempt to answer. Anne felt bound to close the interview if the other would not.

"Good day. And thank you for your help."

The woman looked up, startled, as Anne left the room.

Despite the mildness of the spring day, Anne felt cold. It was not going to be easy to find employment. She walked on unseeingly until suddenly, there was a commotion ahead. She saw she had taken a wrong turning and blundered into a narrow street, now filling up alarmingly with a noisy, jostling throng.

The centre of interest proved to be a fight between two women. Repulsed, Anne tried to back away but found her way blocked by a surge of people all pushing forward to glimpse the spectacle and forming a tight ring around the contenders.

The two women had progressed from catcalling to fisticuffs and were now brawling in the ugly, clumsy manner of amateurs. Their hair was down and their clothing torn. The younger of the two threw herself at the other and with a shriek, clawed at her shoulders. As she pulled back, there was a ripping sound as the bodice gave way, exposing the woman's pendulous breast with its large brown nipple and areola. At this, the crowd became even more excited, shouting and screaming.

Anne was crushed up against a man whose face was contorted with what looked like pleasurable venom. Sickened, she pulled away and, crouching down, pushed herself head first out of the scrum of bodies.

She had freed herself from the crowd and was starting to hurry away when there was a retching sound close by. A drunken man lying at the side of the street had vomited close to her feet. He rolled over on to his back and their eyes met – his, staring and bloodshot in a swollen, purple face. Pulling her skirts away in disgust, Anne fled, only slowing down when the streets became familiar once more.

Anne received two letters the next day. The first was a brief note from Mr Pearson's son in Kent. He expressed his father's condolences but added that Mr Pearson, being in poor health, had decided to retire immediately from his profession. He would not be returning to the house in Victoria Park which had now been put up for sale. In the circumstances, he hoped she would quit the premises by the end of the month, a date only ten days hence.

Anne felt hollow at the news. It would be a wrench to leave. Where would she go?

The second letter was from the Church School Governors. It dashed two of Anne's hopes simultaneously. First, there was no possibility of a permanent post at the school. It had already been filled. Secondly, and here the language was less direct, it would not be possible to provide Anne with a reference relating to her previous, temporary employment at the school.

"Not possible?" Anne went hot with fury. Of course it was possible. She knew her work had been satisfactory. There could be only one explanation – Erskine, the headmaster, had said something against her, had destroyed her good name with some invented slur. It was not difficult to guess his motive. If only her mother had been here! Anne bit her lip to keep back the tears. She knew very well what her mother's reaction would have been. She would have insisted on seeing the Chairman of the Governors and giving him her version of the situation. Few people could withstand her mother when she was fired by a sense of injustice.

But she was not here – and never would be. Anne had never felt so alone. She felt like a boat which had lost its mast, rudder and all. How was she going to cope on her own?

Her eyes misted with tears and she lifted the hem of her apron to wipe them. As she did so, she glanced down and, to her horror, saw a smear of vomit on the hem of her skirt. Nauseated, she leapt up instantly, poured water into a bowl and began sponging the garment vigorously. But she still found it repellent and with hands quivering, she pulled off her dress and underskirt.

Standing there in her chemise, Anne suddenly felt a desperate yearning to get away from the East End, from its teeming streets, its drunkards, whores and beggars and the still-present threat of the cholera. What had her mother said about Castle Hill? "Your mind seems washed clean." There, in that Yorkshire village, she had family, even though she had never met them – an aunt, an uncle and two cousins near her own age.

How to get there? Yorkshire seemed like the end of the earth to Anne, who had never been out of London in her life nor travelled on a railway train. Then her mother's voice again – "Fifteen shillings and a halfpenny, Anne. That's how much it costs to get to Wakefield. Never mind, we'll keep saving and one day, we'll both go."

Feverish now with excitement, Anne emptied her purse, the jug on the mantelpiece, the tin at the back of the drawer. In total, a couple of shillings – scarcely enough to keep her warm and fed until the end of the month. But all these years, her mother *had* been saving, Anne was sure of it. She had never given up her plan to visit Yorkshire and she was a practical woman, not a dreamer. Somewhere in these rooms were her mother's savings, her Yorkshire money.

Frantically, Anne began pulling out drawers, rooting in cupboards, looking under the mattress. Nothing! But she must find the money! It had suddenly become the most, the only, important thing in her life. Redoubling her efforts, she went on searching, this time, more thoroughly, until in a flash, it came to her – the memory of a rug being lifted and her mother bending over it. She flew into the bedroom and threw back the rug. There, sure enough, was a loose floorboard and under it, a small bag of coins.

Aware that this might decide her fate, once and for all, Anne lifted out the bag with trembling hands, up-ended it and shook the coins out onto the floor where they rolled and settled. With heart beating fast, she counted them – one, two, three...

Taking a deep, necessary, breath, she sat back on her heels. She could do it. There was just enough to get her to Yorkshire. How to get back, if she needed to, she did not know. She'd find a way somehow. Of one thing she was sure, however. It was what her mother would have wanted.

CHAPTER TWO

"It's the best thing you could be doing, my dear. Going to claim kin, the best thing, to be sure."

Anne was not so convinced, despite Mrs Dooley's assurance. The excitement she had felt when she wrote to her aunt for the second time, announcing her intended journey to Yorkshire, was fading fast. True, there had been a condolences card from Agnes which had crossed this letter in the post but after that, complete silence.

Anne's hopeful anticipation turned to anxiety as the end of the month, and her tenancy, approached. Could her second letter have got lost? Or worse, did her aunt and uncle want nothing to do with her? Perhaps they feared she was planning to foist herself on them as a poor relation. Anne's cheeks burned with embarrassment at the thought. Had she made it clear enough that this was just a visit? As she remembered the money, her spirits sank even lower. It was true. She *was* a poor relation. And if there was no work for her in Yorkshire, what then? She would be forced to beg for some money to get her back to London. It was too shameful. Whatever had she been thinking of – announcing her arrival before being invited?

But there was no turning back now. After a tearful farewell from Mrs Dooley, Anne set off for Kings Cross station the next morning, carrying a large cloth bag and a wooden box bound with twine. Hackney Road and Old Street were already swarming with life, the air filled with the noise of horses' hooves and the trundling of cart wheels, the shouts of tradesmen unloading goods, rolling barrels, teasing and abusing passers-by in equal measure. She clasped her belongings tight as street-sellers pressed up close to her while ragged urchins clung to her skirts, begging to carry her luggage for a farthing.

Anne had never been inside a railway station before. The nearest thing to it, she thought, must be a church, or rather, a cathedral, with its vast, soaring roof and sense of grandeur. Clouds of steam rose into the vaulted space overhead while below, the great engines crouched, momentarily at rest, before their next excursion northward. Anne felt a thrill of excited pride as she made her way towards the express train to Edinburgh.

This was an experience to be relished whatever the outcome. A piercing whistle, a wave of a green flag and they were off! Soon the outskirts of London were left behind. The train gathered speed once it was out in open country, settling into a steady, monotonous rhythm as it forged its way through towns, villages and miles upon miles of fields and farmland.

The day wore on. Sometimes, weary of her book, Anne felt as if they would never get there. After changing trains at Doncaster, she reached Wakefield, where she climbed down the steps and felt, for the first time that day, stiff and weary from travelling.

But there was one more stage to go – a journey by road coach to Huddersfield. A railway porter told her the name of the inn yard where the coach would be waiting and pointed the way. Anne set off, nervously aware of the strangers on the streets as she passed them. Once she took a wrong turn and found herself in a dead end, a foul-smelling courtyard from which she fled, pursued by a barking dog and a mouthful of unintelligible abuse from a blowsy woman on a doorstep.

At last she found the inn and the coach drawn up outside. On the box sat an old coachman in a long travelling coat and a hat pulled down over his ears.

"Pardon me," said Anne. "Is this the coach for Huddersfield?"

The man looked at her but said nothing. Anne repeated her question.

"Aye."

"Please can you set me down as near as possible to Almondbury? It's a village this side of Huddersfield."

She might have been speaking a foreign language for all the response she got. The man stared at her blankly.

"Almondbury. Almondbury," she said slowly. "Near Huddersfield."

Suddenly the man's face cleared.

"Tha' means Aimbry, lass!" he declared.

Anne was happy to agree that she did. Climbing into the coach, she met her travelling companions – a distinguished-looking man, who read his papers as long as the light lasted, and a stout, older woman with a small grand-daughter about four years old. They heard the flick of a whip, the words "Walk on!" and the coach began to trundle over the cobbled streets of Wakefield.

It was warm and stuffy inside the carriage. Anne, in her mourning clothes, was hot. So was the child, who pulled off her bonnet and cape despite her grandmother's words. As it grew darker outside and there was nothing to see from the window, the child became bored. With a yawn, she threw herself across Anne's lap and after a couple of twitches, fell asleep. Her grandmother made a move to lift her off but Anne indicated she was quite happy as things were. They both looked down at the child who lay still, her curls clinging damply to her flushed cheeks.

Soon the grandmother was nodding herself. The gentleman removed his pince-nez, rubbed the bridge of his nose and closed his eyes. The coach rumbled on. Anne strove to keep awake in case she missed her destination. Once she reached the village church, she would know how to find the farm from what her mother had told her.

What would she discover there? A friendly family, glad to see a relative they had never met? But if that were the case, why had no-one replied to her letter and extended some kind of welcome? Perhaps they wanted nothing to do with her, in fact, resented her effrontery in assuming a right to a place in their home? If so, how would they show it? Anne shivered. An image flashed into her mind, of herself knocking on a door, to no avail. As she had done at the vicarage, on the day her mother died.

Suddenly, the carriage swung violently to one side and jolted to an abrupt halt. The swerve flung Anne forward onto her companions, throwing the sleeping child to the floor where she awoke and began to cry. Outside, the terrified neighing of horses was followed by angry voices. Opening the door with difficulty, Anne clambered out.

It took a moment for her eyes to focus in the darkness. Then she saw the coachman, alternately calming his horses and shouting over his shoulder at a woman on horseback whose sudden appearance from a side road had apparently forced the coach to swerve. His fury, coupled with a broad dialect, made it difficult for Anne to understand him. Not so the rider who screamed back, then, leaping down from her horse, rushed at him, whip raised.

Anne sprang forward, appalled.

"Stop! Stop! What are you doing?" she cried.

The woman spun round. For a moment, it seemed as if the lash of the whip might fall on Anne's shoulders. Unflinching, Anne stood her ground. The woman, taller than her, dark and dressed in a riding habit, glared at her.

"Keep out of this!" she sneered. "This is none of your business."

"Is that so?" retorted Anne. "Stopping you whipping a coachman is my business. What kind of woman are you?"

"What? What?" The woman almost spat at Anne. Her large front teeth glinted in the moonlight.

"What right have you to whip a man who's only doing his job? He knows the road – he travels along it every day. It's probably your fault."

"How dare you speak to me like that!" the woman shouted.

"I dare because a child may be hurt. She has been thrown to the floor by the sudden stop."

"So – ?" said the woman, insolently.

Anne was furious. The callousness of the woman!

"So you ought to care! Or do you only think of yourself?"

The woman seemed lost for an answer. Instead, she turned away with a dismissive snort and addressed the coachman roughly.

"As for you, you doddering old fool! You're not fit to drive this coach. Next time, stay awake and watch where you're going. If you're sober enough."

With that, she swung herself back into the saddle, wheeled about and cantered off. Muttering, the driver turned to his horses again and checked their legs for injury. Fortunately, there appeared to be no damage. One of the wheels had gone into the roadside ditch but was soon righted once the driver urged the horses forward gently.

Inside the carriage, all was well, the child shocked but unhurt. The grandmother tutted.

"Nasty temper, that one."

"Still, no great harm done, I think," said the gentleman, who had got out to look.

They resumed their journey without delay. Anne felt slightly dizzy. Perhaps it was the shock of the recent encounter, at the end of a long day. And it was a long time since she had eaten anything. What an unpleasant woman! She didn't regret what she had said to her. What could she have been doing riding out alone at night? And so fast that she had nearly collided with a coach which bore lamps at the front and back? Yawning, Anne found herself fighting against the tide of sleep that threatened to overwhelm her. The other passengers were nodding, unable to resist the swaying of the carriage and the regular sound of the horses' hooves on the road.

The driver's sudden rapping of his whip against the side of the coach startled them all.

"Aimbry! Stop for Aimbry!"

Bidding goodbye to the other travellers, Anne climbed out. Her box dropped from the roof of the coach with a thud on the stony ground.

"Here y' are, lass!" said the driver gruffly but not unkindly. "Follow yon lane for about half a mile. You can't miss t' village."

With a slapping of the reins, he drove off, leaving Anne alone with her belongings in near-total darkness. She watched the coach disappear, the light of the lamps dwindling to pinpoints. She had never felt so friendless.

Anne shivered. There was a sickly feeling in the pit of her stomach. If she were to be attacked and killed by footpads here, who would know – or care? She stood still, straining her eyes to see all she could in the dark. There was no living soul in sight nor any habitation. All was quiet save for the faint rustling of night creatures in the woods which bordered the lane.

There was nowhere to go but forward, whatever Almondbury or the Stott farm had in store for her. If her Aunt Agnes was anything like her mother, then all would be well. Even with this attempt to cheer herself up, Anne could not stop herself wishing she were two hundred miles south and knocking on Mrs Dooley's door for company.

The silence was like nothing she had ever experienced before – thick and oppressive. Picking up her wooden box, with her bag in the other hand, Anne began walking. Her luggage was heavier than it had seemed when she started out. Sometimes she stumbled, twisting her ankles on the rutted, uneven surface of the lane, and was forced to stop and rest.

She was now so exhausted that time and time again she felt tempted to simply lie down and sleep. But something kept her going. Eventually, after toiling up a steep lane, the moon emerged from behind clouds and revealed the centre of the village – a church, a fine old building opposite, some cottages and a public house from which muffled shouts emerged.

Passing in front of the church, Anne began to trudge up yet another slope, the twine around her box now cutting painfully into her fingers. A small group of rough-looking young men, who were lolling against a wall, fell silent and stared at her. Fearful of provoking them in any way, Anne dropped her eyes and quickened her pace to get past them.

She was about ten yards further ahead when she suddenly felt a thud of something heavy between her shoulders. It was a clod of earth. Surprised but not fearful, she stopped and turned, only to meet a volley of stones. One of them struck her sharply on the cheek. Shock was greater than pain, however. As she stood, more stones followed, one a sizeable rock that hit her on the knee.

Anne could scarcely believe this was happening. Disbelief and a sense of outrage banished her faint-heartedness in a flash. How dare they? What had she done to deserve this? Dropping her box to the ground, her hands found some of the missiles. She could see her attackers dimly now so she hurled two of the stones at them as hard as she could. There came yells, curses of some kind and, worst of all, laughter. She barely had time to consider what her next move should be when another young man appeared and threw himself at the youths.

"What do you think you're doing, yer daft buggers?"

He struck one of them so hard that he fell heavily onto his back with a groan. Fists up, the newcomer challenged the others.

"Come on then! Who's next?"

Swearing and grumbling, the others clumped away, their iron-shod clogs ringing on the cobbles.

Anne's defender came towards her, wiping his hands, which were bloodied, against his jacket.

"Are ye hurt, lass?"

"No, not really. Thank you for helping me."

He seemed embarrassed.

"They want a good hiding. A young lass, out on her own. Where are you bound?"

"I'm looking for Stotts' farm. Agnes Stott is my aunt."

"Right," he said, picking up her box as if it weighed nothing. "I'll take you there, in case them buggers – those fools trouble you again."

They set off, side by side. The road began to rise steeply. Anne was finding it hard to breathe.

"Hilly. Again," she ventured.

"Aye, it's all hills and valleys hereabouts."

The clouds moved away from the moon. The young man was tall, dark-haired and plainly dressed, not a gentleman but not a ruffian either. When he spoke again, there was a warmth in his tone that Anne found very appealing.

"You'll be tired and hungry, I warrant. How long have you been travelling?"

"Since early this morning. From London."

As she spoke, her strength seemed to leave her and she stumbled. His arm was around her waist instantly and then, just as quickly, withdrawn.

"Here, take my arm. It'll help you."

As Anne slipped her arm through his and felt the warmth of his body through the woollen cloth, she experienced a strong sense of security, a feeling she could not remember ever having had before. It felt not just good but natural, how it ought to be. For the first time that day, she did not wish the journey to end.

They did not speak again for a while but walked on, the man fitting his stride to her shorter steps for which Anne was grateful. As they reached the top of the hill, he spoke.

"This is Broken Cross. The Stotts' farm is down there." He pointed down to the right.

"Thank you. I can manage now."

He remonstrated.

"Nay, I'll come wi' you. This box is heavy enough."

They began their way down the hill. Anne's legs suddenly felt very weak. She did not want to let go of this young man and have to face the unknown Stott family. But the moment of separation from him grew nearer with every step.

The farmhouse and its buildings were long and low and completely dark except for one lighted window downstairs. As they walked up a pebbled path to the door, Anne could see her companion more clearly. She saw him steal a quick glance at her too, making her heart beat faster. Putting her box down on the path, he began to back away.

"Well, I'll be off now."

Wanting to hold him there a little longer, she took his hand, a firm, warm hand.

"Thank you again. I'm afraid I don't know your name."

"John. John Brook."

For the first time, their eyes met. The moonlight illuminated a strong face with dark, expressive eyes and a full, curving mouth which looked both aggressive and vulnerable at the same time. Anne knew it was a face she could love.

"I am Anne Graham. Emma Ramsden's daughter. She was Agnes Stott's elder sister."

She saw him register her use of the past tense.

"I'm very sorry," he said gently. "Is it recent? Your mother's death?"

"Yes," said Anne, feeling the grief begin to well up again. "About two weeks ago."

"Then," he said, putting his arm round her shoulders, "we must get you inside. With your kinfolk."

Stepping up to the farmhouse door, he gave it a solid thumping.

To Anne's dismay, the response was not the swift opening of the door but a more unpleasant one. Suddenly, as if from nowhere, two dogs rushed towards them, one barking loudly, the other, more terrifying, crouching low and making little runs towards their legs, snapping and snarling as it did so.

Anne was really frightened. Instinctively, she cried out and clung to John Brook in her terror.

"Nay," he said calmly. "They're only doing their job. Don't be afeard."

But she could not control her trembling. The next moment, he had bent forward and lifted her up bodily so that she was completely out of the dogs' reach. Cradled against him, with his arms clasping her round the waist and under the knees, she pressed her face against his throat and wished that everything would disappear, except for her and John Brook.

At that moment, however, the door opened a little and a woman appeared. Her voice was timid, hesitant.

"Who's there?"

Anne lifted her head. Even in the gloom, there was no doubt that this was her mother's sister. Reluctantly, she slid down from John's grasp.

"It is Anne. Anne Graham. Is that you, Aunt Agnes?"

"Yes, yes," replied the woman. "Can you come in quickly? I don't want to wake your uncle."

There was nothing Anne could do except part from her protector. Before she stepped inside, she turned to him once more.

"I hope we shall meet again, Mr Brook?"

"Yes indeed. Perhaps at church?"

"Oh yes," said Anne, joy flowing through her at the thought that this man was not lost to her for ever. "Oh yes, I'm sure we shall. Thank you. Good night."

"Goodnight, Miss Graham. Mrs Stott."

As he moved away, he spoke calmly to the dogs who, quiet now, wagged their tails and followed him out on to the road.

The woman backed away as Anne entered the low-ceilinged farmhouse kitchen. There was no sense of welcome.

"Aunt Agnes? I hope you will forgive my coming like this. I do not wish to be a burden and will leave if it is not convenient."

"What? Oh no, not at all. I'm glad to see you."

Her aunt's behaviour belied her words. She stood with her back to the kitchen range, nervously twisting her apron between her fingers. She seemed to be frightened of something or someone. Anne could see her quite clearly now in the lamplight – the same slim build as her mother, the faded auburn hair. Like my mother, she thought. In looks but not in spirit.

Her aunt's arm jerked towards a chair.

"Sit down, do. Will you have something? A bit o' bread and cheese? Some milk?"

"Thank you. A drink of milk would be very nice."

Her aunt seemed glad to have something to do. Putting a mug of milk in front of Anne, she spoke more confidently.

"Your cousin Sarah has been in bed these two hours. You'll see her tomorrow when she gets in from the mill. Ned is still out but should be in soon."

And what of your husband, my uncle, thought Anne, sipping the milk. Why do you not mention him? Is he the reason you did not answer my letter?

Her aunt hesitated.

"I was very sad to hear of our Emma's death. She was no age. She was always right kind to me. I was grieved, we all were, when she went off to London all them years ago."

"I see," said Anne, who knew very little about this phase of her mother's life.

"Did she – did you have anyone to help you at the end? Would a doctor come?"

"Yes, but he said there was no treatment for the disease. The parish men came and took her. They wanted to bury all the cholera victims rightaway. But she was properly buried at Hackney Church."

Anne stopped, choked with the memory of those dreadful last days, her mother wasting away before her eyes, ravaged by the fever, the relief when all suffering stopped, the unbearable sense of loss which followed it. Reaching for her handkerchief, she blew her nose in an attempt to prevent the tears coming. Her face felt painfully tender as she did so, reminding her of the reception she had received at the hands of the village youths.

At that moment the back door was flung, or perhaps kicked, open and a young man of about twenty lurched in. With a shock, Anne saw, as he moved into the lamplight, that he bore a bruise on his cheekbone, as fresh as hers but bigger and more livid. This must be one of her attackers, one she had hit with a stone or who had been struck by John Brook. It had to be. A sense of fearful uncertainty gripped her.

"Ned," said his mother, "this is your cousin Anne. Come from London."

Anne murmured a greeting. It was not returned. Ned was too busy negotiating his way round the kitchen, holding on to the backs of chairs for support, cramming a chunk of cheese into his mouth. Clumsy, drunken lout, thought Anne, her fear changing to contempt.

"You'll be wanting your bed," her aunt said. "I'm afraid you'll have to share Sarah's. Her room is over this one. Shall Ned carry your box up?"

"No, thank you, I can manage," replied Anne firmly. She had already decided to keep that particular cousin at arm's length. From now on, she would not trust him with anything – not even her luggage.

Anne woke in the dark and, for a frightening second or two, could not think where she was. Someone was moving about slowly in the room. There was a slight rustle of clothing and then, as the door was opened, she glimpsed a young girl, head lowered, stumbling out.

Realising it was her cousin Sarah going to work, Anne rolled over to the middle of the bed, feeling the warmth left by the other body. Burying her face in the pillow, she met a strange, oily smell, one she could not place. Meaning to rise in a few minutes, she fell into another deep sleep.

When she woke again, sunlight was leaking round the edges of the shutters. Dressing quickly, she went downstairs and found her aunt sweeping the stone-flagged floor.

"Good morning, Aunt. I seem to have slept long. What time is it?" It was eleven, mid-morning. "Goodness! I don't think I have ever slept so late. Please forgive me," she said, mortified in case her aunt thought this was how she meant to go on, getting up late like a lady while everyone else had been at work for three hours or more.

"Never heed, lass." Having put the rag rugs back on the floor, her aunt fetched bread and butter and began to brew some tea.

"My uncle and cousin Ned – ?"

"They'll be in soon. For their dinner."

While Anne ate, her aunt stood at the table opposite her, wrapped in a large apron, kneading bread dough in a crock. She seemed reluctant to meet Anne's eyes.

Anne said nothing, though still puzzled by the situation, and concentrated on eating her breakfast. In the daylight she could see how small the farm kitchen was, dominated by the black range with its open fire and two oven doors alongside. Only now did she notice a curtained alcove in the corner.

Her aunt saw the direction of her gaze.

"Ned sleeps there."

"Oh, I see!"

"We've just the two bedrooms upstairs. Next door, you'll see when you go out, there's a small cottage adjoining. Jack's mother lives there."

Anne thought she understood. There was really no room for a guest, certainly for any length of time. Perhaps that was the reason for her aunt's uneasiness which showed no sign of disappearing.

"Your uncle –" Agnes's words were interrupted by the gruff sound of men's voices outside. She flinched, wiped her hands clean of the dough and swiftly set about laying the table with thick plates and cutlery.

The door was pushed open with such violence that Anne jumped. Jack Stott entered, continuing to shout over his shoulder to a man outside. She understood not a word of what he said but its abusive tone was unmistakable.

He came in, a lean, wiry man, his thin mouth twisted into a sneer, obviously still angry.

"Well, he can go if he's a mind to, th' idle bugger!"

No-one spoke. Rubbing his hands down the sides of his trousers, he sat down at the table. Anne watched in amazement as Agnes produced a mug of ale almost as he did so, putting it just where his right hand could lift it without stretching.

"So you're Emma Ramsden's child." His stare was intimidating, the eyes fierce with hostility.

Anne was aware of her aunt, hovering behind him nervously.

"Yes," replied Anne. She had no objection to being addressed in this way, by her mother's maiden name. It was probably how she was still known. She returned his look, her eyes steady. "I'm pleased to meet you – Uncle."

He responded with a grunt, bending his head to the steaming plate of vegetable stew which Agnes had slid in front of him. Anne saw that he had left a trail of mud from the door to the table.

The door opened and closed again with another bang. This time it was her cousin Ned who joined his father at the table and began eating noisily, tearing off a hunk of bread and mopping up his broth with it.

Anne stole a glance at him. He was not bad-looking, brown-haired and blue-eyed, and lacked his father's thin lips. Then he looked up at her, eating with his mouth open, and she saw the broken and blackened front teeth. The bruise on his cheek was less swollen and turning blue. He kept on looking at her, unabashed, then turned his attention to wiping his plate with the bread and sucking it.

Jack picked at his teeth with a thumb nail, fixing her with an unpleasant stare as he did so.

"How long are ye thinking of staying?" Out of the corner of her eye, Anne saw her aunt lower her head, as if ashamed.

What a brute, thought Anne. Not a word about her mother's death. But she would meet his ill manners with courtesy. After all, she was an uninvited guest.

"Three or four weeks – if that is all right," she replied. When he did not answer, her pride made her say, "I should be happy to pay for my board and lodging."

Her aunt intervened, her face flushing as she spoke.

"We won't hear of it! The idea! Emma's daughter! After all this time!"

There was silence. Jack said nothing. Ned grinned unpleasantly. Agnes's colour was still high.

"Thank you, Aunt. I should be very grateful to be a guest for a while. If I could find a teaching position, I would take it straightaway."

Jack laughed mirthlessly.

"Reckon you've come to t' wrong place for that kind of work. There's not much of that hereabouts. More in London, I would say."

His wife protested.

"We can't be sure. I've told Sarah to ask about."

Jack gave Agnes a withering glance as if he thought she was an idiot. Anne was distressed to see how affected her aunt was by her husband's treatment of her. The older woman's colour rose again and she shrank back, like an animal that had been kicked.

When the men returned to their work, the atmosphere eased. Anne showed herself ready to help Agnes with any of the household tasks, clearing away, washing up, collecting the eggs from the hen-house. She was pleased to feel her aunt relax in her company.

In the afternoon they sat companionably together with tea and oatcake. Agnes brought out a drawing of her mother, Emma, as a girl, holding a lamb in her arms, standing in front of the farmhouse.

"A sketcher came to the door one day and showed us portraits he'd made. It was Emma's birthday and she begged for a portrait as a present. So Father agreed."

Anne was moved.

"It would be lovely to have it framed," she said, gazing at it. Her mother looked so happy.

To her surprise, Agnes took the drawing from her and put it back in its folder.

"You wouldn't like it framed?" asked Anne, disappointed and curious.

"I would but your uncle wouldn't." Her aunt looked embarrassed. "It's perhaps hard for you to understand, Anne. Farmers can be ...their feeling for land is very strong. Jack knows that Father wanted Emma to have the farm, to marry the man he'd picked for her and stay here. But she wouldn't. She went to London with the Crowthers. She was always very determined."

Anne recognised the description.

"So what happened then?"

"Well, nothing. Father was very angry, very cold. He wouldn't answer her letters from London. Then he fell ill. He had to rely on his farm-workers entirely. One of them was Jack."

Now Anne understood.

"And Jack married you. When your father died, it became your farm."

"*His* farm." Agnes's tone was icy. For the first time, Anne saw a flicker of self-assertion in her aunt. She liked her the better for it.

The men returned in the late afternoon and after a hearty tea, cleaned themselves up and left the house.

With their departure, the sense of freedom was palpable. As they washed the dishes together, Anne told her aunt of Mr Erskine's attempted assault. In the telling, it became farcical. The two women were still laughing when Sarah came home from the mill.

Anne immediately felt a pang when she saw her. The girl looked worn-out and fell exhausted into a chair. But sympathy was the last thing she wanted. When Anne began to offer it, the girl bridled.

"It's same for everybody. And I like to earn my own brass."

When Agnes made fresh tea, Sarah sat and drank a pint mug of it.

"Thirsty work. In t' mill." Then she went upstairs, carrying a jug of water.

"This is for your benefit," whispered Agnes. "She doesn't always bother."

When Sarah re-appeared, she looked much better. She had washed herself, put on a clean blouse and skirt and brushed her hair, which was reddish in hue, although not the same colour as Anne's. She returned to the only comfortable chair in the kitchen.

Anne could feel Sarah's gaze on her, taking in every detail, from the brooch at her throat down to her neatly laced-up boots. Her clothes were not expensive but they probably had a little of London fashion about them. But if Sarah was impressed by her cousin's appearance, she did not show it.

"So you want to find a position hereabouts. Teaching."

"Yes," said Anne. "In a school or with a family."

"Well, you won't find any in t' local schools."

Anne wished her cousin could sound less pleased.

"How do you know?" asked her mother.

"Because Mary Wood, Lizzie Wood's sister, 'as been looking for one 'erself. She's 'ad to go nearly as far as Leeds to get one." Looking up at Anne, Sarah added, "There's plenty educated folk round here."

"I suppose so," murmured Anne, disappointed.

"But!" Sarah pronounced the word decisively. Assured of full attention, she went on. "Mr Blezard, who owns t' mill, 'as got a daughter, Charlotte. About same age as me. Sixteen or thereabouts. She's been at boarding school for long enough. But she must be about ready to come 'ome. Rich folk 'ave governesses sometime for girls that old, don't they?"

"They do indeed, Sarah. Thank you for your help. I appreciate it."

Anne smiled warmly at her cousin, inviting a similar response. But the girl just shrugged and looked away.

Agnes seemed to notice her daughter's offhand manner.

"It would be grand if you could get taken on by Mr Blezard, Anne.

He's building a new house in Wood Lane, only about fifteen minutes' walk away. Go tomorrow, Saturday afternoon. You'll likely find him at home."

CHAPTER THREE

Anne was happy with anticipation as she set off the next day. She knew that her expertise in literature, history and geography would be appropriate, as would music. Fortunately, she played the piano quite well but she knew no French, which was highly regarded as a suitable accomplishment for young ladies. Still, it was worth a try.

Reaching the top of the hill, she came to a lane which dropped steeply down to the right towards Longley and soon came upon the Blezards' house in Wood Lane - large, handsome and recently built in the local golden-grey sandstone on the brow of a hill overlooking Huddersfield. As she went up the drive, she could see gardeners working in the grounds, attending to a well-laid out garden. She did not need to knock because a man she assumed to be Mr Blezard was standing at the front door talking to a tradesman who looked decidedly aggrieved.

"I'm sorry, Tom, but there it is," said Blezard. "Mrs Blezard won't have the stair carpet laid until the cabinet-maker's finished. Because o' t' dust, do you see?"

"That's all very well, Mr Blezard, but I'd like to have had word, before I came all this way from Brighouse."

"Aye," replied Blezard. He pressed some coins into the man's hand. "Take this for your trouble. I'll mek sure we let you know when we're right ready next time."

The scene had attracted a few children and idle passers-by who watched with mild interest as the man, still glowering, took up his reins again and turned his horse and cart round.

Blezard caught Anne's eye.

"What a mercy it wa'nt raining!" They both laughed. "Now, missy, what can I do for you?"

"My name is Anne Graham, Mr Blezard. My cousin, Sarah Stott, works in your mill."

He nodded, non-committally.

"I have been living in London but am hoping to find work in this area. Where my mother came from," explained Anne. "I have taught at a Church School and should like to offer my services as a governess, if you need one."

"I was going to say," replied Blezard. "I didn't think you looked right sort for a mill girl."

Anne understood this was by way of being a compliment. Blezard suddenly leant forward, screwing his eyes up in concentration.

"That's a nice bit o' cloth you're wearing. Is it West Country? Or possibly French?" Before she could answer, he apologised.

"I'm sorry, lass. I should have seen you're in mourning, not made personal comments about your dress."

"That's quite all right, Mr Blezard," Anne replied gently, seeing the man was genuinely sorry for his bluntness. But he was contrite. Putting his hand under her elbow, he drew her into the porch.

"Nay, come in, do, and have a drink o' tea. We'll talk inside."

Anne followed him into the hallway, which was lofty and impressive, with etched glass window panels and a gleaming mosaic floor of deep blue and ochre tiles. Her gasp of admiration obviously pleased him.

"It looks very well, dun't it? And so it should, brass I've spent on it! Mrs Blezard likes quality. And so do I."

They sat down in a handsome, freshly decorated parlour. George Blezard was in his early fifties, Anne thought - stocky, well-fleshed and with a ruddy face. He looked less comfortable here than he had done outside talking to the tradesman.

"To tell you the truth, I hadn't thought of Charlotte having a governess."

Anne's heart sank. But he hadn't finished.

"When her mother died, it seemed best to leave her where she was, at school with her friends. But I do miss her. And she might like to come home and join in things here now she's that bit older."

"I understand. As for references – "

Blezard flapped his hand.

"Nay, never heed. I can tell what you're like without references. I think you'd suit right well, that is, if we think of having a governess. I shall speak to Mrs Blezard about it rightaway."

"Of course," said Anne, thinking this was the moment to leave.

"Nay, sit down and let's have some tea." Blezard rang the bell for the maid. He looked pleased. "The more I think about it, the more it suits. Isabel, Mrs Blezard, might be glad of a bit of female company. She gets a bit stalled with my being out all hours. And then talking about mill stuff when I get in."

Anne relaxed. She liked this bluff, kindly man who seemed willing to imagine the feelings of others. They drank tea out of pretty china and chatted pleasantly till the sound of the front door opening halted them.

"That'll be Isabel, I warrant," he said, rising. Anne stood up too, the smile on her face freezing as, with a mixture of surprise and dismay, she recognised the woman who now entered the room. Once again, she was dressed in the height of fashion, although this time not in the riding habit she had been wearing two days earlier on the road to Huddersfield.

Isabel Blezard recognised Anne a moment later. Her face flushed slightly.

"This is Miss Anne Graham, my dear," said Blezard. "She's looking for a post as governess."

"Indeed?" said his wife, as if the news could not possibly have any interest for her. She kept her eyes down, carefully tweaking each finger of her soft leather gloves one by one until she had removed them.

Anne saw that the other woman did not want to admit that the two of them had met before. Considering Isabel's behaviour that night, it was not surprising. There was no point in prolonging the meeting.

Anne put out her hand, hiding her disappointment as best she could.

"Thank you for listening to me, Mr Blezard. I am staying at Stotts' farm in Kaye Lane should you wish to contact me."

"Aye, aye," replied Blezard, looking somewhat mystified. Isabel turned her head, looking for the maid, but Anne was already on her way out, eager to escape an embarrassing situation. As she stepped out on the stone flags, she could hear behind her the beginnings of an argument. She quickened her pace to avoid hearing any more.

Anne's hopes were shattered. Just when she felt that she had been getting on well with Mr Blezard and had begun to imagine how pleasant such a post would be, it had all come crashing down. That dreadful woman! What a pity that kind-hearted man was married to her! And poor Charlotte too, with such a stepmother.

She retraced her steps, climbing up the steeply twisting slope of Longley Lane until she reached the outskirts of Almondbury once more, high above the town of Huddersfield. It was a fine spring afternoon and she felt reluctant to return immediately to the dark confines of the Stott farm. Ahead of her was Castle Hill, skirted by a lane that would take her down into the Woodsome Valley, then curving back into the village itself. What was it her mother had said about this spot? "All your troubles vanish?" Admittedly, her troubles were very slight. She had been disappointed by what had happened at the Blezards but there would be other opportunities no doubt.

The deep breaths she was taking were having effect. She felt instantly better in every way – stronger and more cheerful. This magnificent landscape was all that her mother had said it was. Castle Hill stood at the crest of the long raised plateau that was Almondbury, like the huge clenched fist of some resting giant's arm. The towering earthwork, the Hill itself, was a huge grassy mound, its peak sliced by ditches and hollows, its surface darkened by patches of gorse.

Anne's excitement grew. Nothing now would satisfy her but to climb the great hill. Seeing rough stone steps set in the hillside, she began to mount them until she reached the summit where there was a large, flat area and a tavern. Anne stood on the rim and looked about her. The view it commanded was staggering. It felt like standing on top of the world. Far across to the left was the bony outline of the Pennine ridge – bare, mysterious, unknown. In front, hundreds of feet below in the valley basin, which spread from left to right almost as far as the eye could see, stood the town of Huddersfield with its great mills and chimneys sending up a grey pall of smoke. Halfway down, on a green apron, lay a cricket field. Grey ribbons of dry-stone walling edged the patchwork of fields where cattle grazed. Here and there, church and chapel rose above the huddled houses.

Some of the cottages had rows of windows, on both floors, separated by stone mullions. But the farm cottages bordering Castle Hill were low, bedded down into the earth, their small windows facing away from the prevailing wind. Even now, on a sunny day, the wind was keen, piercing Anne's clothing. She walked on and then, turning left into Lumb Lane, entered a calmer world. Castle Hill still loomed up by her left shoulder but it felt as if someone had closed a door and shut out the wind.

As she followed the lane round, Anne found herself in the softer, richer landscape of the Woodsome valley which nestled in Almondbury's southern flank. Here the foliage thickened and bloomed. Dog roses and brambles caught at her skirts as she passed. Bluebell leaves were pushing up through the leaf mould in the woods alongside. The sun, now low in the sky, threw long shadows across the fields, highlighting the chestnut brown and white cows grazing with their young.

Anne had never seen this kind of countryside before. Her experience was limited to the parks and open spaces of London. She felt, as she knew her mother had done, a sense of belonging to the sturdy farmland around her. Surely there was a life, and happiness, for her here?

Turning towards the village once more by this circular route, she climbed a hill, passing the quaint buildings of an old grammar school and then up an even steeper incline until she reached the centre of the village and its ancient parish church. Pausing near Wormall Hall, a timbered building inscribed '1631', she looked through a large stone archway to a courtyard beyond which was lit by late afternoon sunshine.

Sounds of work issuing from a barn-like structure ahead drew Anne forward. The doors of a woodshop were wide-open on this fine day, revealing John Brook working at his bench, planing and smoothing a long piece of golden-pink wood. His shirt sleeves were rolled up and his body wrapped in a long hessian work apron. Specks of sawdust floated in the gauzy sunlight around him, which lit the soft hairs on his muscular fore-arms. He did not hear her approach but remained bent over his task, his strong hands stroking the timber as gently as a lover.

Anne felt herself grow warm as she watched him. She had never thought a man could look so beautiful at his work. She found herself wanting him to continue, so that she could go on observing him, and at the same time, wanting him to stop and notice her. A moment later, he did so and straightened up. As their eyes met, her heart leapt and refused to calm down.

Laying his tools down carefully on the bench, he came forward, wiping the sawdust off his hands with a cloth.

"Good afternoon, Miss Graham."

He smiled at her. Anne found it hard to concentrate. She felt she had a silly, joyous grin on her face but could do nothing about it.

"Good afternoon, Mr Brook."

"Are you inspecting the local trades?" He made the words sound friendly, welcoming.

"Not really. I have just been taking a walk around Almondbury, to Castle Hill and now back to my aunt's."

"And what do you think to it then, Miss Graham?"

"Please – call me Anne," she entreated. "I like it very much. It is just as my mother said and I seem to feel –" She stopped, aware of the confessional nature of her speech, but went on, secure in her trust of the listener. "I feel close to her here, where she grew up and was happy as a girl. And I love the countryside. Castle Hill in particular."

"Aye, it's a grand sight. And right pleasant today, I should think. When the wind blows up there, by, it really blows."

He laughed and Anne found herself joining him.

"So have you a mind to stay in these parts?"

"Well, yes, I hope so. I don't want to go back to London. I should like to teach." She hesitated. "I hoped to gain a position at Mr Blezard's, as governess to his daughter, but – I did not suit."

"Never mind 'em," he said cheerfully. "I dare say there'll be other posts coming along. There's plenty of folk roundabout doing right well for theirselves, building big houses and the like, who might well be glad of your talents."

Anne looked up and smiled into the dark brown eyes. She felt incredibly, unaccountably, cheered.

"Yes, I hope so. Well," she said, backing away. "I mustn't keep you from your work."

"Nay, I've done enough for today." He took off his apron and shook his shirt sleeves down. "I'll walk up with you."

After securing the workshop premises, he accompanied her up the village street. Without quite understanding why, Anne felt wonderful, as if she were walking on air. Several people were about on this fine spring evening, standing in their cottage doorways. She noticed how John spoke to them all and was acknowledged, if not by words, by a nod.

"You've lived here all your life, I suppose?" she asked.

"Aye." He smiled at her again. "Man and boy, as they say."

Anne felt a sensation of dizziness of the most delicious kind.

Struggling for self-control, yet at the same time rejoicing in the emotion, she turned her head away. They began the climb up Kaye Lane towards Broken Cross, the same route they had taken, in darkness, only days earlier.

"I can see it's a big village – now, in daylight."

"Aye, it is. Spread out. Several hundred folk. And an old one. Been here a lot longer than Huddersfield."

"And do the inhabitants usually greet strangers with a volley of missiles?"

"I'm sorry to say some of 'em do. Young louts. And beer addles what little brain they've got."

There was a pause. John was bound to know Ned Stott was one of the louts in question, Anne thought. But he maintained a tactful silence. She steered the conversation onto safer ground.

"And the woodshop? Do you work for someone, John?"

She could hear the pride in his answer.

"Nay, it's my own business. Though – " he paused and then went on – "I've had to borrow money to set it up. But I shall pay it back before so long."

"Business is good?"

"Aye, pretty good." He sounded hesitant, as if afraid of seeming to boast.

"How did you come to start? Are you following your father's trade?"

"No, not at all. He's a weaver. I served an apprenticeship to a cabinet-maker. I like working with wood. Always have. Seems natural, somehow."

"What kind of thing do you make?"

"All sorts. Chairs, tables, sideboards. Fancy carving."

Anne was fascinated.

"I should think it's satisfying work."

"It is. It's grand to take something and fashion it into something new. Something beautiful. And feel you've made it."

They had stopped walking for a moment. She looked at John wonderingly and found that he was looking at her in the same way. For a while they were silent. Then Anne spoke.

"Where do you live, John?"

"In a weavers' cottage down Lumb Lane. In the valley."

He gestured to the left.

"You can tell weavers' cottages by the windows, banks of them with mullions, to let more light in. For the handloom weavers. Like my parents. Weaving pieces at home that were taken somewhere else to be finished and then sold in the Cloth Hall in Huddersfield. But there's hardly any demand for it now. Not since the power looms came in."

"That's a pity."

"I suppose so. But these things happen. Progress. It can't be stopped. And working conditions for most folk are better than they used to be."

"Do your parents still do any weaving?"

"My mother does a bit but my father's eyesight's too poor now. And he had a stroke a while back. He's not got proper use of his right side. He's quite a bit older than my mother. Used to work hard for weavers' rights, when he was younger. Years ago, they were experts, fancy weavers, not just making plain cloth but with all sorts of patterns, silk and cotton as well as wool. It was a skilled trade round these parts."

As they reached the crest of Broken Cross, Anne stopped to catch her breath. The road ahead of them was like a switchback, dipping down and then up again towards the summit of Castle Hill. Down to the right was the Stott farm with its fields stretching out behind it.

"How far does the Stotts' land extend?" asked Anne. "As far as we can see?"

"Nay, it borders the Haighs'. Their farm is at the top of Longley Lane, that steep lane you went down today on the way to the Blezards. They're grand folk, the Haighs. Hannah, Mrs Haigh, was a friend of your mother's when they were young. You'll meet them before so long."

"I hope so," said Anne, smiling up at him.

But this time, he did not meet her smile, turning away with what looked like embarrassment. He seemed to be struggling with what he was about to say next. Finally, he spoke, looking, for the first time in their conversation, unsure of himself.

"You'll mebbe meet her next month. When I get wed. To Molly Dyson."

Anne felt as though she had been hit in the face. Speechless with shock, she stared at him. But he had dropped his head and was scuffing a clump of turf with his boot.

"I see." The voice did not sound like hers.

"You'll come, will you? To the wedding supper?"

Now he looked at her like a boy longing to be forgiven, his dark eyes full of pleading.

Though hurt herself, Anne could not resist his appeal.

"Yes, I'll come," she said. "Thank you for your company, John. I have enjoyed talking to you.

His wide smile looked full of relief.

"It was my pleasure. I bid you good-day." With a nod, he turned away and headed for the footpath which led to his home in the valley.

Anne watched his tall figure gradually disappear into the distance and then walked slowly on towards the Stott farm, trying to compose the turmoil of her feelings. It is not to be wondered at, she reasoned. An attractive young man like that, he was almost bound to be betrothed to some local girl. I should have foreseen it. Indeed, I was foolish not to. But the feeling of disappointment was intense, almost as intense as the grief she had so recently suffered. Standing still, she took several deep breaths. This will not do, she told herself. The young man is promised to another and that is the end of the matter.

Opening the little gate that led up to the farmhouse door, a melancholy voice suddenly seemed to wail inside her. If only I had met him years ago!

John walked slowly home. For the first time in his life, he failed to look across the valley and admire the splendid view across the fields to where the land swept up to Castle Hill on the horizon. His mind was too full.

In the first place, he was stunned at how much he had said to Anne Graham. He couldn't remember talking about himself like that to anyone, ever. It had seemed so easy talking to her, as if they had known each other for years. But he knew it was more than that. He had found her extremely attractive, he could not deny it. She had a particularly beautiful smile which lit up her face. And her skin had a glow about it, and her eyes, and her mouth ...

He pulled himself up with a jolt. This was not right. He was betrothed to Molly Dyson, had been, unofficially, for years. They had promised each other they would marry when Molly reached eighteen. Now her birthday had come and gone and the wedding was planned for next month.

He had never thought before to question his love for Molly. Indeed, he felt shocked to find himself doing so now. They had been sweethearts since childhood – a long, unbroken relationship with much mutual affection and almost no disagreements. He had sometimes observed other couples with amazement, at their passionate quarrels, jealousies and subsequent reconciliations, and wondered at them. He and Molly were not like that, not at all.

He thought of Molly now, with her pretty face and dark curly hair. She had changed remarkably little since the day he first met her, when she was eight and he was eleven years old.

One fine Sunday afternoon, he and his friends had been playing in Penny Spring Wood, climbing trees, building a dam in the stream, when another lad, face bright red with running, thundered down the banking.

"Come quick! There's a lass stuck in t'mud in Stott's field!"

Excitedly the gang scrambled up, hands, boots and trousers wet, and followed him in anticipation of death or rescue. Either would do.

They heard the commotion before they reached the scene. A small girl was jumping up and down, screaming and crying at the sight of her elder sister who was trapped in a muddy ditch which ran alongside the hedge bordering a field. As she struggled to pull one leg out, so the other sank deeper. The mud now reached her knees and there was a look of panic on her tear-stained face.

"What made you get in there, yer daft thing?" asked one lad incredulously.

For answer, she looked shame-facedly at a clump of white flowers known as milkmaids which she had been trying to reach. The younger girl was inspired to further explosions of terror.

"Our Molly's going to die! She's going to be sucked under and die!"

"No, she's not," said John calmly. "We're going to get her out. Easily."

It was not quite so straightforward. The muddy patch looked dangerously deep and soft and the girl was at least six feet away from firm ground.

John took command.

"Ben! Run up to t'farm and fetch us two planks!"

The boys ran off as fast as they could. John squatted down to be on the same level as the girls.

"There! We'll soon have you out. No! Don't struggle or you'll go deeper." This was already happening. John began to wonder if he should have told the lads to bring some men with them to help.

"What do they call you?" he asked the prisoner.

"Molly. Molly Dyson," she replied. "And that's Cissie." Cissie resumed her wailing.

"Now Cissie, stop that," said John. "Won't this be a grand tale to tell your Mam and Dad when you get home?"

Cissie was not convinced but fell silent.

"They told us not to come this far," confessed Molly. Her eyes, filled with tears, were quite bloodshot. But she was bonny, thought John, with dark tumbling curls and a glowing pink and white skin.

After a while, during which John talked about whatever he could to take the girls' minds off their predicament, the lads returned with two long pieces of wood. John laid them over the mud and, with Ben holding his ankles, lay on his front and wriggled forward until he reached Molly.

"Not so tight," he pleaded as she clutched his neck. "Just hold on, don't let go." Loud sucking noises were heard as he pulled one leg out of the mud and then the other, delighting the lads who scampered about, imitating the sounds as rudely as they could.

"Never heed'em," advised John. Molly was now on firm ground but a sorry sight, her skirt and boots thickly plastered with mud. He cleaned her up as best he could with handfuls of grass, noticing that she had suddenly lost all her colour.

"Now then! Back to t' farm, lads, with the planks!" Then, turning to the girls who clung to each other, sobbing, "Where do you live?"

"Northgate."

"Good! It's on my way home," he lied. Taking a girl in either hand, he strode forward across the fields.

Leaving them outside their cottage, he was taken aback when Molly reached up and gave him a moist kiss and an adoring look. He remembered walking home, feeling more pleased with life than he had ever done before. That feeling, of manly pride at saving a young lass, had never really left him.

Absorbed in his memories, John turned into Lumb Lane. There was no point in thinking about Anne Graham in that way. He was committed to Molly and happy to be so. He thought of their recent love-making – the fervent, passionate kisses leading to the overwhelming, almost unbearable, desire for complete fulfilment. But he had held back, out of a sense of what was right. They would wait until their wedding night. He knew Molly respected him for his restraint. No, any thoughts or feelings about another woman were dishonourable. He would banish them from his mind.

As he turned the corner towards his home, he was just in time to see a horse and cart, with two people on the box, pulling away from the cottage and accelerating into the distance. Vaulting over the small gate, he was indoors a few strides later.

"Wasn't that the Haighs just leaving? Ben and his mother? What did they want?"

Only when his question was greeted with silence did he notice the strained atmosphere in the room. His father sat in the carver chair, his knotted hands clenched on the wooden arms; his mother stood stiffly by the fire, looking away from him.

This was strange. The Brooks were on friendly terms with the Haighs although only John ever spent any time at the farm. He could not imagine any kind of disagreement springing up between them.

"You might well ask," said his father. "Beats me why she's being so awkward."

John looked at his mother for explanation. But she said nothing, her lips pursed tight.

"Well, I hope someone's going to tell me what this is about," said John. "It's not bad news, is it?"

"No, not at all," replied his father, still looking at Martha who had relaxed slightly and turned towards her son. As she still did not speak, Walter went on, although the effort was visible.

"They came, Hannah particularly came, to offer their farmhouse for your wedding supper, yours and Molly's. Not just the house but to provide the food as well. A right handsome offer, I thought it. But *she*" – indicating Martha, "was ready to find fault wi' it. Why I don't know."

"Did you want to have it here, Mother?" asked John. "Did it upset your plans?"

She shrugged and refused to be drawn. The two men looked at each other, non-plussed. Walter continued.

"I think it's a right good idea. And a generous offer. Your mother's enough to do with th' ouse an' all, and bit o' weaving she does. Not to mention looking after me."

This was so patently true that John hesitated to endorse what his father had just said. He remained silent, knowing his mother could not be browbeaten. Eventually she spoke.

"I just had a mind to have it here. Just us and Molly's family."

"Why, there must be going on a dozen on 'em! If they all come, cousins and the like!"

"They won't all come. You know very well, Walter," said Martha crossly.

"It'd be grand to have it at the Haighs. They won't be at the wedding, I should think, but they've been like cousins to John all his life. Haven't they, lad? Made up for us not giving you any real ones." The old man, white-haired, frail-boned, shook slightly with the exertion of speaking.

Martha seemed to notice this and soften. She turned to John.

"What do you want, lad? Just a small do here, at home? Or a bigger one, up at the Haighs, with all their family? We know Molly's parents can't do it theirselves." This was not in question. Molly's family lived in very poor circumstances in a tiny, dark under-dwelling in the village.

John thought the Haigh offer both generous and enlightened. Firstly, the farmhouse was large with ample seating in the kitchen and secondly, Hannah was an excellent cook who would produce a splendid spread and enjoy doing so. But he knew of his mother's pride and sensitivity, even if he did not quite understand her motives.

"It would be nice to have it here, Mother. And you'd do us proud, I know. But I wouldn't like Hannah's feelings to be hurt if we turn down her offer. And I'd be glad to think you had less work to do."

"You'd be happy to have it at the Haighs? And Molly?"

John spoke gently.

"Yes, I would. And I'm pretty sure Molly would like it too. I'll ask her tonight when I see her."

Martha took a deep breath.

"Then we'll thank Hannah for her kind offer and accept. So long as it's what you want. Now sit down. You must be ready for your tea. You're later than you usually are on a Saturday."

As she was speaking, she was tying on her apron and lifting a meat-and-potato pie out of the oven. John helped his father up to the table and then sat down himself, glad that the difficulties, whatever they really were, had been smoothed away.

His mother, however, remained unnaturally quiet and picked at the food on her plate. John did his best to cheer her up.

"This pie's champion, Mam. I hope Molly's will be as good, eh, Father?"

His father murmured agreement. Eating seemed an effort for him. He struggled with his meal although Martha had given him only a small helping.

Martha looked pleased.

"I'm glad you like it. I hope for your sake Molly can cook. If she can't, she can always come to me for advice. But you know, mothers-in-law have to tread carefully in these matters."

John grinned at her. She smiled back and John felt the atmosphere in the room lighten.

"Oh, I nearly forgot," she said, getting up. "There's a letter come for you." She handed John a thick white envelope. "Is it payment from one of your customers?"

"No," said John, opening it and scanning the handsome sheet of paper inside. "It's from Isabel Blezard, Wood Lane."

"That'll be George Blezard's new wife – married not long since. What does she want?"

"Seems she's very pleased with the staircase I put in at their new house. No expense spared so I spent a good long time on it. Fine bit of mahogany. I was quite pleased with it myself. Wants me to call and see about making some fireplace surrounds for them."

"That's good," said Martha. "He'll have plenty brass I should think, with owning a mill. What does Molly say about working there?"

"She doesn't say much. It's mostly about her friends on the mill floor. Though they were right interested when they heard Mr Blezard was getting wed a second time. Seems they met in Scarborough."

"Yes, I heard that too – from Willy Fowler when he came for my pieces. George Blezard went there on holiday – he'd not been right well since his wife died. And then he comes back, engaged to this young woman. I should think there were a few disappointed lasses and mothers round here when they heard about it. He'd be a good catch, I should think."

"A bit old?" asked John. "He must be over fifty?"

His mother laughed.

"You're showing your ignorance, lad! Over fifty and a mill-owner! Just right, for some. Old enough to know better, others might say."

"I'll go and see her on Monday afternoon, as she asks," said John, lifting his father's chair away from the table as his mother cleared the dishes.

"And let me, and Molly, know all about her when you get back. We like a bit o' gossip."

His mother seemed perfectly all right now, thought John. He still couldn't fathom why she had been so reluctant to accept Hannah's offer to do the catering for the wedding supper and have it at the farm. Perhaps it was something to do with feminine pride, after all.

John presented himself at the Blezard home with a book of drawings and a bag of wood samples and was shown into the parlour where Isabel Blezard was seated on a button-backed, velvet chair. She rose as he entered and came towards him, holding out her hand.

"Mr Brook! Thank you so much for coming."

The phrase that sprang to John's mind was "a handsome woman." She was taller than average, dark, full-bosomed and carried herself confidently. The white hand she proffered bore two expensive-looking rings.

"Mrs Blezard."

He took her hand and was surprised at its warm pressure against his.

"Do let us sit down." She gestured him towards the couch where he sat, legs apart. Then she re-positioned herself on the chair and arranged her full-skirted, lilac dress in becoming folds. John did not feel at ease, despite the sumptuousness of the upholstery.

Isabel Blezard appeared to be enjoying herself. She looked back at John boldly, without dropping her gaze, a smile on her wide red lips. When she spoke, he could see her large white teeth were slightly prominent, but not unattractively so.

"We have seen the over-mantel you made for Mrs Beaumont in Edgerton, Mr Brook, and thought it very fine. We should like something similar here, with perhaps a smaller, simpler one in the dining-room."

"Can you show me which one you mean, Mrs Blezard?" asked John, lifting the pattern book and opening it on his lap. Before he could hand it to her, she got up, crossed the room and joined him on the couch. She sat so close he could smell her perfume and feel the warmth of her body beside him.

"The one I liked was, I think, a mixture of walnut and mahogany, with carved foliage. And some repoussé work. The surround was rose granite or something similar."

"This will be the one, I think," he said, turning the pages until he came to a particular design. "I have a mason I work with if that is all right with you."

"Yes, of course," she purred, stretching her arm across him so that her fingers touched the book on his lap.

John felt himself go hot. He was equally embarrassed by her nearness and by the thought of edging away from her. As he felt his face reddening, she stood up and ran her hands down the sides of her bodice, leaving them resting on her hips.

"Shall we look at the other room now? Perhaps another design? And you will want to take measurements." The look she sent him was challenging and coquettish at the same time.

Relieved at being able to move, John stood up and began to note down the dimensions of the two fire-places. All the time, Isabel hovered behind him, praising the beautiful work he had already done for them.

When he had finished, he declined her offer of refreshment and made his escape as politely as he could.

A hunted man – that was what he felt like, he thought, as he climbed Longley Lane. It made him uncomfortable and also, if he was honest, somewhat physically aroused. He was glad of the walk home in the fresh air.

Later, when he saw Molly, he called Isabel "handsome and well-dressed" and was unwilling to be drawn further. He could have said something about George Blezard having his hands full but thought it wiser not to. Molly would have wanted to know the reason for his comment.

He also said nothing about his walk through the village with Anne Graham. He could have described her in considerable detail — taller than Molly but not as tall as Isabel Blezard, more slender than either, graceful, pale-skinned, blue-eyed, with light auburn hair that curled about her temples, ladylike but spirited. And that from the back her narrow waist and swaying walk were very pleasing to the eye. He could have said all these things. But he knew he would not.

Anne lost no time in placing an advertisement in the Education section of the local weekly paper, '*The Huddersfield Examiner*'. It read : "A Young Lady Governess, with experience of teaching, would be glad to instruct junior or senior pupils in Reading, Writing, Arithmetic, History, Geography, Religious Instruction and Music." It was followed by a Box Number. Now she could only wait.

She did not want to apply for work in any of the textile mills in the area. There were several reasons for this, the main one being that she wanted, above all, to teach and was in some measure qualified to do so. She also knew mill work was dirty, noisy and entailed long hours of standing. More importantly, she felt that the other workers would not welcome her.

One evening she had been walking through the village when she passed a group of girls in clogs and rough clothes who were talking and laughing loudly outside the public house opposite the church. When they caught sight of her, there were whispers and then jeers. Anne supposed they recognised her as Sarah Stott's cousin from London. The experience was not pleasant and Anne quickened her step.

As she moved away, one of them shouted, "Look at them booits!", referring to her neat leather boots. Then another voice growled, "They wouldn't last five minutes in t' mill!" and after a pause, "Nor would she!" There was a burst and then a gale of raucous laughter. Flustered, Anne walked on as calmly as she could.

The weather had been cool, wet and windy for a fortnight. Anne had rushed out into the farmyard many times to bring in half-dry washing from the line as a blustery shower swept by, pulling out the pegs as fast as she could, holding some of them in her teeth in her haste as large raindrops plopped onto her back and shoulders, drenching her within seconds.

But then, as May moved into June, the weather became warmer and more settled. During a welcome dry spell, farmers began hay-making. The smell of new-mown hay hung in the still air, haystalks drifted along the lanes where laden hay-carts had passed and clung to the boots of passers-by. Casual labourers, unemployed men and others who could afford to leave their own work for a short while appeared at the farms to help cut and bring in the hay while the dry weather lasted. Ned Stott's cronies turned up, shuffling their feet and sniggering when Anne came to the door. Once out in the fields with the older men, they changed, wielding pitchforks and handling horses and wagons with great confidence and some skill. When Anne and her aunt brought out bread, cheese and ale, they took them without thanks, as if these were their due, needing no recognition.

Anne had been living at the farm for more than the four weeks originally proposed. There had been no reply to her newspaper advertisement but her aunt seemed keen that she should stay on. Her uncle had made no objection. No doubt he could see what a useful and unpaid helper she was at this busy time. Anne did not expect him to voice any appreciation of the fact; she was simply grateful that he left her alone.

One evening, hearing the sound of voices and the tramping of feet on the road, she went to the gate to see who was going past. There were six or seven men walking down the hill, no doubt from one or other of the farms near Castle Hill, returning from a stint of haymaking. John Brook was among them and as she had not seen him before, in old, sweat-stained clothes which clung to his body, a ragged shirt open at his throat and his hair tousled and dusty with pollen. He did not pause as he went past but gave her a brief nod as he kept in step with the other men. She felt herself go hot and her pulse quicken at the unexpected sight of him. She stood looking at his back view as long as she could see him, at the same time scorning her foolishness in doing so.

Anne had never spent so much time in the fresh air before. Her white skin flushed and then became a light golden colour, with a dusting of freckles on her nose and cheeks. She slept more deeply than she had ever done. Sometimes on the hottest nights, she would wake in the small bedroom, seeking a cool spot in the bed she shared with Sarah. Once she woke to the light of a full moon and listened to the sound of a fox barking in the distance. Then the birds began calling to one another, before the break of day.

She had almost forgotten the early morning sounds of her London street, of horses' hooves and wheels on the road, of people's voices and footsteps. She thought about them now and the house in Victoria Park which her mother had kept spotless for so long. It was a tall house with a small garden at the back and at the front, a basement area and wrought-iron railings. She had been aware of the seasons passing as a change from warm to cold, and by her mother's response to them; spring and spring cleaning; summer and the dust; autumn and leaves clogging the drain outside their window; winter and the drawing of curtains in the afternoon. She had been ignorant of farming life and its bond with the soil, the sun and the rain.

CHAPTER FOUR

John Brook married Molly Dyson when haymaking was over. The vicar conducted the simple ceremony in All Hallows' Church with few people present. Then the bridal couple, together with John's mother and father, Molly's parents and sister, made their way out of the village up towards Castle Hill in a horse-drawn cart belonging to Eli Haigh of Lane Farm.

As they passed the Stott farm, Anne was standing at the gate. She smiled, waved and then began walking up the hill after them. A few moments later, she met her cousin Sarah on her way home from the mill.

The girl looked cross and tired. She seemed surprised to see Anne.

"Where are you bound?"

"The Haighs' farm. I'm invited to the wedding supper for John and Molly Brook. They've just gone past."

Sarah's eyes narrowed.

"Does my father know you're going?"

"I don't know," replied Anne, nonplussed. "I told Aunt Agnes. She said nothing."

"Well, she wouldn't," sneered Sarah. "My father'll not be right pleased when he hears about it. We have nowt to do with the Haighs."

"Why not?"

Sarah shrugged.

"I don't know. Never 'ave done."

"Well, I don't see that it's any concern of mine," said Anne crisply. "John invited me after church one Sunday and I accepted. I will see you later." She turned away and continued walking up the hill.

It came as a surprise to her, this animosity between the Haighs and the Stotts. Remembering that John had spoken of the Haighs as "grand folks", she supposed the fault lay with her uncle. But it did not deter her from going to the wedding supper.

How she would cope, emotionally, with the occasion was another matter. At first she had determined to stay away, feeling it would be the less painful option. But she had decided to go, mainly because she wanted to meet the Haighs, particularly Hannah whom her mother had often spoken of with affection. Secondly, it would be cowardly to stay away for fear of emotional pain. If she was going to remain in the area, as she intended, then she would have to accept the fact that John was someone else's husband. Lastly, and she felt shamefaced at what she knew was weakness, she wanted to see John again, in whatever circumstances.

The Haighs' farm was at the top of Kaye Lane, set well back from the road. Like the Stott farmhouse, it was an old building under a stone-slated roof but altogether less forbidding in appearance and more spacious, with flowerbeds under the windows. Once through the five-barred gate, the approach was across a well-swept courtyard, a good distance away from the nearest cowshed.

Despite the confidence of her words to Sarah, Anne felt slightly nervous as she stepped into the yard where two pony and traps were tied up. Sounds of talking and laughter emerged from the open farmhouse door through which three small boys suddenly erupted. They were followed by a young man, presumably their father.

"Now, lads! Calm down! See!"

Any effect he might have had vanished when two small girls, in Sunday best clothes, ran out behind him, hesitated for a moment and then chased after the boys, shrieking as they went.

The young man smiled at Anne.

"It's their cousins. They don't see them that often and when they do – !" He held out a large hand. "I'm Matthew Haigh."

"Anne Graham," she replied, her hand lost in his.

"Come in, come in, before the Haighs eat everything on t'table."

The scene inside was a heart-warming one. Too many people were crammed into the long kitchen but were so obviously enjoying themselves that their number increased rather than diminished the air of merriment. The new Mrs Brook, rosy-cheeked, sat in the place of honour, wearing an ivory silk dress in the fashion of twenty years ago. John stood by the window listening to a young man while the Haighs, Dysons and Brooks chatted and helped themselves to the spread laid out on the table. There was cold fowl, boiled ham, pork pie, pickled onions, beetroot, bread and butter and on the sideboard, dishes of stewed gooseberries, jugs of cream and short-bread biscuits.

"Come in, my dear. I'm right glad to meet you." Anne found herself embraced by a large, friendly woman. "I'm Hannah Haigh. Your mother was one of my dearest friends. Sit down, my dear, and have some supper."

Anne squeezed into the space made for her on a wooden bench while someone filled her plate. As she studied the guests, she found she could distinguish the Haighs from the rest because of their strong physical resemblance to one another. Their look could be traced to Eli Haigh, Hannah's husband. In his mid fifties, he was still a handsome man, strongly built, with high cheekbones, a square jaw and broad brow. Fair-haired, his eyes were a light, bright blue, and wide-set in his ruddy face.

There was some moving about and changing of places to Anne's left as a young woman about her own age manoeuvred herself into the space next to her. This was Rachel Haigh who lost no time in identifying everyone in the room for Anne's benefit.

"There's my three brothers, Matthew, Joseph and Ben. Matt and Joe are married and live away. Ben and I still live here, at home."

"I've been here a month," said Anne. "But we've never met?"

"No. We're chapel-goers, not church folk like you and John and his mother. My parents are Methodists."

"Were they always so?"

"My mother was. Like her family. But my father wasn't religious at all — like most farmers, you'll hear people say. Then he was "saved" — not long after my brother Ben was born."

Anne was intrigued. She looked at Eli who sat with a small child on each knee, the picture of calm contentment. Who would think he had ever known spiritual turmoil?

"And do you work on the farm?" she asked, turning back to Rachel.

"No. Ben does but I work as a nurse at the Infirmary."

"Do you?" Anne was impressed. "Then you do brave work. More than I could do."

Rachel said nothing. Anne had noticed before that local people seemed to find it hard to accept compliments.

"Does the Infirmary treat all cases?"

"It's mainly for folk injured at work. But we see many more in the Dispensary, who go home with whatever treatment we can give them."

She warmed to the subject, which was clearly close to her heart. "But there are so many we can't help, from the poorer classes. Some live in appalling conditions, worse than beasts. If there was better housing, there would be better health."

This conversation was cut short by a Haigh grandchild, a small girl who climbed on Anne's lap and began pulling at her curly hair.

Rachel laughed. "She's not used to that colour. All the Haighs have flaxen hair as you can see."

"Not Sam," said the child, pointing to the young man who was still talking earnestly to John. The latter had the air of a man listening politely but awaiting the moment when he could, just as politely, move away and talk to someone else.

"True," said Rachel. "That's Samuel Armitage. He, John and Ben were friends at school. Sam's the cleverest person we know. He's an engineer."

Anne looked at the young man, who carried on talking obliviously. He had a plain but clever-looking face, a strongly freckled skin and ginger hair much brighter than hers. The physical difference between him and his taller, darker companion was very marked. With a pang, Anne recognised once again how deeply attractive John Brook was, especially now, in his best clothes, a wave of his glossy dark brown hair falling forward over his forehead. Would she ever be able to look at him calmly, dispassionately, in the way she was able to look at Sam Armitage? When John eventually moved away to talk to other people, Sam remained where he was, by the piano, all by himself, making no attempt to talk to anyone else. Anne caught his eye at one point but he looked away immediately, as if embarrassed.

Anne had hoped she might be able to exchange a few words with Hannah Haigh and talk about her mother but she soon realised this was not the right moment. Hannah was on the go the whole time, refilling plates and mugs, encouraging everyone to eat up and have some more, constantly taking more food out of the oven or getting one of her sons to bring up fresh supplies from the keeping cellar. She had an open, pleasant face, fair-haired and blue-eyed like her husband but without his distinctive cheekbones and jaw.

When Rachel turned to speak to one of her sisters-in-law who sat on the other side of her, Anne stole a glance at the bride, Molly, now Mrs John Brook. She was undeniably pretty, with dark curly hair and a beautifully clear complexion. She looked as if she had never been happier. As well she might, thought Anne wistfully.

John's mother, Martha Brook, seemed to have said very little to anyone. A small, trim woman with the same dark colouring as her son, she spent most of the evening attending to her husband Walter who looked old and frail in the midst of so much youth and bloom. As Anne watched the couple, she saw Martha touch John on the sleeve and speak to him a lowered voice. It must have been something to do with leaving because he then spoke to Molly, her parents and the hosts.

There was a general stirring. Some people got up and began to look for shawls and coats while others spread out along the settle or moved to a vacated chair. Two of the Haigh grandchildren were found hiding under the table and were dragged out, beaming and highly pleased with themselves.

At that moment Anne saw John was listening intently to some news brought in by one of the farm-workers. After a word with Sam, he came across to Anne and Rachel.

"Anne! Would you allow Sam Armitage to accompany you home? He goes home your way."

"What is it?" asked Rachel.

"Seems there's dog-fighting planned on the Hill tonight. Alfred says he's seen some rough lads going by and some dogs in muzzles. It's against the law and cruel but it happens. Best get home now before there's any trouble."

Anne rose at once, bidding farewell to the assembled company. She kissed Rachel who seemed as pleased as she did at their meeting one another.

Drawing her shawl around her shoulders, Anne stepped out into the darkening farmyard. Sam Armitage stood stiffly, apparently ill-at-ease with his mission. He escorted her down the hill to the Stott farm, walking by her side but keeping a yard of space between them. He spoke little and then only in response to Anne's questions. Had she not received testimony of his cleverness and seen him talking so animatedly, she would have thought him a dull fellow.

The door of the Stott farmhouse was opened by Sarah. She seemed maliciously pleased.

"You'd better come in. My father's got summat to say to you."

The signs were ominous. Jack sat in his chair, glowering at her, legs apart, his roughened hands clasping his thighs. Ned lolled beside him, one foot on the fender, a look of cheerful anticipation on his face, unlike his mother who stood leaning against the far wall, nervously pleating her apron between her fingers. Her uncle scowled at Anne and spoke viciously.

"What were you doing at the 'aighs? Don't you know we 'ave nowt to do wi' em?"

Anne removed her shawl and folded it over one arm. Quiet tact might be the best course though she could feel her anger rising. She spoke as evenly as she could.

"It was a wedding supper. Not a Haigh wedding but John Brook's. I think you know him. I was invited some time ago, at church."

"Pssst!" The farmer spat. It was not clear which word or words had provoked him most. "You've to keep away from 'em, do ye hear?" He got up and came so close that Anne could feel his breath on her face, see his reddened eyes, the open pores of his skin and yellowing teeth. She trembled, not with fear but at the thought that her gentle aunt had to put up with this bully every day of her life.

"Do ye hear what I say?" he repeated.

"Perfectly," said Anne, her heart thudding. "But I don't see what right you have to say it to me."

"What! What!" Jack looked as if he was likely to explode.

"Whatever quarrel you have with the Haighs is your business, not mine."

"You'll do as I say, as long as you live under my roof, my girl!" he roared.

Something snapped inside Anne. Her rage spilled out.

"I am not your girl! As for it being your roof, remember I am your wife's niece – the wife who brought you this farm!"

The man stared as if he could not believe what he was hearing. Anne's heart was racing so fast she reached for the back of a chair to steady herself. She would not be threatened. But her angry words had fallen on fertile ground. Jack's face was purple with fury.

"And a bloody good job I was 'ere to tek it on," he snarled. "It'd 'ave gone to rack and ruin if it'd waited for your mother to see to it. No," his face twisting with malice, "she was too busy runnin' off to London with her fine friends! With nowt to show for it – 'cept a bastard bairn!"

For a moment, Anne was speechless, stunned. Behind her, she heard a gasp from her aunt. Feeling the blood rushing to her face at this insult, Anne shouted back,

"How dare you say that! How dare you! I am no bastard! My mother was married to my father! She told me so!"

"Pah! You've only her word for it," Jack replied with a sly nastiness that made Anne hate him. All the love, all the grief she felt for her mother came surging through her veins.

"What right have you to say that? You – you brute!"

Jack was crouching in front of her, as if ready to spring.

"What did tha' call me? Say that again!"

"Brute! I said brute! And that's what you are –".

Anne stopped abruptly, at a sudden strange noise behind her. It was her aunt fighting for breath and half-collapsing on a chair. Anne moved towards her but Agnes shook her head as if to say "Pay no attention." Neither of her children moved – Sarah, her eyes round, her mouth hanging open, Ned, lip curling, listening to the argument with evident enjoyment.

Anne gave both cousins a scathing look. But she would say no more. Not out of fear of her uncle but because of the distress to her aunt. Turning her back deliberately on the others, she addressed herself to Agnes.

"I shall not trespass on your hospitality any longer than necessary, Aunt Agnes. I thank you for receiving me into your home." She hoped this reference to the ownership of the farm was not lost on Jack.

Her aunt nodded. Turning, Anne unlatched the wooden door to the staircase and mounted the stone steps with as much calm as she could muster.

Once in the bedroom, she found her heart still thudding from the confrontation. One thing was clear. She had to find work and somewhere else to live. Without delay.

Agnes was sitting close to the window, her head bent over her darning, when Anne came into the kitchen next morning. Swiftly she dropped to her knees by the side of her aunt and put her arms round her, feeling the thin, bowed shoulders beneath her blouse.

"Aunt! I'm so very sorry about last night."

Her aunt did not respond.

"Aunt Agnes? Do you hear? I'm sorry I angered Uncle Jack and that you suffered because of me."

Her aunt's expression, when she looked up at Anne, was weary.

"You've no need to apologise, Anne. Jack's bad tempers come without anyone provoking 'em."

"Well, if you say so. As long as you're all right," said Anne lamely.

Agnes did not reply but lowered her head once again to her work.

"But I feel I can't stay here any longer. Not after what was said."

Agnes looked up sharply, a flash of fear in her eyes which vanished as quickly as it had appeared.

"Must you, Anne? It's been grand having you here."

"I think I have to," replied Anne, moving around the room, uncomfortably aware of her aunt's distress. "As long as I'm here, there'll always be conflict between me and my uncle. It's not fair on you."

Agnes was silent and stared ahead, stony-faced.

"I thought, if I could get some mill work – any sort, I could get a cheap lodging nearby. I doubt I shall hear anything from my advertisement in the newspaper. It's been a few weeks now."

"Oh, my dear! I'd be sorry to see you go into t' mill. The work's hard and they're a rough lot."

"They won't all be," said Anne, forcing a smile. "I thought I'd call in at the one at the bottom of the village and ask if they need anybody."

Agnes said nothing.

"And I'll see you every Sunday. At church. Let me make us some tea."

It was a good idea. The tension eased as they sat together sipping the hot liquid. Anne felt she had to mention the ugly slur voiced by her uncle.

"Agnes. Do you think my mother married my father?"

Agnes looked startled.

"Oh, I think she did. At least – I remember she wrote to Father telling him she was about to marry a bandsman in the army. He didn't tell me but I saw the letter."

"And then?"

"That was all. He never replied to any of her letters, he was so angry with her for going off to London. She stopped writing after a while."

"And you?"

Agnes flushed.

"I wanted to write but Father forbade it. Then he fell ill and Jack took over the running of the farm. I did write. Later. She wrote back saying your father, Arthur Graham, had died before you were born. I always assumed they had been married."

"I see," said Anne, although she was no nearer the truth than before. "Do you know why Jack is so against the Haighs?"

"I don't know the whole of it. I know it all began when Father blamed Eli Haigh's father for some bad advice about buying railway stock. I think they both lost a good deal of money. More than twenty year since."

"Is that it?" asked Anne, incredulously. "All that time ago?"

Agnes smiled grimly.

"That's nothing unusual. In these parts."

Anne felt sure there must be more to it than that. Like her parents' marriage, it was a matter that had been described but had not convinced her. Perhaps she would never know the full truth of either.

The two women turned their attention to household tasks, Agnes preparing dinner for the men's return at midday, Anne tackling a pile of ironing. Picking up the flat iron from the range, she spat on its surface to test its heat. Tiny balls of spit bounced off immediately. Pressing down on the damp garments, and exchanging the flat iron for another when it grew cool, she worked until the laundry basket was empty and the clothes folded and left to air near the kitchen range.

"I think I'll go down to the mill now, Aunt, and see if there is anything."

Anne put on a light bonnet and shawl, opened the door and was surprised to meet the letter-carrier coming along the path. To her delight, the letter he brought was from the vicar of the church she had attended in London, now back in his parish. Full of apologies for his delay in responding, he now compensated for it by providing a testimonial overflowing with praise for her learning, dedication and integrity of character. Anne's cheeks burned with delicious embarrassment.

"Surely you won't go down to the mill now, will you?" asked Agnes. "Now this has come?"

"Oh, I think I must, Aunt. Perhaps it won't be long before I can use this for a teaching post. But I need to earn some money now."

Reaching the village several minutes later, she passed John Brook's woodshop, shut up and with no sign of him. She carried on, turning right down the steep drop of St Helen's Gate until she reached the mill.

The long building was several stories high with many windows cut into its solid stone walls. Anne picked her way over the cobbled yard, avoiding a great wagon being unloaded of its bales of wool by workmen, while the cart-horses stood motionless, impervious to the clanking of machinery and the roaring noise of the steam engine from within. Stepping up to an open door, she looked about for someone to speak to. As she waited, she caught a glimpse of the interior, of men rolling baskets on wheels across the dirty floor while belts and pulleys above their heads slapped and whirred, and louder than anything, the constant clacking of the looms attended by women in drab overalls, standing at their work. Those nearest the door turned to stare at her.

"Yes?"

It was a middle-aged man, in a hat, grubby shirt, waistcoat and thick trousers.

"I wondered if there was any vacancy for a mill-worker. Female," said Anne, feeling extremely foolish and out-of-place.

The man looked her over for what in polite company would have been an impertinently long time.

"Ever done any before?" he asked, moving a wad of tobacco he was chewing from one side of his mouth to the other.

"No. But I'm willing to learn."

The man sniffed.

"Nowt doing, lass."

"I see. Thank you."

She hurried away, feeling both relief and disappointment. Regaining the narrow causeway outside the mill, she turned left towards the valley. She would get some fresh air and walk back to the farm the long way round. A few moments later, she crossed the bridge over the Rushfield Dike, a mere trickle at this time of year, then prepared to turn right again.

As she came to the junction, she was surprised to meet a small boy, about six years of age, purposefully making his way towards her. Too well-dressed for a village child, he carried a leather bag across his back. He greeted her with the kind of confidence that came from speaking to servants.

"Good afternoon. Can you tell me if this is the road to London?"

Anne considered. It was, but in the other direction, at a distance of two hundred miles.

"Yes, but the other way. And it is a very long journey."

"Yes, I know," he said. "But I have brought money and provisions." He lifted the bag off his back and, struggling with the buckles, opened it to reveal a cloth-wrapped pie and a bottle of ginger beer.

Anne held her lips steady.

"You are well-provided. But I cannot advise you to make this journey at present."

"Why not?" The boy lifted his chin.

"Because you need to consult a timetable to find out the times of the connections you would need to make. To reach Doncaster and catch the train to London, you must first get to Wakefield. I know because I travelled here that way myself some weeks since."

The boy looked doubtful.

"I see. Well, on your advice, I may – " He stopped, as if recalling the reasons he had set out so determinedly.

Anne spoke gently.

"I think your mother and father would be glad to see you and hear of your change of plan."

The boy's face brightened.

"Yes, perhaps they would."

"Might I perhaps accompany you home?"

"Very well. I live at Dartmouth Hall."

Gathering up his supplies, he turned round and they began the walk back together. Dartmouth Hall was about half a mile ahead, set in extensive grounds. Together they went through an impressive gateway and along a drive between an avenue of trees. As they drew near to the house, the boy's legs moved more slowly. Whether this was from reluctance or tiredness, Anne did not know, but a moment later, she felt him slip his hand into hers and hold it tight.

Anne knew there were two or three grand houses in the valley but had not seen any of them, so sheltered were they from the roadside. Dartmouth Hall was a magnificent building of Tudor origin by the look of it but she had no time for closer inspection. As they went up the steps to the main door, an elderly servant ran out and grasped the boy with a cry of relief.

"Thank God! Susan!" she called to a maid who came running out. "Tell them Master Edward is found!"

Holding the boy ever more tightly, she rushed indoors with him to a room where his mother was having hysterics while another maid tried to calm her down. Anne followed hesitantly. When she saw the boy, the mother flew at him, sobbing, and clasped him to her. He submitted, twisting his head to look at Anne. It was a while before the mother collected herself.

"Now, Edward! You have been a very naughty boy to distress your Mama so. What do you mean by it?"

The boy looked sulky and said nothing. At that moment, his sister, about two years younger than Edward, ran into the room, ringlets bobbing, and heard the question.

"He was rude to Miss Paget," she announced. "She smacked him and he smacked her back."

"What is this, Edward? Insolent to your governess?"

"She's a foolish woman, Mama. And she's always drunk."

There was a gasp of disbelief from the children's mother and a peal of laughter from the little girl who began jumping about, squealing "She is! She is!" at the top of her voice. Anne felt a sudden desire to laugh but controlled herself just in time.

"It's true, Mama," said Edward. "She keeps a bottle in her bureau and takes a drink when she thinks we're not looking."

"Out of the mouths of babes..." thought Anne. It all sounded very convincing.

The mother was rescued by the sound of a horse's hooves on the gravel outside the window. Anne saw a well-dressed man, erect of bearing and with a fine moustache, dismount and speak to the groom at his side.

"We shall see what Papa thinks of this," cried the mother, sweeping out of the room. She could be seen talking excitedly to her husband who went striding up the stairs, two at a time. His wife, fluttering, remained at the bottom. Instinctively, everyone else, including Anne, moved out into the hall behind her.

Above their heads, the father could be heard rattling the handle of a locked door and shouting to the person inside. Getting no response, he summoned two menservants to force the door open.

With her husband in control, the mother sent the children upstairs with a maid. Now in command of herself, she apologised to Anne and drew her into the parlour, introducing herself as Ellen Thorpe. Fashionably dressed in blue silk, she looked to be in her early thirties, with light-coloured hair and eyes, her pretty face marred by a slightly petulant expression.

"We owe you our gratitude, Miss Graham. Had Edward chanced upon someone unscrupulous, there is no knowing what might have happened. His father will see that he is punished."

"I hope he will not be too severe," said Anne. "Your son was very sensibly prepared but very willing to return when reminded of his parents."

Mrs Thorpe looked pleased.

"Dear boy! I think he would have missed his Mama before very long."

The door opened and Frederick Thorpe entered, flushed and straightening his jacket. As his wife began to question him, he held up his hand.

"I shall spare you the details, my dear. All you need to know is that Miss Paget will be leaving directly, without a reference. The maids are helping her to pack and William will take her into Huddersfield when she is ready. I suggest the children be kept out of the way until she is gone."

Silently, Anne admired his efficiency. His wife was more voluble.

"Thank you, my dearest love," she simpered. "What would I do without your strength and authority?"

She gazed at him adoringly. Thorpe ignored her. Turning to Anne, he bowed politely.

"I hear we have you to thank, Miss Graham, for returning our little runaway."

Anne smiled. He continued.

"I have heard all about you from one of our maids. Visitors from London do not arrive in the village every day."

His wife gave a high-pitched laugh.

"Of course! You are from London as I am! And do you miss it, my dear, as I do? The fashionable shops, the elegance of the people?"

A look of irritation flickered across Thorpe's face. Before Anne could reply, he went on as if his wife had not spoken.

"The fact is, Miss Graham, that you come to us at a most opportune moment and highly recommended by your conduct. I believe you may be seeking a situation as a governess?"

"Indeed I am, Sir."

"You have seen the two young rascals for yourself – "

"Frederick, Frederick, how can you say such a thing?" protested his wife.

" – so you know what you have to contend with. I suggest that if you are interested, you return tomorrow morning when we can discuss it further. You will no doubt have a reference you can bring?"

"Yes, sir, I do."

"Excellent. Till tomorrow, then. Shall we say nine o'clock?"

He took her hand and looked into her eyes an instant longer than was necessary. A man who feels himself attractive to women, thought Anne. But what matter?

As she walked down the drive, she glanced back at the house and waved to the two children who were at an upstairs window. Instead of waving back, they put their tongues out and goggle-eyed, flattened their faces against the glass.

Anne was not deterred by this grotesque display. Anyone who had coped, as she had, with a huge classroom full of small Cockney children, was not dismayed by the prospect of teaching these two, however much they had been spoilt by their mother.

At a quarter to nine the next morning, Anne was approaching Dartmouth Hall along the avenue of sycamores, this time on her own. When she reached the front entrance, she paused to take in the impressive sight. The Hall was indeed a handsome old manor house with Tudor gables, stone mullions and latticed windows. Entering the porch, she was shown into a large entrance hall, its great open fireplace surmounted by the elaborately carved names of the original owners. From here, she was taken into a small breakfast room where Frederick Thorpe was awaiting her. There was no sign of his wife.

"This seems satisfactory," he said, swiftly reading the reference from the vicar of her London parish. "You like children? They can be tiresome."

"Yes, I do. They are not tiresome when they are busy doing something."

"Exactly so. And what I want to see Edward doing is reading. He is past six years old. At his age I could read the newspaper."

"Perhaps I could look at the schoolroom, Mr Thorpe?"

"By all means."

He led her up the grand stairs and along a galleried corridor. Anne looked down at the magnificent entrance hall they had just left.

"A beautiful house," she ventured.

"Yes, indeed. But I must tell you, before the servants do, that we do not own the Hall. We merely rent it by the quarter. The owner intends to return here some time in the future and restore the house and estate for his own use. We shall move to one of the new houses being built on the other side of Huddersfield in Edgerton. Mrs Thorpe has friends there. So you see, I cannot promise that your post here will be long-lived. Edward will be going to school soon, and Georgina too."

"I understand, sir."

"In the meantime, I should be heartily glad if you could interest Edward in the rudiments of English and arithmetic in particular."

By now they had reached the schoolroom, a large pleasant room beyond a line of bedrooms. Like the rooms downstairs, it had the characteristic oak panelling of the period as well as latticed windows with diamond-shaped panes.

Anne moved to the cupboards, easel and table. As she suspected, the reading books were of the dullest, the stationery scant.

"Could you purchase some items, sir, for Master Edward and Miss Georgina?"

"By all means. Paper, crayons and the like?"

"Yes, sir. And could you visit the bookseller for a copy of '*Boys Own*' magazine? And perhaps one of the complete stories they publish. There is one called '*Shot and Shell*' which may appeal to Master Edward."

Thorpe smiled.

"If he resembles his father, it will. One of the benefits of the Hall is the profusion of game on the estate lands. I expect a shooting party here next month when we hope for some excellent bags."

Anne said nothing. She disliked the shooting of creatures for sport but saw that any comment to that effect would be out of place. After discussion of pay and conditions, they shook hands and Anne left, with instructions to return next morning with her belongings.

She walked briskly up the hill with a greater spring in her step than had appeared since her arrival. This was all she could have hoped for – some form of independence, away from her surly relatives at the farm, working with children and not least, a room, and a bed, of her own! She had to restrain herself from skipping or bursting into song as she ran down the hill from Broken Cross.

Returning to the Stott farm, it was hard to contain her exuberance but contain it she had to, out of respect for her aunt's feelings.

"So Mr Thorpe thinks I would suit and asked me to come straightaway. Tomorrow morning. It has all happened very suddenly. Please forgive me."

Her aunt made an attempt at a smile. Anne noticed how very tired she looked.

"Not at all, my dear. You must go now you've t' chance."

Anne sensed a wistful note in her aunt's voice. Agnes's gentleness and timidity did not fit her for the life she had to lead. Anne felt a pang of guilt at leaving her to the mercies of Jack Stott and her uncaring children.

Her uncle and cousin Ned received the news that Anne was leaving with a grunt or two. Sarah, learning of it when she came home that evening from the mill, had more to say.

"Well, you *will* be mixing with some fine company and no mistake. I expect you'll be well suited with that. But don't be giving yourself airs, Mrs Thorpe does enough of that herself. Thinks folk round here aren't good enough for her. The 'all doesn't belong them, you know. They're nobbut tenants."

"So I understand," said Anne. She kissed her aunt lightly on the cheek. "Thank you for your hospitality, Aunt. And Uncle. I hope I shall see you, Aunt Agnes, before long. Certainly at church."

Her aunt gave her a wan smile. Anne then retired to bed, glad to be out of the Stotts' kitchen. Upstairs, she packed her belongings ready for the morning when Mr Thorpe was sending the carriage for her. She could scarcely believe her good fortune. But her happiness was clouded by the thought of her aunt's sad face. She must do all she could to help her in any way possible.

Anne settled in very quickly at the Hall. Her room, though simply furnished, was a delight, with a polished wood floor, a dark oak chest for her clothes and best of all, casement windows opening out onto the gardens. When she had put her books and her mother's likeness on the mantelpiece, it felt like home. The first night she fell asleep as soon as she got into bed, savouring equally the bliss of clean sheets and solitude.

Her relationship with Edward had got off to a good start. He had not been punished for his attempt at running away and seemed to believe that in some way he had Anne to thank for it. Besides that, he had thoroughly disliked her predecessor, Miss Paget, regarding her with the contempt that comes easily to children for those they know do not really like them.

Georgina tolerated her. The little girl's main enjoyment came from playing with her numerous, beautifully-dressed dolls but she was willing to concentrate on learning her letters for short periods of time, as long as Anne allowed her to skip off in search of Mama when the fancy took her.

Anne knew, from what she had read and discussed with her colleagues at the Church School, that the position of the governess in a large household was a delicate one. She belonged neither above nor below stairs. An important person to consider, and one who could be friend or foe, was the nursery maid who had possibly looked after the children since they were babies and still slept with them in the nursery. To her, the new governess could well be seen as an interloper. Fortunately for Anne, this was not the case with Susan who had not been with the Thorpe family for very long. She was a small, cheerful young woman of decided views, particularly on the subject of the previous governess.

"That Miss Paget! She thought she wa' sumbody but she wa'nt – she were nowt! Thought I wa' 'er servant, she did. I soon put her right!"

The maids lost no time in telling Anne that they liked Mr Thorpe for his directness and efficiency but were less keen on his wife. Mrs Thorpe undoubtedly thought of herself as "somebody" and perhaps she was, down south. She expected the staff to show her a deference that did not come naturally to them. Anne once heard her complaining to her husband.

"Frederick! You really must speak to the maids. Tell them they must wait outside a door for the word "Enter" before they come in. They seem to think they can just knock and walk in. And I've told them time and time again that I wish to be addressed as "Ma'am" – not "Mrs Thorpe", or even worse sometimes, as "Missus.""

"My dear Ellen, it is for you to train them to do these things, if that is what you want. You forget this is not an established servants' hall, such as you had in your parents' home in Chelsea. These are simply local people I recruited when you insisted on our taking a short lease on this place. You can't expect them to behave like those who are born into service. Just be grateful, as I am, that they seem to be honest."

Anne thought Frederick's judgment sound. The staff at the Hall appeared to be decent people, glad to have found employment yet still independent-minded, and prone to plain speaking and acting. They knew of Anne's circumstances and treated her, as she treated them, as equals.

In this congenial environment, Anne turned to her main task, that of educating the children, with enthusiasm. Although Georgina's attention easily wandered, Anne was pleased to find that the child enjoyed writing and listening to stories and was soon able to write her own name and those of her dolls.

Edward needed handling with greater tact. Anne soon discovered that he was a highly intelligent child who was secretly mortified by his inability to read. Taking care not to humiliate him with infant primers, she tried to find word and letter games to appeal to him and by degrees, was able to lead him gently into reading simple sentences. He mastered these so quickly that she was soon giving him more difficult things to read until, a few weeks later, he was ready to tackle a tale of real interest to him, namely, the adventures of Captain Carstairs of the 6th Hussars. The day he was able to read part of the familiar tale to his parents was a proud one.

"Oh well done, my love!" gushed his mother, covering him with kisses. But it was his father's approval that counted with Edward.

"Yes indeed, my boy," said his father. "And well done to Miss Graham also," he added, glancing at Anne. "I think some celebration is called for. What do you say, Edward? Shall we ask Miss Graham if she would care to accompany us to the cricket match at Lascelles Hall tomorrow? My wife will probably see precious little of the game, if her past conduct is anything to go by, when she meets the ladies of her acquaintance."

Ellen Thorpe gave her high, fluting laugh. Anne smiled.

"Thank you, sir. I should like it very much, although I have never seen one before."

"Don't worry, Miss Graham," Edward reassured her, brimming with importance. "I will explain it all to you."

Anne was still wearing black in mourning for her mother but the Thorpes were decked out in new, fashionable clothes for the occasion. Mother and daughter were in toning outfits, Mrs Thorpe in a blue and white striped foulard with a dainty bonnet with matching parasol and Georgina in a miniature, shorter version of the same, father and son in silk-striped caps atop a striped blazer for the man and a long-sleeved shirt with floppy silk bow tie for the boy.

It was a sunny afternoon and as they drew near to the cricket ground, a sizeable crowd was making its way along the narrow lanes. Most were working men in shirt sleeves and there was some shouting and jostling as the carriage attempted to get through. In common with the servants at the Hall, the men showed no particular deference for those wealthier or of a higher social class than themselves, more like a cheerful contempt. Anne liked them for it.

The cricket field at Lascelles Hall was a fine, level one enclosed by low stone walls. Families were making themselves comfortable around the perimeter, the better-off gathering in front of the pavilion where rows of canvas chairs had been set out. Ellen Thorpe was soon happily chatting to her friends while her husband, as one of the contributing supporters of the club, began talking knowledgeably to the officials.

"The visitors are Hunslet Union Club," said Edward. "They have won the toss and have chosen to bat first."

At that moment the home team walked out on to the pitch and took up their positions. With a start, Anne recognised John Brook among them. All the players wore creamy-white shirts and high-waisted trousers with braces. To Anne's eyes, none looked so handsome as John. He was one of the tallest, slim but strongly built across the shoulders, his muscles emphasised by the close-fitting braces. When the ball was thrown to him to open the bowling, he rolled up his sleeves, revealing tanned, shapely fore-arms. She felt herself shiver with pleasure as she feasted her eyes on him, imagining touching his arms, feeling them warm and firm around her. As he ran forward, his thighs strained against his clothing. A deeply stirring, yearning sensation ran through her body which she was powerless to resist.

"That's John Brook from the village," said Edward.

"Yes, I know," said Anne. She would have found it difficult to say more.

"He used to play for a Honley team but Jed Thewlis from Lascelles Hall saw him and got him to play here instead. It's a more important club."

Edward's father had bought him a score-card book and for the next hour or so, he concentrated hard on the play and carefully wrote down the runs scored in every over. The effort kept him from speaking to Anne. But she was completely occupied, entranced even, watching John on the pitch, the graceful wheeling of his upper body as he bowled, his speed when fielding, his power and accuracy when he threw the ball in.

Around her, onlookers shouted praise or criticism, children and dogs chased each other, people gossiped but she was oblivious to them all. As she gazed at him, a voice spoke inside her head. It said "You are in love with John Brook."

"In love?" Had this really happened to her? For a moment she was ecstatic with breathtaking joy and abandoned herself to the torrent of feeling that gushed through her. Yes, there was no denying it – these were the only words to describe the feeling of passionate affection mingled with desire that seemed to possess her entirely. What else could explain the overwhelming satisfaction that came from simply looking at John Brook?

All too soon, reason returned her to reality. "But he is married to someone else and does not love you." It was brutal but the truth. She felt as though her heart would break with the pain and for a while, had difficulty in breathing. Feeling her emotions were so strong they must be visible to others, she stole a glance along the row of spectators on either side of her. But no, none of them seemed to have noticed anything; they were still watching the match, dozing or chatting as they were before, while Edward's curly head was still bent low over his scoring book. By now, her heart was thudding and tears were pushing into her eyes. Pulling her handkerchief out, she took a deep breath and blew her nose. Gathering herself together and wrenching her eyes from the cricket pitch, she spoke briskly to Edward.

"Well, Edward. How are the opponents doing?" Before he could answer, there was a great roar as the last man was caught out.

"All out!" cried Edward. "For 93!"

The players trooped off the pitch to join everyone in the celebration which was tea. Frederick Thorpe brought Anne and his wife a tray of refreshments, behind him a tea tent heaving with people.

After the interval, the innings of the Lascelles Hall team proceeded at a swifter pace. There were some excellent batsmen who smacked the ball to all areas of the field, the cry of "Four!" ringing out regularly in the late afternoon.

John, looking like some graceful warrior, was still batting, although five partners had been dismissed already. As the score rose to the high eighties, many of the crowd stood up, impelled by an energy they felt they could will into their team.

The Hunslet bowler walked away, spitting on the ball and rubbing it on his trousers, then turned, began his run up and bowled straight at the wicket. With a resounding crack, John smote the ball with the centre of the bat and with a great swing, sent it soaring up and out across the boundary without touching the ground.

Cheers and applause greeted this winning shot.

"He's top scorer, top scorer !" exclaimed Edward excitedly. Of course, of course, thought Anne, smiling down at him.

The two batsmen led the procession off the field to a standing ovation, the older one, heavily bewhiskered, swinging his bat and grinning broadly. John followed with his head down but as he passed Anne, her hands raised in joyous clapping, he looked up and met her eyes. Her heart lurched for that instant and then he was gone.

"A good day," said Thorpe, as the carriage came to a halt at the terrace steps. Anne was relieved when Susan and another maid ran out to meet them and lifted the two sleepy children down. She climbed the steps slowly and then summoned her energy to mount the stairs to her room, thankful to be relieved of any further responsibility that day.

On waking next morning, Anne's mind was, for a moment, mercifully blank. Then it all came rushing back – the cricket match, images of John and the stunning realisation of her feelings for him, feelings which she acknowledged had been growing stronger ever since their first meeting.

She was tempted to ask "Why? Why has Fate dealt me this blow, leading me to the man I love but denying me the possibility of happiness?" But she knew this was pointless. It was a question to which there was no answer. Searching for one would only lead her to self-pity and despair.

She tried to be rational and to tell herself that she was not bound to meet him very often. Their paths only crossed at church. Now she was employed by the Thorpes, her place was with them; there would be little or no time for social chat with other churchgoers after the service on the paved walk outside. A smile or nod of recognition would be the extent of her contact with him. In any case, her Aunt Agnes had first call on her attention.

Unfortunately, not seeing him face-to-face had little effect. However hard she tried, she thought about John Brook for more hours than she knew was sensible. It was a good day that tired her out so thoroughly that she fell asleep quickly from sheer exhaustion. If this did not happen, then this was the worst time – when all other distractions were gone. Thinking about John was a pleasure so intense she could not prevent herself indulging in it even though the experience brought its own pain. Anne was reminded of how, as a child, she would push her tongue under a loose tooth. Imagining herself in his arms filled her with the torments of unfulfilled longing; thinking of him with his wife introduced her to the horrors of jealousy, which followed her into her dreams.

Why was falling out of love so difficult when falling in love was so easy? She was comforted when she realised she must be one of many, of thousands of fellow-sufferers. She remembered her mother saying "What cannot be cured must be endured." Enduring pain must bring one some kind of maturity, surely? Even if it didn't, believing it did might help. Better than wallowing in misery, at any rate. Time would help her, would soften the hurt. For the moment, she was glad that her suffering was secret and would remain so.

What mattered now was to gain an unblemished reference from her present employers which would help her find a new position elsewhere as a governess next year, a long enough period ahead to establish herself as a trusted employee and short enough for her to hope that her heartache would soon be lessened by a change of scene.

In the meantime, the education of Edward and Georgina was her priority. She managed to establish a pattern of schoolwork in the mornings, leaving the afternoons for play and walks. Even so, distractions arose. Edward's concentration was severely disturbed by the arrival of the shooting parties his father organised once the season began. The estate extended over several hundred acres of field and woodland; more men were taken on as beaters and grooms.

Edward was very keen to accompany the shooters but here, fortunately, his mother's over-protectiveness coincided with his father's cooler judgment that a rising seven year old would be a dangerous addition to any group. He had to be content with watching the men gathering at the start, excited beneath their apparent calm, talking of dogs and guns and birds, their new hunting jackets, hats and breeches contrasting with the shabby everyday clothes of the working men. If he was lucky, he was allowed to run out to meet them as they returned, the smell of powder still on them, and hold a swinging brace of game birds, necks twisted together, golden plumage still gleaming.

Further distraction came from Mrs Thorpe's tea-parties. Anne would be summoned to bring the children downstairs, clean, well-dressed and ready to recite or read aloud.

Georgina loved these occasions.

"Should I dance as well, Miss Graham? Will you play the Fairy Dance for me?" She pirouetted as she spoke, leaving Susan to disentangle the hairbrush.

"I don't think so, my dear. Keep that for when you are alone with Mama and Papa."

Edward grumbled as his top shirt button was fastened.

"They're stupid women. I don't see why we have to go downstairs and see them."

"They are not stupid women, Edward," said Anne, holding him still. "And if they were, it would be impolite of you to say so. Now bring your books."

Down they went, Anne in her best black gown with a brightly dressed child on either hand. Their appearance was greeted by exclamations of pleasure.

"Here they are!" cooed their mother. "Say good afternoon to my visitors." They obeyed, Georgina willing to be kissed, Edward decidedly not.

Anne took a chair in the corner of the room. She expected to know none of the women there but recognised Isabel Blezard at once. Isabel treated her as if she were invisible, not even glancing in her direction when Mrs Thorpe introduced her as the new governess.

"I hear your last one lived up to their reputation," said a plain young woman with strong, pointed features. She sat beside an older woman who was clearly her mother.

"I'm afraid so," said Ellen Thorpe. Her eyelids fluttered nervously.

The young woman pursued her line of thought despite the small girl at her knee.

"A drunkard, I hear. Not to mention any other sins we know nothing of."

Edward looked interested. Anne thought the woman very vulgar and was relieved when the older woman intervened.

"Are we to have the pleasure of hearing the children?"

Georgina, happy to be first, sang a nursery rhyme, rolling her eyes about as she did so which detracted slightly from her performance. Obligatory applause and a hug from Mama ensued.

Edward had agreed to read a piece from his *'Boys Own'* monthly magazine to demonstrate his recently-acquired ability. Anne had chosen a suitable passage, a description of the cavalry being inspected by their general. Edward's preference was for a later passage in which a native bearer was gored by a wild beast. Anne prayed he would stick to her choice and fixed him with a long, hard look to make sure he did.

As he read to the group of languid women, Anne thought how strange it was that she should be sitting in this sunny Yorkshire drawing-room at the end of summer when less than six months ago she had been teaching poor London children in a church school and living, not in comfort, but happily, with her mother in the narrow house in Victoria Park. Was life fated? Surely not, for it had been her decision to strike out on her own up here.

Her musings were cut short by a smattering of applause. Edward, really rather proud of himself, was now demonstrating his manliness by cramming as much cake into his mouth as he could. Anne, sipping tea, could not but overhear the conversation.

Isabel Blezard was describing, with evident satisfaction, the work she had commissioned for her new home.

"We are very pleased with all the new woodwork. Mahogany, a particular favourite of mine. I do so love its rich hue. I really must show you the carved over-mantel in the parlour – quite beautiful. The rose-coloured granite just sets it off. And I've had a shield carved in the centre. For our initials, you know."

"How splendid!" said Ellen Thorpe. "I am quite envious. The Hall is very fine, of course, but one can't exactly put one's mark on it, so to speak. Still, it is very pleasant and reminds me so much of my happy childhood days with Mama and Papa. When we acquire our new home next year, I shall certainly accept your recommendations, Isabel, about who to commission for such work."

Isabel looked gratified.

"Oh, I recommend John Brook, here in the village, for any kind of cabinet-making. His work is exceptionally fine. As good as anyone in London, I would say."

"I too have heard that John Brook's work is very fine," said the sharp-featured young woman suggestively. Anne recalled that she was a Miss Littlewood, daughter of a local doctor. The young woman giggled. "In fact, everything about him is rather fine, I would say."

Her mother looked displeased while Isabel's eyes registered interest.

"Did you see him at the cricket match?" Miss Littlewood went on. "And even better, when he was helping with the hay-making?"

Head down, looking at her sewing, Anne felt her cheeks grow hot. She could imagine what the young woman meant, although she hated her for saying it.

Mrs Littlewood grasped the initiative.

"Dear Ellen, your hair is looking very well. Has your maid dressed it or have you visited the new establishment in John William Street?"

"Thank you. I have arranged it myself as usual. Have you visited it?"

"No, indeed. Grace and I passed it last week. I would not wish to sit, so exposed, with four other customers."

"But Mother," interrupted her daughter, "those who have patronised it spoke most highly of Professor Lin. And they have the latest styles from Paris."

Anne was to learn no more of the latest fashions in hairdressing as the children became fidgety and needed to be withdrawn. Any further lessons were out of the question. A brisk trot around the nearest garden was the only option before them.

Anne gained great pleasure from the extensive grounds around the Hall and felt herself grow stronger from the daily exercise she took with the children. In July the children had enjoyed gathering flowers, in

August they hunted for spent cartridges and now, as the days shortened, they picked up the conkers where they had fallen from the chestnut trees.

One blustery October day they had walked further than usual. The wind, blowing in gusts, seemed to make the children excitable. They had raced ahead and scrambled down a steep bank which fell right down to a dry-stone wall bordering the Woodsome Road. Anne followed, more carefully.

A man with a dog was walking towards them along the road. With a start, Anne recognised John and waited, with her heart racing and her mouth going dry, until he drew level. After the exchange of polite enquiries, his gaze rested on Edward and Georgina whose cheeks were pink with exertion.

"They're bonny children, Miss Graham. And are you enjoying teaching them?"

"Oh yes!"

Anne turned and smiled at them. John was still speaking, with a hint of embarrassment. He spoke so softly Anne could only just catch his meaning. Then she understood. He was telling her that Molly was expecting their first child in the spring. She gave him an automatic smile, said something appropriate and then moved away, shepherding the children in front of her.

Was this part of her fate? Assuredly part of the fate of John and Molly Brook. But did it have to come so soon, before the pain of her unrequited love had had time to diminish?

The children ran home, whooping and brandishing twigs. Anne walked behind them, tears running down her cheeks unheeded, until she reached the house once more and assumed her professional face.

CHAPTER FIVE

Christmas morning and All Hallows' Church was almost full. As the organist played the opening bars of 'O Come All Ye Faithful,' the congregation stood and began to sing.

Anne, standing in the pew behind Edward and Georgina and their parents, was impressed, as she always was, by the hearty singing coming from all parts. The people seemed to sing at greater volume and with greater zest than the London congregation she was used to.

Looking down, she was pleased to see the children standing quietly, heads bent. A special toy had been promised if they behaved well in church. Their father, Frederick Thorpe, was singing lustily in his fine tenor voice, obviously enjoying his role, though temporary, of local squire. Ellen Thorpe seemed less at ease. Preparations were being made for a lavish entertainment later that day with a dinner served exceptionally in the Great Hall, which had already been hung with garlands of greenery from the estate. As the party was leaving for church, Ellen had been fretting lest the lofty chamber would not be warm enough for their guests and had left strict instructions for the servants to keep the fire in the vast stone fireplace built up high all day.

As the carol came to an end and the churchgoers rustled and fidgeted in making themselves comfortable for the sermon, Anne quickly scanned the congregation for her Aunt Agnes. At last she picked her out, sitting at the very back near the church door. She must have arrived late, probably getting a Christmas meal ready for her ungrateful family while they slept in. But I must not be uncharitable, thought Anne, not this morning of all mornings. However, that was easier said than done when her glance took in the Blezard family sitting in the pew across the aisle.

Isabel Blezard was wearing a magnificent fur-trimmed cape and matching bonnet, which looked new, as all her clothes did. Anne saw her peel off her kid gloves in order to turn the pages of the hymn book. As she did so, the precious stones in her rings winked in the sunbeam in which she stood. Isabel looked very pleased with herself this morning, unlike her husband who appeared anxious. He frequently murmured something to a young girl on his other side. That must be Charlotte, his daughter from his first marriage, come home from boarding school. Her broad face and ruddy colouring were like her father's. The girl stared fixedly ahead and made no attempt to sing. It could not be easy, being Isabel Blezard's step-daughter.

Anne felt certain that John, his wife Molly and his mother Martha Brook, were seated somewhere behind her but it was impossible to turn round and look for them. And did she really want to? The sight of Molly on John's arm or of his attentiveness to his pregnant young wife sent a shaft of pain through her. Better not to look. But even as she decided this, kneeling in prayer, she knew her eyes would seek him out, nonetheless.

The service over, the organ music continued as the congregation filed out. People greeted each other cheerfully and chatted as they emerged into the chill winter sunlight. Anne was always amused to watch those who sought out the vicar for his individual attention. Who were they? Those committed to church work, undoubtedly, but also those who thought their social position demanded it, like Frederick Thorpe, as he made his way purposefully towards the vicar. But there was no harm in it. She was sure the church funds were benefiting handsomely from the contributions of the temporary tenant of Dartmouth Hall.

"A most pleasant service, Vicar, most pleasant!" said Ellen Thorpe with a smile and a proffered hand. Her husband looked pleased. Ellen Thorpe was at her best in social situations such as these.

"Thank you, thank you, Mrs Thorpe," replied the vicar. "And are we enjoying our Christmas morning?" he asked, stooping down to the children. Georgina obliged with a sweet smile, Edward simply nodded. The Thorpes moved on and began to speak to other acquaintances.

This was the moment for Anne to speak to the Brooks, if she wished. She saw them emerging from the church porch, or rather, she saw John, head and shoulders above the people around him. But before she could make a move, she was pushed to one side by the elbow of Isabel Blezard who bore down on the group in a determined manner and remained standing talking to them, blocking Anne's view as she did so. Anne had just a moment to greet her Aunt Agnes as she hurried past when she saw the Thorpe party moving along the paved walk towards their carriage. She had no choice but to follow them.

John spent most of the church service worrying about his wife. Although she had made no complaint, Molly had obviously found the walk up to the village from their cottage in the valley very taxing. She had been forced to stop and rest several times on the way. John's mother, however, had said nothing so he assumed that this was perhaps not unusual for a woman in the fifth month of pregnancy. He was relieved when they reached the church and he could get her to a pew.

John could see Anne Graham several rows ahead, her bright hair just showing under her black bonnet. He had thought of her several times during the last few months. By all accounts, which travelled swiftly along the Almondbury lanes, she was well thought of at Dartmouth Hall. Indeed, he would have been surprised to have heard otherwise. She had a lively, energetic air about her and seemed ready to enjoy life. He was sure the children would like her as their governess.

When he had seen her a few weeks earlier in the woods at the edge of the estate, he had thought she looked in better health. She was probably enjoying more food, fresh air and exercise than she had had in London. He would speak to her after the service and wish her a happy Christmas.

His intention was thwarted, however, once they had left the church. Isabel Blezard, looking very expensively dressed, with her husband and step-daughter hanging back behind her, swooped down upon them.

"Good morning, Mr Brook. Mrs Brook. Molly. I wish you all the compliments of the season."

"Thank you, Mrs Blezard," John replied. "Mr Blezard. Miss Blezard. We wish you all the same."

Isabel, bright-eyed, turned to Molly.

"How are you, Molly? You look a little tired if I may say so."

"I'm well enough, Mrs Blezard, thank you."

John looked at his wife doubtfully and then back at Isabel.

"We shall be glad when we can get her to rest a bit more."

Isabel's face lit up.

"I do understand. I wonder – " She stopped, as if an idea had just occurred to her.

"I wonder if Molly would like a shorter working day in our household from now on? I'm afraid it would only be general maid's duties but as a temporary measure, it might suit. Better than the mill, at any rate."

John did not like her final remark. It sounded patronising to Molly and critical of him for allowing his pregnant wife to go on working there. He bridled.

"Thank you for the offer, Mrs Blezard. We will let you know directly." With that, he put his arm round Molly and steered her away from the Blezards and towards the church gates.

Little was said as the Brooks made their way home. Once indoors and warm, John re-considered. He had perhaps been a bit too hasty.

"What do you think to Mrs Blezard's offer, Molly? I know you've never fancied going into service."

"No, right enough. T' mill pays more and I like the company."

"Why don't you stop at home now? I'm earning enough. I wish you would."

"No! You've said this before and I've told you what I've decided. I want to work another month – at least. I'm saving all my wage so this child can have all new stuff, not other people's hand-me-downs, like me and Cissie always had. And I can't expect you to do it. You've still to pay off that money you owe for the woodshop."

"You've no need to worry about that," said John, his face darkening. "There'll be enough money for all we want."

"I'm not saying there won't. I'm just saying I want to find some extra, for what *I* want. I've never 'ad that before. All my wages 'ave allus 'ad to go straight to my mother – to feed t' family."

John said nothing. The Brooks had never known real poverty, had never been completely without work but he knew the Dysons had not fared so well. He understood exactly why Molly felt and spoke as she did. He also knew there was no point arguing with her once she had made her mind up.

His mother now came in from the little scullery where she had been tactfully keeping out of the way. Walter was dozing by the fire until she shook his shoulder very gently.

"Now then, what about some dinner? This bit o' beef's just asking to be eaten! John! Are you going to carve for us?"

John and Molly bustled to get things ready, laying the table, serving up the vegetables. John stood, a tea cloth tucked in his belt, sharpening the knife on the whetstone and then slicing through the crunchy surface of the joint to the fat-glistening meat inside. Whatever there had been of disagreement in the room melted away under the influence of food, warmth and a sense of well-being.

"By, you were in t' best place this morning, Father," said John. "Wind were bitter cold."

His father nodded.

"Eh, I thought so mysen. Reckon it's what my father used to call a Burtoner."

"A Burtoner? What's that?"

"A Burtoner. A wind from Kirkburton. An East wind. Coldest o' t' lot. Sign o' snow."

John and Molly burst out laughing.

"What's so comical?" asked Martha.

"Well," John explained. "Kirkburton's nobbut three mile away. Reckon t' wind comes from a bit further away than that!"

Soon they were all chuckling, his father included. When they were quiet, Molly turned to her mother-in-law.

"What do you think, Martha, about me working?"

Martha spoke carefully.

"Well, why don't you just work about a month for Mrs Blezard? Shorter hours'll do you good. And you might get to sit down a bit as well. We'll soon be into t' worst o' t' weather. Going up and down Lockwood Scar to the mill will be hard enough for t' fittest. I should take Mrs Blezard's offer. You can always stop when you want."

The truth of this was evident. Lockwood Scar was one of the steepest hills in the area and nearly half a mile long.

Molly considered.

"All right then. I'll stop working at t' mill and go to Mrs Blezard's."

The weather remained cold after Christmas. Then, as January wore on, the temperature dropped still further.

It had been near freezing all that week. On the Sunday, the Thorpe family were confined indoors with heavy colds. Anne went to church by herself. As she walked towards the village, there was a chilling dampness in the air that made her draw her cloak more tightly around her body.

It began to snow while the service was in progress. People coming out of church drew their cloaks and shawls more tightly around them and hurried home, heads down, snowflakes melting on faces and eyelashes. Those with horses reined them in to tread more carefully and most dismounted as soon as the roads became steeper.

Isabel, resplendent in a wine-coloured coat and skirt with matching hat, stood waiting just inside the church gates for her carriage. It edged forward until it was alongside, the horses tossing their heads and snorting steam. She climbed into the vehicle and, wrapping herself in the rugs, gave instructions for the coachman to drive straight up the hill as usual.

Anne, who had hung back to avoid Isabel, was about to leave the churchyard when she saw John and his young wife approaching. She knew that the sight of him, tenderly solicitous of the other woman, would make her wince but nevertheless, she could not deny herself the fulfilment of her longing to see him close to.

He passed her, as she feared he would, without seeing her, with eyes only for his pregnant wife whom he supported carefully with his arm around her waist. Angry with herself, Anne turned blindly out of the gate and began to walk back to the Hall.

Leaving the church, John and Molly picked their way slowly along the village street with other churchgoers and then turned down the lane into the valley, treading carefully as the snow flurried around them.

"It's settling," he said. "If it snows all day, it'll be too deep for you to get to the Blezards' tomorrow. Best stop at home."

"No, no! I'm fit to walk. And I don't want to lose any money. I've not been there two weeks yet."

"We'll see. If it's thick, mind, I'll come with you and see you safe."

All his life John would remember that Sunday. It continued to snow steadily all day until the cottage seemed becalmed in a vast white ocean. After Sunday dinner, they had sat companionably round the fire, his parents in the two carver chairs with John and Molly between them on the upright ones. His father tried to make Molly take the more comfortable chair but she would not. She sat knitting, a cushion in the small of her back while John read a periodical. His father soon dozed off while his mother sat quietly, her head bent over her crochet. The only sounds were the tiny click of needles, the turn of a page and the shifting rustle of the coals in the grate. As the sun went down, a carmine glow briefly lit the snow-covered fields.

"It's like a picture!" exclaimed Molly, gazing out of the window, her smooth skin shining in the reflected light. And as beautiful indoors as out, thought John, looking at her, his heart full. Here about me are those I love most in the world, safe and well. I would not change places with any man in the country, however rich he might be.

His father stirred; his mother fetched bread, cheese and ale. The room became warmer as the fire reddened and gave out greater heat. Reluctantly, a short while later, they left the warm room for their beds upstairs, John banking up the fire for the night with slack.

Molly fell asleep in her husband's arms almost at once. John listened to the soft sound of her breathing until he too succumbed to sleep.

They were up very early the next morning, woken by the unnaturally bright light.

"It's not snowing now but there's plenty more up there," said John, peering out. "We'd best look sharp and get out before it starts again."

The snow was almost a foot deep in places and as they entered the drive of the Blezard house, it began to snow again, at first finely and then with large flakes. John spoke.

" Molly! You mustn't try to get back tonight. I'll speak to the housekeeper."

So saying, he went in by the servants' door and began looking for Mrs Drew. She appeared, a severe figure in black, and listened impassively.

"Good morning, Mrs Drew. I'd be much obliged if my wife could stay in the house tonight. I think we're in for a deal more snow and I fear for her safety if she tries to walk home."

Mrs Drew said nothing. John continued, as if he had not noticed her lack of response.

"If not, she'll go straight back now."

The housekeeper met his gaze. She understood the situation perfectly.

"Wait here. I must ask Mrs Blezard."

As she mounted the staircase, Molly began to loosen the cloth bindings round her feet. John stopped her.

"Leave them be. Show her we're ready to leave if they won't be reasonable."

Moments passed. Then Isabel appeared, wearing an oyster silk robe, trimmed with swansdown, her long dark hair falling in curls about her shoulders. She stood still, smiling, as if happy for the observers to take in the full picture.

John had never seen her with hair down or indeed, in such intimate garments. He was not aware of detail, only of a general impression of beauty, rosiness, silkiness, shine. Almost at once, he felt a flush of confused pleasure and embarrassment.

"I am sorry for the early hour, Mrs Blezard, but I am concerned for Molly's safety if the snow continues. We get some heavy snow in these parts and if it drifts, it can be treacherous."

"I understand. Of course." Isabel gave him her most winning smile. "Molly may stay overnight. There is room in the maids' attic. Mrs Drew will see to it."

"Thank you, Mrs Blezard." Molly had spoken but Isabel did not take her eyes from John's face.

"In fact," Isabel went on, "she may stay more than one night if it is necessary."

John's face cleared.

"Well, I'd feel better if she could. To know she's safe."

"That's settled then," said Isabel pleasantly. "Molly may stay until you come to collect her. We must take care of her, especially as she is with child. How long...?"

"I am six months gone. But I am fit and well." There was more than a touch of truculence in Molly's voice.

"I am sure you are. With such a good husband to take care of you."

Isabel's smile was directed at John alone. Suddenly he wanted to be out of the house. Why, he did not know, except for a feeling of being unable to cope.

"Thank you. Good morning, Mrs Blezard. Mrs Drew. Molly."

And then he was gone, without any final tenderness to his wife, a fact they both noticed, and regretted, moments later when he had gone striding down the drive.

It continued snowing heavily all Monday. By the evening, the outlines of roads were indistinguishable. Only those who knew the area well ventured out. Workers at the mills walked home in large groups, keeping together for safety. There was some larking about and throwing of snowballs but getting home mattered most. Farmers and shepherds had already secured as much of their stock as possible and prepared themselves for a snow siege. Pennine weather was to be taken seriously.

By Tuesday morning, the world as seen from Castle Hill was a virtually unbroken sea of white. By Tuesday afternoon, the wind increased in power, sending fresh flurries of snow which piled up in deep drifts wherever it was blown. Walkers wrapped mufflers and shawls across their faces to avoid the wind's keen bite, stumbling and cursing at journeys that took them so much longer. No-one stirred abroad unless they were bound to.

Molly spent Monday and Tuesday nights sharing an attic room with Jessie, the maid-of-all-work. Each morning they had to break the ice in their water jug before they could wash.

She found Jessie a foolish chatterbox and did not look forward to spending another night in her company. Once Molly was in bed, she was ready to go to sleep. Not so Jessie, who seemed unnaturally wide awake and excited by the presence of a companion.

"Have you seen all Mrs Blezard's clothes? She's got trunks of 'em, some not even worn yet. All o' the best quality. And so they should be when your husband owns a mill. There's a coat and skirt, a port wine colour, I dote on. And her evening gowns! I don't think she wears t' same one twice."

Molly shut her eyes, said nothing and hoped Jessie would think she was asleep. As she lay awake in the hard narrow bed, hearing the snuffling noises made by Jessie who had fallen asleep at long last, she felt an overwhelming desire to go home. Perhaps if it stopped snowing and the wind dropped the next day, she would be able to make her way there. If she went early enough and kept to the main path, she could do it. It would be grand to surprise John and see his delighted face.

She was woken by a shaft of sunlight stealing round the edge of the roller blind. It seemed a good omen. Rising, she went to the washstand. The water was cold but not frozen. Another good omen. Now dressed, she roused Jessie from her deep sleep.

"Get up, Jessie. It's a fine morning. I hope to go home today."

Jessie opened her eyes reluctantly, the way she greeted each new day. She raised herself on one arm, looked at the snowy landscape and then fell back on her pillow, groaning.

"You're not right in th' ead. When you can stay 'ere for nowt." Grumbling and moving like an old woman, she eventually sat up. "I 'ate Wednesdays. It's scrubbing day, kitchen floor and all t' pots as well."

Downstairs in the kitchen Mrs Drew waited impatiently for the young women to finish eating. Jessie prolonged the event as long as she could, leaning on her elbows, chewing her bread slowly.

"Get a move on, Jessie Lodge. You're paid to work, not eat."

Jessie sighed heavily as she and Molly wrapped themselves in the rough cleaning aprons. The two young women worked all morning, scrubbing the cooking utensils, the range, the deep sinks, the wooden draining-boards and the stone-flagged floor. Unlike Jessie, Molly worked without complaining, although she found herself tiring as she dragged the sodden scrubbing brush back and forth. She and Jessie began working on the floor from opposite sides. After a while, the stretching and pulling made Molly feel dizzy. Conscious of the baby heaving inside her, she stopped, sat up and took deep breaths. At once, Jessie stopped as well.

"Don't leave it all to me!" she complained.

When the floor was done, they rested and ate some bread and cheese. Molly was alarmed at the fluttering of her heart but told herself it was only to be expected. She was relieved that the next task was cleaning the silver, which enabled them to sit at the table, still rubbing hard and polishing, but in a more comfortable position.

Having been up for about six hours, Jessie now became better-tempered and her normal talkative self. It was the one afternoon in the week when she was allowed to leave the house for a few hours and visit her invalid mother in Longley, a few minutes away.

"She's never nowt interesting to say to me, 'cept 'Brought me owt to eat?' " Here Jessie rolled her eyes, indicating that she had some cheese wrapped in a cloth in her apron pocket.

"She's right glad I work 'ere now. I couldn't stand t' mill – it were too noisy for me.

Will you go back to t' mill after t' baby's born? Or will your husband keep you – like he should? John Brook's not afraid of work, they say."

Molly rose to her husband's defence.

"They say right. John works as hard as any man, and harder than most. I'm proud to be his wife."

At that moment Isabel Blezard appeared at the kitchen door, half a dozen cambric blouses over her arm.

"Where is Mrs Drew?" she snapped.

"She's in the wine cellar, madam," replied Jessie, slipping off her stool and wrapping her shawl round her shoulders. "I'm just off to visit my mother, madam. Wednesday afternoon. I shall be back at six."

Molly spoke quickly.

"I should like to go now as well, Mrs Blezard, if I could. Because of the snow. I'd like to surprise my husband."

Isabel's face went hard, the eyes narrowing.

"No doubt you would. But I expect a servant to work for the hours agreed. You can go now if you want. And not come back."

Molly bit her lip. One part of her wanted to march out, there and then; the other told her she had three, or more, weeks' wages she could earn – and save.

"Well, what is it to be?" asked Isabel crossly. "I want these blouses properly laundering. They're so badly done they need washing and pressing again."

Molly made up her mind. If she worked quickly, she could be away before it was dark.

"I will do them, Mrs Blezard."

Isabel did not reply but simply smacked the blouses down on the table and swept out.

Moving carefully, Molly put more water on to boil. There was nothing wrong with the blouses except that a few of the pin-tucks were not quite flat. A damp cloth and a hot flat iron was all that was needed but that, no doubt, would not satisfy Mrs Blezard.

Two hours later, the blouses had been washed, dried on the creel over the range, pressed and replaced on the creel to air. Molly found the housekeeper.

"Please, Mrs Drew, might I go now? I have laundered the blouses as Mrs Blezard asked."

Mrs Drew did not speak but went upstairs to see her mistress. A minute later, she returned.

"Mrs Blezard says the stairs are dusty. You may go when you have swept them – properly, mind. Top to bottom."

Molly's heart sank. Tears of anger and exhaustion threatened to come but she held them back, collected the dust-pan, brush and dusters and climbed the two flights of stairs. Mercifully, the stair carpet was not dusty at all but the action of brushing, on her knees whilst going backwards, was extremely tiring. She found herself sweating heavily and was obliged to stop and rest several times.

As she reached the last few steps to the downstairs hall, the clock struck four. Feet in black velvet slippers appeared at eye-level. Looking up, tired and dishevelled, she saw Isabel Blezard, her eyes hard and unfriendly.

"I've finished now, Madam."

"So I see."

There was a pause. Molly was coming to the conclusion, reluctantly, that it was now too late to attempt the journey home. She hated having to ask a favour but swallowed her pride and did so.

"Mrs Blezard. Could I, please, change my mind about going home? And stop another night?"

Isabel's mouth twisted into a sneer. When she spoke, her words dripped venom.

"Not so keen to rejoin your husband after all? Begging another night's free board and lodging? You sound like Jessie."

Molly's face went scarlet. She drew herself up.

"You are quite wrong, Mrs Blezard. I will go at once."

The cold hit her like a blow. Hot from her exertions and drenched in sweat, Molly pulled her shawl up round her mouth to avoid breathing in the icy air.

The snow was about three feet deep and to begin with, she was able to trudge along Wood Lane in a channel made by other feet, with miniature glaciers piled high on either side. It was now almost dark. As the temperature dropped, the surface of the snow froze and glinted in the moonlight. There was nobody about.

Molly was not afraid, buoyed up at the thought of seeing John again. But her progress up Longley Lane was painfully slow because of the steep gradient which forced her to stop and rest every few yards. When she finally reached the top of the hill, she leant against a dry-stone wall for a while out of the wind which had sprung up afresh.

Feeling slightly rested, she turned right and set off once again. Deep though the snow was, it was still possible to see the great mound of Castle Hill looming up ahead of her on the left. On the right, where the ground fell away sharply hundreds of feet towards Huddersfield, she could see nothing but a white-grey fog.

The way ahead was faintly marked by footprints and ruts made by cart wheels, blurred by further snowfall. Now it was Molly's footsteps making fresh tracks. But not for long. The wind, which seemed to be growing stronger by the minute, whipped across the surface of the snow, scattering it and taking Molly's breath away. She stumbled from side to side, occasionally plunging her feet into wayside drifts which were deeper than they appeared to be. By now, her feet and legs were sodden, as were her skirts which seemed to become heavier with every step.

Soon, however, she saw, with relief, the place ahead known as Catterstones at the foot of the earthworks, the cottage windows small squares of misty light in the gloom. Should she give up her attempt, stop and ask for shelter here until morning? It was sensible but not what she wanted to do. She was over halfway home already and in any case, she was still looking forward to seeing the surprise on John's face when she appeared. Instead, she turned left towards the valley and the Brook cottage. It was still possible to guess the whereabouts of the path which ran along the base of the earthworks even if she couldn't see it.

She battled on, fighting equally for breath and a secure footing. But then, to her dismay, it began to snow again, not gently, but whipped by the wind that stung her eyes and cheeks. She had seen no-one throughout her journey. Now she would not have seen them had they been yards away so blinding was the snowstorm. Gasping for breath, she found her mouth instantly full of snow.

Suddenly, stepping forward, her foot found nothing but soft snow and she fell headlong, deep into a snowdrift. Struggling up, soaked from head to foot, she felt the first stab of fear, of dread that she would not reach home. Surely, if she simply kept going, she would be bound to reach the cottage? She plodded on.

"By 'eck, I don't care if I never see snow again!"

George Blezard came stamping and blowing into the hallway, taking off his hat and cape and shaking them vigorously.

"George!" protested Isabel, emerging from the parlour. "Not all over the floor!"

"As I paid for it, I reckon I can spill a bit o' snow on it if I've a mind to," he retorted, running a hand over his hair. "Get me some brandy." Staggering into the parlour, he collapsed onto the nearest chair and sat, legs apart, gulping it back. "By! I've seen some bad weather but this beats all. And it's not over yet, not by a long chalk." He looked at Isabel. "I don't suppose any of you have been out, have you? Are we all right for meat and drink?"

Isabel moved impatiently.

"Of course we are. Mrs Drew sees to such things."

"She might do but if we stay snowed up, you'd be surprised how greedy folk get. Have her come here."

Mrs Drew appeared, impassive as usual.

"See 'ere, missus, is there plenty in t' pantry cupboard?"

"You may rest assured, sir. We have all we need."

"But look here. Send someone over to Haighs' farm tomorrow. Ask 'em to kill us a pig and send it over. Tell him I'll see him right. Then you can salt half on it, for later."

"Very well, sir. I'll go myself if neither of the two girls arrive tomorrow morning. Jessie's not come back yet and Molly went home earlier."

"I'd be surprised if you ever get Jessie Lodge to do owt on time. But that lass Molly. What time did she go?"

Mrs Drew looked at Isabel for confirmation. Isabel spoke quickly.

"She went soon after Jessie. About one o'clock."

Mrs Drew said nothing.

"Well, I hope she got home all right. It's treacherous up there on t' top. When it's light, never mind in t' dark."

As he got up, he swayed and had to clutch the back of a chair for support. He hoped Isabel hadn't noticed. He'd got enough to worry about without having her nagging him about his drinking habits.

The snow did not prevent John getting to work; it merely slowed his walk up into the village and to his woodshop opposite the church. By the end of Tuesday, however, there was not much more he could do. Finished items – a fireplace surround, a carved armchair – were ready for transport to customer and upholsterer but he needed the carter to come and collect them.

On Wednesday, he tidied up, checked his wood orders and brought his accounts up to date. Then, rather than remain idle, he walked over to Kirkheaton where he knew of several people who had expressed interest in his carved decorative work, carrying his pattern book and wood samples. As he passed the road that led to Dartmouth Hall, he thought of Anne Graham. He was glad she had found a post there, even though it sounded to be temporary; he would not wish an enemy to be forced to share the company of Jack and Ned Stott any longer than was necessary. When he had said this to his mother, she had agreed but had pointed out that it was sad for poor Agnes Stott who needed a friend more than most.

John regretted he had not been able to speak to Anne after church the previous Sunday, just as it came on to snow, but he had fancied that Molly seemed slightly blue around the mouth. When he had looked up, Anne had disappeared. Perhaps the absence of the Thorpe family meant there was illness at the Hall and she had to get back to the children.

He was kept busy with his customers till late on Wednesday afternoon. As he sat in one fine drawing-room, his samples spread out around him, it began to snow again, swirling thickly against the window-panes, "as if it meant business" as his customer, a stout merchant, said.

Persuaded to wait until the snowstorm eased off, it was evening before he walked back from Kirkheaton. Almondbury was like a ghost village as he passed through it, with spectral shapes and smashed snowpiles now hardening under the frost. Houses were shut tight against the cold, as if they would never open again. All was silent save for the noise from the taverns, fuller than usual with customers there either by necessity or choice.

When he reached Lumb Lane, all the cottages were in darkness except for his parents' house where a light was still burning. He was knocking the compacted snow off his boots when his mother heard him and opened the door.

"John! Thank God you're back. We thought you might not be coming home tonight but staying somewhere."

"Nay, I wanted to get back."

"And 'ave you to go back there again in t' morning?"

"Nay, that's one good thing. I've finished there."

"Well then, 'ave a sleep in. You deserve it."

"I might. Then I'll go up and see our Molly and bring her home. I reckon she's ready for a rest. I'll go early afternoon. Surprise her. I can give Ben Haigh a hand while I'm waiting for her to finish."

For John, Thursday bore the cheering aspect of an unexpected holiday, like an extra Sunday which had come and taken him by pleasant surprise. It had stopped snowing and a bleak sun shone thinly on the snow-covered land. A few determined children played and shouted in the snow while their elders worked to clear pathways. For them, the novelty had worn thin; they now wished for a rapid thaw and a return to normality.

John spent the morning shifting snow for himself and their neighbours, chopping and carrying wood, shovelling ash from fire-grates and spreading it across footpaths. Beyond the small garden gates, Lumb Lane was filled with snowdrifts like a great white eiderdown billowing on and on so that there was no telling where the borders of the lane began and ended. But John knew the route as well in darkness as in daylight having trodden that way up to Castle Hill and on to the Haighs' farmhouse since he was a child. Taking a walking-stick, he pushed through the snow, clearing a narrow path he would be able to find on his way back. It did not seem as if it would snow again that day. It was too cold, for a start.

Reaching the row of cottages at Catterstones at the foot of Castle Hill, his progress became easier. The local farmers and cottage-dwellers had already cleared a pathway so it took John only a few minutes to cover that part of the journey. When he came to Longley Lane, he trod cautiously as he descended its steep, curving corner. At the Blezards' house, he went round to the back and knocked at the door. It was opened by Mrs Drew who looked at him without interest.

"Good afternoon, Mrs Drew. Excuse my disturbing you but I wondered if my wife was ready for leaving yet."

Some kind of reaction flickered in the woman's eyes but was gone in a moment.

"You are mistaken, Mr Brook. Your wife left for home yesterday."

"Yesterday? When?"

"In the afternoon. About one o'clock. We have not seen her since."

John was dumb with shock and for an instant, motionless. Then he turned hastily, gouging up the gravel with his boots, and walked away as fast as he could without running.

He strode up the hill, his heart thudding, holding back the panic welling up inside him. Two voices clamoured in his head. "She left here at one yesterday. Why didn't she reach home? Where is she now?" The other voice strove to combat the rising terror. "There'll be some explanation. She must have stopped somewhere, taken shelter." But the first voice was now screaming. "Then what is delaying her? It's more than twenty-four hours. Why have we heard nothing?"

He scarcely noticed that he had reached the Haighs' farm, only felt a flood of relief as he burst into the farmyard. Ben was carrying hay across to the barn, his father Eli emerging from the farmhouse with a pint pot in his hand, the boy sweeping with the yard broom.

"Ben! Eli! Will you help me? Molly's not come home. She left Blezards yesterday afternoon. I fear she's mebbe trapped in t' snow!"

One look at John's face was enough. Ben and his father seized pitchforks, spades, a carriage pole, anything to penetrate and shift the snow. They all hurried off along the route they thought Molly must have taken, a sheepdog at their heels.

"She can't have come to harm, surely?" said Ben. "It wa' light till four. She'd have got past Catterstones and turned into Lumb Lane before so long."

"But there's some deep drifts that side of the hill," John replied. He fought back the image of his wife, choking, engulfed by snow, which kept forcing its way into his mind's eye.

Eli spoke quietly to the boy.

"Go and ask all them at Catterstones if they saw a lass go by yesterday afternoon." The boy disappeared into the first cottage.

Four young people were playing about on the lower slopes of the hill. The boys were tussling in the snow, rolling over and over, while the girls watched and laughed. As the group of grim-faced men began sinking the farm implements into the deep snow, they stopped and watched, at a distance.

They worked methodically, moving forward together in a line, the dog running back and forth at their feet. Every time John raised the pitchfork and plunged its handle into a drift, he feared the worst. Again and again they were forced to stop and use the spades to dig to the bottom of the drifts which in places were ten feet deep.

No-one at Catterstones had seen Molly go by. But that might not signify. Two men from the cottages joined them and began digging alongside. The sky had clouded over and it was now bitterly cold. The young observers had become bored and wandered off, engrossed once more in each other.

The men toiled on, hoping yet dreading to find what they were seeking. John was aglow with exertion but inside he was frozen, his mind gripped against feeling anything. No-one spoke; there was nothing to say. All their breath went into prodding the snow, seeking solid ground, moving forward and repeating their actions.

And then Ben stopped. The dog, crouching, whined and barked. Eli hooked his fingers in its collar and pulled it back. Ben uttered one word.

"Here."

Taking the spade, he began scooping the snow away to left and right. The others watched him. As the heavy iron tool met the snow, its touch was as delicate as the lightest, finest blade. He swept the snow very gently to one side, exposing the form of a young woman, curled up in her shawl like a sleeping baby. He put down the spade and stepped back.

John moved forward like a man in a dream and with his hands, stroked the snow away from his dead wife. She looked so beautiful, so defenceless. His grief was like a block of stone, deep in his chest. Stooping, he slid his arms under her body and lifted her. Then he turned and began the final part of his journey, towards home. The others followed.

As he carried her down the path he had cleared just a short time ago, a searing flash of pain went through him as he realised he was also carrying their dead child in his arms. Shuddering sobs began to well up inside him but no tears came. Only a thought which went round and round in his head – "If I had gone to fetch her, she would still be alive."

When the group reached the door of the cottage, Ben stepped forward, knocked loudly on it and then stood to one side. The door opened and John went slowly in, sideways to avoid banging his wife's head on the doorpost.

Inside the cottage, his parents stared, transfixed with horror at the sight of John with his dead wife in his arms. All he could say was –

"It is my fault."

Something strange happened. It was as if everything seemed further off and he, John, was somewhere else. Martha was talking quietly to Ben at the door but it all felt far away. He became aware that his mother was plucking at his sleeve.

"John! John! Can you carry her upstairs?"

He felt his mother pull him towards the corner of the room and propel him, very gently, up the steep, narrow, stone steps. Once in the bedroom, she persuaded him to lay Molly on the double bed. When he had done so, they both stood, looking down at her where she lay as if asleep. For the moment, he felt empty, frozen into feeling nothing.

Then his mother was pulling him out of the room, all the time making soothing noises as if he was a hurt child. Downstairs she made him some tea and poured something into it, brandy, he supposed. He sat by the fire, his wet boots and clothes steaming, his hands slowly losing their swollen redness and returning to normal. His father sat across from him, silent, picking at the rug on his knees.

Overhead John heard the sounds of his mother moving about from one side of the bed to the other. Something knocked against a floorboard. After a while, which could have been five or fifty minutes, his mother came downstairs carrying a bundle of Molly's clothing. She went straight through with it into the scullery but not before drops of melted snow had dripped in a line across the floor.

"Son? John? You can go up and see her now."

He stood up, his legs as heavy as lead. Deep down he wanted to cry, desperately, but the tears seemed blocked. All he could feel was a physical pain in his chest.

When he opened the bedroom door, he saw what his mother had been doing. Molly lay on her back, dressed in a clean white nightgown. Her arms were crossed over her breast while the lower part of her body was wrapped in some sort of quilt covered with a white sheet.

John knelt down by the side of the bed. Two locks of her wet, black hair had been combed and lay on each shoulder; even now, in death, each one ended in a curl. Her dark eyelashes were perfect half-moons on the ivory cheeks. John laid his face against hers, willing it to become warm, and kissed the cold lips. As he put his hand on her body, he felt the unmistakable solid curve of the unborn child. Now the hot tears came splashing onto Molly's face and throat. There was a strange, animal noise. It came from him. His sweet wife! Molly, his childhood friend, and the woman who would have been the mother of his child! He sobbed on, so full of anguish that he felt nothing would ever make it go away.

Some time later, there were no more tears left. Getting to his feet stiffly, he went downstairs where his anxious parents awaited him.

"Oh lad! What can I say?" His mother wrapped her arms around him and buried her face against his chest. He found himself patting her on the back.

"Thank you, Mother. For what you've done."

His mother's eyes were red with weeping.

"It was an accident, John. A terrible accident. Sometimes they happen."

He looked at her unseeingly.

"If I had gone to meet her, it wouldn't have happened. So it must be my fault."

His mother's face twisted in pain.

"Oh my son, you mustn't think that! How could you know? Wasn't she supposed to wait until you collected her?"

"I ought to have known. What she was likely to do. I should have known she would have wanted to surprise me. As soon as the weather was better. As it was yesterday morning."

He stopped, choked with guilt and grief. What had he been doing on Wednesday? When he could have walked over to Wood Lane easily enough? He had been visiting comfortable homes, enjoying tea and cake and the praise of people who had seen his work and wanted some for themselves, as the snow started again, swirling about in their well-kept gardens. And all the while, Molly had been struggling home by herself as the blizzard worsened and deepened the drifts along her way. He shut his eyes tight in an attempt to ward off the dreadful picture in his mind.

"John?"

He opened his eyes. His mother went on.

"I've been thinking. If Molly left Wood Lane at one o'clock as they say, then it seems unlikely it was just t' snow that killed her."

"What do you mean?"

"If she'd been fit, she could have struggled out of a snowdrift. In the daytime. I'm sure of it. Suppose it was her heart – that gave out. If it'd been that, then nothing would have saved her. Even if you'd gone to collect her, she would still have died. If her heart couldn't stand much more." His mother paused, as if debating whether to go on. Eventually, she did.

"I thought, once or twice, that she didn't look well. Round the mouth."

John felt as though someone had driven a knife through his own heart.

"I thought the same!" he cried in anguish. "So why didn't I make her stop working? If she'd stayed at home and rested, she'd be alive now!"

Martha bit her lip. John knew what she was thinking – that Molly was stubborn and no-one would have been able to stop her working. But he didn't want her to say it.

Then he saw her look at the clock and back at him.

"John. I know it's hard but I think it best you go up to the village tonight and tell Molly's family what's happened. With their being other people that know about it already, news'll be around the village before long. It's only right they hear it from us. Unless you want me to go."

"No, no. I'll go. Mother. You've done enough already."

He stood up.

"And perhaps you'd better mention the funeral. When'll be best for them. Then you can see the vicar tomorrow."

John's heart sank at the thought of what lay before him. He didn't know how he was going to bear it. But bear it he must.

His mother found a dry coat for him and made him take off the wet one. It wasn't wet all over, just on the arms and across the front where he had clasped Molly's cold, wet body against him. His mother hung it round a chair and stood it in front of the fire to dry. If only he could remove his feelings as easily!

He kissed his mother and then struck out along the dark lanes, his heart heavy with what he had to tell the Dysons – that they would never see their elder daughter alive again, nor their first grandchild – ever.

Later that night, after a heart-rending hour spent with Molly's family, John lay awake in front of the dying embers of the fire on a bed his mother had made up for him downstairs. He knew she had meant well when she spoke of Molly's possible weak heart but in fact, she had added an extra dimension of guilt to the burden he already carried. Round and round it went in his mind, always ending with the same words – "If only."

Tomorrow he would go back to the Blezards and try to find out more. But what else could he learn? The housekeeper said that Molly had left at one o'clock and it was unlikely that she would have gone anywhere else but straight home. What more would they be able to tell him?

He must have fallen asleep because the next thing he knew, he was suddenly wide awake. It was a bright moonlit night and despite the thick cloth curtains, a shaft of moonlight pointed its finger onto the kitchen floor. The silence was almost tangible.

He had been dreaming of Anne Graham. She had been standing at an altar, a shadowy bridegroom at her side. He saw himself in the congregation, flinging up an arm, meaning to shout "No!" at the top of his voice. But no sound issued from his throat and when he tried to reach her, his legs were rooted to the spot.

He found he was sitting bolt upright, trembling and sweating. How could he think, even in a dream, of re-marrying when his poor young wife lay upstairs, as yet unburied? How could he be so despicable? He was disgusted at himself. All his recent life seemed a catalogue of shame. For the first time, he admitted that, had he met Anne Graham years ago, he would not have married Molly Dyson. He also knew that, in the last few months, he had sometimes wearied of Molly's stubbornness and her prattle about her friends at the mill. He had been ashamed to feel that then; he was doubly ashamed now. Had he ever loved her, in the way that you were supposed to love, the way people loved in songs and stories? But, even if he hadn't, and that was bad enough, how could he not have married Molly after all the years they had been together as sweethearts? To have done that would have stained her honour, and his. It would have been unthinkable.

He lay on his back looking at the ceiling, now lightening with the approach of day. Perhaps all that had happened was punishment for the sins of his heart and mind. One thing was clear. There was only one person to blame. And that was John Brook.

CHAPTER SIX

At eight o'clock, Anne went into the nursery as she did every morning. Susan was just finishing dressing Georgina. Edward was already dressed and playing with his soldiers. After exchanging a few words about the weather, the young woman went downstairs to collect the breakfast. Anne laid the cloth on the nursery table and looked out of the window. The snow still lay thick on the ground, its even surface untouched apart from some recent tracks made by the children and the dogs. The trees looked beautiful, the snow lying on the branches like white blossom.

A slight rattle in the corridor told Anne that Susan was outside the door. Moving swiftly, she opened it to find Susan holding a large tray laden with porridge, milk, jam and toast. The look of shock on the nurserymaid's face made Anne seize the other side of the tray to steady it.

"It's Molly Brook, Miss. She's been found dead in the snow."

Anne was stunned but very quickly turned to see if the children were listening. Fortunately, they were engrossed in looking out at the snowy landscape.

"When? Who found her?"

"Her husband, Miss. Yesterday. In't it a dreadful thing? I can hardly bear to think about it."

There was no time for explanation. The children ran to the table and began to eat their porridge. Susan stood behind Edward's chair and mouthed more information in which the words "Blezards" and "walking home" figured. But Anne was now so shocked herself she could take nothing in. She tried to eat but her throat refused to swallow properly.

Mercifully, the children were willing to draw and colour pictures quietly for a while with the promise of a play in the snow later. It was not of the dead girl Anne thought but of John and his present state of mind. The pain he must be suffering was terrible to contemplate. The desire to wrap him in her arms and comfort him was overwhelming. If he had been close, she felt nothing would have stopped her doing so.

Her eyes kept filling with tears. Seeing her raise a handkerchief to her face once again, Susan took the initiative.

"Now then, children. What do you say to a game in the snow?" Her words were met by joyous yelps and jumping.

"Is that all right, Miss Graham? Master and mistress are not expected back till late."

"I'm sure it will be, Susan. In any case, I will take responsibility for cancelling their lessons today."

Bundled into woollen hats, leggings and mittens, the children burst out into the garden and began stamping about and churning up the even surface of the snow. Susan went out with them and was soon joined by the gardener's boy and a young stable groom. After some snow throwing by the lads, they quietened down and set about making a giant snowball.

The rest of the household staff – the maids in their black dresses and white caps and cuffs, the housekeeper in her black, the cook, the coachman – all came to the windows to watch the children at play, their own work suspended in the fraught atmosphere. It felt like an extraordinary day when all the usual routines and constraints could be ignored. All of them knew John, Molly and their families. Edith, one of the maids, had been Molly Dyson's best friend; she was so distressed that the housekeeper sent her home to her family for a few hours.

After a while, Anne slipped away, relieved at being able to escape to the schoolroom and be on her own. The others were coping with their feelings by talking, endlessly, about John and Molly and what they knew of their childhood, their courtship, marriage and the expected child. It only intensified Anne's pain.

Alone upstairs with the shouts of the children heard faintly in the distance, she wrote a letter of sympathy to John. It was not difficult to write from the heart when it was so full. However, when she re-read it, she toned down some of the expression. John might not be the only person to read it.

The children were brought indoors, protesting, noses and chins chapped with the cold, mittens, boots and stockings wet through. After their boisterous play, bathed and dressed in their night-clothes, they submitted to resting on the couch while Anne read them a story. They went to bed sooner and with less clamour than usual, for which she was grateful.

Even so, it was several hours before she was calm enough to sleep. It was not long after the news of Molly's death had reached her that she had come to the inescapable conclusion – that John was now a widower and free to re-marry. But as soon as this thought came to her, she had gone hot with shame. How callous to let one's mind run on those lines! She must not give in to such fantasies. In any case, he might never marry again. Grief could do strange, unforeseen things to people. And even if he did decide to take a second wife, why should it be her? The one, terrible truth was that his eighteen-year old wife, expecting a child in three months' time, had met a cruel and tragic death.

Anne found herself weeping again. She had to admit that in those weeks before the wedding, she had sometimes thought –"If only Molly Dyson didn't exist!" But not in this way, no, not this way! At last, turning over the pillow once more, she fell asleep in a state of nervous exhaustion.

In the early hours of the morning, she woke with a start, unnaturally alert. She thought instantly of John. Was he awake too? Where was he? Was Molly lying, cold, in their bed upstairs? Wherever he was, she was sure he was not asleep. She had such a strong sense of him, she felt as though her mind could reach his across the silent valley that lay between them. After another wakeful hour, she drifted off to sleep.

Charlotte Blezard was grateful for the snow. It meant she had a good excuse for staying with her school-friend Helen for a few more nights than originally planned. But today, Friday, there was no more putting it off. She would have to go home. Reluctantly she gathered her belongings together.

"Will you be all right walking back?" asked Helen. "I don't think the carriage can get out until the roads are clear."

"Oh, yes," replied Charlotte. "I'm glad of the walk." It would postpone the moment of return a little longer.

Her friend Helen Shaw, the only child of well-to-do, educated parents, lived in Northgate, Honley, about a mile away, in a handsome old house looking out across fields. Charlotte had never envied her before, in fact, had never envied anyone. Until her father had re-married and brought Isabel home.

"Perhaps it won't be so bad. If she goes out a lot. Are you bound to see much of her?"

"I suppose not. Except at supper-time. What she calls dinner. When Father's back."

"Well then!"

"She's not so bad when he's there. It's when she gets me on her own. She makes me feel – worthless, somehow."

"How ridiculous!" Helen spoke angrily. "Of course you're not worthless. It's much more likely that she's jealous of you!"

"Jealous? How could she be?"

"Very easily. She's a second wife, she's only known your father – how long? A year? Less? And she can probably see how fond your father is of you."

"I never thought of that," said Charlotte. "Do you think that's it?"

"Yes. I do. It's probably harder for her with you being a young woman. Perhaps if you were a child, she would find it easier."

"Perhaps."

Charlotte remembered how she had felt when she'd come home from school for Christmas. She had already reconciled herself to the loss of the old house in Lockwood near the mill, the house where she had grown up, but was unprepared for the shock of the room Isabel had furnished without consulting her. It was pretty, suffocatingly so, full of knick-knacks, china ornaments, stuffed creatures under glass domes, a cradle overflowing with toys and the final insult, a huge, grinning doll which was sat up, legs sprawled, on the frilled cushions decorating the bed. It was a room for the sort of young girl delighted by playthings and feminine frivolities, in short, for a girl totally unlike Charlotte. She hadn't known whether to laugh or cry.

"Well, what do you think of that then?" her father had said, his arm round her shoulders, beaming.

Charlotte hadn't the heart to upset him.

"It's very fine," she answered, wondering where she was going to put her books. And now it was going to be more difficult if she was to leave the school where she was a termly boarder and be at home all the time.

"Tell them what you want to do," advised Helen. "Mother and Father think it an excellent idea. Come next week and tell me how you have got on."

Charlotte left Helen cheerfully enough but as she got closer to home, she could feel her confidence ebbing away. The maid was taking her outdoor things when Isabel came downstairs. She was, as always, beautifully dressed. Charlotte had to admit that she was a handsome woman with a good figure and posture.

Charlotte suddenly felt terribly dowdy. Worse still, the look in Isabel's eyes suggested that this was her stepmother's opinion of her as well. Charlotte felt her face go hot.

"Good day, Isabel."

"Good day, Charlotte."

It was best to speak now, thought Charlotte. Arguments over supper were upsetting, and unfair to Father.

"Isabel, might I speak to you for a moment?"

"Of course."

Isabel opened the door of the parlour where a splendid fire blazed in the grate surmounted by some of John Brook's exquisite carving. She sank into a richly brocaded chair, its deep plum colour toning with the rose madder of her day dress. One shapely hand lay gracefully along the arm of the chair; the other played with a dark ringlet.

Charlotte sat tensely on a sofa opposite.

"I wish to speak to you and Father about leaving the boarding-school."

Isabel raised an eyebrow.

"And why should you want to do that?"

Charlotte's answer came clearly; she had given it some thought.

"I do not think I shall learn any more at Miss Broadley's. I have noticed how the lessons repeat themselves, as they are bound to do for the new girls each year. And although Miss Broadley and her assistants are well-meaning, they are not very highly educated themselves – that is to say, they are very knowledgeable in some areas but not in those I am really interested in." She paused for breath.

"Which are?"

"Mathematics chiefly – and science." As Isabel said nothing,

Charlotte went on.

"I should now like to stay at home, continue my studies with my friend Helen at her house and attend lectures in Huddersfield. And Leeds, and Bradford. And possibly Manchester as well."

Charlotte was still flushed but this time it was from animation, not embarrassment.

"Really?" commented Isabel, as if it was the most boring subject in the world. "And this is what you see as appropriate, is it, for a young girl in your position, a girl of – what is it ? Fifteen? Sixteen?"

"Seventeen."

"I should have thought the best way to show your gratitude for all that your father has done for you is to equip yourself as well as possible for the future. Although he hopes someone will make you an offer of marriage, I do not think we can assume this will happen soon. If at all."

She paused, as if allowing time for the insult to sink in. Charlotte felt as if she had been stung. Isabel continued.

"Husbands, in my experience, are not looking for a wife on the basis of her knowledge of mathematics – they seek accomplishments of the kind your boarding school provides. I must say I'm surprised at your ingratitude."

She stopped, possibly halted by something in Charlotte's face. Charlotte's feelings were in turmoil. She felt hurt, angry, powerless, all at the same time. She struggled to take control of herself.

"Father will not regard it as ingratitude. He will understand –"

She stopped. Would he? And if he did, would he take her part against Isabel's?

Isabel raised her eyebrows.

"I shall speak to Father myself about this. Please tell him I shall not be joining you for dinner this evening."

Isabel's rejoinder came with the speed born of malice.

"As you wish. A few missed meals might improve your figure."

With a gasp, Charlotte's mouth fell open. She got up clumsily, rushed out of the room and ran up the stairs.

George Blezard, well-wrapped against the cold in his overcoat of best cloth, was sure Newsome Road was getting steeper. He stopped on the corner to catch his breath before making the final ascent to Wood Lane. When he was a young man, he'd have thought nothing of this bit of a hill. Kept you fit, hills did. If they didn't kill you first. A moment later, he set off again. Someone had cleared a path down the middle of the road and scattered it with grit and ashes. Sort of thing he used to do as a lad. Good job people went on doing these things.

As he drew near the house, he allowed himself some satisfaction at its appearance – soundly-built in good stone, solid and handsome. Isabel was right. It did look like the house of a prosperous mill-owner. Pity he didn't feel like one. Still, he couldn't deny it looked very welcoming. In the parlour, the red-shaded lamps had been lit, making the whole window glow with rosy light. Very nice, with dark hollies and laurels against the white snow of the front lawn.

At that moment, someone drew the thick curtains, blotting out the light. George decided to go round to the servants' entrance and take his snow-caked boots off there. Isabel had made that much fuss last time he took them off in the hall. Mind you, she'd once scolded him for coming in by the servants' door. Some women were just contrary – at least, some of the time.

He padded upstairs in his socks. When he entered the bedroom, Isabel was sitting at the dressing table, deciding on the best position in her hair for an artificial flower. She spoke to his reflection in the mirror.

"What have you been doing all day? I thought you were coming home early."

George took off his coat, opened the wardrobe and took out one of the soft jackets Isabel liked him to wear in the evenings. His daytime work jacket now lived permanently in his office; Isabel said it smelt too strongly of the mill to be brought home.

"What have I been doing ? I've been doing the accounts, or at any rate, trying to."

Isabel moved her head sharply. He knew this was not a conversation she wanted. But it had to be said.

"It's no good, Isabel, this spending's got to stop. You've done a grand job here in the house and you know I'm right proud of you in all your finery but the bills never stop! There's just been one for nearly twenty pound. For a velvet opera cloak and all the trimmings! How many times will you wear that? And another bill from Fillans! How much more jewellery do you need?" Before she could answer, he continued. "I don't think you understand how bad trade is at the moment. And wages have to be paid just t' same."

"You should lay off some of your workers. Other people do."

"I know they do. But I'm not doing that unless I have to. I know what it's like to be poor. Even if you don't."

This was one of their regular disagreements. They continued to dress for dinner in silence. Isabel decided against the flower. Instead she pushed a diamanté clip into the thick, dark ringlets which she had looped up on one side. After turning her head from side to side in front of the dressing-table mirror, she spoke again.

"So, are you saying we must economise? Why not start in this house? Get rid of some of the staff. Make a start with Jessie. In my view, she's idle, stupid, and a gossip. I should be glad to see the back of her."

George bridled. This was not so simple. He had grown up living next door to Jessie's mother, Ida. Her family had been good to him, when he needed it, when he was a child alone in the dark rooms, waiting for his mother to come home from work. Now Ida was poorly and near-destitute. When he had offered to take Jessie into service, she had wept tears of gratitude. According to Ida, Jessie was "too delicate" for mill work. "Too idle" was probably nearer the mark and he had already decided to move the girl onto to some other work elsewhere. But he would do it when he was ready and not before.

"I shall deal with Jessie when I've a mind to. As far as I can see, all t' staff have their 'ands full. Why, it's only a month since you told me we needed a bit more 'elp in t' kitchen. That's why we took on Molly Brook."

Isabel looked angry but said nothing. George went on, doggedly.

"I'm just saying we need a bit of economy in our outgoings. If you could just decide not to buy any more stuff this month, it would help."

He peered at her face in the mirror but she got up, flounced away and started fiddling with her jewellery boxes. It was clear she had no intention of answering. Eventually, George felt bound to speak.

"Well, shall we go down now? I'm ready for my supper. I don't know about you."

Once seated in the dining room, George made an effort to lighten the atmosphere. Isabel's silence was a fearsome thing.

"Well, there's nowt like cold weather for giving you a good appetite. What have we got tonight then?"

"Roast lamb, sir," said the maid, lifting the lid of the soup tureen. "And pea soup."

"Champion!" beamed George. "You can start serving. Hang on a minute. Where's our Charlotte?"

Isabel did not meet his eye. She unfolded her napkin daintily.

"She won't be down this evening. She spent the day at her friend's. Presumably she ate there."

"Well, I hope I see her before bedtime. I don't see enough of the lass as it is."

Isabel said nothing. They finished their meal with a minimum of conversation. Later, as they were leaving to take their coffee, and in George's case, brandy, in the parlour, they became aware of raised voices beyond in the servants' part of the house. A maid appeared, bearing news instead of the expected coffee-pot. She looked agitated.

"Please Sir, Madam. Someone's just come to tell us. It's Molly Brook. She's been found dead. In the snow."

"Nay! I am sorry to hear that!" George was extremely shocked. "Do you hear that, Isabel?"

Isabel shook her head and said nothing.

"Such a bonny lass. And expecting. What a terrible thing! How that young man, her husband, is feeling dun't bear thinking on."

At that moment, Jessie Lodge, unable to contain herself, burst through the servants' door.

"I were one o' last people to see 'er alive, sir! She were fair looking forward to going home. But I told her she were best stay here a bit longer. She might still be alive if she'd listened to me, sir!"

Mrs Drew now appeared and, looking displeased, restrained the voluble Jessie and half-pushed, half-led her back to the servants' quarters.

"The coffee will be with you directly, sir, madam," she said, smoothing down her black apron.

George found it difficult to leave the subject of Molly. He was genuinely distressed. Having had to face the death of a wife himself, he sympathised deeply with the suffering of John Brook. He walked round the room, leaning on the backs of the chairs or the mantelpiece, unable to settle.

"He won't get over this in a hurry, I fear. And to think of the poor dead child. Never to be born."

After he had gone on in this vein for a while, Isabel interrupted him impatiently.

"Shall I write a letter of condolence? Now?"

"Aye, do, do. And mind you send a wreath for t' funeral - a good 'un."

George gradually lapsed into silence with his second brandy. Isabel sat at the pretty walnut writing-desk and wrote several drafts before she was satisfied with both content and appearance. She wrote on heavy, embossed paper, black-edged like its envelope, which she addressed to 'John Brook, Lumb Lane, Almondbury.'

The evening wore on. The clock on the mantelpiece kept up its monotonous ticking, chiming away the quarters and the hours. George fell into a doze, head back and mouth open, making puffing sounds with each breath.

Suddenly the door opened and Charlotte appeared. George sat up and rubbed bloodshot eyes. He noticed that Isabel looked none too pleased.

"Good evening, Father."

"Charlotte! Come in, love! It's grand to see you. Come sit down and tell me what you've been doing with yourself."

He patted the sofa close to him. Charlotte sat down, sideways on, with her back to Isabel, her face tense.

"I hear you've been at your friend Helen's. You must ask her over here sometime. I like to see you with your friends."

"Yes, Father, thank you. In fact, that's what I wanted to talk to you about."

George knew, from the expression in Charlotte's eyes, that it was something important. He also suspected she had already had words about it with Isabel who kept her head down over her magazine as if it was the most interesting thing in the world.

"Go on then, flower."

It was his pet name for her, a sign he was on her side.

"I'd like to leave the boarding-school, Father, and continue my studies at home. And with Helen."

"Well!" said George. "Would you now!"

"I'm very grateful, Father, for all you have spent on my education but I would really –"

"Nay, lass. There's no need to thank me – that's what brass is for." He patted his daughter's hand.

"And what now, my love? What do you want to do with yourself now?"

Charlotte's face was bright with enthusiasm.

"Helen and I want to pursue our studies to a higher level."

"Eh up, d'ye hear that, Isabel? And what sort of thing will you study?"

"Mathematics and science – chiefly chemistry, with some physics and botany."

George roared with pleasure.

"By! There'll be no talking to you when you're a professor! Nay lass!"- when he saw her face cloud over –"I'm not laughing. I'm fair proud of you. Mathematics eh? Well, I could do with some help there mysen. You've allus been good with figures. Like your mother."

He did not often refer to his first wife, out of regard for Isabel. But he felt it right to do so, at this moment.

"Well then, you make the arrangements and tell me what I've got to sign. It'll be grand to have you home again."

The next moment Charlotte was embracing him. George felt happier than he had done for some time. He reflected that, money worries apart, he was a very lucky man.

The snow lay on the ground well into February. Villagers trudged along the icy paths uncomplainingly; it was what they expected of their winter weather. No-one lingered out of doors any longer than was necessary but sought their fire-sides as soon as they could.

Anne had not seen John since the tragedy. She had heard that Molly's funeral had taken place, quietly; after that, all was silent. She longed to see him again but no opportunity ever arose. He had not appeared at church nor had she walked up from the Hall and through the village for weeks. Caring for the children had taken up all her time. While the snow lasted, the children had enjoyed it. However, when the thaw came, they developed sore throats and she and Susan had been kept busy attending them.

One bright, cold morning at the beginning of March, Ellen Thorpe decided that the children were sufficiently recovered to venture outside, or at least, into a carriage warmly dressed and swaddled in woollen rugs. They were to visit a friend of hers in Shelley and much to her delight, her husband had agreed to accompany them.

"Georgina! Keep wrapped up, put your hands in, do! Edward! Be a good boy and please Mama!"

Frederick Thorpe was more to the point.

"Edward, leave your sister alone or you'll go back upstairs!"

Edward stopping poking his sister and sat still. Anne and Susan stood by the carriage, shivering. Eventually, Frederick Thorpe noticed them.

"Thank you, Miss Graham. Susan. We shan't need you until later this afternoon."

As the two young women began to retreat gratefully towards the front door, he appeared to be struck by a fresh thought.

"Miss Graham! Feel free to take some exercise yourself. For a change of scene, after your weeks in the sickroom."

As the carriage rolled over the gravel and moved away, Susan ran indoors, seeking the warmth of the fire in the kitchen, closely followed by Anne. This was her chance to call on John. A few minutes later, she emerged again, this time wearing her outdoor clothes, and began walking briskly along the drive and then up towards the village.

As she slowed her pace to climb the last, steepest incline of St Helen's Gate, heart beating fast with excitement as much as with exertion, she tried to think of what she would say when she knocked at the door of John's woodshop. "How are you? Why haven't you been to church lately?" The obvious questions seemed so crass. What could the poor man say in reply? "I'm prostrate with grief" as an answer to both questions? If only she had a legitimate business enquiry about some work she wanted to commission from him! But if she didn't try to speak to him now, it might be weeks, perhaps months, before she had another chance to resume contact with him.

The woodshop was shut up as she expected it to be. But he might be inside all the same. Hoping passionately that he would be in, Anne knocked firmly at the door, still not sure what she was going to say. When he opened it a few moments later, she was shocked by his pallor and tense expression.

"Good morning, John. I – I haven't seen you for some time."

"No."

He seemed to have difficulty speaking.

"I'm sorry I haven't seen you at church," Anne said softly.

He did not reply. Had she gone too far? It was not uncommon for someone who had suffered a great personal loss to turn away from religion, at least for a while. As she pondered, he struggled to say something.

"Perhaps...soon."

Anne smiled gently.

"I do hope so."

He looked at her then and seemed to see her properly for the first time. His features relaxed a little. Anne's heart lifted. She smiled again and was just about to say more when the sight and sound of a carriage turning into the archway distracted them both. As the horses came to a halt, blowing down their nostrils, the carriage door opened and Isabel Blezard emerged, with one well-shod foot on the step and both hands lifting her full skirts before her. Anne was irritated, in the extreme, and even more so when she saw that Isabel did not attempt to get down until John moved forward and offered his arm as support.

"Good day, Mrs Blezard," said Anne, angry that the moment had been spoilt by the other woman's arrival. Isabel gave Anne the briefest of nods and turned the full beam of her attention onto John.

"Mr Brook. John. I know I said eleven o'clock but as I had to come down to the village this morning, I thought I might press you to return with me. And save you the trouble of walking up that long hill."

There was little John could do but fall in with her plan, and excusing himself, with an eloquent look towards Anne, he went inside for what he needed. Outside, Anne remained standing at the door but Isabel walked straight past her and stood looking out at the valley view behind the woodshop.

Anne looked at the other woman's back and, for a wild moment, felt a strong desire to punch it. The impulse caused her to recognise what her true feelings were towards Isabel – annoyance, dislike and jealousy. This greedy woman, she thought, married, wealthy, wanted it all – including John! She fumed in silence. There was nothing she could do if Isabel was genuinely engaging John to do some more woodworking for her.

He came out, looking slightly embarrassed, locking the door behind him.

"I'm sorry, Anne. I have to go."

"Of course," she said, as pleasantly as she could. "I hope to see you again before very long. Good-bye. Good-bye, Mrs Blezard."

Isabel walked past her again without turning her head, her eyes fixed on John. Anne hurried away to avoid seeing them go off together.

As she walked back to the Hall, she found herself struggling with mixed emotions. Would it have been better not to have called on John? By doing so, she had re-opened a wound that, while not healed, had given her little real pain of late. Now, the joy of seeing him again face-to-face had been quickly dispelled by the jealous anger aroused by the intrusion of Isabel Blezard. Was the woman just as predatory towards other young men? Or was it only towards John? While Anne came close to hating the woman, she was forced to admit she understood the reasons for her conduct.

The bad mood caused by this encounter soon melted away. One could not remain cross when, all at once, it felt like spring. Anne opened her bedroom window and leant out, breathing in the fresh, sweet-smelling air. Daffodils were budding, birds calling and there was an unaccustomed softness and warmth in the lengthening days. It seemed a good moment to speak to Frederick Thorpe.

"I hope you are pleased with the children's progress, sir."

She smiled, knowing this was the best way of approaching her employer.

"Yes indeed," he replied, looking up from his desk and meeting her smile with one of his own. "Mrs Thorpe and I will always be grateful for what you have done – for Edward in particular."

"Thank you, sir. I wondered whether, now that I have been here over six months, I might be allowed an afternoon and evening off a week – to visit my aunt and attend choir practice at the Zion."

"The Zion, eh? Not the church?"

"No sir, they have sufficient choir boys and men. The Zion has a mixed choir and has need of sopranos. My friend Rachel Haigh is already a member."

"Well then, it would be churlish of me to deny the choir its chance of a new, and I have no doubt delightful, soprano." Thorpe smiled again, as if pleased both with his generosity and turn of phrase. "I will speak to Mrs Thorpe directly. I am sure she will be agreeable to the arrangement."

"Thank you, sir." Anne ran upstairs, light of heart and foot.

The following Thursday was a fine, bright day with a strong breeze sending the clouds hurrying across the sky. Anne found herself walking towards the Brooks' cottage in Lumb Lane and as she drew abreast of the gate, she saw Martha Brook, John's mother, pegging out some sheets. She stopped when she saw Anne and came forward.

"Is it Miss Graham? Emma's daughter? You were at the wedding supper at the Haighs?"

"Yes," Anne replied, her heart beating a little faster. It was disturbing seeing someone whose face resembled John's so closely, with the same brown eyes and full, curving mouth.

"I have to thank you, Miss Graham, for your letter."

"Oh yes. How is Mr Brook? John?"

The older woman's face saddened.

"Still very down. He blames himself almost entirely. It will take some time, I fear."

"Yes, yes, I'm sure."

"I did what I thought was best, Miss Graham. I cleared everything away that was Molly's. Except for the baby clothes. I couldn't bring myself to get rid of them.

Some day perhaps – " Mrs Brook paused and attempted a bleak smile. "Some day perhaps they'll be needed."

Anne smiled back, in sympathy. Mrs Brook smiled more fully, looking even more like her son.

"Would you care to come inside, Miss Graham, for a drink of tea?"

Anne felt sure the cottage room would be as clean and neat as a new pin but suspected that this was a token politeness, not to be taken seriously, especially on a wash day.

"Thank you very much, Mrs Brook, but my aunt Stott is expecting me."

"How is Agnes? I haven't spoken to her for some time."

"Nor have I. But I hope to now that I am released from my post on Thursday afternoons."

"I'm glad to hear it. Please give her my best regards. I bid you good afternoon."

At the farm, her Aunt Agnes looked very pale and tired in contrast to the bright-eyed Mrs Brook, although Agnes was much the younger. Apparently she had been ill with a low fever for several weeks. She said very little during the visit, which disappointed Anne, who had been expecting a warmer welcome. After tea, Anne did some ironing and put some washing to steep. Then she kissed her aunt goodbye and promised to visit her the following week. Perhaps Agnes had problems she knew nothing of.

Her spirits were restored by her reception at the Haighs' farm. Everyone seemed pleased to see her, especially Rachel. Hannah piled food onto her plate as if she thought the Thorpes had been starving her.

As the two young women walked down to the village, Anne asked if they had seen John at the farm lately.

"No. We're worried about him. It's nearly two months since. He used to call in all the time and we've hardly seen him at all."

"I suppose you might see more of him when the better weather comes?"

"Well, that's what we're hoping. He's always helped on the farm, has done all his life. He's almost like another brother to me." She stopped, distressed.

"In time perhaps," said Anne, squeezing her hand.

They had now reached the Zion Chapel, the light from its long windows illuminating the village street. Inside it was very handsome with highly polished light oak floors, pews, pulpit and an imposing bank of pews for the choir below the organ.

Rachel was greeted and Anne introduced. The choirmaster, a young man with fierce eye-brows, beckoned her to the piano. On the stand, a large hymn book was open at a well-known hymn.

"Do you know this?" he asked, playing the introductory chords softly.

"Oh yes."

"Would you sing it for me?"

Anne did so, effortlessly, in a clear, pure soprano voice. At the end, the conductor looked at her keenly.

"Very good. Do you read music?"

"Yes."

"We'll be pleased to have you join us, Miss Graham. Now then, ladies," he called out, "A new recruit for the ranks. Miss Anne Graham. Soprano."

The chatter subsiding, the choir took their places and practice began. Anne, at the end of the sopranos, recognised the young man next to her, at the end of the row of tenors. It was Sam Armitage, the shy, ginger-haired young man she had met at the Brooks' wedding supper. Diffident at first, he relaxed as they both smiled at the conductor's demands and laughed at his weak jokes. By the end of the evening when they had to share a music sheet, he seemed to be positively enjoying himself.

Later that week, at Dartmouth Hall, Anne and Susan were coping with a problem as calmly as possible. The evening had been going well until Georgina, freshly bathed and dressed in her nightwear, realised that Edward was not being prepared for bed as usual.

"It's not fair!" she wailed. "I want to stay up too! I want to see the ladies and gentlemen as well!" She stamped her foot and burst into tears.

"Now Georgina," said Anne, drying her tears, "It is disappointing, I know. But when I tell Mama that you have been a good girl and gone to bed without a fuss, then perhaps she will let you stay up another time."

Georgina appeared to be weighing up the two options open to her.

Fortunately, she decided against the full blast of outraged injustice and chose to go quietly.

"All right then," she said, breathing heavily. "All right. But I'm going to the next party, I am."

"Good girl," said Anne, kissing her and propelling her gently towards Susan and away from Edward who, dressed in his best clothes, had to be restrained from smirking at his less fortunate sister.

It was hard for the children not to be disturbed by the dinner parties their parents gave. Delightful suspense began the day before when tradesmen began delivering extra supplies of food, at the same time as the housemaids gave the reception rooms an extra clean. Silver was polished, chandeliers wiped and fireplaces cleared and re-laid as servants brought in fresh flowers and foliage for decoration.

The Thorpes were generous hosts. Anne suspected that Ellen Thorpe wished to show these northerners a bit of London style while Frederick used the occasions to further his numerous business deals. Tonight, in addition to their regular guests, the Blezards and the Littlewoods, they were expecting the Broomfields as well as two other business men. One of them had a dowdy wife but Seth Broomfield, a factory owner, was bringing his young wife, Jemima, a remarkably pretty and lively brunette, whom Frederick ensured sat next to him at the table.

The dinner had been well received, as it usually was. Ellen Thorpe thought further training was still needed in the serving of vegetables but Frederick had found Jemima Broomfield as delightful as she looked in her becoming cherry-red gown. He would have chatted to her all evening except for the times his attention was wrenched away by the demands of Isabel Blezard on his left.

"Is this another one of your contracts, Frederick? Eh?" called Dr Littlewood across the dinner table and over the buzz of conversation.

"What? Which one do you mean?" asked Thorpe, turning away with some reluctance from his attractive female guest.

"This new road to Huddersfield. From Almondbury village."

"No, no, nothing to do with me," replied Thorpe. Road-building was not one of his interests. "But it'll be a good thing. A better road than down the Old Bank. Too steep for comfort."

"You're right there," said George Blezard. "It's dangerous enough as it is, without having to look out for t' big stones blasted carters keep leaving behind 'em."

"George!" muttered Isabel reprovingly, putting her hand on his arm. He was already on the second bottle of red wine placed in front of him by the Thorpe servants.

"The main disadvantage," began Grace Littlewood shrilly. The noise of conversation did not drop so she began again, this time more loudly. "The main disadvantage will be the hordes of Irish navvies engaged for the work who will be brought up into the village as a consequence."

This time she was more successful at being heard. The behaviour of the Irish in the town was a common source of complaint.

"Nonsense!" growled Broomfield, his face flushed. "Better they've got summat to do than festering in their pigsties in town. And if they spend their wages on victuals and drink here, well, so much the better for village trade!"

His remark met with approval, expressed by cries of "Hear! Hear!" and the pounding of fists on the tablecloth. Ellen Thorpe, seeing her crystal glasses shivering, judged the moment had come to separate the gentlemen from the ladies. Catching her husband's eye, she stood up and smiling winningly, said "Ladies! Let us retire. The gentlemen, no doubt, will join us later."

At this, the ladies, six in number, rose and with considerable manoeuvring of voluminous skirts and petticoats and the gathering up of personal finery, left the dining table with its guttering candles, half-empty bottles and scattered dishes of fruit for the well-ordered calm of the drawing-room. As they left, a servant fetched the decanter of port from the sideboard and placed it in front of the host. Meanwhile, the ladies settled themselves in chairs and sofas, ready for the tea and coffee being offered by the maids.

Anne had been playing a quiet card game with Edward close by. This was her cue to bring him into the room for a few words with the female guests.

"How he is growing, Ellen!" said Mrs Littlewood. "A fine boy!"

Ellen looked gratified. Anne saw that Isabel Blezard gave the child less than a fleeting glance and returned to her absorbing conversation with Jemima Broomfield on the subject of fashion, judging by their frequent gestures to their own beautifully stitched and decorated evening gowns.

Anne sat unobtrusively in a corner of the room. Edward was being invited to help himself from a dish of sweetmeats – biscuits, candied fruits and chocolates. She was pleased to see how politely he was behaving but less sanguine about the effects of what he was eating.

Left with nothing to do but watch in silence, she found herself thinking of John as she so often did. Indeed, he was in her mind most of the time except when immediate matters demanded her concentration. What would he be doing now? Sitting at home with his parents? She wondered, as she did time and again, how well he was recovering from his bereavement. When summer comes, she vowed, I will see him, no matter what.

At that moment, John was walking, as he did nearly every night, walking until he was fit to drop. He was aware that he was in a rut but could not bring himself to get out of it. Each weekday he worked as long as he could and then returned home where his parents greeted him with an anxious sympathy that was beginning to set his teeth on edge, although he knew it was ungrateful of him. He tried to eat the meals his mother cooked for him but he was never hungry and after a few mouthfuls, could manage no more. His mother's worried look pained him further. To escape the unspoken words which hung in the air, he would beckon to Meg, his Border collie, who would leap to her feet eagerly and follow him outside. Then he would walk and keep walking so that when he returned home, he fell asleep instantly from exhaustion. He prayed that he would sleep through till morning but too often, he awoke in the early hours, prey to the demons he had lived with since Molly's death.

When out at night, he kept mainly to well-worn paths because it was easy to fall and twist an ankle in the darkness. One route he could not bring himself to follow was the one which led from his cottage in Lumb Lane up towards Castle Hill which passed the point where he had found Molly's body in the snow three months ago.

Tonight the moon was almost full, casting its silvery light across the valley. Had John been in a fit state to appreciate it, he would have marvelled at the beauty of the night sky, of the shapes and textures of tree and shrub and the gentle soughing of the wind in the foliage. As it was, he plodded on unnoticing, lost in his thoughts.

Coming up from Bank Foot, he bore left into Farnley Line, the long road that swept down along the valley, skirting Almondbury and passing the grounds of Dartmouth Hall on its way to Woodsome Bridge. For a while the only sound was the noise of his boots on the road until suddenly it was eclipsed by a terrible, blood-curdling scream that came from the edge of the Dartmouth estate. John, a countryman, knew the night calls of bird and beast and recognised at once that this was a human cry and almost certainly that of a child. He began to run and the dog ran too. The cry had now changed to a moaning sound that was no less terrible.

Vaulting over the dry-stone wall that bordered the estate, John crashed through the undergrowth led by the sound of human pain. Seconds later, he found its source. A boy of about nine lay on the ground clutching his leg which was fast in the jaws of an iron man-trap.

Rage flooded through John's veins but he made an effort to speak calmly so as not to frighten the boy further.

"Now lad, you've got yourself into a pretty pickle," he said, bending down to work out the mechanism of the trap. The boy turned to him in relief, sobbing.

"I were only looking for rabbits."

"I know you were, lad. Don't worry, I'll soon have you free."

John found a section of the trap where the serrated teeth did not quite meet and prised the end of his walking stick between them.

"Listen, lad ! When I say "now", I'm going to try and open the trap. I need both hands so when I say the word, you must pull your leg out. All right?"

The boy twisted round to look and muttered his assent. The metal was so stiff with rust it took all John's strength to lever the contraption open. Leaning with all his weight on the opening jaws, he shouted "Now!" The boy moved with agonising slowness. His leg was only just clear when John was forced to let go. The trap sprang together again, this time with shreds of cloth, skin and flesh between its teeth.

The boy lay quite still in a dead faint. Lifting him gently, John carried on in the direction he was heading, towards Dartmouth Hall. Those responsible for this instrument of torture should be made to witness its terrible consequences.

Edward could not sleep. Anne thought this hardly surprising. He had been allowed to stay up much later than usual, had become excited by the party atmosphere and eaten all the sweetmeats offered him by the indulgent female guests, as well as those he had already chosen for himself. Anne left him sitting up in bed with a book while she slipped down the kitchen stairs. Perhaps a hot drink would relax him.

She was quite unprepared for the scene that met her in the kitchen. Instead of finding the staff washing and clearing away the dishes and utensils used for the evening's dinner party, every single one of them stood round a table on which lay a dirty young boy, apparently asleep. As she drew nearer, she saw that one leg of the boy's trousers was ripped at knee level and below that, a purple and blackening wound on his pale flesh was oozing blood from V-shaped cuts.

"Is he – ?" she whispered. Susan reassured her in a hoarse whisper.

"He's asleep. Cook gave him a drop of laudanum."

Only then did Anne notice John standing at the boy's head. Some of the staff began edging away; one of the maids felt sick and was pushed down with her head between her knees. Anne turned to the cook.

"Do you know what to do next?"

The cook shook her head.

"He were in such pain I gave him some stuff. I have it for the toothache."

No-one else had anything to offer. Anne had an idea.

"There's a Dr Littlewood upstairs. Perhaps he would come down and look at the boy. I'll go and ask him."

She ran upstairs to the drawing-room where she turned the doorknob carefully and slipped inside as silently as possible.

The gentlemen had now rejoined the ladies. She did not know all the guests but recognised Isabel Blezard talking vivaciously to Frederick Thorpe, George Blezard standing with a group of business men and Dr Littlewood, with a foolish smile on his face, listening attentively to Jemima Broomfield. The whole picture was vibrant and pleasing to the eye – the rich colours of the women's silk gowns, the dark clothing of the men and the glow of the oil paintings in the lamp and candle light. But Anne had only a moment to register this response. She touched the doctor's sleeve gently. He turned and looked at her with displeasure. She spoke softly so that only he could hear.

"I'm sorry to disturb you, sir, but a boy has been injured on the estate. We have him downstairs and would be very grateful if you could take a look at him."

Dr Littlewood glowered. He did not speak.

Anne repeated her message and added "He's just in the kitchen, sir. We would value your advice. I will wait outside the room for you." Thinking he might need to make his excuses, she left the room quietly and stood outside in the corridor.

The minutes passed. She was puzzled. Had he not understood her? Was he perhaps deaf? She was just about to go back into the room when John joined her.

"Where's the doctor? Have you spoken to him?"

"Yes. I don't understand why he hasn't come out."

"I do!" he replied, his lip curling and an angry flush mounting in his face. "We'll see about that!" Then he was gone, re-appearing a minute later with the boy, still unconscious, in his arms.

"Open the door!" he commanded.

Anne did so, holding the double doors wide open so he could get through. She saw him glance quickly round the room, locate Dr Littlewood and then make straight for Frederick Thorpe. Conversation suddenly died away. Someone gasped.

"Are ye satisfied? Are ye?" blazed John, swinging the boy under Thorpe's gaze. The man paled. John thundered on.

"What right have you to lay man-traps? Isn't it enough to shoot the game for your sport? Are ye after trapping men, and bairns, as well?" He then turned and unleashed the full force of his wrath on Dr Littlewood.

"As for you. A man who heals the sick, are you? As long as they've plenty of brass and fill your belly with meat and drink!"

Anne was stunned. She had never seen John like this, like a man possessed. But she loved him for it. Out of the corner of her eye, she saw Isabel Blezard staring at him, eyes wide and lips wet.

Thorpe tried to lower the temperature.

"Mr Brook – it is Mr Brook, isn't it? We are all extremely distressed by this accident, especially, I can see, the ladies. I assure you the mantraps were not set by my instruction. No, indeed." He turned towards his wife as if seeking confirmation of his words. But she looked sickly and shrank back.

To Anne's amazement, Isabel Blezard stepped forward until she was standing close to John. She put one hand gently on the boy's forehead and looked soulfully into John's eyes.

"The poor child! How fortunate that you were near, Mr Brook. And were able to rescue him."

Anne went stiff with rage. What a hypocrite the woman was! Pretending to feel compassion for another when it was obvious she hadn't a sympathetic bone in her body! Even for children! Especially for children!

Isabel had not finished. She stroked the boy's brow and looked up at John with an expression of pitying sorrow. To Anne's relief, John appeared not to notice this performance put on for his benefit but continued to glare at the doctor.

Skilfully, Thorpe assumed command of the situation.

"Dr Littlewood? If you could just take a look at the child? Mr Brook, if you would carry him downstairs, Dr Littlewood will examine him and recommend some treatment."

As he spoke, he was carefully guiding John towards the door. Grasping the doctor by the shoulder, he managed to manoeuvre him outside as well. Anne took over, saying "This way, sir," holding on to the doctor's sleeve so he could not escape.

Downstairs, John laid the boy back on the kitchen table where he rolled his head from side to side, moaning softly.

The doctor gave the gashed leg a cursory inspection.

"There is nothing anyone can do," he said, with a touch of complacency. Anne wanted to slap him. "The wound may heal but blood poisoning may well set in. I suggest you take him up to the Infirmary tomorrow."

With that, he turned on his heel and returned to the party. The staff, the women in particular, muttered amongst themselves. Anne felt something had to be done that night.

"John! Rachel is a nurse at the Infirmary. They deal with injuries at work like this. Shall we take him up to the farm and ask her advice?"

John agreed. The boy was wrapped in a warm cloak and carried out into the courtyard. Without seeking permission, William brought one of Thorpe's horses out and saddled it up.

"Wait! I'll sit in front of you and hold him," cried Anne. She scrambled up and held her arms out for the boy.

The horse walked slowly with his extra burden and it was over thirty minutes before they reached the Haighs' farm. Anne felt enormously relieved when Rachel, calm, capable Rachel, came to their aid.

"All I can do is clean the wound with this tincture," she said, dabbing the boy's leg gently. "Fortunately we keep some at the farm in case of accidents."

"Will it heal?" asked Anne.

Rachel looked at her.

"It may do. It depends on the child's own healing power. If not ..." She did not elaborate. Anne knew of the dangers of gangrene, and of amputation which carried with it as many dangers as it aimed to cure.

Afterwards, John, Anne and the boy, his leg now bathed and bandaged, remounted the horse and made their way slowly back to the village. When they came to the boy's home, John carried him in and told the parents all that had happened. He looked stricken with anguish as he climbed up behind her and took the reins.

"All we can do is pray," he said. No more words were spoken. Anne was choked with emotion. Mixed with her sorrow at the evening's disaster was the joy of feeling the warmth of John's body close behind her, his arms alongside holding the reins and his breath on her neck. It was some time before she was able to reach the oblivion of sleep that night.

CHAPTER SEVEN

George Blezard emerged from the bank in St. George's Square in the centre of Huddersfield and stood blinking in the spring sunshine. Across the square to his left stood the handsome entrance to the railway station with its neo-classical portico and columns. "This is Huddersfield" it seemed to say, "Gateway to an important town!"

In the station forecourt, there were several cabs either setting down passengers or waiting for a fare from among those arriving by train. Men in overcoats and tall hats stood chatting outside the George Hotel; women passed, baskets on their arms, going to and from the market. To his right, carriages and carts transporting all manner of goods rumbled along John William Street in front of the Lion Buildings.

If George had been in the right mood, he would have felt proud as he walked along the streets of the town centre. Some of the commercial buildings were nothing more than functional but among them were splendid pieces of architecture, stylish as well as substantial, which declared the town's growing prosperity.

However, not for the first time, George felt as if everyone in the town was making money except him. He had tried to ignore the facts over the past year but his financial position was growing steadily worse. Fluctuations in the wool trade were to be expected but times generally picked up sooner or later, often from a fortunate war somewhere abroad which called for strong but cheap woollen cloth for uniforms in pleasingly large quantity. But no such luck had occurred recently. Or if it had, some foreign beggar had got in there first and seized the contract. George's cloth was not selling well and he still had to find for wages, maintenance, overheads and even for outright replacement of machinery. Only that morning Sam Armitage, his chief engineer, had come to see him in the noisy, dusty office George inhabited at the mill, at the top of a flight of stairs where he could see the mill floor and its busy looms.

"Can I have a word, Mr Blezard?"

"Aye! Come in, come in, lad!"

Truth to tell, George was glad of some male company, especially that of Sam Armitage whose cleverness George held in high esteem. Many men understood their engines and how to put them right but Sam seemed also to understand the theory behind them. He could look at a drawing of a machine and work out its efficiency from that alone.

Sam looked as if he was bearing bad news.

"I'm sorry, Mr Blezard, but I'm worried about the steam boilers."

"The steam boilers!" George sounded disbelieving. "It's not five year since they were put in. And they were good ones too."

"I don't doubt that, Mr Blezard," replied Sam gloomily. "But if you remember, you told me you extended the mill soon after that, added more looms."

"Yes, yes, I know," said George testily. "It were t' best thing to do, at the time."

"The point is, Mr Blezard, I think the steam boilers are working beyond their capacity." Sam paused. He had technical drawings with him but judged this was not the moment to bring them out. There was no need. The facts, unfortunately, spoke for themselves.

"There's nothing wrong as yet but they're having to work flat-out, there's no reserve. And in time, that's going to increase wear and tear on them. And they won't just wear out sooner – there's the danger of explosion."

He stopped again. Of all the things mill-owners understood and feared, the first was fire. Mills were notorious tinder-boxes. Wooden looms, wool and cotton threads and highly inflammable oily waste could, with the merest touch of a flame, produce a deathly inferno. Then there was explosion, which was fire and destruction together, of man and machine.

George's face was tense. Sam Armitage was not a man given to exaggeration; when he pronounced, it was based on facts.

"I've been investigating recent explosions at other works – at Upper Aspley Mills and Learoyd's Old Mills off Leeds Road. In both, the steam boilers exploded and in both, demand for power had recently been stepped up."

There was no point in arguing.

"So what's the solution then?" George asked wearily.

"New steam boilers - bigger ones. In the next six months – sooner if possible. I've seen some suitable – and costed 'em." There was no withholding this piece of paper. Sam handed it over gravely.

George sighed.

"Well thank'ee, lad. I'll look it over later." Which he did, and which led to his visit to the bank in Britannia Buildings in the centre of town.

The bank manager looked at George over his expensive spectacles.

"I understand your position, Mr Blezard, I understand it entirely. But coming right now, so soon after our most recent advance... For a considerable sum, I see."

George's heart sank. The bank manager paused to re-read George's file. As if it was new to him, thought George crossly. The man had nowt to do but sit in this fancy office and read a few figures. It was all very well for him. He didn't have to deal with the everyday problems of running a business, relying on suppliers, mill hands, machines and worst of all, customers and the fickleness of fashion. He had probably never had any worries about money in his life, this self-satisfied looking man, sat at his fine desk with the sun streaming in through big windows overlooking the Square.

The bank manager's words roused him from his reverie. There could be no further advance for at least three months, when they would review the position.

Walking down Chapel Hill on his way back to the mill, George ruminated on his present state of affairs. He was an honest man, honest to himself as well as to others. He knew that responsibility for his mounting debts was only partly due to the vagaries of trade. He had to admit he had brought most of his misfortune on himself by taking a second wife, a young woman from away, who did not understand the realities of business. Or if she did, and this was where George's honesty pained him, she did not care enough about him to heed his pleas for financial restraint.

Isabel had seemed so tender, so loving when they were courting. He had met her in Scarborough, a fashionable resort on the East coast where she helped her mother run a small hotel on the South Cliff, a few streets back from the Esplanade where the most distinguished residents and hoteliers lived. He had been at a low ebb after Betty's death. Usually the most robust of men, he had had to visit the doctor when he had been unable to throw off a succession of heavy colds and bronchitis.

"You need a change of air, George," said the doctor, an old friend of his. "You work too hard. Go somewhere bracing. Where there's a bit of life. I recommend Scarborough."

George hadn't needed much persuading. He and Betty had made their wedding journey there so the place aroused happy memories. But this time, he'd stay somewhere cheaper. No point in wasting brass.

So he had gone to Rowe's Hotel where Miss Isabel Rowe, the receptionist, had welcomed him warmly. She seemed right interested in hearing about his life in Huddersfield and his textile mill. She was a fine-looking young woman, just the sort he liked, dark-haired and built on the generous side.

The weather had been fine and he had walked about a bit. But you couldn't really enjoy yourself much on your own. Well, he couldn't. He remembered attending evensong at a nearby church. For somewhere to go, really. When he came out, he found that Isabel had been at the same service and they walked back to the hotel together.

Later that evening, she had served him his supper quietly and efficiently. He was the only guest. As she removed his dessert plate, she invited him to share a glass of cognac with her in the parlour.

"The nights are coming cooler," she said. "I think it is in the long dark evenings that we miss our loved ones most."

"It is that," he replied, looking into the fine dark eyes not three feet away.

"But time heals, they say," she added, laying her well-groomed hand very lightly on his.

George felt himself go hot.

"Warming. That brandy. I fancy a breath of air. I don't suppose you would like to accompany me?"

Together they stepped out into the cool sea air and walked down to the front until they reached the Esplanade where the big hotels were ablaze with light.

"We stayed in that one," indicated George, his voice gruff with emotion. "On our wedding journey."

"And were you happy together?"

"Oh yes. Very happy. She was a grand woman."

"Then she would have wanted you to be happy again," said Isabel, slipping her arm through his and leaning her breast against him. He remembered how good it had felt, a woman on his arm once again.

Over the next few days, George was delighted by the attention Isabel paid him. After being fine, the weather turned wet. Rain lashed against the windows all day without a break and the sea came smashing against the sea walls, sending great plumes of foam across the Marine Parade.

George went for a walk, determined to show a true Yorkshireman's disdain for inclement weather, but when his good wool overcoat became saturated, he took the wise course of returning to the hotel. Isabel's concern for him touched his heart.

"Goodness me, you're wet through, Mr Blezard! Let me have your hat and coat. I'll dry them in the kitchen. Now sit down by the fire and I'll bring you some tea."

He did not need much persuading, sinking into a deep armchair in front of a roaring fire. Isabel knelt down in front of him. Before he realised what she was doing, she had unlaced his boots and eased them off gently. Without a word, she put them in the hearth and taking hold of his right foot, wrapped both her hands round it, holding it so close to her body that it was almost resting on her bosom. When she looked up into his face with her dark, lustrous eyes and her full, red lips slightly parted, he felt a strong throb of desire spreading up through his body in a thoroughly alarming and delicious manner. It was a long time since he had felt like that.

"Your poor foot is cold," Isabel said, massaging it with her warm, young hands. Then she released it and did the same with the other one. When she stood up, with a rustle of silk underskirts, it was all he could do not to pull her towards him between his parted legs and kiss her.

Later, she brought him tea and crumpets which she toasted on the fire.

"Careful! The butter is running down your chin!" she laughed, dabbing at his face with a linen napkin. Then she sucked the butter off her own fingers. George felt deliriously happy.

In the evening, after serving him his dinner, she sat with him, at his invitation, in the cosy parlour.

"And do you like the hotel trade, Miss Rowe?" he asked.

She wrinkled her nose prettily.

"I do and I don't. It is very pleasant when one has congenial guests such as yourself, Mr Blezard" – she smiled at him, winningly, –"but less so when one has to serve people who – what can I say? – are not of the best quality. I should think your work in the mill is more satisfying. You have something to show for your efforts at the end of it."

"Yes, to be sure, there is that. It does feel satisfying, right enough, seeing t' wool coming into t' mill, in bales, and going out as fine pieces of cloth. It's a grand sight. Folk say it's a dirty, noisy job but I say it's like nature, which is often mucky, but no worse for that. If you'll excuse the word, Miss Rowe."

She laughed a silvery laugh.

"Of course, Mr Blezard. And what is it they say? "Where there's muck, there's brass.""

He joined in her laughter as if he had never heard the saying before.

Then it was the last day of his holiday and the weather was no better. "Nay lass, it's not your fault," he said when Isabel began apologising for it. "'appen I'll go for a ride in a carriage or summat." Seeing Isabel's face alight with interest, he added, "Perhaps you would do me the honour of accompanying me?"

It took Isabel only a few moments to find her mother and arrange for her to take over the reception desk. George closed his ears to what sounded like "words" in the kitchen before the older woman appeared, looking red-faced and flustered. But Isabel seemed all composure and it was not long before they were bowling along.

Their first stop was further along the promenade on the South Cliff. Here they got out of the carriage and inspected the building of the Grand Hotel, which was projected to be the biggest and best seaside hotel ever.

"It looks to be a grand job," said George, surveying the footings of the enormous building on the sea front.

"How right you are, Mr Blezard!" simpered Isabel. "Grand by name and grand by nature!"

The rain began to ease off as they drove along the Forge Valley, admiring the views. All too soon, it seemed to George, they were on their way back to the hotel. Isabel was silent.

"Are you all right, lass? I mean, Miss Rowe?" George was concerned.

She did not answer but pressed a handkerchief to her eyes. When she still did not reply, George got up from his seat and moved across, in the swaying carriage, to sit beside her. He saw that she was weeping very quietly.

"Miss Rowe! Isabel!" he found himself saying. "What ails you, my dear?"

Suddenly she was in his arms and he was inhaling the scent of her hair and feeling the warmth of her against his chest.

"Don't cry, my dear! Please don't cry! What is it, my love?"

For answer, she looked up at him, her eyes full of pleading.

"I can't bear to think of parting from you – George."

What else could he have done? He did the only thing possible – bent and kissed the warm, inviting lips and said, "Then don't, my dear. Don't let us part. Ever."

There was more kissing and murmuring of endearments. By the time the carriage reached the hotel, they were firmly betrothed, to their mutual satisfaction.

George had returned to Huddersfield on a wave of euphoria. He announced his wedding plans to his relatives who accepted the news with pleasure or resignation. Even his daughter Charlotte, who mattered most in the world to him, had shown no objection. True, her eyes had filled with tears but her words had allayed his doubts.

"As long as it makes you happy, Father!" she had said, hugging him.

George had gone back to Scarborough three weeks later. During that time, he received frequent letters from Isabel which amazed and delighted him with their passion. They were married in her local church and then he had brought his bride home, to Huddersfield.

Home was a solid, unpretentious villa in Lockwood, a few minutes walk from the mill, where George and his first wife had lived all their married life. But it didn't suit Isabel. For one thing, the streets were thronged with rough working people on their way to and from the local mills and factories. So a brand-new house it had to be, higher up in Newsome, with a view over the town and Castle Hill a short uphill walk behind it.

It had certainly kept Isabel busy and interested for months, choosing everything about it from doors to doilies. He had tried to tell her it were best to let Charlotte choose all her own stuff for her bedroom but Isabel had turned a deaf ear and done what she wanted anyway. She was good at that.

He sighed, thinking, as he had done more and more lately, of the good wife he had lost, Betty, the mother of his only child. She had been a stoical woman and had borne years of increasing pain with immense fortitude. Even during the time when she had been virtually an invalid, she had always been ready to listen to him and support him as best she could. Moreover, she had had a good business head on her shoulders; her advice, whether to tighten the purse-strings or to speculate and spend, had always been sound.

Charlotte, their daughter, had inherited her mother's talent with figures. As a child, she liked nothing better than to be given a list of numbers to add up. When she got the answer right, as she invariably did, it was hard to say who was the more pleased, the father or the child. He remembered Betty chiding him gently for rewarding the child with sweetmeats.

"You'll spoil her appetite, George! She'll never eat her dinner!" But she always did and he recalled how this would please him and his wife equally.

It was true that Charlotte would never be a fashion plate. If she inherited her reckoning talents from her mother, it was clear she took after her father in appearance and from being a chubby child, was now on her way to being a plump young woman. Like him, she had a rosy, cheerful face which he had always found beautiful, though he understood that others had different standards of beauty.

At this point, the face of his second wife, Isabel, came into his mind. Somehow he did not wish to spend the evening in her company. He thought this was the night she went to Jemima Broomfield's to play cards but he could not be sure. In any case, she'd play heck with him if she found out he'd been into town and forgotten to collect her new pair of boots from Shaw's in Westgate.

They were just locking up at the mill when he arrived back.

"Nay, you can give me t' keys," he said. "I've a mind to stay a bit and do some work while everything's quiet."

It was only when he settled himself at his familiar desk, with its scratches and stains from the past, that he realised he had eaten very little all day. Never heed, he thought, pulling the bottle of brandy out of the desk drawer, time enough when he got home. Mrs Drew could get him some cold meat and pickles.

Two hours passed without his realising it. George had covered several sheets of paper with his untidy figuring. But with a bit of economising over the next three months, it looked as if he might be able to satisfy the bank that a loan for new steam boilers would be a good investment.

Leaning back in his old, cracked leather chair, stiff with sitting so long, he rubbed his hand across his face in an effort to focus his attention and his eyesight. He hadn't felt well all day. Not surprising, with all the worry he had. He could see almost nothing through the dirty windows that looked out onto the mill floor, the pool of golden light cast by the oil lamp on his desk rendering everything else well nigh invisible.

When he opened the door, he could barely see the stairs-steps below him. Holding the oil lamp high with his left hand, he felt for the hand-rail with the other and pushed one foot forward until it met the edge of the top step. He began descending the flight of stairs very carefully and had almost reached the bottom when a fierce pain in his chest shot through him so searingly that it paralysed his left arm. And then he was falling, crashing down the stairs, the lamp flying from his grasp and smashing on the floor. Terrified, pinned by the pain in his chest, he watched in horror as the flaming oil snaked away from him.

"Help! Help!" he croaked, although he knew there was no-one there. Desperate to stop the fire spreading, he tried to launch himself forward to smother it. But a second, greater pain hammered him and he slumped to the floor, powerless.

The flames ran on, fed by the trickle of oil and the loose threads which lay profusely in their path. Within minutes, tongues of fire were running up the legs of the looms and feeding on the oily waste.

One corner of the mill was now lit up. But George Blezard was past seeing it, lying dead on the floor, his sheets of figures still on the desk where he had left them.

"You didn't expect to see me, I warrant," said Sarah with a look of grim satisfaction. She was right, Anne didn't. Thursday afternoons were now spent with Aunt Agnes, and at their most pleasant, were tranquil times when Agnes would reminisce and tell Anne all she could remember of her mother's early life. Today she had been met on her arrival by her cousin Sarah obviously bursting with news.

The three women sat in the farm kitchen, Sarah in her father's chair with her feet in the hearth, close to the kitchen range. Her mother was laying the table for tea and parkin. Anne, warm from walking, removed her shawl and took a chair by the small window.

"Been a fire at Blezard's Mill. 'Aven't you heard?" Anne hadn't. Sarah seemed mightily pleased.

"Last night. About nine o'clock. Place were locked up but Mr Blezard were still there, doing his books. Anyway about nine o'clock, people across t' road saw flames in t' downstairs windows. Fire brigade were fetched but fire were well on by then. As luck would have it, it were raining and they soon got fire under control. It were only at one end o' t' building though."

"But there must have been considerable damage?" asked Anne, full of concern.

"Oh yes! When we got to work this morning, we were right shocked. All t' windows were broken. And inside! It were all blackened and a terrible smell! And where t' water 'd been pumped in, it were sodden underfoot. It'll tek some cleaning up, I can tell you. We've been told to stay off all week. We'd best get paid. That's all I hope. Still, old Blezard's bound to 'ave been insured."

"And Mr Blezard? Is he safe?"

"Oh no! They found him dead at t' bottom o' t' steps. Seems it were his oil lamp that set place on fire. He must have fallen down t' steps holding it. Could've been drinking. He were allus fond of 'is brandy."

Anne was horrified.

"Dead? Oh! His poor wife and daughter! He couldn't have been very old."

"About fifty, we reckon," said Sarah, her tone indicating that she regarded this as very old indeed. Anne and her aunt exchanged glances. Sarah was now satisfied. Rising, she wrapped her shawl round her shoulders and tucked her hands under her arms. "I'm off to Nelly Schofield's. I'll be back late."

Anne moved to the table where her aunt was pouring tea.

"Poor Mr Blezard! And his wife! They'd not been married long, had they?"

"Not eighteen months," replied her aunt who had visibly relaxed with the departure of her daughter. "But it's Charlotte I feel sorry for. She lost her mother less than three years ago. She was away at school when her father re-married. She can't have been too happy about that, I think. The second Mrs Blezard is not what you would call motherly."

"Motherly!" Anne exclaimed. "Not at all, I would say. From what I've seen of her, she's a vain, selfish woman who does nothing but spend money on herself and her new house. I've only spoken briefly to Charlotte at church but she seems quite a different sort of girl."

"Yes, she is. She's like her father to look at but she's like her mother too, Betty Gledhill as she was. I knew her when we were girls. Her father owned t' mill. She was a grand woman, very straight, you knew where you were with her."

"And how are you, Aunt?" asked Anne, helping to clear the table. "You look very pale, even paler than we people with auburn hair usually do."

"Oh, I'm well enough," said her aunt hastily. They were standing at the scullery sink about to wash the tea things. If Anne had not happened to look down, she would not have seen what she did – a purple bruise just above her aunt's thin, freckled wrist.

"What's that? How did you do that?"

"It's nothing," said her aunt, keeping her eyes down. Anne put her hand on her aunt's other sleeve and gently pulled it up. There was a similar bruise on the other arm, this time showing clearly the outline of someone's fingers on the white skin.

"Who has done this to you?" she demanded. "Uncle Jack? Ned? This is no accident."

Her aunt seemed frightened and backed into the room, away from the force of Anne's enquiry. Anne followed her.

"You've had other bruises, haven't you? I've seen them. And you said you did them yourself, banging into things. But you didn't, did you? Tell me!"

Agnes bit her lip, the colour rising in her cheeks.

"It's nothing. It's what happens – in some families. It always has."
When Anne began to question her again, her aunt shook her head.

"It could be a lot worse. Jack just doesn't know how strong he is."

"Well, someone should tell him. And I will."

"No, no, please don't! It will just make matters worse. It's just – when he comes home, when he's drunk a bit too much and, I think, lost some money gaming. When things don't suit."

"So he takes it out on you!" Anne was angrier than she had been for a long time.

"Believe me, Anne, things will be all right. I ask you not to say anything."

"I won't promise," replied Anne, hotly. "But I don't want to make life more difficult for you than it is already. Just tell me if he does it again. I have to go now, Aunt. Rachel is expecting me. Till next week then. Take care of yourself."

She left the farmhouse with some reluctance and began the walk to the Haighs' farm. The more she thought about Jack Stott's treatment of her aunt the more outraged she felt. Men who "knocked their wives about" were all too common. She had more than once felt pity for some woman in that situation. But they had never been her own flesh and blood before. She remembered her mother speaking of her younger sister's timidity. Anne's mother had had a strong will which blazed into boldness at any sign of unfairness. Agnes was patently not the same.

Leaving the Stott farm and entering that of the Haighs was like going into another world. The Stott farmhouse was dark, poky and low-ceilinged even though kept clean and neat by Agnes. The farmyard behind it was untidy and cluttered with rusted implements. In the milking-shed, the cows stood in liquid manure which seeped in runnels across the cobbled yard almost to the farmhouse door.

At the Haighs' farm, light found its way easily into the courtyard and windows of the farmhouse. The farm was worked in the same way as at the Stotts', by a father and son with the help of some more labourers, but there was a purposeful air about the place quite absent from the farm lower down the hill. Anne had to admit that the vital difference lay in the atmosphere created by the families in question. There was a warmth at the heart of the Haigh farm totally lacking in the other one. Eli Haigh was a kindly if somewhat silent man, but his wife Hannah was the epitome of the good countrywoman. Cheerful and buxom, she responded to everyone with generosity and interest. She was never happier than when she was feeding people; her pleasure was palpable and, thought Anne, it nourished her own spirit at the same time without her knowing it.

She welcomed Anne as usual.

"Now look who's here! Come in, my dear, come in and have some supper. You need some building up after walking all that way uphill."

Broth, tea-cake, cheese, cold meat, red cabbage, apple pie – all were put in front of Anne. She smiled.

"I'll do my best, Hannah. Where is Rachel today?"

"To tell the truth, my dear, I've made her go up to her bed. She's taken a bad cold in th' ead. Just this morning. See for yourself."

Rachel was sitting up in bed, the quilt pulled up around her, attempting to stem a streaming cold with a quantity of soft rag.

"Hallo, Anne. I'm sorry I won't be coming to choir practice tonight. They'll have to be a contralto short."

"Never mind," said Anne, perching on the end of the bed. "I hope you'll soon be better. Have you heard about the fire at Blezard's Mill last night? And about Mr Blezard?"

Rachel had heard the news, Ben learning of it when he delivered the milk that morning.

"It's Charlotte I feel sorry for," said Rachel. "She and her father were devoted to each other. It seems a pity he married again but it's a man's privilege, I suppose."

Anne had a sudden image of Charlotte and George Blezard on Christmas morning, standing close together while Isabel queened it in her finery.

"Yes. I wonder how she will get on with her stepmother now. They seem very different."

Their conversation was brought to an end by a fit of coughing from Rachel. Promising to make her excuses to the choirmaster, Anne went downstairs and joined Hannah, Eli and Ben at the supper table where the talk was of George Blezard and his unhappy accident. Hannah was full of sympathy, Eli hoped the mill was fully insured while Ben reckoned they had a good man in Sam Armitage who would deal properly with restoring the mill to working order as soon as possible.

"He's got a good head for business as well as engineering," he said. "They're lucky to have him."

"He sings in the Zion choir," said Anne. "The tenors. He seems to be enjoying it."

"Good, good," said Hannah. "I'm glad to hear he's getting out more."

Anne hesitated. She wanted to speak of John Brook but feared she might blush. Taking a deep breath, she moved the conversation in the direction she wished it to go.

"Have you seen much of John, John Brook lately? When I spoke to his mother last, she said he was still grieving very badly."

Hannah's face saddened.

"Not as much as we would like, have we, Eli?" Eli shook his head. She went on. "We must try to get him up here when the family come over – cheer him up a bit if we can."

"Do you think he might like to join the choir? Now that Sam goes." Anne felt embarrassed. She knew that her motives were not pure, less designed to draw John out of his mourning than to give her a chance to see him.

"He might," said Hannah. "What do you think, Ben? Does he like singing?"

"I'm not sure. We all sang at school. It's worth a try."

"It's a very good idea of yours," said Hannah, smiling at Anne. "Singing lifts the spirit – and that's what he needs. I'll have a word with his mother if I don't see him soon. Now, what about a piece more pie, my dear? I'm sure you've a bit more room for some."

There being no question of Rachel attending the choir practice that evening, Anne set off by herself soon after supper for the walk back down to the village. As she came abreast of the Stott farm, where a feeble light shone from the downstairs window, she felt troubled once again. The day Agnes wed Jack Stott had been an unlucky one for her. The marriage enabled him to take over her father's farm; it had given her a miserable existence which she seemed to accept without complaining. It was said that one should not interfere between husband and wife but Anne was sorely tempted. In another minute, she had given way to temptation.

As she walked past the farm, she heard a strangled cry from within as if the sound had been stifled the instant it was uttered. It was unmistakably the voice of Agnes, her aunt.

Turning, Anne ran up the path and threw herself against the door latch. The scene inside made her blood boil. Agnes was cowering in a corner, her arms up, protecting her face. Jack stood over her, threatening her with his fists raised. Anne was carrying a heavy Bible and without a second thought, she swung it up with both hands and slammed it as hard as she could against the side of his head. He staggered, dumbfounded. Before he had time to collect his wits, Anne flew at him like a tigress. Now it was his turn to fling his arms up in self-defence.

"You coward! You beast! How dare you strike her!" And she swung the Bible at him again, from below this time so that she delivered an upper-cut to his jaw. The blow did not fell him but he lost his balance and crashed to the floor.

Anne was on fire with rage. She helped her aunt up and propelled her into a chair and then turned on her uncle and lashed him, this time with her tongue.

"This is your wife who works for you day in, day out. And what thanks do you give her? If it wasn't for her, you would have no farm. It was hers before it was yours. If my mother was still alive — " She stopped because of the horrible certainty that if she continued talking about her mother, she would burst into tears.

Jack shook his head and rubbed his hand across his unshaven chin. Fortunately for Anne, he looked stunned. She noticed, for the first time, that her cousin Ned was lurking in the scullery. She contented herself with giving him a withering glance.

"I'm going now to choir practice," she said to her aunt. Turning to her uncle, "If I hear from my aunt that you have ill-treated her again, I shall tell everyone just what kind of man you are – the vicar, the minister, the constable, the doctor, all the farmers hereabouts and as many other people as I can. Then we'll see how they treat you. And there are men in the village who'd be only too happy to give you a thrashing."

She had no idea if her last threat could be carried out but she felt it ought to be. Jack had still made no attempt to get up. Bending over her aunt, she kissed her.

"Goodbye, Aunt. I will be here as usual next week. You know you can always get a note to me at the Hall if you need help." Glaring once more at the two men, Anne left the house.

She was glad of the walk to the village; it gave her time to compose herself.

As she neared the chapel, she saw Sam Armitage hovering outside. Only then did she remember that it was his family Bible she was carrying that she had used as a weapon.

Her face must have revealed more than she knew because he came forward quickly, looking concerned.

"Are you quite well, Anne? You look..." He stopped, as if unused to such intimacy.

"Sam. I do hope your Bible is as it was when you gave it to me."

"What do you mean?" he asked, drawing her to one side. Other choir members were arriving and going in.

"I — I've just hit Jack Stott with it."

Sam gave a hoot of laughter.

"Don't laugh! It's true. It's not how the good book should be used."

"It may not be but it's probably done some real good this time. I'm sorry, Anne. You know I'm not a believer. I couldn't pretend otherwise. I just brought the Bible because I thought you'd like to see the illustrations."

"I did. Thank you for lending it to me." She handed it back and took a few deep breaths. Sam stood waiting for her.

"Are you recovered? Shall we go in?"

Anne smiled at him. "Yes indeed. I think a few choruses of "And He Shall Purify" are just what I need."

Chuckling, he put his hand under her elbow as they went in together.

Ned Stott sat with his legs stretched out, his feet in the hearth. As soon as Anne Graham had gone, his mother had cleared the table and gone upstairs to bed without a word. He could hear his father outside in the yard, pumping water, no doubt to stop his face from swelling where

Anne Graham had hit him. Ned grinned to himself. It had been a sight worth seeing, that young lass hitting his father.

There had been a time, many years ago, when he had stood up to his father when he first saw him slapping his mother. But the beating Jack had given him had stopped him ever doing it again. When his father got a bit rough with his mother, as he did now and again, he just kept out of the way. She never complained so he reckoned she was used to it. Anyroad, giving the wife a few slaps was nothing out of the ordinary. They probably expected it. And deserved it, most like.

His father came back into the kitchen, dabbing his chin with a ragged towel, the neck of his shirt dark with water. The look in his eyes was dangerous. Ned knew better than to say anything to him. He watched as his father poured some tea into a pint pot and then, after tasting it, spat it out. Rubbing his mouth with the back of his hand, Jack went back into the scullery. Ned could hear him banging pots about and clanking lids. He returned, scowling.

"There's no bloody ale." Still grumbling, he felt for his coat. Only when he had his hand on the door latch did he speak directly to Ned. "Well, are ye bloody coming or not?"

Ned got up and followed him. There was no need to ask where they were going. They walked up the road to Broken Cross and then down the other side into the centre of the village without speaking. Ned thought it best to say nothing about Anne Graham and the Bible. It was a pity he couldn't tell his mates about it. It'd make a grand tale. But he knew what his father would be like if he breathed a word of it. She was a fiery lass and no mistake. He remembered how she'd thrown a stone that had hit him, quite hard, the night she came. He didn't think any the worse of her for it.

When they reached the beer-house, they went in and joined their own groups, Jack with some of the older men and Ned with lads from the village. For the next two hours or so, there was no contact between them until Jack came up and with a jerk of his head, indicated it was time for off. Ned wasn't bothered. He'd run out o' brass a while since.

The fresh night air hit them as they left the fug of the beer-house. As they began walking up towards home, they saw some folk coming down Westgate from the direction of the Zion chapel.

"Eh-up. Zion's loosing," said Jack.

"Nay," said Ned, who was better informed. "It's choir practice night. It's choir. One Anne Graham goes to."

"Right enough," replied Jack unpleasantly.

The two men halted and stepped back in the shadow of a stone gateway. Across the road, they saw Anne walking past, accompanied by a ginger-haired young man. When the couple came to the road junction, they stopped. It was clear that the young man was offering to walk home with her and just as clear that she was telling him not to. At last, she succeeded and they parted to go their separate ways. But not before the two watchers saw him take her hand and hold it for a while.

The Stott men walked slowly up the village street. Then Jack spoke.

"Summat goin' on there?"

"What dost tha mean?" growled Ned, as if he did not understand, although he did.

"Them two. Graham lass and that chap. Dost tha know 'im?"

"Sam Armitage. Engineer at Blezard's."

"Looked a bit fond, to me."

Ned grunted. He thought the same. It was the first he'd heard of it. They continued walking up the hill in silence.

"What dost tha think to her?"

"Who?"

"Anne Graham. Thi cousin. Could tha fancy her?"

Ned considered. It wasn't owt he'd given much thought to. But she was quite a bonny lass, he reckoned, if you liked that sort. And any lass who'd clouted his father, twice, had summat about her.

"Reckon I could. I like a lass with a bit o' spirit."

Now it was his father's turn to grunt.

"Never mind that. Tha wants to think on. She's Emma Ramsden's child."

Ned said nothing. He knew his father hadn't finished, was working his way round to something important. Sure enough, after a minute or so, Jack came to it.

"I'm just saying. Thi grandfather, thi mother's father, Nathan Ramsden, wanted th'eldest child, Emma, to have t' farm. But she went off to London. And niver come back."

There was another, longer, pause.

"The old man left it Emma in 'is will."

Now Ned understood. Indeed, he would have been a fool if he hadn't. That must have been what his cousin meant when she said "If my mother was still alive." Farm were really hers. And his – if he married her.

"So tha sees, lad. It meks sense. 'er and thee. Bastard or not. Think on't."

Ned didn't need telling twice. He clumped up the road towards the farm with his father without another word, imagining what it would be like to have Anne Graham in his bed. He'd had a few tumbles with local lasses so he had no worries of that sort. Anne Graham! By, he should have thought of it before! If she were here now, why...

As if reading his mind, his father had one more bit of advice.

"Tha wants to get in there, lad — afore sum'dy else does."

CHAPTER EIGHT

Behind the gleaming black hearse came the first funeral carriage bearing the widow and the daughter. Charlotte had been crying quietly for most of the journey from Wood Lane. She knew that she was not only crying for the untimely death of her dear father but for herself and what his loss would mean to her. He had been her shield in these last difficult months, when he had taken a second wife. With considerable skill, he had managed to keep the peace between the two women. And he had done all this when, Charlotte knew, he had more worries about his business than he had had for a long time. Making an effort to stem her tearfulness, she tucked her handkerchief away.

As the cortège entered the village, the undertakers' men climbed down and led the procession at walking pace. The followers carried wands draped in black crape with scarves of the same fabric across their chests, the line of their black-draped top hats echoed by the plumed head-dresses of the high-stepping horses behind them.

Isabel had spent the journey playing with her gloves and adjusting her veil. As the carriage door was opened and a helping hand proffered, she pressed a black-edged wisp of lawn to her eyes. She stood still for a moment, just long enough, thought Charlotte, for onlookers to take note of her new outfit, the mourning dress trimmed with black ruffles of lace forming a deep frill which swept down from each epaulette to a flattering V at the waist. A half-cape, similarly trimmed, and a bonnet with streamers, completed the picture. Taking care to keep just ahead of her step-daughter, their mourning veils fluttering slightly in the breeze, she followed the pall-bearers into the church.

It was almost full. George Blezard had been well-liked. He was one of those rare mill-owners who had done mill work themselves as a child and seen his mother driven to an early death by its relentless grind. He had never forgotten his good fortune in marrying Elizabeth Gledhill of Gledhill's Mill nor did he forget what it was like to work on the mill floor. Indeed, had he been able to forget, he might have made a better business man. Most of his fellows with their eyes more firmly fixed on profit thought him soft but even some of them had turned out today to honour a man who demonstrated virtues they respected but did not practise. His bank manager was there, the relatives of his first wife and some of the craftsmen who had worked recently on the new house in Wood Lane. John Brook was not there but he had written to Isabel and to Charlotte expressing his condolences.

For Charlotte, the funeral service passed in a blur. It was barely three years since they had held the funeral service for her mother in the same church and the memory of how she had held on to her father's arm and willed her comforting strength into him was painfully fresh. She had believed then that she, and she alone, would bring him from grieving into a state, perhaps not of happiness, but of acceptance. She had not foreseen that, on his visit to Scarborough the following year, he would be captivated by another woman and make her his second wife.

She had tried hard to like Isabel. Charlotte possessed a rational mind and she understood that a wife could be more to a man than a daughter could. So she had struggled to overcome her initial jealousy and tried to see the situation from her father's point of view.

At the beginning, he had seemed happy, lifted out of his misery by Isabel's undeniable beauty and sparkle. But as time went on, his happy moments were fewer and it seemed to Charlotte that Isabel's conduct added to, instead of lessening, his cares. Even so, she could have forgiven her step-mother's lavish spending had she ever seen any sign of genuine affection for her father. True, there were gestures, in public – the squeezed hand, the cuddled arm – but at home, these were almost totally absent. She did remember one occasion, entering a room unannounced, when she had come upon Isabel sitting on George's knee kissing him but it was clear from the subsequent conversation that he had just agreed that they should give John Brook a further commission for more fireplaces. Of spontaneous, disinterested fondness, there had been no evidence.

As they came out of the church, friends and acquaintances thronged around the two women. Most wanted to speak to Charlotte and tell her how much they had thought of her father.

Mercifully, the interment in the churchyard was brief and the mourners began to disperse soon after. Charlotte had not been surprised at John Brook's absence. His wife's funeral had taken place at All Hallows only a few months earlier; it was not to be wondered at. However, as the family moved back towards the carriages, he appeared in the distance and came forward to speak to them, addressing his remarks, Charlotte noted, to her.

"I was sorry I was unable to attend your father's funeral, Miss Charlotte. Please accept my apologies. He was a fine man."

Charlotte was shocked at how gaunt and haggard he looked. The expression in his eyes was tortured, painful to witness.

"Thank you, Mr Brook. And thank you for your letters. We are very grateful."

This seemed as long an encounter as the young man could manage. He was moving away when Isabel spoke to him, preventing his leaving.

"Thank you again, Mr Brook."

He muttered something and began to back away.

"I hope your parents are well?"

Why doesn't she let him go? thought Charlotte. The poor man has done all he can for the moment. But Isabel persisted.

"Your wood-carving has been much admired. I have recommended your work to several of my friends."

"Thank you, Mrs Blezard. If you will excuse me..." He made an attempt at a polite smile and then walked away.

Isabel and Charlotte watched him go, now joined by Jessie Lodge.

"It's a tragedy, that's what it is," said Jessie, referring obviously to the departing John Brook rather than to the man they had just buried. Charlotte turned aside but she could hear the conversation quite clearly.

"He's just wasting away, there's no sense in it."

"You mean the loss of his wife, I suppose?" asked Isabel.

"Yes. A grand young man like that. There's plenty lasses I know of who'd cheer him up if they had chance."

"No doubt," said Isabel drily.

"He's been invited to all manner of things but he won't go to any of 'em. All he does is walk that blessed dog. Up Castle Hill, by Mellor Wood and then back home. Every night, even in t'rain." Jessie dropped her voice to a dramatic whisper. "But he never walks up top o' Lumb Lane – where they found Molly – dead."

154

Charlotte thought this was enough. There was no knowing what vulgarity Jessie might come out with, given any further audience.

Turning to Isabel who was still gazing after John Brook's departing figure, she said, "Shall we go now, Isabel? I have already thanked the vicar."

The two women walked slowly back to their carriage which was waiting nearby. Just a few close relatives were coming back to the house for a funeral tea. Charlotte had arranged with Mrs Drew for the provision of boiled ham, shortbread biscuits and port wine. She had held back initially, thinking this was a matter for the widow, but Isabel was too busy seeing her dressmaker to attend to such details.

As the carriage swept into Wood Lane, Charlotte took a deep breath. The worst was over. Or was it? Tomorrow the family solicitor was coming to read George's will. Charlotte knew its contents. She had an idea that Isabel did not.

Isabel found the journey back to Wood Lane from the church tedious in the extreme. On the way there, she had been able to enjoy anticipating the response her new mourning clothes would provoke in the onlookers as well as the pleasure that always came from being the centre of attention, which, as the widow, she clearly was.

Now there was just a boring tea party to be endured.

A further irritation was the excruciatingly slow pace of the carriage. Isabel hated being in a slow-moving vehicle, although she conceded that a funeral procession was a special case. She liked to travel fast, either in a single gig or on horseback. She recalled the night she had been riding home on her black gelding. The whip had set the beast galloping so hard that Isabel had not seen the old coach rumbling along Wakefield Road until it was almost too late. The stupid driver had probably been half asleep. Still, she had managed to get home before George's suspicions were aroused.

That evening, over a year ago now, had not been a successful one. She had met Frederick Thorpe as arranged in a private room upstairs at a country inn. But he had apparently changed his mind since their encounter at the Hall a few days before. Then, he had seemed more than willing.

It had been that tedious time after dinner when guests had begun playing cards or gossiping or sitting quietly by themselves getting drunk. Her husband had belonged to the latter group. Bored by the conversation, Isabel looked round for their host, Frederick Thorpe, who had been giving her meaningful looks throughout dinner. There was no sign of him. Remembering that he liked to smoke, she had gone outside and down the steps towards the shrubbery. There, behind a rhododendron hedge, she had found him, quite alone, puffing on a cigar. As Isabel approached, he took it from his mouth, his moist red lips visible beneath the luxuriant moustache. What he had seen in Isabel's eyes must have been unmistakable because he had immediately thrown the cigar down on the path.

A moment later they were clutching each other, fiercely kissing again and again. Savage with lust, Isabel pressed herself against him, devouring him, running her hands over his body. She felt him respond as she spread her legs and drove her tongue into his tobacco-tasting mouth.

They writhed, locked together in passion until they could go no further, at least, not then, in those circumstances. Panting, Isabel had pulled away and told him where she would be one evening later that week. Shaken, he had agreed to meet her. Stumbling back indoors, she slipped upstairs to re-arrange her dishevelled hair, leaving Thorpe in the bushes where, she suspected, he was hunting for the dropped cigar.

But when the assignation materialised, it had all been quite different. Thorpe had kept his distance and told her, bluntly, that he had thought it over. She was a very attractive woman but ... She hardly heard what he said, something about "wife" "children" "old friend George" and "reputation, yours as well as mine." She had simply turned on her heel, stamped down the narrow inn stairs, remounted her horse and spurred it away.

Perhaps he was right. Perhaps he would have been unable to cope with the affaire and her regular visits to the Hall to take tea with his wife. Personally, she thought it would have added a little piquancy. There was nothing like a little danger to spice things up.

Still, perhaps it had all turned out for the best. With George gone, she was a free agent. If she had been saddled with Frederick Thorpe, who knows how difficult it would have been to get rid of him? No, she thought, leaning back against the upholstery with her eyes closed, the way was now clear for the greatest adventure of all – the capture of the most attractive man she had met since coming to this dreary town – John Brook, tall, handsome, athletically built, with manly charms he seemed quite unconscious of. When he first came to the house in Wood Lane, she had noticed his dark, compelling eyes and his hands – strong, tanned, shapely. It would be exciting to be caressed by those hands.

She remembered the ridiculous Grace Littlewood simpering over him at one of Ellen Thorpe's tea-parties. What had she said? "Very fine!" While that smug minx of a governess, Anne something or other, sat in the corner, listening.

She had not seen him playing cricket as Grace Littlewood had, but she had seen him helping in the hayfields as she walked past one sunny day carrying her parasol. Some of the young men had stripped off their shirts and were shouting at him to do the same. Laughing, he had pulled his shirt over his head, flung it to one side and resumed his work. She could remember the look of his body even now, the firm muscles rounding his upper arms and shoulders, the ripples of his back as he plunged the pitchfork into the hay, the tantalising glimpse of naked hips as he stretched up and tossed it onto the waiting wagon.

Thanks to that gossip Jessie, she now knew where he was likely to be most evenings. It was only a matter of time.

She yawned. Thank God the journey was over. Just the tea party and then freedom. And tomorrow they would hear the will. What could be better?

"Fifty per cent? Do you mean half?"

Charlotte saw Isabel's face become ugly with shock. The solicitor, who was used to reactions of this kind, waited a moment before repeating the words.

"Yes, Mrs Blezard, that is what it means. "My wife Isabel Blezard and my daughter Charlotte Elizabeth Blezard are to have fifty per cent each of the assets." Mr Blezard intended that you and Miss Charlotte should have an equal share of the house, cash and investments."

"But this is outrageous!" stormed Isabel, the colour mounting in her face. "Surely it is usual for the wife to inherit the whole, with a bequest of some kind to any children of a former marriage?"

"Not necessarily," said the solicitor smoothly. "That is one way of doing it, to be sure, but it is not uncommon to have an arrangement of this kind."

Thank God Father doesn't have to hear this, thought Charlotte, aware immediately that this was illogical, to say the least. She kept quiet.

"What about the house then?" asked Isabel aggressively. "Presumably we could sell it?"

"Only if you both agree to the sale."

"And the same with the mill? "

"Aah!" said the solicitor, turning over the pages of the document. Charlotte suspected he was enjoying himself.

"There are restrictions on the mill and what can be done with it. It has been in the family a long time. The first Mrs Blezard's family, that is." The solicitor did not look up to witness Isabel's look of cold fury. "Miss Charlotte is to have the controlling interest in the mill." He looked at Charlotte. "He entrusts her with a managerial role."

Isabel gave a contemptuous snort.

"So what of the cash assets? The investments? Have they been calculated?"

When the answer came, it was no shock to Charlotte who had been expecting as much.

"There are a number of small investments which will guarantee a sufficient, if moderate, income. As for cash, I'm afraid Mr Blezard left very little. His expenditure over the past eighteen months has been as great as his income. Indeed, there are some unpaid bills still outstanding."

For once, Isabel was speechless. She stood up, knocking things off the desk in her haste and left the room with a sway of her full skirts and a rattle of her jet jewellery.

Charlotte released the breath she had been holding and took a sip of water. She was glad that part of the will-reading was over. The solicitor, who had known the family for many years, waited for her to compose herself. For Charlotte, there were investments and stock from her mother's estate to do with as she wished. Fortunately, Isabel had no claim on these.

Minutes later, they heard the door bang and saw Isabel leading her horse past the window and out on to the road.

"Mr Blezard also left a small bequest to Mr Samuel Armitage," said the solicitor.

"Did he? Good! I know he deserves it." Charlotte was pleased, especially as that gentleman was expected at Wood Lane later that afternoon. "Might I be the one to tell him about it?"

"You could perhaps ask him to call and see me at my chambers in town for the exact details. But I have no objection to your giving him the news in general."

When Charlotte told Sam that her father had left him some money, he looked stunned.

"He had no need –" he began, then stopped, as if afraid of appearing ungracious.

"No, but I'm sure he did so to show his appreciation of your work, Mr Armitage – Sam," said Charlotte. Seeing he was still in the grip of embarrassment, she asked him what needed to be done to restore the mill to working, and profitable, order.

"My suggestion, Miss Charlotte, is to turn this fire to advantage. I'd only recently advised Mr Blezard that the steam boilers were having to power too many machines."

Charlotte was interested. He went on, confidently.

"I suggest we get rid of the looms at that side of the building which has been fire-damaged. That'll reduce the demand for power and should mean the steam-boilers will last that much longer."

"What might we use the cleared space for?"

"Well, I've been to one or two mills lately where they've had samples of their cloth laid out, nicely-like, in a sort of display. Instead of folk just going into the office and looking at 'em there. Like they've always done."

"A good idea! And how did my father keep up with what was going on in the cloth trade?"

Sam mentioned the activities of the Cloth Hall in Huddersfield, the trade magazines and the exhibitions held at home and abroad.

Charlotte was excited.

"I shall make it my business to find out all I can. Blezard's has been a respected name in cloth for too long to let it fail now. With your help, of course," she added, giving him a shy smile. When she shook his hand in farewell, she felt hopeful for the first time since her father's death.

She was reading by the fireside when Isabel returned, coming into the room noisily and striking the door panel with her riding-crop.

"I thought you would like to know – " she declared, "that Ellen Thorpe has invited me to accompany her to London in two weeks' time. We are to stay with some friends of hers and then accompany them to Paris."

"That will be very pleasant for you," said Charlotte. "How long will you be away?"

"A couple of months or so, I'm not exactly sure."

"I see. Well, I'm sure it will be very interesting."

Isabel pulled the door to and disappeared. Two months! thought Charlotte gleefully. The bliss of so long a time without Isabel! She decided that, on her return, her stepmother would find that changes had been made to the living arrangements. If the house were really jointly owned, then she, Charlotte, needed more than the bedroom she occupied at present. Not that she would do it behind Isabel's back. She would tell her what she planned to do before she left and carry it out during her stepmother's absence. She supposed that Isabel would be too full of excited anticipation to care too much one way or the other.

Perhaps it was his mother's words.

"John! Eli could do with some help, up at the farm. Hannah was telling me. Can you look in some time?"

Perhaps it was the weather. On this May evening the valley bottom was bathed in sunlight. All the trees were full and green and the grass lush. It was so warm the Brooks had moved their chairs outside after supper and now sat, John and his father in shirt sleeves, Martha in a cotton blouse, in the tiny garden in Lumb Lane.

Perhaps it was time. After he had lost his wife in January, John had found himself gritting his teeth when he was told, again and again, "Time is a great healer". Yet it seemed to be true. There were moments now when he was not consumed with grief and they seemed to be lengthening. He found himself saying, "Yes, I will," almost without realising he had done so. His dog wriggled forward and laid her head on his feet. He stroked her unthinkingly and then said, "In fact, I might walk up there now. It's such a beautiful evening."

His mother did not respond straightaway. When she did speak, it sounded deliberately casual.

"Yes. Why not?"

She and Walter sat quite still while John washed himself under the pump and put on a clean shirt. Only when he had left did she relax.

"Thank God!"

Her husband was less sanguine.

"I see he's gone t' long way round again. Still avoiding top o' Lumb Lane."

Martha shook her head.

"Give him time, Walter. He'll come to it one day."

As John strode along the familiar footpaths, he was aware of a new lightness in his step. In the early weeks following Molly's death, these evening walks had been a painful necessity, a way of avoiding the suffocating sympathy of his parents and his own obsessive thoughts. As great as his bereavement was his sense of guilt. If only he had gone to the Blezards' house the day before or met her by arrangement, then Molly might not have perished. The image of her small figure struggling through the snow and then falling, never to get up again, would not leave his head but returned to torment him, causing him fresh anguish every time.

But tonight, he seemed able to dispel it, if only for a while. As he reached higher ground, he looked back at the green landscape behind him. Here, on the edge of the Pennines, this particular valley was sheltered from the prevailing wind which blew strongly from the north-west. Buildings were few, only a scattering of weavers' cottages like his own and farmhouses and barns, all of stone, looking as if they had been there for ever. When they were boys, Sam, a mine of information even then, had drawn his attention to the still-visible lines which ran across several of the fields, evidence of strip-farming by the peasants in medieval times. It pleased John to think that people had farmed this land before his time and would do after he was gone.

The sun had set but there was no drop in temperature. If anything, it was more sultry. No doubt it was the weather which had brought out more walkers than usual, mainly young couples, John noted with a pang. A pair were coming towards him now, their progress encumbered by their need to stop and kiss each other every few yards. As John came alongside, they paused and the youth, looking at him with a mixture of pride and embarrassment, spoke as if to re-establish a connection between men.

"Eh-up. We shall 'ave a storm afore t' night's out."

"Aye. That we shall," replied John. He walked on without a backward glance.

Instead of striking up towards the summit of Castle Hill and its comforting isolation, he broke away from his customary route and made for the Haigh farm at the top of Longley Lane. He did not realise until he was opening the farm gate that this was the first time for months that he had come to the farm. Something he did not understand was impelling him to rejoin the company of friends.

Irritably, Isabel pushed the dinner plate away. It was too hot to be eating beef stew. After watching her nervously for a moment, the maid removed the plate, slowly, and then left the dining-room as quickly as she could. Isabel toyed with some blancmange. Charlotte was out again, presumably at her friend's. It was a relief to be free of her company, and her snivelling over her father, for a while.

Upstairs Isabel's trunks were almost packed, ready for the excursion to London and Paris with Ellen Thorpe. She could hardly believe her luck. Still, it was no more than a proper reward for the many afternoons she had spent at the Hall, enduring the company of its insipid hostess.

She watched as Jessie and another maid carried several cans of hot and cold water into the bathroom. As she expected, it was Jessie who spoke.

"Is that enough, Mrs Blezard?"

Isabel glanced at the level of the bathwater.

"No. At least three more cans. Each."

Jessie stomped off down the stairs. When I get back, thought Isabel, I shall dismiss that girl at the first sign of laziness or rudeness. I should not have to wait long.

At last they were finished. Isabel stripped off her clothes and dropped them in a heap. Slipping down into the water was an exquisite pleasure. Languorously she slid the cake of French perfumed soap over her body, working up a frothy lather with the sponge. Rinsed and patted dry, she surveyed herself in the pier glass. She looked as good as ever, the hips perhaps a little plumper but her body still hourglass-shaped, her breasts full, her nipples large and firm. She turned sideways and admired the turn of the ankle, the dimpled knee. Running her hands over her curved belly and thighs excited her.

It was so humid she felt herself sweating under her breasts already. She powdered her body profusely, then re-dressed choosing a lace-edged cotton underskirt and a lavender blue cotton gown which was low-necked and tight-fitting at the bodice. Then she combed her damp hair and secured it with a single hairpin at each side. Finally, leaning close to the looking-glass, she bit her lips until they reddened and swelled. She could not resist smiling at herself – a slow, inviting smile. Tonight perhaps she would be lucky.

The farmhouse door was propped open. Stepping inside, John saw the Haighs sitting at the kitchen table finishing their meal. When they saw him, they all stood up and greeted him like a long-lost traveller. Hannah was not content until she had bundled him into a chair and put something to eat and drink in front of him.

"See! Get that down you. You look as if you haven't eaten for months. I shall have something to say to your mother."

They all knew she was joking. To please her, John ate some cheese and a scone. They tasted wonderful.

"It's fair grand to see you," Hannah said, beaming. "Now Rachel. Tell him about that choir."

"Will you come? We practise at the Zion on a Thursday night. It doesn't matter if you're a church-goer. So is Anne. We don't just practise hymns for Sunday, we sing all sorts."

"Anne Graham goes, does she?" asked John, cheered at the news.

"Yes, she's been a while now. She has a beautiful voice, soprano. You should hear her. And Sam's joined as well."

"Sam? Sam Armitage?"

"Yes. I was surprised too. Different from those other evening classes he goes to. But he's enjoying it. So would you, I'm sure."

John laughed.

"You've more confidence in my musical ability than I have."

"Nonsense!" declared Rachel, sitting down at the old piano. "Come on! What are you? Tenor or bass?" She played the first line of the hymn 'Guide Me O Thou Great Jehovah'. The music drew them all to her. She began again.

"Now - John, Ben, Father. Sing it in this key." She played it for tenor voices. Gradually each man joined in, singing to the end of the verse. Hannah's face was suffused with joy.

"Father's really a bass, I know. Try it lower."

Rachel played the opening bars again, this time lower down the scale.

"Now! "Guide me O...."

The three men began together but Ben stopped almost at once. Eli and John continued, their deep, rich tones very similar.

"Bread of Heaven! Bread of Heaven!

Feed me till I want no more!

Feed me ti - ill I want no more!"

"Splendid! Splendid!" cried Hannah.

"Yes, it was," said Rachel, swinging round on the piano stool. "You will come, won't you, John? You'll know a lot of the people there."

"Very well," said John, finding himself smiling. "If I can, I will."

Ben loosened his collar.

"By! It's thirsty work, this singing!"

Still laughing, they carried the old wooden settle outside the farmhouse door and were soon sat on it in a row, drinking Hannah's home-made cordial.

"Look at that moon!" exclaimed Ben.

It had emerged, silvery-white, from behind a bank of purple-grey cloud. The sky was an opalescent mauve, fading to golden-grey on the horizon.

"I don't remember it being this hot for a long time," said Rachel, plucking at her sleeves.

"There's a storm up there somewhere," said Eli. "Can you feel it? I'm sure the beasts can."

All fell silent. As if on cue, jagged lightning streaked across the sky and was gone as soon as the eye registered it. Rachel drew in her breath. John looked at Hannah's happy, up-turned face.

"How are Matthew and Joe? And their families?"

"Well, all well, I'm glad to say," replied Hannah. "Both have another baby expected, one very soon." She stopped and bit her lip.

"Good, good. I'm glad to hear it," said John, although the tone of his voice belied his words.

"I do believe it's cooler indoors than out," said Rachel, getting up.

"I must be going," said John, looking round for his dog.

"It's been grand seeing you," said Hannah. "And we'll see you again before so long?"

"Yes indeed. Eli's going to let me know when he starts cutting the hay. I'll be glad to give a hand."

Hannah patted his shoulder.

"Give my best wishes to Martha and Walter."

"And I'll see you on Thursday?" asked Rachel. "I know Sam'll be pleased to see you."

"Don't you be so sure," chuckled Ben. "I think Sam's already very happy at choir practice. I wager he wishes it were every night." The others looking to him for explanation, he went on. "I hear he's only got eyes for Anne Graham. I shouldn't be surprised if those two started walking out together soon. They say he's a changed man."

"Well, that's good," said Hannah. "I'd be right glad to hear he had a sweetheart. He deserves one."

There was a general murmur of agreement. John suddenly felt very low. He made his farewells as quickly as he could. Leaving the path to the farm, he stepped out on to the road home. Like Rachel, he could not remember such a hot, sultry night. It was weather foreign to these parts. His shirt was wet through with sweat, not just under his arms but running down his spine. When he licked his lips, his mouth was salty with it.

He decided to walk back across the fields and then cut through Mellor Wood to the path he had taken virtually every night since Molly's death, the dog at his heels. Reaching the wood, he plunged in among the trees, his feet sinking into the thick bed of dry leaves, twigs cracking as he brushed past them.

Gloom engulfed him. How could he have been foolish enough as to think he could so easily recover from his misery? Once again he felt terribly alone. Only this time it was worse. He was in one place and over there, far off, were the happy people, the lovers in the valley, the Haighs and their burgeoning family, and now, Anne Graham and Sam Armitage. Anne Graham and Sam!

Should he have seen this coming? Sam had never shown any interest in lasses before but then, he hadn't met Anne Graham. Could it be true? John racked his brains, trying to recall if he had ever seen them together. It was at the wedding supper. But that was nearly a year ago. Much could have happened since then. While he, John Brook, had been mourning, by himself, away from village life.

Hadn't it been his suggestion, that they walk home together for Anne's protection? He had noticed Sam's embarrassment and the look of their heads next to each other, Anne's light coppery hair next to Sam's violent ginger. Suddenly a picture flashed into his mind, unbidden, a picture of them making love, of Sam's mouth on hers, of Sam's hands on her body, gliding over the pale naked shoulders, down over the small, firm breasts, the pink nipples. It was unbearable. He wrenched his mind away from the vision but it kept returning to taunt him. Despite himself, he felt a tightening in his loins.

As he came to a small clearing in the wood, the scene was suddenly illuminated by a flash of sheet lightning, followed by a crackling and then a sputtering like falling fireworks. A moment later, he heard a woman's cry which seemed to come from a dip in the land close by. At first he could see nothing but then a brief, secondary flash of lightning erupted and to his amazement, he saw Isabel Blezard, outlined in yellow light, half-sitting, half-lying on the ground. She was holding her right ankle with both hands. Coming closer, his eyes were drawn to the folds of a lacy petticoat which was pulled back above her right knee.

"Mrs Blezard! What are you doing here? What ails you?"

She looked up at him, appealingly, eyes and lips glistening in the moonlight.

"Thank goodness it's you, John! I've fallen and twisted my ankle. So stupid!"

He knelt down beside her and put his hands gently either side of her ankle.

"Is it here?"

Isabel gave a tiny bleat of pain.

"Yes, yes. Just there."

He frowned.

"Best leave the boot on, I think. Can make it worse if you take it off."

He sensed that Isabel wasn't listening. Her skirts had fallen back still further, revealing the whiteness of her thighs above her stockings. Her nearness was overwhelming; he could feel her warmth, her breath, smell her female scents. To his dismay, she began to weep.

John couldn't bear to see anyone cry, especially a woman. Moving closer, he put his arms round her and drew her head towards his chest. She clung to him, her nose and mouth burrowing into the hollow of his breastbone. Instinctively, he stroked her hair.

"Hush! Don't cry, Mrs Blezard. Please don't."

She leant back slightly. He could see her eyes and teeth shining in the darkness.

"Oh John! It's not the ankle. I am so lonely, so lonely! Hold me again!"

The thought that he was becoming more involved with this woman than he wanted to be flickered through his mind but it disappeared without trace. The desire to hold her warm, pleading softness was overpowering.

He had forgotten how it felt to hold a yielding woman in his arms. He inhaled the smell of her hair and as he did so, she straightened up and, pulling his head down towards hers, pressed her open lips against his mouth.

All thought was banished as his body responded. At her gentle pressure, he sank onto his back in the undergrowth. Now she was straddled across him, exploring his mouth with her tongue. All he was aware of was her body cleaving to his, her hands touching him, pulling at his clothing until she found his straining flesh. Then all consciousness became one as he abandoned himself to the great surge of desire which swept through him, released after months of repression.

There was a moment, when he had entered her, when the thought of who she was and what he was doing, came to him but it was too late.

Passion pulsed to its conclusion.

Later, when he opened his eyes, it was very dark and silent. The lightning had moved away to the next valley. John's dog was some distance away, her fore-paws stretched out in front of her. She whined at him. Isabel was standing up, leaning against a tree, looking remarkably composed. Her ankle did not appear to be giving her any pain.

John instantly regretted what he had done. Scrambling to his feet, he refastened his clothing as quickly as possible and brushed the leaves off his back. Speaking was out of the question. He put out his arm for Isabel to lean on and they began to walk back towards her home in Wood Lane.

Neither had spoken. When the moment for leave-taking came, Isabel tried unsuccessfully to make John look at her.

"Good-night, John."

He mumbled a reply and hurried away. He tried not to think about what he had done as he made for home, the dog at his heels. It did not occur to him to wonder why Isabel had been where he had found her on that warm May night.

CHAPTER NINE

"Miss Graham! Miss Graham!"

The two children came racing along the path leading to the shrubbery where Anne was strolling. Ellen Thorpe had had visitors all afternoon, elegantly dressed women like herself who had moved from the drawing-room to the terrace to take tea under large sunshades. As usual, Anne waited until the children, invited to join the ladies, appeared to be settled. Then she slipped quietly away, remaining close by in case she was needed to remove them from the adult gathering.

Anne thought the children had developed very pleasingly. Georgina was better at concentrating; Edward had become more responsible. Not only that, he had become an avid reader and showed signs of being an excellent all-round scholar. She had come to love them both in the past ten months.

Edward reached her first though Georgina was not far behind.

"Miss Graham! Where do you think we are all going next week? Not Father – but the rest of us?"

"Can you guess, Miss Graham? You should be able to," cried Georgina, hopping from one foot to the other.

"I really don't know," replied Anne, truthfully. "You must tell me."

"To London!" they chorused. Georgina chattered on. "Where you come from. We are to stay at Grandmother's in Chelsea and we shall go to the parks and on the river."

"Really?" said Anne, delighted. It was the first she had heard of it.

"Yes. Mama did not tell us of it sooner in case we should become too excited," said Edward. "As if we should! And Mama and her friend are going to Paris as well. But we shall not, we shall stay in London till they come back."

"Well, this is exciting," said Anne, allowing herself to be pulled along the path and back to the house. As they reached the terrace, she saw that almost all the guests had gone. Only one remained. Ellen Thorpe's mousy-blonde head was tilted towards another, a dark-haired one. As the two woman laughed and straightened up, Anne saw their expressions and jumped to a conclusion she felt to be true.

"Ah, Miss Graham!" Ellen Thorpe looked as though this encounter was less than welcome. "The children will have told you our news. A trip to London."

"Yes, Mrs Thorpe. I'm sure they will enjoy it."

"Very good for their education," said Isabel Blezard. The look she gave Anne could only be described as a smirk. Like Anne, she was wearing black but the widow's dress gleamed with jet embroidery, the bodice lavishly seamed, the skirts full and glossy.

"Though we see this as a holiday, most definitely," Ellen Thorpe stressed. Anne noticed the beads of perspiration on the woman's forehead. She thought she would rescue her from embarrassment.

"So they will not need any lessons during the visit? My services will not be required?" asked Anne, speaking with a calmness she did not feel.

"Exactly." Ellen Thorpe smiled, looking relieved. But Edward was listening, if Georgina was not.

"What, Mama? Is Miss Graham not to come with us? But she would enjoy it so much. And we should like her to come."

Anne could have hugged the boy. Instead, she said "Think how I shall enjoy your letters, Edward. And I will write to you and tell you how things are at the Hall."

The boy's brow was still clouded. He was obviously prepared to go on arguing. His mother intervened before he could speak again.

"Edward! Perhaps you would go and find Father? Miss Graham, would you mind going to the schoolroom? Mr Thorpe will be with you directly." She fanned herself rapidly. "It really is too hot to be out, too hot. What do you think, Isabel? Shall we go indoors?" They did so, with much gathering up of skirts, silk shawls and fans.

Anne walked along the panelled hallway and up the oak stairs. She had known this day would come but she could not help feeling downcast. She wondered how influential Isabel Blezard had been in forming Ellen Thorpe's decision not to include Anne in the party going to London.

Frederick Thorpe's handling of the situation was smoother than his wife's.

"My dear Miss Graham. Do let us sit down. First may I say how pleased my wife and I are with your teaching of Edward and Georgina over the past year. They have improved not just in their learning but in their general conduct. All credit to you! You will remember I spoke of Edward's attending a school for boys in the near future? I think you will agree that he is now ready for this – after your excellent teaching. When he returns from London, he will start straightaway."

Anne had a sense of things dropping away from her. But her pride helped her appear composed. He continued.

"In the circumstances, we shall not need your services after the end of this month, although you are at liberty to remain living here for the next two months as we arranged. Which I hope will give you time to find another situation. I shall of course be happy to write you a reference in the highest possible terms."

"Thank you, Mr Thorpe. I shall of course be most sorry to leave Master Edward and Miss Georgina. I hope I shall be as fortunate next time." Anne was surprised at the intensity of her distress. But she would not show it.

"Anything I can do, Miss Graham, I will. If I hear of a suitable vacancy, I shall recommend you and let you know at once." With a smile, he left the schoolroom.

Anne stood at the window watching the children playing with Susan. It was foolish to be regretful. Governesses, like nursemaids, had to face the fact that their charges would grow up and no longer need them. However, knowing something was inevitable did not prevent one from feeling its effects when it happened. Losing her position, room and salary was bad enough but the thought of being separated from the children filled her with pain. They had come to feel like her own, especially Edward who was demonstrative in his affection for her. I've learnt more about the pain of loss in the past fifteen months than I ever knew existed, she thought, leaning her forehead against the window-pane. Will it always be like this?

At that moment, the children caught sight of her and began waving at her with both hands, grinning and hopping about at the same time until they saw her laugh. Her misery eased. How could one be sad in the face of so much joy?

She would not let the children know she was disappointed at not going to London. She would make the best of her few last weeks here and set about looking for a new post without delay. With a deliberately bright smile, she ran down the back stairs and out into the garden. Susan rushed up to her, full of excitement.

"'Ave ye heard, Miss Graham? I'm to go wi' t' children to London next week. And stay two month! I don't know how I shall get on!"

"How splendid, Susan! I know you will enjoy it! What an opportunity!"

As Georgina pulled Susan away, Edward looked up at Anne. He suddenly came close and, wrapping his arms tightly round her waist, pressed his face against her body. Before she could say or do anything, he released her and ran off to join the others.

Later, getting ready to attend choir practice, she decided the time had come. She had been ready for it for some weeks. Now seemed appropriate. Removing her black blouse and skirt, she washed thoroughly and then lifted the new dress from its box and laid it on the bed. It was a lavender-grey silk, quite plain except for the rows of piping which curved down from the shoulders to the waist. It fitted beautifully.

She looked at herself critically in the mirror. Her appearance was healthier than when she arrived from London a year ago, her complexion rosier, her figure a little more rounded. She dressed her hair as was fashionable, looping up the long curls and securing them at the back of her head. The final touch was a silver and amethyst brooch that had belonged to her mother which she pinned at the base of her throat on the white cambric collar. Picking up her musical scores, she allowed herself a secret smile at her reflection before setting off.

As she approached the Zion building, she suddenly felt self-conscious and afraid of being over-dressed. However, the reactions of Rachel and Sam dismissed her fears. Rachel was delighted.

"It's lovely, Anne! It's grand to see you out of black!"

Sam said nothing but his look expressed his admiration as effectively as any words.

Light of heart, Anne took her usual place among the sopranos. They were singing some pieces from Sterndale Bennett's 'The May Queen', a recent work. Latecomers were arriving. Raised voices and some joking by the door attracted her attention. With a mixture of shock and pleasure, she saw the tall figure of John Brook amongst a group of men. Someone was teasing him about joining the basses without an audition. She heard him say that was his only chance of being accepted. Someone else slapped him on the shoulder, saying he was welcome.

Anne looked down at her song-sheet but the notes were jumping about. She felt her face and neck grow hot and her heart began to thud. When she regained control, she dared to look up across the space between them. He must have felt her eyes upon him because he stopped speaking to his neighbour and returned her gaze.

It seemed as though an invisible line held them locked together. How long the moment lasted, Anne could not say but it sent the blood surging through her body, giving her a singing sensation that had little to do with the music around her.

As always, she enjoyed the choral practice and the social atmosphere it generated. She now knew most of the other singers, in particular, those she stood next to. Sam Armitage always seemed to manage to position himself at the end of the tenors so that he stood close to her along the same row of pews. In between singing, he would catch her eye and smile.

But this evening brought an added bonus. Directly across from her, standing next to the contraltos were the basses. When she wished to raise the level of her happiness, which was already at record height this evening, she would glance up and without fail, meet the eyes of John Brook and hold them. Occasionally, he would be concentrating on the score and fail to see her looking at him but when he did, he would return her gaze so expressively with his dark eyes that she feared her heart would dance right out of its new, pearl-buttoned bodice.

The practice over, the choir members stood milling about outside chatting. The younger ones gathered together and began to walk up Kaye Lane in the direction of Castle Hill. Beside Anne, Rachel, John and Sam, there were about half a dozen others who lived in Almondbury or the villages nearby.

Sam walked next to Anne, giving her news of Blezard's Mill.

"And how is Charlotte?" she asked.

"Quite well, I think. She's taking a real interest in the business."

Rachel, overhearing, began to ask him more. Anne turned to John who was walking behind her.

"Are you playing cricket again this season, John?"

"I haven't done so far but yes, I think I shall. Jed Thewlis has already asked me to."

"I believe he was the one who persuaded you to play for Lascelles Hall?"

"Yes, he did. Right enough. They're a big cricketing family. Last year a whole team of eleven Thewlises took on Chickenley Club. By themselves."

Anne laughed aloud at this and in turn, set John chuckling. They both became sober at Anne's next enquiry.

"What happened to the boy who got his leg caught in a man-trap a few months back? Rachel said he recovered but didn't know any more."

"Well, he lived through it," said John, his face darkening at the memory. "But it's left him with an ugly scar and a bit of a limp. He'll likely carry those all his life."

"I cannot bear to think of the cruelty. Not to people or to animals."

"Nor me. When I hear of louts setting dogs on one another, to fight until one of 'em's torn apart and like to die, it makes my blood boil. Whether they do it for money or pleasure. There were a few of them up on Castle Hill the other night. I scared 'em off. Made 'em think constables were coming." He stopped abruptly.

Anne looked at him sharply.

"Was someone I know there?"

He did not answer.

"Was it Ned Stott, my cousin?"

"Never you mind, Anne. Just make sure and keep out of their way."

Engrossed in their conversation, they had not noticed that they had reached the lower slopes of Castle Hill. Sam appeared by Anne's side again as the group began to climb the steep grassy ramparts between them and the summit. When they reached the top, they walked round admiring the view on all sides. At the edge of the flat green expanse, on the side overlooking Huddersfield, the tavern was doing a good trade. Shouts from noisy drinkers reached them whenever someone opened the door. The members of the choir moved away and found a sheltered spot on the lower slopes.

The talk was of a projected outing to the Lake District in the near future.

"It's 4s.6d each. Or you can pay 10 shillings and go First Class." Sam's words met with cheerful derision all round.

"You'll come, won't you, John?" asked Rachel. "I'm sure Sam can get another ticket."

"Yes, I'd like to," replied John. Anne was thrilled. She was already looking forward to the railway trip; now it promised to be even more pleasurable.

"I hear some people are going to London – and Paris as well," said Sam. There were cries of "Who?" "Who do you mean?"

"Charlotte Blezard tells me her step-mother is to go to London next week with Ellen Thorpe and her children. And be away two months."

Rachel turned to Anne.

"Are you going too, Anne? We shall miss you."

"No, I'm not going," said Anne uncomfortably. "In fact, my employment at the Hall is coming to an end. Edward is to go to a school when they return."

"So where will you go?" asked Rachel. Both Sam and John appeared to be listening.

"I'm not sure yet. I need to look for a new position. And lodgings too perhaps."

Rachel put her hand on Anne's arm.

"You can always stay at the farm. Perhaps you can find a post not too far away."

The light was now fading. The group got to their feet and began to take leave of one another. At that moment they heard a commotion up above them. A gang of drunken youths was being thrown out of the tavern. Shouting and swearing, they came nearer. Two of them started fighting and, locked together, rolled down the banking towards Anne and her friends. John took hold of Anne's arm and steered her out of their way. Looking over her shoulder, she saw that one of the pair now throwing punches at each other was her cousin Ned. Gasps of pain were heard as they progressed to kicking one another, using their clogs as weapons.

"Why don't their friends stop them?" she cried. But the rest of the rough-looking bunch were urging the pair on to further brutalities from their vantage point at the top of the hill.

Suddenly a blow to Ned's head felled him. He dropped like a stone, tumbling down the banking out of control. For a moment, the onlookers were silent as he lay still. Trying to stand up, he lost his footing and staggering like a clown, slithered down the grassy slope until, legs apart, he met a gorse bush where he remained, stuck.

Up above on the ridge, his mates bellowed with laughter. Anne made a move towards the hapless youth but John held her back.

"Keep out of it. I should."

As he spoke, Ned disentangled himself and slid even further down the hill until he was almost at their feet, his face swollen, his nostrils clotted with dark blood. Anne shuddered at the hatred in his expression as he looked at John and allowed herself to be drawn away.

For a few minutes, the choir members were silent, concentrating on picking their way across the stone-set paths which led back to level ground. Then normal chatter resumed and spirits rose again at the prospect of the trip to Lake Windermere.

Anne, John and Sam found themselves walking down into the village together. With the young men either side of Anne, conversation was equally maintained as far down as the parish church. There, Sam reluctantly turned left towards his home while Anne and John bore right into St Helen's Gate and down into the Woodsome valley. When they reached the lane that led to John's cottage, Anne paused, ready to say good night. But he would not leave her to walk the last quarter of a mile to the Hall in the growing darkness and insisted on accompanying her as far as the gates.

"Good night, John. Thank you."

"It has been a pleasure," he said, smiling down into her eyes. Her step was light as she went in by the servants' door and told the housekeeper she was back. Who would have thought the day would end so happily?

Leaving Anne at the approach to Dartmouth Hall, John walked back to Lumb Lane in a contented mood. He was glad he had taken the step of joining the Zion choir. But he almost hadn't.

After the night of his encounter with Isabel, he had remained in a pit of self-loathing for several days. He was disgusted with the way he had behaved – like a coarse village lout or a rutting animal. True, she appeared to have been a willing partner but that was not the point. Her conduct could have stemmed from her own, more recent, bereavement to which he should have been more sensitive. He felt he must have taken advantage of her, to his shame.

His parents said nothing but he sensed their uneasiness. The atmosphere in the cottage, where no-one could escape anyone else except by going out or going to bed, had been heavy with unspoken words.

Finally he came to his senses. One day he had stayed at his work much later than usual. He told himself it was because the light was still good but knew he really wanted to reduce the time he had to be at home in his parents' company.

Coming home he was surprised to find them both in the tiny front garden, sitting on kitchen chairs, his father, bizarrely, swaddled in blankets.

"What are you doing out here?" he asked in amazement.

His mother's expression was both angry and tearful.

"I got your father out here this afternoon. To cut his hair. I thought you'd soon be back. Then it came cold and when I tried to get him back in, he couldn't manage it. And I couldn't lift him."

John knelt down. His father, dozing, opened his eyes.

"I'm sorry to be late, Father. Now let's get you inside." Removing the blankets, he lifted the frail figure and carried him up to bed.

The incident felt like a penance. John cleared the plate of supper his mother brought him, although it was dried up with being kept warm.

The next morning, eating his porridge, he spoke to his mother, still feeling the need to make amends.

"Is it tonight, the Zion choir practice?"

"Yes. I believe so. Are you thinking of going?"

"I thought I'd give it a try. If they'll have me. I'll be home by six. Is that all right?"

She had been agreeable, not to say pleased, as he knew she would.

Now, as he opened the front door, still thinking of Anne and how she had looked, his mother was just coming down the stairs-steps. Her face was grim.

"It's your father. He took bad again this evening." As John made to go upstairs, she put out her hand to stop him.

"Nay, leave him. He's just fallen asleep. It'll do him good."

Automatically, she set food out on the table but John could not eat. Instead he came and sat opposite her by the fireside. He noticed how tired and worried she appeared. Seeing his concern, she made an effort.

"How have you got on, then? At the choir."

"Quite well. I'll be glad when I know the music a bit better."

"Sam was there, was he?"

"Yes. And quite a few others I knew." He mentioned some names.

"Good, good. And then you went walking, did you? That's what we used to do. After Bible-reading class."

"Yes. We went up to Castle Hill."

"Well, that'll given you an appetite."

To please his mother, he ate some of the food she had put on the table. Once she saw him eating, she went upstairs to bed.

It was not long before John did the same. He fell asleep at once into a deep dreamless sleep from which he awoke refreshed and calm. To his surprise, his mother was sitting on the small wooden chair next to his bed.

"Mam! How long have you been there?"

She shrugged and he saw how weary she looked.

"Is it Father? How is he?"

"He's gone. Not long since."

She got up and went into the other bedroom. John followed her.

His father, Walter Brook, was lying on his back in the double bed. His nose and cheekbones seemed more prominent in death, his waxen pallor making him look other-worldly rather than old. Martha had lifted his arms over the sheet and crossed them on his chest. The sight of his pale, freckled hands, now so defenceless, moved John most.

"He looks at peace," he said to his mother, putting his arm round her. She did not move but remained stiff and still, looking down at the figure in the bed.

"I'll go to my work, put a note on my door and then come back. Mam?"

She shook herself then.

"Yes. And knock on Mrs Keen's door and ask her to come and help me lay him out."

Martha took the death very quietly. She was not seen to cry, even at the funeral which took place at All Hallows within the week. John was not surprised. His mother did not show her feelings readily. He had no memory of much affection being shown by either parent towards the other. But the same could not have been said of their treatment of him, which had been warm, consistent and on his mother's part at least, verging on indulgence. He wondered whether the strongest bond between his parents had been their mutual love of him, their only child. In other respects, they seemed to have had little in common. On Martha's side of the bedroom hung a print of a religious painting; on Walter's, a shelf holding his political reading matter.

As John stood with his mother in the pew, waiting for the coffin to be carried in, he felt ill-at-ease, knowing how his father would have hated the thought of a Church of England funeral. Hearing the tread of footsteps, he turned round. Following the coffin were six or seven old men, neat-looking in overcoats. He did not know all their names but recognised the faces of Walter's friends and colleagues from his Chartist and Fancy Weavers' Union days. As the coffin was brought alongside him, John's throat swelled with emotion at this evidence of loyalty.

His mother remained calm and dry-eyed throughout. She spoke politely to the mourners after the burial but there was no funeral tea nor was it expected. Anne and Hannah Haigh, who had sat at the back of the church, expressed their sympathy and then quietly disappeared.

Back home in the cottage, his mother seemed restless, unable to sit still. She went up and down the stairs several times, bringing down bundles of clothes for the workhouse and making piles of Walter's books and papers.

"Sit down, Mother. There's no need to do that now."

She continued to move things about.

"Perhaps you'll sort through these things tomorrow and see what you want to keep."

"I will, I will. Now sit down or you'll wear yourself out."

At last she gave in and sat down in the chair opposite John. As she did so, she felt something behind the cushion. It was Walter's spectacles.

John put out his hand.

"Don't give those away. I'd like to keep them."

She handed them to him without a word. But something was wrong, or just not being said. Martha seemed to be caught in some sort of mental struggle. At last she spoke.

"I don't know what to do for the best," she said, twisting her fingers. "I've always thought "Least said, soonest mended." But it might be wrong to go to my grave..." She broke off, distressed.

John was alarmed.

"Are you ill? Is that what you're saying?"

"No, no!" She shook her head wearily. "I knew this day would come and now that it has, I must face its consequences. For truth's sake."

John kept silent. He had no idea what she meant. His mother continued, keeping her eyes on the fire, away from his.

"I feel shame and yet – I know I would do it all again. The truth is, John, that Walter Brook was a good father to you but –" Here, she looked up at him warily. "He was not your real father."

For a moment, John found the words meaningless. Before he could question her, his mother went on.

"I shame to tell you that I went to another man, someone else's husband, and gave myself to him. Oh!" Her face was contorted with pain. "Oh, I so longed for a child! We'd been wed over ten years and you know Walter was a good bit older than me. I kept hoping and hoping but nothing happened. And it seemed so unfair. Everywhere you looked, there were women with babies. Why not me? Why was I being punished? And she, one of my friends, who was married after me, had just had a third son. I could hardly bear it."

The truth flashed upon John then.

"Third son? Then – are you saying – Eli? Eli Haigh?"

"Yes, I am," she replied, looking down at her hands in her lap, a dull red flush staining her neck.

The shock was enormous and pleasurable. Pictures of the past flooded into his mind, the farm where he had always felt welcome, where he had enjoyed playing and then, later, helping to feed the stock, milk the cows, make hay, gather in the harvest. The loneliness he had sometimes felt as an only child had been dispelled by the companionship of the Haigh children, most of all by Ben who had seemed, always, more than just a friend.

"So Ben and I are half-brothers! And Matthew, and Joe! And Rachel, my half-sister!" John declared, beaming, delighted.

A look at his mother sobered him. What she had told him was obviously deeply shameful to her and to the memory of Walter. Walter!

"Did my father, did Walter know the truth?"

The answer was fierce.

"No, he did not! He was never told. He loved you as his own."

John felt a rush of conflicting emotions – relief that Walter had never known the truth but had loved him as his own son and died without disillusionment – and sadness at the great lie that had been perpetrated on him, a man of immense integrity and sense of justice. John had no time to consider his feelings towards his mother before she spoke again. He did not wish to hear but now she had started, there was no stopping her.

"It was harvest time and Walter had gone to Leeds on Chartist business. Hannah was still lying-in after the birth of Ben; she was poorly all the way through with him. I went to see her but it was hard. A third baby son and just as bonny as the first two.

"It was right hot that September and heavy with it. You could feel thunderstorms about. Everybody was out in the fields, getting the corn in before the weather broke. The men worked right on until it was too dark to see what they were doing. I was helping, seeing to the men's thirst. And didn't they drink some stuff!

"When they'd cleared Long Field, we all got together and had some supper. There was a fair bit of larking about. I was dizzy with the sun being on my head all day. And I'd drunk some ale on top of that.

"I remember there was a great moon. I followed Eli into the barn. He was checking that all the farm's tools had been put back. There was no-one else about. And I felt – so lonely, so wretched. And he – well, I don't know how he felt but I think he was hungry. For a bit of love."

She stopped. John was feeling very uncomfortable. He did not wish to hear any details. But his mother meant to finish her story.

"Anyroad, I thought, "This man has fathered three grand little lads. Why should Hannah begrudge me this one night? And she need never know." And so – that's what happened.

"We never spoke of it after, Eli and me. Weeks later, I knew I was expecting. I didn't tell him, only Walter. He was the happiest man alive."

"Did Eli never suspect?"

"I don't know. I never said anything. And you don't look like him. You look like me, dark-hair and brown eyes."

True, thought John, but in some ways, I am a farmer's son. I love the land, and all creatures. If I'd grown up on a farm, I doubt I would ever have turned to woodworking. Aloud, he said "And did Eli ever say anything, after I was born?"

"No. We were never alone. I made sure of that. But I think he was ashamed – of what he'd done that night. He started going to chapel soon after."

For the first time, John thought about Eli and what it might have meant to him. There were still so many unanswered questions.

"Did anyone else know? Your mother? Hannah?"

"No, no-one. It was the only way. I was never going to breathe a word of it to a soul, even you. Did I do wrong?"

The question was ambiguous. But the looked-for answer was clear.

"No," replied John, kissing her on the forehead. "No, you didn't do wrong."

His reply seemed to soothe her. For the first time, she looked as if she might burst into tears. He was not surprised when she embraced him and then left the room quickly, going upstairs to bed before him, something she never did.

John sat for a while longer, gazing into the embers in the grate. When Walter died, he had not anticipated that, less than a week later, he would be hearing his mother describe the night that led to his birth. He thought no worse of her for what she had done. How could he? Woman's desperate desire to have a child was well known. No man had the right to question it. Nor did he blame Eli. He understood how difficult it would have been to resist the feelings aroused in him by a woman hungry for the act of love.

CHAPTER TEN

As Anne walked along the drive at the Hall, the sun was just coming up. The air was cool but with the promise of warmth to come. She kept to the centre of the lane to keep the hem of her skirt dry but her boots were already wet with the dew. Anticipating a warm day, she wore a cream cotton blouse with her dark blue jacket and skirt, and carried her provisions in a small bag.

The valley was fresh and green, gilded here and there by the rising sun. As she passed by, cattle were stirring in the fields whose dry-stone walls swept up as far as the skyline where the great mound of Castle Hill stood, dominating the landscape.

She was thinking, as she so often was, of John. Was he truly recovering from his bereavement, as he appeared to be doing? Her feeling of hope was immediately followed by one of self-reproach. How could she be so selfish, so insensitive? Molly had been dead less than six months. A husband who had loved her could not recover so quickly. And yet, and yet... She knew she was caught between the desire to believe him a man of deep faithfulness and the equally strong wish that his heart was now whole and ready to be given to another woman, and that woman herself.

She was so deeply engrossed in her thoughts that it came as a sudden but delightful shock when she saw John coming towards her. Confused, she hardly knew what she said.

"John! Why! Good morning! I did not expect to see you so soon, here!"

"It's very little out of my way," he replied, blushing.

They both fell silent, using their breath to climb the steep slope up into the village. Anne could not have spoken had she wished to. The fact that John had come to meet her rather than taking the direct route in the opposite direction could only mean that he wanted to be with her, not just to protect her in the hours of darkness as before but for the sheer pleasure of walking alongside her.

As they reached the church in the centre of the village, Sam Armitage stepped forward, the sun glinting on his ginger hair. His face fell a little at the sight of John but he greeted Anne cheerfully and the three of them walked on together.

As they passed the small stone cottages in Westgate, two young women emerged, clutching their parcels for the journey. Dora and Eva Taylor attended the Zion Chapel and were members of its choir. They both worked in a local mill as menders, a skilled job that gave them an edge over the other mill girls.

"A grand morning!" cried Dora, while the younger Eva giggled. "We're that excited!"

At the bottom of Longley Lane, where a carter was awaiting them, they were joined by Rachel and another choir member, Sidney Mallinson, who worked as a clerk in Huddersfield. When they were all aboard, the carter flicked his whip and they began the last stage of their journey to the railway station. Sam, with an air of importance, collected the tickets from the Booking Office and the party moved on to the platform. They had not long to wait.

With a mighty roar, the excursion train burst through the tunnel and slowed to a halt with a loud hiss of escaping steam. Momentarily overwhelmed, Anne clutched John's arm. Helping her up the steps and into the carriage, he deposited her carefully by the window with her back to the engine and then took the seat opposite her. Dora and Eva scuttled in behind them, Dora securing the favoured place next to John. Sam, entering the carriage last, looked disappointed to find the seat next to Anne had been taken by Rachel. But he was on his feet several times during the journey, pointing out places of interest, always addressing his remarks to Anne.

She meanwhile found the whole experience delightful. This was not the Yorkshire she had seen from the train between Doncaster and Wakefield but a more magnificent one of wild moors and green valleys, and stone-arched viaducts striding across them with giant steps. North and then north-west they travelled, stopping to pick up more trippers at stations along the route. The landscape opened out, became more rolling, and lighter-coloured from the pale limestone walls bordering the fields. Content with the present moment and anticipating happiness in the day ahead, Anne was carried along on a tide of joy.

Her fellow passengers filled the carriage to capacity and there was considerable joking, particularly between Eva and Sidney Mallinson, at the fullness of the women's skirts overlapping and entangling the men's legs. When Eva dropped a humbug which got lost amongst the yards of fabric, she became quite hysterical at Sidney's efforts to retrieve it.

Anne sat quietly, enjoying her position next to the window, looking either out at the view or across at John who smiled at her whenever she caught his eye. It was too noisy for intimate conversation but there was no need for it. The Taylor sisters sought his attention frequently so that he was obliged to turn and speak to them.

After a while, Dora, flushed with excitement, wanted the window open. Lifting and then releasing the leather strap, John opened the one next to him obligingly but within minutes, was forced to shut it again because of the smuts which flew in and speckled his face. Dora immediately produced a handkerchief.

"'Ere, lick this," she said. She proceeded to dab the smuts off John's face.

Anne felt unreasonably annoyed. Then, leaning back in the seat, she shut her eyes. Anne Graham, she thought, you are a silly woman! Jealous of another for touching his face! How foolish you are! The voice of Sam made her open her eyes.

"Are you well, Anne? We're almost there."

The train was full and the platform was soon thronged with people moving about in the clouds of steam. Windermere station was tiny compared with that of Huddersfield but just as pleasing in its own way, built in local slate with high arched windows and doorways. Cabs were lined up waiting as the passengers stepped out under a canopied roof with slender, fluted columns.

There was some hesitation among the group. Most of the other travellers were climbing into conveyances of some kind. Sam explained.

"The lake's a bit off. Down at Bowness. I thought we'd walk down, so as to have a good look round, and then get a lift back up in a wagonette. Is that all right with everybody?"

All the group, thrifty as well as sturdy, were well used to walking up and down hills. Sidney Mallinson answered for everybody.

"Fair enough. Legs downhill, wheels up."

Soon they came to the shores of the lake which extended as far as the eye could see to left and right, and was studded with small, wooded islands. Straight across the lake, the trees grew thickly and away to the right, towered the bare, high fells.

The lake was alive with craft. A packed ferry boat was crossing the lake towards Hawkshead, propelled by boatmen pulling on huge oars. There were rowing boats, small steam launches bearing one or two passengers and large, private steam yachts where revellers could be heard as well as seen, chatting and drinking in their panelled saloons, the ladies outside sheltering from the bright sun beneath their pretty parasols.

"Just imagine having your own boat!" exclaimed Rachel.

By now, the group had joined the queue at the Bowness pier. Alongside, hawkers offered pasties, hot potatoes and sweetmeats while others cried out the attractions of a nearby wrestling match.

But the lure of a sail on the lake took precedence. Steadied by the rough but welcome hand of one of the crew, Anne climbed aboard the paddle steamer '*Rothay*', its polished teak seats and decking gleaming in the spring sunshine. With the Bowness band playing loud and clear, the steamer moved away from the pier and out into the centre of the lake before heading up towards Waterhead and Ambleside.

Holding the rail, Anne found the fresh breeze on her face very welcome after the stuffiness of the railway carriage. Sam, who had been at her side since arriving in Windermere, had disappeared below, having a particular interest in steam boilers.

"Are you enjoying this?" asked John at her elbow.

"Oh yes," she replied, looking up into his face. "How lovely it is!"

For a moment, John's eyes continued to rest on her face before he turned to look at the landscape. Above the shimmering waters of the lake, the mountains rose, first green and then, further off, lilac-grey. At the head of the lake, they disembarked and began climbing the hillside until they found a suitable spot, dry and in dappled shade, for their picnic lunch.

As they finished eating, Sam touched Anne's arm.

"Anne! Have you finished? Come and look at this view."

Obligingly she got up and followed him, leaving the rest of the group behind. Sam led her round a headland until they came upon a fresh view of the landscape, with the lake framed by trees on either side.

"How beautiful!" Anne exclaimed. She turned to find Sam looking intently at her, his face slightly flushed.

"As you are," he said, going even redder.

Anne laughed.

"Nonsense! But thank you for saying so!"

Sam laughed too, seeming relieved.

"I'm very glad you could come, Anne."

"So am I."

"And that you joined the choir. It's made a lot of difference to me."

"It has to me too, Sam. A wonderful difference. It has made me very happy."

Sam's mouth trembled. Further words seemed beyond him. He took Anne's hand for a moment until, gently, she retrieved it.

"I think we ought to get back to the others now. But thank you for showing me this view."

"Thank you for coming, Anne."

Turning, they retraced their steps. Anne sensed Sam's feelings towards her. She hoped they were not strong; she would not want him to be hurt. They soon rejoined the others who had packed up and were ready for some more walking. But a little later, Eva came to a halt.

"I'm jiggered," she said. "Can't we stop for a rest?"

After discussion, it was agreed that the ladies should rest while the men went ahead. Sam and Rachel possessed watches so a meeting an hour and a half later was agreed upon.

Anne settled down with the other women although she would have liked to have accompanied the men. But it seemed polite to fall in with the general will of the group. Rachel, tired after an emergency at the Infirmary, lay back on the grass and was soon asleep while Dora and Eva amused themselves with whispered comments interspersed with squeals of laughter. Anne tried not to listen and to attend to her magazine but it was difficult to concentrate especially when it became clear that the two sisters were talking about John.

"Nay, it's you he likes," said Dora, thus provoking Eva into a further fit of giggles.

"What makes you say that?" asked Eva. For answer, Dora leant towards her sister and whispered in her ear. More squeaks. Recovering herself, Eva went on.

"There's a few at t' mill that'd 'ave him tomorrow."

"Well, can you blame 'em?" retorted her elder sister.

Eva, sobered for the moment, spoke seriously.

"But it's not six months since he buried her."

"Yes, but time, you know. You know what they say about time," said Dora sagely. And then, rolling her eyes, "And you know what they say about men!" This led to smothered laughter and snorting so loud that it woke Rachel up.

Sidney Mallinson appeared, glowing with exertion.

"We've had a right good hike, we 'ave," he declared. "You can see for miles, from t'top, right across peaks. Them two beggars are still up there."

He gestured behind him. On the top of the nearest fell, two figures could be seen, the tall dark frame of John Brook and the smaller, slighter one of the red-haired Sam Armitage. They were not walking but sitting down, apparently deep in conversation.

"What's John doing up there?" demanded Eva. "He'd better look sharp."

Time was now running out if they were to catch the boat and their appointed train. The gangway was being pulled up as John and Sam ran and jumped aboard. Dora and Eva began scolding them. Anne turned away, happy at the thought of the pleasant journey home that was to come.

But when it came, it was disappointing. Anne took the seat in the corner of the carriage that she had occupied on the outward journey. But Sidney Mallinson darted into the seat opposite, keen to have the best view from the window. He was followed by a determined Sam who sat next to Anne and who was obviously delighted when told by the others to "shove up." The female members got in next, with John taking the corner seat on the same side as Anne, the one place where it was impossible to communicate with him.

The railway journey back passed quickly, more quickly than the outward one. Anne tried to maintain polite interest as Sam pointed out the features of the landscape through which they passed but was relieved when he fell silent. Soon they were in the cart again which this time, for an extra fee, was to deliver them closer to their homes. As they reached the Haighs' farm, Rachel alighted, followed by John who left them all with a hasty "Good night" over his shoulder.

"What a pity!" wailed the irrepressible Eva. "I was 'oping for a bit of a cuddle-up with 'im going down into t' village."

Anne, dejected, had to admit that her sentiments were similar, although she would not have deigned to express them so publicly. She went to bed with her face pink and stinging from the day in the sun but lower in spirits than she had expected.

The Hall felt desolate without the children. Anne set about tidying the schoolroom in preparation for her departure. It did not take her long. The school books and stationery had been kept in good order and when she had thrown away the waste paper and chewed crayons, the premises were neat and ready for future use. Smoothing out the drawings, she found two she thought she would like to keep – a picture of a favourite doll by Georgina and a self-portrait by Edward, shouldering a toy rifle.

Her own room would take very little time to clear, so few were her possessions. But she would miss it, the first room she had had all to herself. In particular, she would miss the view from the window of well-tended lawns, flower beds and the tree-filled horizon.

This morning, the gardeners were already busy outside, digging, weeding, dead-heading roses, tying up stragglers and generally restoring beauty and order. Anne stood watching them, admiring the calm pace at which they worked. It seemed impossible to garden rapidly. As if he could feel her eyes on him, the gardener's boy looked up from his wheelbarrow, waved and gave her a broad smile. Automatically she smiled and waved back. The lad looked completely happy. For a moment Anne could not prevent herself envying him although she was ashamed almost immediately of her self-pity.

She had set such store by the trip to Lake Windermere, had thought it would combine all that was delightful and would make her gloriously happy. Perhaps it was always a mistake to anticipate joy, bound to lead to disappointment? All she could be certain of was that John's attitude to her had changed, cooled during the course of the day. What had she done? What had others done? Or said? Or, worse still, had she misconstrued all the apparent signs of his preference for her, imagining that his feelings matched hers simply because she wanted them to, so passionately? Whenever he had looked into her eyes, it had seemed a deeply significant moment of personal intimacy which set her heart racing and her hopes soaring. Yet she had noticed the day before, in the railway compartment, that this was just the way he looked at someone when he was focussing his attention on what they were saying to him, even when, God forbid, it was one of the Taylor girls.

And yet, when she had rationalised so far, she found her arguments crumbling again. Surely he had shown feeling for her, walking her home, coming to meet her yesterday morning when it was quite out of his way? Or was that merely gallantry? She was desperate to see him and find out the truth.

Thursday evening seemed a century away. At last it came and she made her way up into the village determined to speak to John after choir practice. Sam was waiting outside the chapel as usual. His face lit up when he saw her.

"Anne! It's good to see you! Did you enjoy the trip to Windermere?"

"Yes, yes, I did," she replied. Seeing his face fall at her short answer, she made an effort to give due praise. "It was splendidly organised, Sam. Everything was well planned and executed. How clever of you!"

Sam looked as though he could burst with pride.

By now the choir pews were filling up. Rachel arrived and took her place with the contraltos. As had become his habit, Sam stood at the end of the tenors, a few feet away from Anne.

Anne continued to scan each new arrival at the chapel door but there was no sign of John. Somehow it had not occurred to her that he might not come. When the door was closed, ready for practice to begin, she felt foolish and deflated.

At the break between pieces, she spoke to Rachel as casually as she could.

"I don't see John here tonight."

"No. I don't know where he is."

As they began to sing again, Anne started to suppose that he might be ill or hurt in an accident. So vivid was her imagination, so distressing the picture of John wounded and bleeding that she felt quite faint. Commonsense calmed her. If there had been an accident, she would have heard. News like that would spread quickly through the village. Still, perhaps she would walk past his woodshop tomorrow. Just in case. At that moment the woman standing next to her gently turned over a page of Anne's score to indicate the point they had reached.

She found it hard to enjoy the walk after practice. Everything Dora, Eva and Sidney Mallinson said seemed fatuous in the extreme. Rachel was wrapped up in her own concerns. Sam was full of excitement at the course of chemistry lectures he was attending in Huddersfield given by the eminent scientist George Jarmain. Anne listened politely but it was an effort to match the same level of enthusiasm. The walk up to Castle Hill and back had never seemed so long.

Next day she walked past John's woodshop in the village. There was no sign of him. Not that this meant anything – he could well be out in customers' houses. She took the long, roundabout way back to the Hall with the intention of calling at his parents' cottage but at the last minute, thought better of it and hurried past.

She did not see him in church the following Sunday either. Sitting in a pew near the front, she turned round several times looking for him as the church filled up. At the end of the service, the vicar spoke to her for a few minutes and then she moved out of the church gloom into the sunlight. To her dismay, she saw the figures of John and his mother just walking out of the church gates. She wanted to shout out and run up the paved path after them but could not. When she realised they must have entered the church late and sat at the back, she felt even more upset. John's avoidance of her seemed calculated.

The day dragged by. At about eight o'clock there was a tap on her door. It was one of the maids. Mr Thorpe wanted to see her. He greeted her in the library with the particular charm he reserved for young women.

"My dear Miss Graham! I trust you are well. Good! Good! Now my dear, I have to tell you that my lady wife and her party will be returning very soon. I think it best for all concerned if you have taken your departure before the children return. I'm sure you understand. Could you therefore move into other accommodation by the end of next week? Thank you."

There was nothing to be said except "Of course, Mr Thorpe."

Back in her room, Anne could not sit still. Everything seemed to be vanishing – her position, her home, her hopes, for she knew she had begun to hope that John Brook might come to love her given time and opportunity. Outside the sky darkened. There was a rumble of thunder. Rain threatened but she did not care. She had to get out.

As she hurried along the valley, the first drops of rain began to fall. She scarcely felt them. But as the rain became a downpour, she made for the shelter of the woods. Soon her feet were sodden. She had not thought to change into sensible boots. Water streamed down her neck and through her thin clothing. Then she felt her hairpins give way and the wet rope of hair slip down onto her shoulders. She found herself sobbing, great sobs that seemed to come from deep inside her and racked her whole body. Clutching the trunk of a tree for support, she laid her face against the bark and wept, wept for everything that had ever happened in her life to cause her pain.

All at once, she became aware of something, an animal, snuffling at her feet and whining softly. Looking down, she saw it was John's dog. A few steps away stood John, as wet through as she was. As he came nearer, she saw that he looked as miserable as she felt, the usual light in his eyes quenched, the wide mouth tense.

For a moment they said nothing. John tried to speak, clearing his throat as the words came out cracked and uneven.

"You – you must get home, Anne. This is no weather to be out."

She opened her mouth, aware that she could say the same to him. But she did not. They continued to stare at each other, as the rain fell in sheets around them, running off the trees and forming pools around their feet.

At last she found the breath to speak.

"I have wanted to speak to you, John, since the trip to the Lakes."

He made a slight movement of acknowledgement.

"Have I done something to offend you? It seems you have been avoiding me."

He appeared to be wrestling with his emotions before he could speak again.

"One must consider the feelings of others."

She did not understand.

"What do you mean?"

He looked as if he did not want to say any more. Had he been struck with renewed grief for his dead wife? Were her family and his mother hurt that he had begun to enjoy the company of another woman?

"John, you must tell me. I cannot bear it."

Now he looked deep into her eyes with all the vulnerability of a lost boy. When he spoke, his hurt was palpable.

"I spoke to Sam. On the trip. He told me he loved you. That he had never thought he would fall in love but that he had done so. With you."

So that was it! Everything became suddenly clear. John had been avoiding her because of the thought that she belonged to Sam, a thought that was obviously causing him pain! She felt as if a great burden had been lifted from her. She stepped closer.

"And did he tell you of my feelings? Did he tell you I loved him?"

"No, no. He didn't say that. But...he was so happy. I couldn't..." His voice trailed off.

"It is true, John. I have already pledged my heart."

He made an inarticulate sound. She could not let him suffer any longer.

"It is yours, John, if you want it. It is you I love."

The sense of release was enormous and wonderful. She moved closer still and put her fingertips on his fore-arms, feeling the muscles through the wet sleeves. He looked down at her, still stunned.

"I didn't know."

"How could you?"

Reaching up, she put a hand on either side of his face. At her touch, he lowered his head and gently pressed his lips against hers.

"How long?" he asked.

"Since I first saw you," she replied with a smile.

Then they were melded together, mouths, hands, bodies in one long glorious kiss. Hearts thumping, they were forced to take breath before cleaving to one another once more in a warm, wet embrace that neither wanted to end. Pausing later, they looked at each other in wonderment and joy. Gradually, as they came to, they became aware of their drenched state.

"Look at us!" declared Anne. "We shall catch our death." She laughed softly, then loudly as he swooped down and lifted her up bodily in his arms.

"No, no! Don't carry me! You'll sink!"

But he was undeterred and began picking his way across the sodden ground towards the open fields and the road to the Hall. When they reached the porch that led to the servants' entrance, they clung together, kissing like starving people suddenly finding sustenance and fearful of losing it again. They could only bear to part once they had made arrangements to meet the following evening.

The rain had cleared, with a sunny day becoming a warm twilight. Anne and John walked up to Castle Hill and now sat close together, hands intertwined, in a grassy hollow away from prying eyes. They had talked but now were content simply to look at one another. For the first time, Anne was free to drink in every detail of John's face as if she meant to commit them to memory. As the sky grew darker, they exchanged long, lingering kisses that aimed to satisfy but instead stirred them to stronger desires. Eventually, they stood up and began, reluctantly, to walk back along the valley.

"When can we tell folk?" asked John eagerly.

"Not yet awhile. We must think of Molly's family and what is seemly." Seeing John look a little crushed, she continued, "Tell your mother by all means. I think she will agree that our betrothal could be announced in the autumn."

"And our marriage?" he asked, stopping to kiss her again. For a minute or two, they were beyond words. Taking breath, Anne said, "Perhaps when it is just over a year since Molly's death."

John did not argue and they walked on in sweet silence.

On the following Thursday evening, they walked with the choir members as usual but Anne had a sense that they were a couple apart and wondered whether the others suspected anything. Certainly Sam seemed very quiet. After the stroll over Castle Hill, the sky darkened and everyone set off for home without delay. John and Anne took the quickest route back, dropping down from the earthworks and then along Lumb Lane. It was only when John had delivered her to the Hall and begun his journey back home that Anne realised they had crossed the spot where Molly's body was found, without noticing.

John felt that he now inhabited a different world. His tiny cottage bedroom with its low ceiling and mullioned window had sometimes seemed slightly claustrophobic. But as he got up and dressed, there was no sense of crampedness at all. Instead he experienced a feeling of liberation, of exaltation almost. He could hardly believe his good fortune in meeting Anne Graham, being loved by her and loving her in return. Because there was no doubt that he did. He loved everything about her - her face, her figure, her beautiful hair, her voice. Even her fingernails seemed exquisite. In fact, everything about her seemed perfect, including her character. One part of him knew this could not be true but at this stage, he was happy to acquiesce in blissful delusion.

The desire to make love to her was all-consuming but equally strong was the desire to protect and worship her. How long had he loved her? It was a question he shied away from. His sense of morality told him that his love had only begun to grow after his wife had died but deep down, he suspected the emotion had taken root the first night he set eyes on her.

Downstairs he ate his breakfast with a relish that did not go un-noticed by his mother. Silently, she toasted more bread at the fire and piled it onto his plate.

"It's a grand day!" he exclaimed.

"Yes, a grand one," said Martha.

"Mother. I have something to tell you." He laid down his knife and placed his strong, tanned hands palms down on the table. His mother looked at him keenly, her brown eyes, like his own, vivid and expressive.

"I have been speaking to Anne Graham and we have agreed that we will be wed next year." He was unable to say any more but his broad smile conveyed all that was unspoken.

"Oh, lad!"

Martha rose, put her arms round her son and hugged him. After that, speaking or eating was difficult. In a few minutes, they were both calmer and began to discuss practical matters. She appreciated John's concern for proper respect for his late wife and agreed that there should be no celebration, or even announcement, of betrothal until nearer the time of the wedding.

"Though I must speak to Ethel Dyson," said Martha. "Molly's family must be told, in case they hear it from someone else."

John's face clouded.

"Do you think it all too soon, Mother? Will it be thought that I didn't love Molly?"

"Nay, lad. Only small-minded folk, or jealous ones, would think that. You're a young man." She patted his hand.

A week later John called at the Hall with a cart he had borrowed in order to take Anne and her belongings up the Haighs' farm. Her box and bags were packed, ready for John to carry downstairs. But the two lovers stood pressed together by the empty cupboards, tasting the sweetness of a final kiss in the gracious setting of the Hall, empty save for themselves and a few servants.

"We must go," murmured Anne.

"Yes," said John, kissing her again.

Outside, the first few leaves were beginning to fall. Soon it would be autumn. Anne took one last look out of the window.

"I shall miss the children."

For answer, John drew her towards him and held her close, lifting her left hand to his lips and kissing the inside of her wrist.

At the bottom of the stairs, the housekeeper and two maids came out to say good-bye.

"Good-bye, Miss, and good luck," said Edith.

"Let us know where you get to," added the housekeeper.

"Thank you. I will. And will you say good-bye to Susan for me when she returns?"

A fine misty drizzle was falling as they set off for the Haigh farm. John had a waterproof cape which he spread over their shoulders. The damp was making Anne's hair frizz in tiny curls around the hairline; her wet eyelashes showed clear against the fair, glowing skin.

They trundled along in companionable silence. John was thinking about visiting the Haighs, something he had done all his life. This time it would be different. This time he knew that Eli was his true father. Would it really change anything? Life was not a melodrama, where discovery of parentage usually meant an unsuspected inheritance or perhaps, the loss of one. One could argue that it made no difference at all. In his heart he would always think of Walter as his father because he had behaved like one, playing with him, teaching him things, all, John now realised, with great patience. By acting as his father, he had surely been his father?

Despite these conclusions, John felt nervous as they approached the farmhouse. He knew he would look at Eli with new eyes, seeking for resemblances he had never noticed before.

The farmyard was deserted as they drove into it. John helped Anne down, then lifted her belongings out of the cart. As soon as he knocked, the door was flung open by Rachel, obviously delighted to see them.

"Come in, come in! It's good to see you! I'll take you up."

They followed her up the stairs, John shouldering the box. The large room where the three brothers had slept when they were all at home had been freshly whitewashed and new rag rugs put down for the two young women. Anne had a bed, a shelf for her books and a chest for her clothes. It was simple but clean and homely.

Downstairs Hannah had prepared her usual formidable tea, mostly the result of her own cooking, the wooden table scarcely visible beneath the profusion of pies, pickles, cheese, sweetcake and bread. The six of them sat round the table, Eli in his usual position at its head. John, sitting opposite him, gave him a searching glance, watched his movements, how he spoke, even how he ate. He saw nothing significant. Any stranger coming into the room would have picked out Ben immediately as the son, the same flaxen hair, high cheekbones and blue eyes, a look clearly shared by Rachel. There was no point thinking along those lines. They led nowhere.

He realised that heads were bowed and that Eli was saying Grace. Hannah presided happily over all, encouraging everyone to eat their fill, and more.

"Come on then, John! You're not going to leave that bit o' pork pie all by itself, are you? Ben, you need no urging, I know. Rachel, give Anne some more tea-cake. She's nobbut a reed! We'll put some flesh on those bones, believe me!"

John felt a great sense of contentment. It was good that Anne would be living here until she found a suitable position. He knew there were those who mocked the Haighs for their piety and abstinence but the critics were usually people who conspicuously lacked those qualities themselves. Anyone who had experienced their family life from the inside, as he had, knew that the Haighs were not in the least sanctimonious and welcomed guests whether they shared their Nonconformist beliefs or not.

In the past, Hannah had often said to him, "Tell Martha and Walter we'd be glad to see them for tea on Saturday," but they had never accepted the invitation. Now he understood why. Now his mother's strange reluctance to accept Hannah's offer to hold the wedding supper at the farmhouse made sense. Martha had coped with the truth by keeping Eli at a distance. The wedding supper must have put her under considerable strain. He tried to remember how she had acted that evening. All he could recall was her desire to leave early. Considering Walter's health, that had not been remarkable.

His mother, Martha Brook, had not been one for visiting. The one woman who did call on her for tea and conversation sometimes was Anne's aunt, Agnes, the long-suffering wife of Jack Stott. She was probably glad of a respite from the family home where she was, reputedly, treated badly. It occurred to John for the first time that, by marrying Anne, he would be related to the Stott family. He hoped there would be no trouble from that quarter.

Anne appeared to be enjoying herself in conversation as they continued to sit around the kitchen table. The subject was governesses. Anne had been asked if the thought of yet more spoilt children to control, let alone teach, was a daunting one.

"Not really. It's very satisfying. I've never met any bad children. I had some badly behaved ones in my class at the church school in London but what they needed was love and attention. Not beatings."

"But what if," said Ben, reaching for the cheese, "you find yourself with some very nasty folk stuck out on some deserted moor somewhere?"

Anne smiled.

"It's not very likely. I shall make sure I can afford to bribe someone to post a letter asking you to rescue me. You've been reading too many novels, Ben! I'm a bit tougher than Agnes Grey!"

"Ah!" said Rachel. "And you never know, Ben, she might be lucky like Jane Eyre and find a husband like Mr Rochester!"

"Goodness, I hope not!" cried Anne, bursting into infectious laughter. She caught John's eye and exchanged a meaningful look. As she did so, John felt Hannah's observant glance upon them. But what matter? It would be known soon enough.

As the women began to clear the table, the men walked outside to let their tea get down before attending to a farm job together. The Haighs observed the Sabbath as strictly as they could and apart from essential tasks such as feeding animals, they did not work on Sundays. This being Saturday evening, Eli and Ben were glad of the extra pair of hands and muscles provided by John. Ever since he had been a boy, he had enjoyed working alongside the Haighs. He had never understood why he found it so satisfying. Before now, he had always thought it was simply the contrast with the solitary nature of his own work in the woodshop.

When the work was done, he took his leave. The week ahead shone with promise – seeing Anne tomorrow at church and then as often as they could manage during the week without arousing general suspicion.

At choir practice on Thursday evening, they looked across at one another, oblivious of everyone else. The choir was singing the piece from Handel's 'Messiah' – "For Unto Us a Child is Born." When it swelled to its crescendo –

"And His name shall be call – ed

Wonderful! Counsellor!

The Mighty God! the Everlasting Father..."

John thought his heart would burst with joy.

As he and Anne walked up the road out of the village, up towards Castle Hill, they were silent as the others joked and chatted around them. There was no need to speak. Simply being in Anne's company was happiness enough.

CHAPTER ELEVEN

"Jessie? Would you light the lamps please?"

When this was done, Charlotte and Sam bent their heads once more over the large sheet of figures on the walnut writing-desk. Firelight and lamplight set the room aglow, reflected in the lustres on the mantelpiece, the gold-framed pictures on the walls, the brass of fender and fire-irons and the gleaming folds of the ruby damask curtains.

Isabel called this room "the library" and had filled the shelves with tooled, leather-bound books in tasteful shades. It had soon become George Blezard's private place for smoking and drinking, away from his wife's censorious gaze. Since his death, it had been untouched, except by dustpan, brush and dusters. During Isabel's long absence, however, Charlotte had taken over the room as her study and business office. Back issues of '*The Textile Manufacturer*' stood next to trade reports and journals, while the desk drawers now contained trade accounts, both general and particular, relevant to the work of Blezard's Mill.

It was not the only room on which Charlotte had laid her imprint. A small bedroom upstairs which had not so far been used for anything had been transformed into a miniature warehouse. On deep shelving erected for the purpose, there were samples of cloth and yarn, each neatly labelled with price and origin. Other boxes held advertising material and pinned to one wall, a huge calendar announced the dates of all forthcoming trade fairs and exhibitions.

Charlotte leant back in her chair.

"So you think we should stick with worsted coatings?"

"Well, that's my view," said Sam. "There's novelty lines which do well, like Firth's snowflake carriage rugs, but the trouble with fashion is that it's fickle. A change o' fashion and you can be left with a mound o' stuff you can't shift. Worsted coatings is what we do best and I believe there'll be a steady market. I've heard it said elsewhere as well."

Charlotte sighed.

"I wish I knew more about the trade. It seems that bit harder, being a woman."

"Nay, I think you've done champion! The way you've set it up here I wouldn't have believed."

The compliment made Charlotte blush with pleasure. As a clock chimed behind them, she said, "See what time it is! Isn't this when you go to choir practice?"

Sam looked uncomfortable.

"I've decided to give it a miss. I'm not that much of a singer."

"But you like music?"

"Ooh aye, very much. I like nothing better than a good concert."

"So do I," said Charlotte warmly. Fearing she had sounded too eager, she went on. "You'll stay and eat some dinner, won't you? Cook'll be sending it in any time now."

"Aye. Thank you. That would be very nice."

After some slight awkwardness as they moved into the dining-room with its napery and silver, the couple relaxed as lamb chops and roast potatoes had their cheering effect.

"So when's your stepmother coming back then?" asked Sam, chewing vigorously the while.

"Tonight possibly. Or tomorrow."

"Wouldn't you have liked to go to Paris as well?"

"Oh, I should! What I might have learnt at the Exhibition!"

"Never heed. It's been well reported locally. 'Appen you'll go to the next one."

Charlotte's eyes shone.

"Yes indeed." She wanted to say – "and you must come with me" but didn't. "How are the chops? Are they done as you like them?"

"Grand!" he answered, proving it by helping himself to another from the silver serving-dish.

"So are you still going to Mr Jarmain's lectures?"

"That I am." Sam's face lit up at finding an interested listener. He was explaining how chemistry, in the shape of artificial aniline dyes, would benefit the textile industry when they heard the sound of the front door opening.

Charlotte put down her knife and fork and went out into the hallway. It was, as she expected, Isabel, pale but handsome in a long black travelling cloak with a velvet hood.

"Isabel! It's good to see you. How are you?"

"Very tired," replied her stepmother. "These last few miles in Yorkshire

201

have been the worst of all." At that moment, Sam emerged from the dining-room and gave Isabel a slight nod of acknowledgement.

"Mrs Blezard."

A slight smile, almost a sneer, crossed Isabel's face.

"Mr Armitage. Good evening. No doubt Charlotte is seeing to you."

"Yes, thank you, Mrs Blezard."

As if he were a tradesman, thought Charlotte angrily.

"Good, good. I expect you have business matters to talk about. Now, if you will excuse me, I will go straight to my room. Charlotte, you will see that all my boxes are brought in safely."

Her command infuriated Charlotte. It was not her job to see to the luggage. She deputed the task to Mrs Drew and returned to the dining-room. But the relaxed mood of the evening had gone and, declining dessert or coffee, Sam took his leave not long after.

Next morning there was no sign of Isabel at breakfast nor even at lunch-time. Charlotte was enjoying a few final hours of freedom and happily engaged with her ledgers in the library when Isabel flung open the door. One look at her face told Charlotte that she had been into the spare room.

"What is all that stuff upstairs? How dare you take over that room? I need it for my new things."

"I did ask you, Isabel, before you left for London, if I might use that room for my own purposes."

Isabel obviously had no recollection of the conversation.

"What is it anyway? Looks like a rag factory."

"They're samples from our mills and others. Some from abroad. They're to help me keep up with the business."

"The business, the business! It's all you ever think about! Still, no doubt it'll be some consolation to you when you're an old maid!" Isabel had not finished. Looking round the room, she saw that it was fully in use. "So, you've taken over the library as well. You soon got tired of keeping it in your father's memory."

The accusation brought a catch to Charlotte's throat.

"How can you say that? You know he would have liked me to use it!"

"Yes, yes. What do you do in here? Smoke?"

The ridiculous question restored Charlotte's composure.

"No, I use it for studying. And book-keeping. I think that would have pleased Father."

Isabel was temporarily silenced. She was just about to reply when they heard a knock at the front door and the maid's footsteps down the hall. A moment later, the maid appeared at the library door.

"It's Miss Graham, Madam, Miss Charlotte. She's brought a pint of cream the Haighs forgot to deliver with the milk this morning. Shall I show her in?"

"Yes, please do," said Charlotte, before Isabel could answer. "Please show her in and take the cream down to Cook. And bring tea and biscuits for three."

As Anne entered, Charlotte thought how well and happy she looked. She was wearing a dark blue walking dress which suited her very well.

"Anne! How nice to see you! And how good of you to bring the cream!"

"I was glad of the errand. I did not know you were back, Mrs Blezard."

"Yes, we returned last night."

"And you have enjoyed your trip, no doubt?"

"Oh, enormously," gushed Isabel. "London was splendid, of course, it always is. But Paris! Well, Paris capped all."

"And you went to the Exhibition?" asked Charlotte.

"We walked round once but it seemed very dull. Hardly any interesting people at all. Not like the Embassy ball we attended. The Prince of Wales was there, you know. And I heard Adelina Patti sing."

"That I should have liked to hear, I must admit," said Anne pleasantly, now holding a cup of tea. "And did the children enjoy themselves in London? I thought of them often."

"Oh, they had a wonderful time! So much to see. Young Susan is so good with them. You too must have enjoyed yourself. At the Hall. With nothing to do."

"I hear you've moved to the Haighs' farm," said Charlotte quickly.

"Yes, I have. They have made me very welcome."

"Ah! The Haighs!" sneered Isabel. "Most improving company, I'm sure. Take care or they will be turning you into a Methodist."

"I see no sign of their wanting to," said Anne crisply, meeting Isabel's gaze without flinching. "What I do see are good people receiving me generously into their home while I look for further employment."

"Aah yes, of course. The governess," said Isabel. "You must speak with Charlotte who is turning herself into a business woman. I am sure her contacts with tradesmen will prove helpful."

"Perhaps so," said Anne. Then, addressing Charlotte, "I admire the way you're taking over your father's work. It is good for one to be usefully occupied – far better than frittering one's time away with selfish pleasures."

If Anne had meant to sting Isabel's vanity, she had succeeded. Isabel's face reddened. Charlotte rose, almost at the same time as Anne.

"I must be going," Anne said, moving towards the door. Outside, in the entrance hall, Charlotte closed the door behind her and whispered to Anne.

"I will see you when I get back, Anne. I'm going to stay with my friend Helen for a few days. When I return, I may have some good news for you."

"Thank you," Anne whispered back. "I think you very wise to get away from that woman as much as you can. Good-bye."

When Charlotte returned to the library, Isabel was standing with her back to her, looking at the re-arranged books on the shelves, while Jessie cleared the tea things.

"Thank you, Jessie," said Charlotte. "Oh! Here are Anne's gloves. Never mind, I'll return them later."

"She's living at 'aighs' farm now, Miss," said Jessie in a loud, audible undertone.

"Yes, I know."

"My cousin Edith saw that John Brook helping her move her stuff out o' th' Hall last week. Edith reckons they're walking out together. Billing and cooing, they were. Reckons they'll soon be wed. That's my hopes gone an' all."

"Jessie! That's enough!"

The girl left, the china chinking on the tray as she went.

"I know one is not supposed to listen to servants' gossip," said Charlotte, "but I must say that is good news if it is true. I should like to see Anne and John finding happiness together. They deserve it. I shouldn't think there will be any obstacle in their way."

When Isabel turned round, Charlotte was stunned by the look of displeasure on her stepmother's face. The expression in her eyes was fierce and threatening. Thinking that Isabel was about to criticise her further, now that she had had time to notice all the alterations to the library, Charlotte excused herself and escaped to the safety of her own room.

Anne returned to the Haigh farm in high spirits. It was not exactly a pleasure to be in Isabel Blezard's company but she was glad to see that Charlotte was holding her own. It would be grand when Charlotte married and had someone to love and defend her. Perhaps Isabel would re-marry? That would be best of all, especially as it might take her away from Huddersfield.

Anne had never felt happier. Discovering that John loved her as much as she loved him had been the most glorious, incredible moment of her life. She never tired of re-living the moment in her mind when they had declared their love for each other in the rain-drenched woodlands below Castle Hill. And there would be many happy times to come – frequent meetings, then their betrothal, to be followed by their marriage. Anne's heart soared with joyful anticipation. She recalled how it felt to be in his arms. She had always loved the way he looked and the sound of his voice. What she had not foreseen was the tantalising bliss of inhaling his nearness and tasting the sweetness of his flesh. Every surface of her body craved to surround his. One day it would. To be his, body and soul, seemed more than any mortal had a right to expect.

Not least among her present blessings was her good fortune in living with the Haighs. John had called them "grand folks" and so they had proved to be. Although Rachel was her friend, Anne acknowledged that Mrs Haigh, Hannah, was the most exceptional member of the family, possessing what could only be called "goodness." Yet had anyone told her this, she would have laughed with amazed disbelief.

When Anne entered the farmhouse kitchen, Hannah was busy cooking, as she often was.

"There you are, my dear. Did you find Charlotte at home?"

"Yes, I did, thank you, Hannah. I delivered the cream and took tea with Charlotte and her stepmother."

"Oh, Mrs Blezard's back, is she? And had a grand time, I should think."

"Yes, so she said. She saw the Prince of Wales and heard Adelina Patti sing."

"Oh my!" said Hannah, joining in Anne's laughter.

Anne loved watching Hannah cook. Her movements were so sure, so relaxed, that the ingredients seemed to obey her touch. At the moment, her plump fingers dusty with flour, she was holding a pie plate in her left hand and turning it round as the knife in her right trimmed the edge, slicing off the pastry in one continuous piece.

"What can I do to help?" Anne asked.

"Well, I've a couple of apples left. Do you think you might find some blackberries? There should be some ripe. There's nothing John likes more than a blackberry and apple pie."

Holding a large basin, Anne was soon crouching down among the brambles in the hedges behind Castle Hill, pulling the ripest berries from the bushes. She had almost filled the basin when she saw a man approaching in the distance. As he came closer, she saw that it was Ned Stott. He was obviously coming to speak to her so she straightened up and licked her purple finger tips clean.

"Hallo, Ned. Is everything all right? Is my aunt well?"

Ned looked somewhat confused.

"Eh? Ooh aye, she's right enough."

There followed an awkward silence. Anne waited for Ned to say what he had come to say but he just continued to look at her, his eyes large, his mouth dropping open slightly. When he did not speak, Anne grew impatient.

"Well, I must be off. Hannah's waiting for these blackberries."

"Wait on!" Ned stepped forward, the colour rising in his cheeks. "I'm off to Honley Feast tomorrow. 'Appen you'd like to come as well."

"No thank you, Ned. But thank you for asking me." Anne had heard about the fairground entertainments but she had no wish to go anywhere with Ned Stott.

"Nay! Wait on!" He spoke more loudly now and looked angry instead of embarrassed. "We're cousins, tha knows." He laid one hand heavily on Anne's arm, almost pinning her to the hedge.

"Ned! Please!" Anne tried to pull away but found herself held by both arms. Ned was now uncomfortably close; she could feel his hot breath on her face. Behind him, there was nothing but an empty field.

Suddenly she felt his grip tighten on her arms as he lunged forward, aiming to kiss her. Repelled, she twisted her head so that his lips brushed only the edge of her chin. The basin fell from her grasp, blackberries scattering in all directions.

"Get away! Get away!" she shouted until he let her go. "Look what you've made me do!" Flustered, she knelt down and began gathering them up again. Cursing under his breath, Ned stomped off, up the field.

Stupid lad, Anne thought, as she hurried back to the farm. I suppose that's what passes for courtship in his world. Her irritation and discomfort had disappeared, however, by the time she re-entered the kitchen.

She drank the tea Hannah had just made and decided not to mention her encounter with Ned. What had been his motive in making up to her? Was it a calculated ploy, or something softer? She could not tell. Either way, she would take care to keep well away from him in future.

"Take a house in London? After Christmas? For two months?"

Charlotte was appalled. She had just been thinking what a pleasant morning it was, with the sun streaming in through the library windows, and on her desk, sheets of figures in her neat handwriting, the accounts of the mill and other business enterprises.. And now here was Isabel bursting, dangerously, with excitement at a new proposition.

Charlotte's practical mind began running through the likely expense, not just the rental, but everything that went with it – the carriage, the servants, the cost of entertaining and not least, the extensive wardrobe of new clothes Isabel would almost certainly think necessary if she were to move into fashionable circles.

"Oh, at least, I should say!" Isabel cried, her face glowing with anticipation. "To take full advantage of the season! And all the events – the theatre, the balls!"

"Have you any idea how much all this would cost?"

"Oh yes! There are properties to let advertised in '*The Times.*' I've been reading Ellen Thorpe's copy. She takes it, you know. To keep in touch with what's going on."

"That's only a part of it," protested Charlotte. "You'd need very much more than that if you were to stay there that long." She paused. It was not easy to deny Isabel what she wanted. But it had to be done.

"I'm afraid it's out of the question, Isabel."

Isabel opened her mouth to speak but Charlotte went on.

"There's only just enough money to keep up with your spending as it is. Trade is not good at the moment."

"Trade, trade! That's all you can talk about!" snapped Isabel. "If you only knew how tedious that makes you!"

Charlotte, colouring slightly, stuck to her guns.

"I'm sorry, Isabel, but it's impossible. I know how much you would enjoy it and perhaps when trade picks up..."

Isabel had not finished. Tossing her head, she paced up and down the room.

"What about the insurance money? From the fire?"

Charlotte gave a start. It was something she did not like to talk about, mainly because it brought back memories of her father's death.

"You can't pretend you've spent all of it because I know you haven't! You said yourself you hadn't replaced the damaged looms. There must be hundreds left, if not a thousand."

Charlotte felt herself hardening. Before, she had had some sympathy with Isabel, whom she knew pined for more, and more exciting, social life than Almondbury or Huddersfield could offer her. This was different.

"The insurance money belongs entirely to the mill, Isabel. It has nothing to do with our general living expenses."

"How can you say that?" shouted Isabel, her face red with anger. "It's all Blezard money! I've as much right to it as you have!"

She's getting into one of her fits of temper, thought Charlotte. But I'm not going to be bullied.

"You are wrong, Isabel. The mill money is not general money. It is my responsibility, mine. The mill was left to me in Father's will and I refuse to jeopardise its future."

Isabel continued to storm at her, her voice loud and shrill. She flung accusations of selfishness, meanness and provincialism at Charlotte who felt herself become firmer and harder as the onslaught raged on. She's like a caged beast, she thought, watching her stepmother pace up and down the room.

Without warning, her face contorted with fury, Isabel lifted her arm and swept the mantelpiece clear of its contents so that a dark oak clock and two vases fell with a loud, splintering crash on the tiled hearth below. Seizing the door handle, she wrenched it open violently.

"You'll be sorry for this, Charlotte Blezard!" she hissed and swept out of the room and up the stairs.

Charlotte bent over the fireplace. She did not care about the vases which Isabel had bought recently but the clock was an old one which had been a wedding present to her parents. She felt quite ridiculously sorry for its poor damaged face and smashed glass. Perhaps it would mend. Poking the broken pieces with her foot, she rang the bell for the maid.

"Please could you sweep this up, Bella? I think the vases might as well be thrown away but can you put the clock pieces in a box? Thank you. I'm going out now for lunch at the Shaws and will be back about three o'clock."

There was no sound from Isabel's bedroom as Charlotte put on her outdoor things. Perhaps she would have calmed down by this afternoon.

It was wash day, and Anne was helping the farmer's wife to peg out the washing. Wearing one of Hannah's aprons which nearly went round her twice, the breeze chilling her damp arms, she was struggling with a large bed sheet which threatened to take off as the wind filled its sails. Hannah came to her aid, securing the sheet with large wooden pegs, and soon the washing lines were full of household linen, shirts, blouses and undergarments. Finally, Hannah hoisted the lines with the clothes-props, lifting the washing even higher in great loops which flapped and billowed against the blue sky and scudding clouds.

"That's a grand job done!" said Hannah with satisfaction. "Two pair of hands gets job done a lot faster than one!"

Together, carrying the empty wash-basket between them, they re-entered the farmhouse kitchen. Hannah stoked up the fire and, swinging the kettle round on its iron hook, positioned it to rest on the hot coals.

"We'll have a drink o' tea in no time! Now sit yourself down and eat some oatcake."

Anne did as she was told. She had come to love this kitchen, with its display of willow pattern plates on a shelf and the Staffordshire dogs on the mantelpiece. She and Hannah had just sat down when the latch was lifted and Charlotte came in, beaming and carrying documents of some kind. Her face declared she was bearing good news.

"I've been visiting my friend Helen, as you know. Mr Shaw's a businessman in Huddersfield, knows what's going on, who's buying, selling, building and the like."

Anne smiled but she still had little idea of what Charlotte meant.

"I told him about your looking for a post of governess and he asked if I had thought of investing in a local school for girls, like the one at Mirfield. He has been looking about for one for his wife to run. She has all the right sort of experience but would need a junior assistant. So I said you would be just the right person!"

"Oh, Charlotte! I should dearly like to teach older girls, although I like the younger children too. If I were fortunate enough to be appointed. And what would be your role?"

"I would be part of the management board so my connection would be mainly financial," said Charlotte with all the aplomb of an experienced business woman. "And when I heard they were already considering a suitable property in Almondbury, I said I'd be delighted to look at it and take on the contract for re-furbishing it."

Anne was speechless with admiration. In the last four years, Charlotte had suffered the loss of both parents and the imposition of an unpleasant stepmother. But she had pulled herself together, and with the help of Sam Armitage, had taken over the running of the Blezard mill. Now she was branching out into new business ventures.

It was Hannah who said the right thing.

"Charlotte, if your mother and father were living, they'd be that proud."

Going even pinker, Charlotte took out some papers from a portfolio.

"Here," she said. "These are the details of the house in question."

Anne recognised it at once, Northfield, which stood in the centre of the village on Northgate. It was a handsome, flat-fronted house, built in the Georgian style which Anne preferred to the more ornate fashion of the day. She began to share Charlotte's excitement.

"Is it empty? Can we look inside?"

"Yes, it's empty but I can't get the key until later. But we could go and look at it from the outside now. Shall we?"

"Oh yes, let's do so! Is that all right with you, Hannah? If I go with Charlotte now?"

"Of course, my dears. You go off and have a look. There's only a bit of mangling left to do in any case."

The Blezard carriage was outside and within minutes, Charlotte and Anne were rolling down towards Northgate. Knowing the house was empty, they took the carriage right up the short drive and through a stone gateway. The very long, arched window above the front door suggested an entrance and staircase behind it of some elegance. They walked round to the back of the house and discovered it was in fact the front, with columns flanking the entrance and uninterrupted views of rolling countryside as far as Lepton. There was also a pleasant garden which sloped away from the full-length windows of the two downstairs rooms.

"These look as though they would make two grand schoolrooms," Anne said, standing next to Charlotte and like her, cupping her hands over her eyes to get a better view of the interior. "One for senior and one for junior pupils." She began to feel deliciously excited at the prospect.

"What would they need? Cupboards either side of the fireplace for teaching things?" asked Charlotte.

"Yes. I should think so. Would that be a job for John?"

"Probably not. His work's too fine, I think. But he'd know who to get to do the job for us."

Having seen as much as they were able to, the two young women began their return journey up through the village. Anne grew more sober.

"Do you think Mrs Shaw will think me sufficiently well qualified,

Charlotte? My references are good but I worry that I have not taught children older than seven years of age."

"Perhaps that will not matter if you can show you are well-read and capable of doing so," replied her friend stoutly.

"How are things at Wood Lane? Is Isabel any more kindly disposed to your projects? As she should be."

Charlotte pulled a face.

"We do best when we keep out of each other's way. Thankfully, she often dines in her room." She hesitated. "On such occasions, I sometimes invite Samuel Armitage to dinner. We have much to discuss."

"Yes, yes, I'm sure you have. I have always thought him a worthy young man." She was pleased to see the happy look that appeared on Charlotte's face.

When the carriage reached the farm, Anne went straight upstairs to her room. She now owned a good if small personal library, with several books she thought relevant to the curriculum of the proposed school, and spent the afternoon reading, and skimming, through them all. Having done so, she was aware her works of history were scanty and juvenile. She felt sure she had seen some history books on the library shelves at the Blezard home which Charlotte would be only too happy to lend her. Not even Isabel, surely, mean-spirited as she could be, would begrudge her the loan of a few books so she set off for the Blezards', glad of an excuse to stretch her legs.

By now, it was five o'clock, with the light already fading. The sunny morning had become a grey afternoon. There was no sign of life at the front of the Blezard house and when she rang the bell, no-one came. She knew that the incorrigible Jessie was inclined to take an afternoon nap if everyone was out so she walked round the side of the house to the garden to see if she could attract someone's attention. Over in a far corner, a middle-aged man was stoking a bonfire. As Anne approached, he looked up and nodded at her.

"Afternoon, Miss."

"Good afternoon. Do you know if Miss Charlotte is in? I rang the bell but there was no answer."

"As far as I know, Miss, both Miss Charlotte and Mrs Blezard are in. And Jessie. Mrs Drew's gone into Huddersfield."

Bending down, the man shovelled up half-burnt pieces of stuff and dropped them onto the flames where they caught fire and blazed.

For the first time Anne looked down at the bonfire. It was well alight with paper and cardboard and what appeared to be cones of yarn which hissed and disintegrated in the flames. On top, several squares of woollen cloth curled and melted away. One of them bore a label which was still legible. It read "50% wool, 50% cotton." It was one of Charlotte's samples.

There was a strange, roaring sound in Anne's head. What was burning here were the contents of the small room Charlotte had lovingly fashioned into an inventory of the current cloth trade. To reduce them to ashes was an act of outright malice. It could only have been ordered by one person.

A towering sense of the injustice done to her friend took hold of Anne. Impelled by outrage and without quite knowing what she did, she stormed into the house by the back entrance. As she flung the door open, she saw that the mistress's bell was clanging furiously and a drowsy Jessie, rubbing her eyes, was stumbling out of the kitchen with a tray. Startled, the girl goggled at her.

"Is Miss Charlotte in?" Anne hissed at her.

"I think so, Miss. Upstairs, in her room. Wait on..."

But Anne was already racing up the stairs. Hearing sounds, Charlotte came out into the corridor. She had obviously been crying, her eyes red, a crumpled handkerchief in one hand.

"Charlotte! I saw the bonfire – "

"You'd better come up."

In the bedroom, Charlotte sank down into a chair. Anne stood by her, tense with anger.

"I was reading in the library and wanted to check something so I went up to my store room. Everything was gone. I couldn't think what had happened. Then I saw Henry with the bonfire. I'm sorry. It's stupid to cry. They're only bits of cloth and things."

Charlotte blew her nose.

"Isabel, I suppose?"

"I'm afraid so. We had a big quarrel this morning. About money."

"Is she in?"

"Yes. In her room."

Anne flew across the corridor and burst into Isabel's room without knocking. In a flash, she took in the scene : the stuffy heat from a fire banked high up the chimney, the bed scattered with silk cushions, the couch where Isabel reclined, a box of chocolates and a fashion magazine on her lap. She sat up, her eyes wide with shock.

"What do you think you are doing, you cruel, idle woman?" cried Anne.

Isabel looked stunned. Anne raged on.

"How dare you? How dare you destroy Charlotte's work? Isn't it enough that you belittle her and sneer at everything she does? You spend your time and money on nothing but yourself! When she tries to make the business successful, you crush her at every turn. What kind of woman are you?"

Wrapping her gown more tightly round herself, Isabel was beginning to collect her wits. She sat up and swung her feet to the ground.

"How dare you come into my room like this? And say these things?"

"If you had any feelings at all, you'd know that she misses her father. And her mother. But no! You've no feelings for anyone but yourself!"

Isabel began to shout back.

"Get out! I won't be spoken to like this! Who do you think you are? You, a nobody, a governess, and very likely, a bastard!"

"What? What?"

"Who knows who fathered you? Your mother ran off to London. Oh yes, very convenient, and married a man there. If they ever were married!"

Anne trembled with fury.

"Don't you mention my mother! You are not fit to speak her name! She was a good woman, unselfish to the end. You don't know the meaning of the word! I doubt you ever loved George Blezard, you just married him for his money. And helped to ruin him!"

Anne was so angry she hardly knew what she was saying. But her words were having an effect on Isabel. Her face scarlet, she screamed at Anne.

"Get out! Get out!"

"With pleasure!" Anne retorted, pulling Isabel's door open so suddenly that Jessie, who was on the other side of it, almost fell into the room.

It was hard to say which of the women was the most startled. But Anne was the first to recover. She lifted her hand to acknowledge Charlotte, who stood in her bedroom doorway, and spoke as calmly as she could.

"Charlotte, my dear. I wonder whether you have any history books I might borrow?"

Charlotte nodded and led the way downstairs.

Back at the farmhouse, Anne arranged the history books on her bedroom shelf. The events of the afternoon had left her feeling more distressed than she had anticipated. She felt sickened when she thought of Isabel's spiteful destruction of Charlotte's work-room. It had the features of a child's nastiness but with an adult's power.

Anne herself had not escaped the venomous lash of Isabel's tongue. "Your mother ran off to London... very convenient.. married a man there. If they ever were married." Was there some secret that her mother had kept from her? She had brought Anne up to believe that the truth was always preferable to lies. That it was not bound to be so was a concept Anne was reluctant to grasp, if only because it made life more complicated. Perhaps many of the truths we took for granted were really half-truths? She had never really understood the saying "Ignorance is bliss" until now.

That night, she and Rachel, in the room they shared, prepared for bed as they usually did, by brushing and plaiting each other's hair. Anne had the easier task. Rachel's silky blonde hair divided easily into strands and was soon braided but Anne's auburn hair seemed to derive energy from the hairbrush and crackled and curled in resistance as it was pulled into shape.

After saying their individual prayers, the two young women got into their beds. Rachel then blew her candle out, ready to close her eyes and succumb to sleep immediately. Anne continued to read, reluctant to snuff the candle and become a prey to the thronging uncertainties that besieged her in the darkness. Eventually she blew her candle out and lay down, hoping sleep would soon come and release her. But it refused to do so. She found herself turning over yet again and sighing heavily. There was a rustle from the other bed.

"Anne? Is something wrong?"

"Not exactly. But there is something I cannot fathom."

"Tell me," said Rachel. By now their eyes had become accustomed to the dark and they could see each other slightly.

"It's about my mother, Emma Ramsden. And when she left the village to go to London as a nursemaid to the Crowthers. There seems to be nothing known after that – until I was born. The fact is, Rachel, I have had it suggested that my mother was not married and that I am therefore illegitimate." Anne felt a sense of relief at putting the worry into words. "Not that I care very much that I might be but it seems incredible, knowing my mother as I did."

"Did your mother never speak of your father?"

"Very rarely. She gave me to understand he was in the army, a military bandsman, who contracted typhus and died about six months after they were married. Fortunately, she had already become housekeeper to Mr Pearson and he, kind man, let her stay when it became clear she was expecting a child. I think he was prepared to put up with the inconvenience of a child in the house for the sake of keeping a very good servant."

"Are there no documents, marriage lines, your birth certificate?"

"I never saw any. I always meant to find out more but my mother seemed not to want to talk about it so I left the subject alone. And then, at the end, she died so suddenly."

Rachel was silent for a moment.

"Is it possible, I do not mean to be hurtful, but is it possible that there never was a soldier husband? People do sometimes cover things up in this way so as not to upset the child."

"I suppose so," said Anne. She suddenly felt very miserable. "But if that were true, who then was, or is, my father?"

"Well, let us think. Who else could it be? Mr Pearson?"

"Oh, I don't think so. He was quite old. He was a kind employer but no, I'm sure there wasn't anything like that between them."

"What about the people your mother worked for before? The Crowthers? Who came from here?

"Yes, she went to work for them as nursemaid to their two young children and then almost immediately they moved to London. Mrs

Crowther was from there and inherited some property. They asked my mother to go with them because she was so good with the children."

"Could it have been Mr Crowther? Living in the same house?"

"I don't think so. My mother said they were a devoted young couple."

Both fell silent. When Rachel spoke again, Anne sensed she was groping for words that would cause the least pain to her friend.

"I shouldn't worry about it. We may never know the exact circumstances but you know your mother was a good woman and that's what matters. Now stop worrying about it and go to sleep."

It was not so simple.

CHAPTER TWELVE

Sitting in the pew next to his mother, John heard what he was listening for. The noise of several people at the church door, along with the piping voices of children, heralded the arrival of the Dartmouth Hall household. As they walked up the aisle to their pew near the front of the church, John turned his head to meet Anne's glance as they passed by. The look as their eyes met set his heart racing. He watched as she greeted the children and then knelt down to pray. It was both wonderful and terrifying that so much of his future happiness rested on that slim figure with head bent and auburn curls showing under her bonnet.

At that moment, a murmur rippled through the congregation. His mother looked over her shoulder and then whispered to him,

"Goodness me! What a hat!"

John turned and saw the hat in question, a purple boat-shaped hat which dipped forward over the brow with upswept curled feathers at the back of the same rich hue. The hat, presumably from Paris, could not fail to make an impact in the village church where most things, from the stone walls and dark pews to the clothes of the congregation, were some shade of brown, grey or black. All heads turned to get a closer look as Isabel Blezard, now in mourning purple, glided by and then gathered up her voluminous skirts before subsiding gracefully into her pew.

Unlike the rest of the congregation, John turned and looked the other way. The sight of the mill-owner's widow made him feel very uneasy. He had heard that she was back at home after her travels and hoped their paths would rarely cross in future. Now that he saw her again, he felt a despairing premonition that this was a vain hope. He tried to keep his eyes steadfastly fixed on the vicar and on what was going on in front of the altar. Despite this effort, he was guiltily aware of Isabel's presence ahead of him. When the time came for silent prayer, the sign for much shuffling and creaking as the congregation knelt down, he pressed his elbows down hard on the ledge in front and prayed more fervently than he had ever done before.

"Dear God. Please forgive my sin, the sin of fornication I committed with Isabel Blezard. I truly repent and ask for forgiveness. Amen."

Embarrassed, he sat back up in the hard pew and folded his arms to listen to the sermon. He heard not a word. His own thoughts mocked him. "Sin of fornication" "truly repent" "forgiveness"! Conventional words, used by thousands, probably without meaning. How could "repent" convey all that he felt? In truth, what he felt was deep shame and fury at his own folly. How could he have been so stupid, so weak? On that night in May, meeting Isabel by chance, he had behaved like a lust-driven animal. No, worse than an animal because, as well as the lust, there had been self-pity, which had allowed him to feel sorry for himself and justify what he was doing. His conduct had insulted Molly's memory, Isabel Blezard's honour and now, Anne Graham's trust. If only he could undo what he had done!

Then, depressing him further, the image that had haunted him for months, the image of a woman stumbling in deep snow, flashed into his mind. He, John Brook, who had prided himself on his courtesy towards women, had treated them abominably. From boyhood, he had witnessed coarseness and cruelty: lads forcing lasses against their will, then boasting of it afterwards, men reeling out of public houses at night and into homes where wives and children cowered at their return. He had vowed he would never sink so low. Yet that too was a form of pride, perhaps the greatest sin of all.

By the time the service ended, he had recovered himself sufficiently to exchange smiles and a few words with Anne as they filed out of church. Outside, he could not bear to linger. He felt the tall, purple presence of Isabel looming close by and making an excuse, hurried away, leaving his mother to speak to her friends and acquaintances.

He did not know what to think of Isabel's behaviour that night or how she felt now. He could understand her loneliness and her need. Perhaps she had been ashamed afterwards too? Perhaps she wished to forget the incident, as he did? He hoped that was the case. But the sense of guilt and uncertainty would not go away.

He was restless all afternoon. He tried walking up Castle Hill in the hope that the bracing air on the summit would clear his mind. But it was no good. He tried to concentrate on the week ahead. He was to meet Anne tomorrow evening. Now that the days were shortening, the choir members had given up their walks after choir practice. Fortunately, her lodging at the Haighs' farm meant he could call and see her at any time without arousing suspicion.

When he returned to the cottage, he saw a pile of wood that needed chopping and was glad of the excuse to relieve some of his tension. As he swung the hatchet time and time again and felt it bite into the wood, he felt some sort of primitive satisfaction. He never grew tired of the look, smell and texture of freshly cut timber. Even now, as he split the logs, there was pleasure.

Suddenly, a shadow fell across his work. Looking up, he saw Isabel Blezard on horseback, reined in close to the front garden wall. The unwelcome shock hit his stomach. The sun had gone down and Isabel, in riding habit and tall hat tilted to one side, was silhouetted against a darkening sky.

"Good evening, John."

"Good evening, Mrs Blezard."

"'Isabel' please, John." Isabel smiled at him.

"I trust you have enjoyed your travels," said John, striving to appear calmer than he felt.

"Very much. But it is good to see you again, John."

John looked away to escape the suggestive look Isabel was inviting him to share.

"John. I need to speak to you on an important matter. Will you come to the house in about an hour's time? Charlotte is away so we shall not be disturbed." Without giving him time to answer, she went on, "Good! I look forward to seeing you." Wheeling her horse about, she disappeared up the lane.

John washed himself thoroughly under the pump and changed his clothes. Combing his thick wet hair in front of the tiny looking-glass over the kitchen sink, he told his mother he was off to the Blezards.

"No doubt she'll be wanting some more fancy carving done. And 'll like nothing better than having a fine young man to come and do it for her."

If it were only that, thought John gloomily.

When he reached Wood Lane, he was shown into the parlour. Despite his mood, he was impressed by its elegance, from the ornate ceiling rose and fringed lamp-shade to the rich Indian carpet. Both furniture and furnishings looked expensive and new. The elaborately carved arm-chairs were upholstered in plum-coloured velvet, the same fabric showing behind the cut-work front panel of the walnut piano near the window. He allowed himself to note how well his walnut and mahogany fire surround bore comparison with the other pieces in the room.

He was standing with his back to the piano when, with a rustle of silk, Isabel entered and closed the door behind her. She was wearing yet another outfit, this time of a deep mauve colour. A matching artificial flower pinned her dark hair up at one side. She indicated that John should sit down but he remained standing. She herself stood behind a chair with her fingers resting lightly on its back, but then moved to take up another graceful pose elsewhere. To show herself off to advantage, thought John, simultaneously admitting that she succeeded.

"John. This is very difficult for me..."

He did not answer.

"We may not let the world see it but we are lonely people, I a widow and you a widower. Neither of us expected to lose our loved one in so short a time and so cruelly."

John was slightly annoyed. He did not think their situations were very similar. He was sorry that George Blezard had died. Who could not be? But the man was in his fifties, was known to have money worries and to drink heavily To compare his death with that of Molly, not yet nineteen and six months with child! He bridled as Isabel's suggestion of equality sank in.

But she had more to say.

"So it was hardly surprising that the situation in which we found ourselves last May should have occurred. Oh!" Here Isabel became more agitated. "Oh John! I was so lonely! And when you held me in your arms, I felt that loneliness disappear! I trust and hope you felt the same!"

John was speechless. How could he possibly say what he really felt – that he wished the whole episode had never happened? And that it had meant nothing, save for physical relief?

"Going away to London, and to Paris, gave me time to consider, to give thought to my, to our, future." She looked at him beseechingly, the lustrous dark eyes wide open and appealing. "I have always thought you a fine man, John, a very fine man in every way."

John felt himself go red. Without a pause, Isabel moved to the fireplace where she stretched out her arms so that she touched the carved edges of the mantelpiece delicately, even caressingly, with her finger-tips. Then she turned slightly and, looking over her shoulder at him, said, "John. I have to tell you that I am with child."

The softly spoken words were like a thunderbolt. John heard himself say, out of a choked throat, "Can you be mistaken?"

"No," said Isabel, turning fully and pressing her hands against her waist. "No, a woman knows. And it is over three months since that night."

John felt as though he had been physically struck. He did not know what message his face conveyed but Isabel's response suggested it was not the one she wanted.

"Do you not believe me? Is that it? Do you think I am some servant girl telling a lie to entrap a husband?" She looked round the room, wildly. "If there were a Bible here, I would swear on it." She pulled a handkerchief from her sleeve and pressed it to her eyes.

Unconsciously, John took a step towards her. She looked up.

"Think of my dishonour, John. If I were to bear a child. Now. Without a husband."

John's brain was whirling. He wanted to suggest she went away, where no-one knew her, but was aware, even as he thought of it, that his impulse was cowardly. As he wondered what to say, she went on.

"I think you will agree that it would be best if we were to marry soon."

He was silent, dumb with horror. Marriage! To this woman! When he had only just found the love of his life, Anne Graham! How could he tell her he was to marry Isabel Blezard? And why? He felt sick with shame. Then he heard Isabel say, in a voice of amazing calmness,

"You could perhaps begin calling at the house, to make a show of courtship."

He did not, could not, speak but simply stared at this woman who was tearing his life to pieces as if it was the easiest thing in the world to do.

"I do not mean to sound cold," she purred. Crossing the space between them, she put her arms round his neck. He caught the smell of sweat and perfume intermingled as she brought her body so close to his that the front of her skirt billowed between his legs.

"I hope it will not be difficult for us to love one another."

She was so close now that he could see the tiny bloodshot veins in her eyes and the faint suggestion of dark hair on her upper lip. He fought down a wave of revulsion that rose in him.

She must have sensed his reaction because she released him and stepped back. Looking down rather than at him, she said softly, "There is a child to be thought of, John, a child."

He was trapped. A child! Isabel could not know the depth of his grief at the loss of the baby Molly was carrying when she died. She could not because he could hardly bear to contemplate it himself. How was he to reconcile this feeling with his love for Anne?

She was waiting for him to speak. Eventually he managed to, although the voice sounded odd, as if it were not his.

"Very well. We will speak of this later."

"Thank you, John. I vow you will not regret it."

She gave him a swift, light kiss on the cheek and moved away to the door, opening it and letting him pass in front of her. There being no maid in sight, she opened the heavy front door with its etched glass panels and John slipped out into the night.

Halfway up Longley Lane, he was forced to stop, gasping, and realised he had been holding his breath since leaving the Blezard house. Taking great gulps of air, he staggered on, only regaining calm when he reached level ground.

The wind was blowing hard as he made his way home. He was grateful for it. Its noise and the buffeting it gave him went a long way towards blotting out thoughts he could not face up to.

Back home, he lay awake for most of the night, turning the dreadful revelations of the evening over and over in his mind. He knew of young men who, in similar circumstances, had simply fled from the area. But his sense of honour would not allow him to do that. No, there was no escape. He must face the consequences although it would break his heart to do so. And perhaps, Anne's too. For the first time, the thought of meeting her, his beloved Anne, the next day filled him with dread.

After tea, Anne set off, to meet John as arranged. There was a spot among the trees in the Woodsome valley which was 'their place' and her step was light as she made her way there. Slipping through a stile, one made of two large stone slabs leaning at an angle like giant, splayed front teeth, she saw a young couple ahead of her who staggered and laughed as they clasped each other round the waist. They veered off the path, down towards the wood.

Tonight she would tell him of the proposed school venture. It was still only sketchy but she felt very hopeful that it would go ahead as planned Everything – the people, the expertise, the money and now the house seemed to be coming together. It should be congenial work, if she obtained the position, and she would no doubt learn much from Mrs Shaw. And she would still be in the neighbourhood not far from the Haighs, from Charlotte and her beloved John.

Her heart lifted as she spied the familiar figure approaching through the trees. But as he came nearer, she could see by his face and his demeanour that something was amiss.

"John! What is it?"

He stayed where he was instead of sweeping her up into his arms as he usually did. The expression on his face was grim. All Anne could think of to explain his look was a family tragedy.

"What is wrong? Tell me!"

He looked at her for a moment, his face full of misery, and then turned away, unable to meet her eyes.

"I am," he replied, at last, his voice thick with emotion. "I have done wrong and I am ashamed of it."

She stared at him, stunned. He took a deep breath and went on, forcing the words out. "I have done wrong in letting you think - in promising -." He stopped. "We cannot be betrothed, married. I have been reminded of a previous commitment to someone else."

"Someone else?" cried Anne, thunderstruck. "But who?"

He looked down and then to one side, shame-faced.

"To Isabel Blezard."

"Isabel Blezard!" They were the last words Anne expected to hear.

"Yes," said John. He looked at her now, his face tense and haunted. "But...I don't understand," said Anne, tears welling up inside her. "I know. I can only say that I am deeply, deeply sorry." "But when...?" she began. He hung his head in obvious misery and did not answer. Anne was full of questions but she could see, painful as it was to admit it, that he wanted to go.

There was no opportunity to ask questions, however, for at that moment a group of young people could be heard in the distance. Their voices and laughter grew louder as they approached. They seemed to be making for the very spot where John and Anne were standing.

"Do not say any more," Anne said, with more calmness than she felt. "I know you must have good reason to speak as you do. We will talk later." Suddenly pity for herself threatened to engulf her. She had to get away. If she stayed any longer, she knew she would not be able to control the great sobs of anguished disappointment which were rising within her.

She turned hastily and blundered sideways, scratching her face on some twigs as she did so. Recovering her balance, she began walking as fast as she could. Crossing the fields in haste, she came to the stile and instead of turning sideways to slip through it, she let herself fall against the stone slabs, gripping them as great sobs burst from her. Wiping her eyes on her skirt, she took several deep breaths and walked back to the Haigh farm at a steady pace.

When she opened the door, she saw the Haighs clustered together near an oil lamp, examining photographs by its light. Anne was glad of the protection given her by the comparative darkness at the edge of the room.

Hannah looked up immediately.

"I'll be putting supper out in a minute, Anne. Just as soon as I've looked at these pictures of our Matthew and his family, with the new baby."

"No, no, thank you, Hannah. I think I'll go straight to bed."

There was nothing unusual about this and Anne was able to make her escape upstairs easily.

In bed, she went over and over the conversation she had just had with John. It made no more sense now than it did then. The problem was time. When had John had time to become close to Isabel, in a courtship sense? True, Anne had seen nothing of him during the months immediately following Molly's death but she believed he had been stunned with grief, merely working and walking until he dropped. Surely, there could not have been any earlier promise to Isabel?

A dreadful possibility presented itself: that John, since joining the choir, had merely been trifling with her, while Isabel was away. It fitted, in terms of timing and opportunity, but the very notion appalled her. Could she have been so wrong about him?

At last, she came to see there was no end to her theorising; it only led her into unhappy confusion. Accept the fact, she told herself. He is promised to another. But her mind would not be still. To Isabel Blezard? Who would bleed him dry, both in money and feeling?

A sudden bout of passionate crying overtook her, leaving her quietened. When Rachel came up to bed, she lay still and pretended to be asleep. It seemed an eternity before the sky grew light and the sounds of the morning allowed her to rise.

If Hannah noticed Anne's pale face and puffy eyes next morning, she did not say anything. Eli and Ben were already at work. After sipping some tea and eating a little of the porridge which Hannah considerately placed in front of her, Anne pulled herself together and told her of the brief visit to Northfield House. Charlotte was to call for her later that day when they would be able to go inside and make further plans.

Rain fell steadily all morning with no sign of a break in the grey sky. It was so dark in the little parlour that Hannah insisted on lighting a lamp so that Anne could see to read more easily. Even with the illumination, she could not concentrate for more than a few minutes at a time. Instead, the details of yesterday's meeting with John returned again and again. Or rather, they failed to do. She found she could not remember all he had said, if indeed he had said much. All she could recall were the words "commitment" and "Isabel Blezard". What she did remember was the dreadful expression on his face, as terrible as the gaunt look of shock he had borne in the weeks after Molly's death. She was in agony until she could find out more.

She had never been happier to see Charlotte although she knew it was for a selfish reason, that of welcome distraction from the torment of her own mind. Charlotte now had the key to Northfield House for the afternoon and a list of what she thought would need to be done before it was ready for use as a school for girls.

They let themselves into the entrance hall and stood in the finely-proportioned hallway with its panelled walls and fine ceiling mouldings. All the doors were open, all the rooms completely empty. The sense of abandonment made it feel desolate to Anne.

"It seems cheerless," she said, shivering.

"Not really," Charlotte declared. "Bit of sunlight and it'll be quite different."

Anne gazed upward.

"Perhaps a surveyor should inspect it?" she asked gloomily. There was, as expected, a finely-turned staircase from ground to first floor with a slender hand-rail but there was more than a suspicion of rot in the banisters which rocked alarmingly under pressure.

"I think Mr and Mrs Shaw have already arranged that. But the floors seem in good shape. What do you think?"

The polished wood strip flooring was attractive and looked free of any damage.

"A few rugs here and there should be all that would be necessary," Charlotte continued, moving purposefully around the ground floor. "And these rooms, the schoolrooms, wouldn't need curtains. These look to be in working order." She touched one of the shutters which framed the long windows. "And a cook should be able to cater for a dozen or so people here. What do you think ?"

They were now standing in the kitchen with its new-ish looking range.

"Oh yes," said Anne. She shivered again. Houses that had stood empty for a while always seemed so cold and clammy.

Charlotte did not notice. Ticking points off on her list, she looked down at the fob watch pinned to a breast pocket.

"I have to go down to Dalton for a while, Anne. There's a business I particularly want to visit. I shan't be much more than an hour, I think. Do you mind staying here while I take the carriage? Could you be thinking about the cupboards and furniture we should need? And measure the rooms upstairs so we can see how many boarders we could fit in comfortably?" She handed Anne the pad, pencil and measure and was gone.

Realising what light there was would soon be fading, Anne did as she was told. She climbed the stairs cautiously without touching the shaky hand rail and measured the upstairs rooms. The house was symmetrical, like so many built early in the century. Downstairs there were four square rooms, two each side of the central hall and upstairs the same, with the addition of a small room over the entrance which could hold just one bed. Would that be for one special boarder? Or would it be hers? The single bedroom of Anne Graham, spinster, her life contained within these walls?

Time passed slowly. Rain beat against the windows so fiercely that it was impossible to see beyond the garden. She went across the landing into the rooms whose windows looked the other way into the village street. There was little to see save for a few drenched folk hurrying along, heads down. One or two looked up and seemed to notice her at the window as they passed.

There was nothing to do but await Charlotte's return. Anne let herself slide down the bedroom wall until she was sitting with her back pressed against it, her legs stretched out, her boots sticking up at right angles. Like a doll, she thought, with wry amusement. But the comparison she had thought of annoyed her. She was not like a doll, at the mercy of other people's wishes. She had to admit she was disappointed, painfully so, at the loss of the hoped-for future with John Brook but she was no love-lorn maiden, ready to die of a broken heart because she had been rejected by a man. No, indeed. She would gain experience here as a teacher of older girls, if she could, and with a good reference, to join the glowing one written by Frederick Thorpe, she would start afresh somewhere else in England.

But then the thought of John and of how ecstatically happy they had been together swept over her. Reasoning was all very well but it was powerless to withstand the painful emotions now overwhelming her. She drew up her knees, put her head down and sobbed her heart out.

Then a welcome sound from downstairs, the door opening and closing. Scrambling to her feet, Anne smoothed her skirts down and crossed the landing to the top of the stairs.

"Charlotte? Is that you?"

But it was not Charlotte. It was a young man in dark, wet clothing and a cap which he removed, shaking the rain off it. He lifted his head and Anne recognised the face of her cousin, Ned Stott.

"Ned! What are you doing here?"

"I might say t'same to you," he replied, starting to mount the stairs. His heavy clogs sounded loud on the bare steps.

Anne backed away. She was not frightened but did not relish the prospect of being alone with Ned Stott in an empty house.

"I'm measuring up. See!" she said, picking up Charlotte's lists and holding them defensively against her chest.

Ned did not answer. When he reached the half-landing, he turned, his mouth hanging open in a loose grin. He kept on coming.

Anne could see a grey mark across his forehead made by the cap and as he came closer, his broken teeth between the dark lips.

"Why dost tha think o' teaching?" he asked gruffly. "Hasta niver thought o' being a farmer's wife?" He kept climbing the stairs, lifting his hands in front of him. Anne saw that they were rough and scored with scabs and scars.

For a moment, Anne did not move, or think of moving. Then, as Ned reached the top step, she remembered his clumsy attempt at wooing in the blackberry field and started to back away.

It was a mistake. A light gleamed in Ned's eyes as if her resistance thrilled him and he lunged forward, his hands reaching out for her shoulders. Anne sprang to one side, dropping the sheets of paper which scattered in all directions. She thought she was fast enough to escape him but he threw himself after her, catching her round the knees and bringing her crashing to the floor. And then, horrible! He was on top of her, holding her wrists in each hand and pressing them flat above her head. His mouth, wet with saliva, came close to hers. For the first time, she smelt his beery breath.

"Tha's heard tell o' kissing cousins," he said thickly, his face nearly touching hers. Just as he tried to kiss her, she jerked her head violently sideways to avoid him. For answer, he pulled her wrists together and leant heavily on them with one arm. The other hand grasped her jaw and held her still while he kissed her with open mouth.

She thought she would choke or be sick. But he was not finished. Still pinning her arms above her head with his left arm, he reached down with the other hand and groped under her skirts, pulling them up as far as they would go. To her horror, he began to pull at the top of his trousers and she became aware of the hardness of his body on hers. Finding her face free, she screamed as loudly as she could, the scream merging with the sound of boots running up the stairs.

All at once Ned's weight was off her and there was another man on top of him, pulling him over and thumping him in the face. It was John, his face livid with anger, his knuckles smeared with Ned's blood.

But Ned was not easily beaten. He was shorter than John but wiry and used to scrapping. He gave John a quick punch in the stomach and as John's head came down, smashed his fist against his mouth.

With a roar, John lunged at Ned and seizing him by the shoulders, thrust him backwards. As Ned stumbled, John delivered a powerful blow to his jaw, sending the younger man hurtling backwards down the stairs. Coming to a halt on the half landing, Ned tried to get up but John was on him again and grasping his collar, threw him down the next flight. There was a cracking of wood as the banisters gave way and Ned slithered to a stop on the hall floor.

My God! He's killed him, thought Anne. Ned lay motionless for a moment and then slowly got to his knees, felt round for his cap, pulled himself upright and with a baleful glance up the stairs, opened the door and staggered out.

Anne and John descended the stairs slowly, sinking down onto the bottom step when they reached it. John touched his face gingerly.

"Well, I can't be sure but I think you'll need some new banisters," he said.

Whether they began at the same time, or one started the other off, it was impossible to say but within seconds, they were both laughing hysterically. Tears were coursing down Anne's cheeks as she put her arms round John very carefully so as not to press his cut mouth. For a moment they clung together as their laughing sobs died away.

John's top lip was split in one place and oozing blood. Rising, Anne went to the kitchen sink and ran cold water onto the hem of her petticoat.

Returning to John's side on the stair, she dabbed his mouth very gently, his blood staining the white cotton until, gradually, it stopped.

"This is the second time you've saved me," Anne said. For answer, he looked into her eyes, a look more eloquent than any words. She took his right hand in both of hers. Its warmth seemed to make them one flesh.

"John. You must tell me. Do you love Isabel Blezard?"

He looked back into her eyes, his gaze unflinching.

"No."

"Then why are you promised to her?"

"Because we lay together one night last May and now she says she is with child."

So that was it! One night! Before he had come back into Anne's life when he joined the choir. Anne looked full at him. All her love, her pain, her understanding, was in that look. Feeling her eyes fill with tears, she leant forward and kissed him very gently on his wounded mouth, once, and then again.

"How shall we bear it?" he asked, tears now spilling over.

"I don't know," said Anne, "but we will."

They sat holding hands for a few minutes longer, her head on his shoulder, the taste of his blood on her lips. Eventually they stirred and wiped their eyes. John spoke first.

"I'll kill that Ned Stott."

"No, no, John! Leave it be. It would only make matters worse. Please!"

He said nothing but she felt he would do as she asked. She went on.

"I wonder how he knew I was here?"

"Could he, or one of his cronies, have seen you?"

Anne remembered the passers-by in the village street.

"Yes. That must have been it. More to the point, what brought you?"

"Charlotte called in. About half an hour ago. Said you were here and would I like to advise on joinery work. So I cleared away, locked up and walked on here. Seems I arrived just in time."

"You did, John. No doubt about it." Anne shuddered.

Downstairs, a door opened and Charlotte came in. She looked stunned at the sight of the lower section of the banisters lying on the hall floor.

"What happened?"

"An unwelcome visitor. My cousin Ned Stott," said Anne.

"Did he do that, to the banisters?" Charlotte asked.

"Yes, in a way. But I don't think we can charge him. They were already rotten."

Charlotte looked at them both then, sitting close to one another on the stairs.

"John looks like he should be at home. With a cold compress on his face."

They both stood up, Anne surprised at how shaky she felt, John needing little persuasion to be taken home in the Blezard carriage.

Soon they were turning down Sharp Lane on the way to the Brook cottage. Anne savoured every moment that she sat close to John, their arms and thighs touching. Then he was gone, hurrying in, against the rain.

The carriage moved on in silence. Charlotte looked as if she was brimming with questions. But she held her tongue, for which Anne was grateful.

This time Hannah did speak.

"Goodness me, Anne! You're as white as a sheet! What ails you, child?" She put her arm across Anne's shoulders. Anne flinched. Unknowingly Hannah had touched her spine which felt bruised all over. One of her elbows was grazed and swollen and in general, she felt as if she had been thrown from a galloping horse. But she did not want to reveal what had happened the day before. No doubt the evidence of the scuffle would now be visible on both men's faces but in Ned's case at least, it would be nothing out of the ordinary. No, she would not mention it. There was enough bad blood between the Haighs and the Stotts already. No need to add to it.

"I fell. Down some stairs," she said lamely.

Hannah's blue eyes looked at her then, as if divining an honestly-meant falsehood.

"Oh dear. Mind you take it easy today then."

It was better weather than they had had for some time. At Hannah's insistence, Anne sat out for a while, wrapped in a warm shawl, in a sheltered spot where Hannah had cultivated a little garden. There were a few late geraniums and a flourishing clump of Michaelmas daisies which caught the morning sun.

There was no reason to doubt what John had told her. One night in May and now Isabel was expecting a child. Such things did happen. Could Isabel be lying? Of course she could. It was a trick as old as the hills, one of the few open to women of all classes in their bid to secure a husband.

Was John the victim of such a plot? Not, she was bound to admit, an innocent victim. She knew there would be many, perhaps even including the devout Haighs, who would think John a sinner and morally bound to put the relationship on a legal, Christian footing. Anne could not be so severe. She did not like what he had done and could not bear to imagine it but she understood how it could have happened. He had taken bereavement so hard that he had seemed unnaturally frozen with grief for months. An unscrupulous woman, using time, place and circumstances to her advantage, could have melted the defences of a man hungry for love, certainly of a man as passionate as Anne believed John to be. She did not doubt that Isabel had both the female charms and the confidence to use them. Perhaps George Blezard's wife had wanted John ever since she had met him, despite the fact that he was betrothed and about to marry another. Anne knew that if this was wrong, then she too was a sinner.

It would be dreadfully painful to see John and Isabel once they were married and presumably living in Wood Lane. How would she bear it? While she remained at the Haighs' farm nearby, she would be in danger of seeing him there where he was received like one of the family. Therefore, Anne said to herself, standing up and taking in deep breaths of the fresh, hillside air, it is good that I shall be living, I hope, in a school where I shall be fully engrossed in purposeful and interesting work. And if I don't gain the position, I will move away – a long way away. With that in mind, she rose and went indoors more cheerfully than she had come out.

That evening, she noticed Rachel observing her and when they were alone, she spoke.

"Forgive me, Anne, if I'm prying into matters that don't concern me but you've seemed low in spirits just lately. Before that, Mother and

I were hoping that you and John were coming to an understanding. We hoped you would, for both your sakes. You seemed so happy together."

There was silence. As Anne did not reply, she spoke again.

"I'm sorry, Anne, if I have gone too far. I just – "

"No, no," replied Anne, with an effort. "You are quite right – in everything you say." Why should she not unburden herself to Rachel, Rachel who felt like a sister? Anne sat up in bed and clasped her knees with both arms.

"Soon after our trip to Lake Windermere, we confessed our love for one another. We agreed to marry in the spring so that a full year would have passed since Molly's death. And we also thought it right to delay the announcement of our betrothal for the same reason. I suppose we were foolish to think that no-one would notice anything. But then something happened. Isabel Blezard returned."

"Isabel Blezard! What has she got to do with it?"

"Exactly. That was my reaction too. But it seems that one night in May, she and John met by chance in the woods below Castle Hill and – " Anne stopped. She did not know which words to use. She decided not to use any. "As a result, Isabel now says she is expecting John's child. Three months gone."

"Hmm." Rachel made a sound.

"Are you shocked?"

"No. Not in the circumstances. I'm sorry rather than shocked. Knowing what I do of Isabel Blezard, which, I confess, is mainly through gossip, I would guess that it was all deliberately planned by her. In fact, I could almost swear it was."

"How can you be so sure?"

"Because she's a scheming woman and out for what she can get. Everyone could see that was why she married George Blezard, except the poor man himself. And Matthew once saw her..."

"When? Why do you stop?"

"Because it's ugly gossip and I feel ashamed to be repeating it. I never would have except that it seems relevant, now. Some time last year, Matthew was at an inn on the Wakefield Road, when he saw Frederick Thorpe arrive and go in by the back stairs, where they have private rooms. A few minutes later, he saw Isabel Blezard arrive, alone, on horseback, and go up the same stairs. It doesn't prove anything, of course, but such assignations usually mean one thing."

"Goodness! Frederick Thorpe!" Anne was stunned but on reflection, became less so. Of all the men in Isabel's circle, Thorpe was the most attractive and obviously had an eye for ladies. However, she would have said he paid more attention to Jemima Broomfield, who was very pretty, than to Isabel.

"I feel stupidly naive," she said.

"No, you're not," protested Rachel. "Well, naive possibly. But not stupid. My opinion is that Isabel is lying. She'll hold John to his word long enough to get what she wants from him and then have a convenient miscarriage."

"Do you think she could actually carry that off?"

"I've no doubt at all," replied Rachel drily. "If need be, she'd get Dr Littlewood to back her up. He'll do anything for money. "Owt for brass" as we say."

"So what should I do? Speak to John right away?"

"Yes, I would. Tell him to delay everything. Don't let Isabel announce their betrothal. It's not the same as being wed but it tends to be seen as binding. Another couple of months and it'll be clear whether Isabel is lying or not."

CHAPTER THIRTEEN

Charlotte was reading in the library, so deeply engrossed that Bella, the new parlour-maid, had to speak to her twice.

"Shall I clear away the tea things, Miss?"

"What? Oh, yes please. Is it six o'clock already? I must get changed."

At that moment, the front door opened and was then slammed shut.

"Mrs Drew! Mrs Drew!"

At the sound of Isabel's raised voice, Charlotte nodded to the maid to leave. Abandoning the tea-tray, the girl turned pale and fled. Charlotte sighed. This was the evening when Isabel usually went to the Broomfields; her summoning of the housekeeper suggested a change of plan. Perhaps she and Anne were not to have the house to themselves after all.

The library door was slammed open so hard that it bounced back on its hinges.

"So! You're here," scowled Isabel, pulling off her bonnet and cape and throwing them on a chair. Charlotte's heart sank. She knew Isabel in this mood. Something, someone, had thwarted or angered her and now she would react by venting her bad temper on all around her. There was no point in asking her what was wrong; it would emerge any moment now.

Isabel was having difficulty removing her left glove. It was stuck, half inside out, on her hand. Pulling at the cuff so fiercely that the fine leather ripped, she flung it into the hearth, sending the other glove after it.

"Ellen Thorpe has only just told me. She's going to London again, tomorrow. And taking Jemima Broomfield with her."

So that was it.

"I told them how fortunate it was, that it was tomorrow that they were leaving. Then they would not miss my supper party."

"What supper party?"

"The one I'm giving tonight. Quite intimate. Only about a dozen people."

"Do the staff know?"

"They will when I tell them," retorted Isabel sharply.

"But – " said Charlotte, and stopped, aware that opposition only made Isabel more enraged.

Her stepmother lifted her chin and said mockingly, "Don't worry. You're invited!" With that, she swept out of the room and along the corridor to the servants' quarters.

As Charlotte put away her books and picked up the bonnet and cape, she could hear Isabel shouting at the back of the house. With an air of resignation, she went upstairs to her room.

Mrs Drew did not respond well to being shouted at. She raised her eyebrows and tried to maintain the air of implacable calm that was her habitual mode.

"You must know, Madam, that Miss Charlotte has invited Miss Graham for dinner this evening. An arrangement made some time ago."

"Pah! You can forget about that. This takes precedence. About a dozen people. Arriving from eight o'clock. Light refreshments – savouries and sweet stuff. Sherry first. Wine. The best we have."

"But tonight, madam! The one evening when we're short-staffed, when you are usually out for dinner. I'm not sure we have enough food in the house to serve so many. Could you not postpone it?"

"No, I could not!" Isabel's temper flared. "I employ you to carry out my wishes, not question my plans!"

"It's going to be very difficult for Cook. The first Mrs Blezard always gave us ample warning – "

"I don't want to hear about Mrs Blezard! *I* am Mrs Blezard and you will do as I say! I'm tired of hearing about your former employer. Those days are past – and so are you! I have never known servants so insolent! You will leave my employment at the end of the week and unless you do as I say, you will go without a reference. Now get on with your work!"

Charlotte heard the rush of Isabel's footsteps up the stairs, along the landing and then into her bedroom. Past experience told her that her stepmother would be there for at least an hour, especially as the maid who usually dressed her hair was not here this evening.

Anne would be arriving soon. It was too late to put her off and in any case, she would be glad of her company. Unless Anne wished to join the party, they could amuse themselves perfectly well in the library.

Isabel had said not a word about the destruction of her workroom. Not that this was unusual; she did not apologise to anyone, ever. Following the bonfire, there had been a day or two of peace, as if a boil had been lanced. Charlotte was prepared to ignore the matter. She hated arguments, having grown-up without ever experiencing them. If she could smooth away domestic difficulties, she would.

When she entered the kitchen, after knocking and being told to come in, she sensed that Cook had reacted to the late order for party catering in much the same way as Mrs Drew. Both women were sitting down, drinking what looked like sherry. Jessie Lodge hovered close by, in charge of the bottle.

"Mrs Drew, Mrs Burton. I'm sorry you've had so little notice for this supper party. There is of course no need to serve dinner for myself and Miss Graham. We will make do with what you are preparing for the other guests."

The two older women appeared somewhat mollified. The cook answered.

"Thank you, Miss Charlotte. I just wish Mrs Blezard was as considerate as you. We do our best."

"I know you do. My father thought himself very fortunate to have such grand folk working for him."

Mrs Burton stood up and tightened her apron strings.

"There weren't many like Mr Blezard. Don't worry, Miss Charlotte. I'll see what I can do."

"Thank you, Mrs Burton. I'm most grateful. Mrs Drew. Jessie."

Charlotte withdrew, pleased to see the cook set to work but less hopeful about Mrs Drew who looked as if she had already had more drink than was good for her.

When Anne knocked at the front door, Charlotte opened it quickly.

"Come in, do!" As she took Anne's cloak, she went on. "There's a minor crisis, I'm afraid. Isabel has ordered a last-minute supper party. I hope this is all right with you. I've cancelled our dinner and said we'll make do with the refreshments they're making."

"Of course! I understand," said Anne, although she was dismayed to learn that Isabel was at home. She had accepted Charlotte's invitation in the belief that this was Isabel's night out. "What's the reason for this party?"

Charlotte shrugged.

"It's something to do with Ellen Thorpe going off to London tomorrow and taking someone else with her this time. Jemima Broomfield. Isabel only found out today."

"And how has Isabel reacted to that?"

Charlotte raised her eyebrows.

"How do you think? Annoyed. Jealous. But everything should be all right if this evening is a success. She has a beautiful new dress she hasn't worn yet. I think she'd been keeping it for the next trip to London. A watered silk with beaded fringing. I expect she'll wear that. If you don't mind, Anne, I'll go up and change now, before anyone arrives. I think we may have to check how preparations are going on in the kitchen. I'm rather worried about Mrs Drew who seemed not to be herself. You'll be all right here, won't you?" She opened the library door for Anne to enter.

"Yes, of course. You go and get ready."

Anne was relieved. The library would be a safe haven. The glass-fronted mahogany bookcases were full of books, all brand-new and in toning leather bindings. Whether Isabel had bought them as part and parcel of the furnishings or not, they were classic works which made Anne's eyes light up as she studied their titles.

From the library, one could see the drive and front gate and soon the crunch of carriage wheels on gravel attracted Anne's attention. It was the first of the guests arriving, Seth and Jemima Broomfield. After helping his young wife down from the carriage, which involved some flattening and manoeuvring of her full, cherry-red skirt, Broomfield, in tall hat and a cloak over his dress suit, lifted the brass knocker and let it drop. No maid appeared so he knocked again. Anne was just wondering whether to fetch a maid or answer it herself when Charlotte came hurrying down the stairs.

"I think they must all be busy. It's all right, Anne. I'll answer it."

Jemima Broomfield was as pretty as Anne remembered from seeing her at Dartmouth Hall. Her husband, her elder by about fifteen years, looked at the young woman with a mixture of pride and uncertainty.

Fortunately, as Charlotte showed them into the parlour, Bella came through the servants' door, bearing a tray of filled wine-glasses. Charlotte then ran upstairs to alert Isabel of her guests' arrival.

Anne hoped she could now retreat into the library but the Thorpes, finding the front door open, came in, catching sight of her before she could do so.

"My dear Miss Graham! How are you? Well, I hope?"

Frederick Thorpe's charm was unfailing. Ellen Thorpe, in her favourite pale blue, looked rather nervous. As well she might, thought Anne, if she had had a taste of Isabel's displeasure.

"Very well, thank you, Mr Thorpe. I hope you and Mrs Thorpe are the same?"

Ellen Thorpe managed a weak smile.

"Indeed."

"I trust Master Edward and Miss Georgina are well too?"

"Yes, they are," replied Thorpe. "Edward found his new school a little restrictive after the freedom of his own schoolroom but he has settled down and is coping well with the level of study required. Georgina will begin at her school in Edgerton in the New Year."

They moved on and into the parlour, along with the rest of the guests who now arrived – the Littlewoods and their sour-faced daughter and two more couples whom Anne had not seen before. Isabel came sailing down the stairs, her entrance provoking gasps of admiration.

"Just look at the belt!" enthused Jemima Broomfield. "With those three long basques at the back! Is it boned, Isabel? I've never seen one like that before!"

"It's called a Swiss belt. Ellen, you'll have seen one before in London, I expect?"

Ellen agreed.

"Oh yes, certainly. In London. But not here, not in the north."

Isabel's smile to Jemima was sweetly triumphant.

Anne at last saw a chance of escaping into the library when, to her surprise, recalling their last encounter, Isabel moved close to her. The purpose of her communication became instantly clear.

"Where is Mrs Drew? And Charlotte? And the food? Find out!" she hissed.

Anne obliged by going into the kitchen where an atmosphere of crisis could be sensed. Charlotte was tucking Jessie's hair into an organdie cap. The girl, in someone else's black dress, looked extremely pleased with herself.

"Now Jessie," said Charlotte. "Think what you're doing. Wait politely with your tray near the guests until they see the food and help themselves. Don't, I repeat don't, speak to them."

"Aye, Miss," replied Jessie and shot out of the kitchen with her tray as if she had been fired from a gun.

Charlotte sighed.

"What's wrong?" asked Anne. "Is it the food?"

"No," said Charlotte, indicating Mrs Burton deftly arranging small savouries on a plate. "No, we're all right there. But I've had to use Jessie, as you see, because Mrs Drew is – well, I'm afraid to say, incapable."

"Incapable?" It was the last word that came to mind regarding the sphinx-like Mrs Drew.

"Yes. We've told her to go to bed. That's why Jessie's helping. No parlour maid, as you can see. But she'll just have to do."

Charlotte continued pouring out wine as she spoke. At that moment, there was another knock at the front door, only just audible above the sound of voices in the parlour.

"Shall I – ?" said Anne.

"Oh please, would you?"

It was hard to say who was the most startled, Anne or John. He stood on the doorstep, tall, handsome, the jacket collar of his best suit turned up, his dark hair gleaming under the light. The cut on his top lip was almost healed. Anne's heart lurched and his face flushed.

"Anne! I didn't expect to see you here!"

"Charlotte invited me last week. Not Isabel. It's the night she usually goes out. I think it's a spur-of-the-moment party."

"So I gather," he said, stepping over the threshold and turning his collar back. "She left a note for me, asking me to come. I found it when I got home."

"Have you seen her recently? To speak to?"

John understood her.

"Yes. I spoke to her yesterday. She came into the shop. I told her there could be no announcement of betrothal, let alone marriage, until a longer period of mourning had passed. For George Blezard as well as Molly. Not yet, I said."

Anne's spirits lifted. It felt like a reprieve. Time, as Rachel had said, would tell whether Isabel was lying or not. He moved towards her and took both her hands in his, dropping them as Grace Littlewood emerged from the parlour, swaying slightly.

"John! John Brook! Do come in, do!"

She slipped her arm through his and giggled. Throwing Anne an expressive look, he allowed himself to be drawn into the company.

The party sounded to be going well. Anne could hear Dr Littlewood's gruff voice and Ellen Thorpe's shrill laugh amidst the buzz of chatter. Wondering at Charlotte's non-appearance, she went through to the kitchen once more.

Mrs Drew was sitting on a chair, with Charlotte and the cook restraining her by holding an arm each. Charlotte was speaking loudly and clearly as if she were repeating something she had already said.

"We will look together in the morning, Mrs Drew. I don't want to be opening the safe now, not when the house is full of company."

"Mr Blezard said I could keep my savings there. And my valuables."

Charlotte raised her eyebrows at Anne as if to say "She's rambling". But Mrs Drew wasn't rambling. It was rather that the combination of sherry and dismissal had removed her characteristic reserve.

"I'm just saying," said Mrs Drew, trying to fix her eyes steadily on Charlotte's face, "I'm just saying it's not the money. I know how much should be there. It's the brooch. My grandmother's. Rubies and pearls set in gold. I don't want *her* getting her hands on it. I know what she is." As no response came, she went further.

"She's a liar and a cheat and doesn't care what she does to get what she wants."

The cook had broken away to replenish a tray of refreshments.

Charlotte released Mrs Drew's other arm. She and Anne stood looking down at the housekeeper whose usually neatly-braided black hair had tumbled out of its hairpins on one side and whose face was pink and sweating. There was much more she wanted to say.

"That time – that time in January when we had the snow, when Molly Brook stayed two nights..."

What the woman told was no ordinary tale. It was more like a piece of evidence in a court of law by a crucial witness. The monologue went on and on, transfixing the listeners who stood appalled at what they were hearing : a story of spite and cruelty, deliberately willed against an innocent young woman and her unborn child, the whole episode compounded and concealed by lies. The price of Mrs Drew's silence had been her secure position as housekeeper. Now the contract was broken, on both sides. No-one spoke when she finished. Anne was stunned.

"I see," said Charlotte. Anne was amazed at her calmness. "I think, Mrs Drew, that you had best go to bed. You and I will sort this out in the morning."

She took the housekeeper by the arm and edged her out of the kitchen and along the corridor to her room. A few minutes later, she returned.

Anne felt as though she were in a trance. She had picked up a tea towel and had been unthinkingly polishing some fresh glasses that stood on a tray, ready to be taken into the parlour. Now she put the glass down in case she crushed it in the anger which was rising in her. If it was the last thing she did, she would drive a wedge between Isabel Blezard and her beloved John. Nothing, nothing was going to stop her now.

At that moment, the door to the kitchen swung back to reveal an excited Jessie and a slightly more relaxed Bella.

"Champagne! Both bottles!" declared Jessie, giving Bella a shove towards the tray of glasses.

"Champagne?" echoed Charlotte. "What for?"

"Announcement," said Jessie. "I 'eard Mrs Blezard telling Thorpe and Littlewood to open the bottles for her."

"Do you know what this is about?" asked Charlotte.

"Yes," replied Anne grimly. "Or, at least, I think I can guess."

She walked quickly behind the two maids who were returning to the parlour as instructed. Charlotte, hurrying, caught up with her up outside the door.

"What's happening?" she asked.

"Isabel is going to announce her betrothal to John Brook. And I'm going to stop it."

Charlotte looked amazed.

"I didn't know they were – "

"They weren't. Except for one time. She's told John she's expecting his child."

Charlotte stared.

"She can't be."

"Why not?"

"She told Father she couldn't have children. Peritonitis when she was a girl."

The news, true or not, gave a final surge to Anne's determination.

"Right!" she said and opened the door.

The hubbub hit her like a strong gust of wind. There was a sense of people having drunk steadily and long. Anne was aware of flushed faces, of the gleaming silks and jewellery of the women, the dark clothing of the men and of plates and glasses littering the top of the piano. Across the room, distinguished by his silence and sobriety, was John, stuck in a corner, looking extremely uncomfortable.

Anne tried to catch his eye. After a moment she succeeded but reaching him and exchanging words of a confidential nature was another matter.

Suddenly the repeated clinking of a knife on a glass brought quiet. All eyes turned to Frederick Thorpe.

"Ladies and gentlemen, pray silence for Mrs Isabel Blezard. Isabel would like to say a few words."

Standing by the piano, smiling a little, Isabel faced the assembled company.

"Ladies and gentlemen. Friends! Thank you so much for coming tonight. At such short notice." The smile left her face. "All of you here knew my dear, late husband and how much he cared for me." Here she stopped to press the fingertips of her left hand against her lips as if to quell their trembling.

"I know, and so do you, how he would not have wanted me to continue mourning his loss any longer than was necessary."

Anne did not look at Charlotte, close beside her, but heard her intake of breath. Now was the moment to speak or it would be too late.

"Mrs Blezard! I fear you are somewhat premature!" Her voice rang out, clear and harsh.

Shocked, all heads turned to look at Anne.

"Such an announcement needs the consent of both parties. Consent which you have not obtained."

Isabel found her voice.

"How dare you interrupt me? Frederick! Harold!"

She gestured wildly to Thorpe and Dr Littlewood to help her. But they could hardly move for the crush of people, especially since Charlotte had closed the door.

Anne's heart was beating so hard she felt it must show through her bodice.

"There is a time when things are right, Mrs Blezard, and when they are dreadfully wrong. But you were never very clear about time, were you, Mrs Blezard?

"What time was it, for example, when Molly Brook left this house that day in January when she met her death? When the snow was already deep and a blizzard was about to sweep across from the moors? Was it one o'clock as you said? Giving her time to reach home while it was still light and she could see where the deep drifts were? Or was it later, much later, when you had deliberately delayed her, making her work on things that didn't need doing?"

Anne could not stop now. She could feel John's eyes boring into her but there was no going back.

"Isn't it true, Mrs Blezard, that it was actually four o'clock before you let Molly Brook go home?"

There were a number of horrified gasps. No-one moved. Isabel's jaw had dropped open, like a fish.

"Four o'clock. Dark. Too dark to see where she was going. Tired out. And six months with child."

Suddenly Isabel plunged forward, as if to silence Anne with her own hands. Anne spoke even faster, to finish what she had to say, before Isabel could reach her.

"You killed Molly Brook almost as surely as if you had thrust her into the snowdrift yourself!"

There was an outcry at these words, a jumble of shouts of disbelief and cries of "Shame!" Anne felt her arm seized but Charlotte held her secure on the other side. She could have gone on, asserting Isabel's motives, but it was perhaps wiser to leave these things unsaid. Better for John if his name were not mentioned.

She forced herself to look at him now. He looked stricken, white-faced, his dark eyes hollow with shock. Isabel appeared to be fainting. She was being supported by Dr Littlewood and his daughter whose eyes were alight with malicious interest. Slowly, they elbowed their way out of the room and began helping Isabel upstairs.

Ellen Thorpe was making wheezing noises behind her lace handkerchief. Her husband lowered her into a chair and urged her to drink a little wine from his glass. She took a few sips and then got up, leaning heavily on his arm as they left. In the hall, the Broomfields and the other couples were making hasty departures as politely as they could to Charlotte who was doing her best to act like a calm hostess. She despatched Jessie and Bella to the kitchen and then followed them, carrying the two unopened bottles of champagne.

Anne and John were alone in the room. She heard him taking deep gulps of breath and watched as the colour slowly returned to his face. Then he looked at her as if seeing her for the first time after a long absence. She moved towards him and put her hands on his fore-arms.

"Thank God!" he said. "Thank God I heard all this in time. How did you learn of it?"

"Mrs Drew. The housekeeper. Only she and Isabel knew."

"I would have married her. For the sake of the child."

Holding his gaze, Anne spoke quietly.

"There is no child. It was another lie."

The effect on John was instant and transforming. His face seemed to relax as the tension drained away from him.

"Then...then...I am free?"

"Yes, John, it would seem so."

They stood looking at each other as the glorious truth sank in. Deep inside her, Anne had a wonderful, suppressed sense of joy to come. But

John looked as if he had not yet fully recovered from the shock of the disclosures.

Charlotte joined them, flurried but in charge of the situation.

"I've persuaded Isabel to go to bed. Dr Littlewood is giving her something to make her sleep. Oh John! I never dreamt that she had acted so callously towards Molly. What can I say?"

"Nothing, Charlotte. You weren't here. You couldn't have known."

"What will Isabel do now?" asked Anne. "She must become the subject of dreadful gossip. It will be round the village tomorrow. And further afield, I should think."

Charlotte shrugged.

"I don't know. It is up to her. Perhaps she will go to London. She is much happier with that kind of life."

After a pause, Anne said, "I will go now, Charlotte, if that is all right."

Charlotte hugged her.

"Thank you, Anne. For everything you did tonight."

"I hope I was right to do it."

"I will see you tomorrow. About eleven?"

"Yes. Till then."

As Anne walked up the hill, she was glad of John's arm for support, her legs suddenly feeling as if they could not bear her. By the time they reached the Haighs' farm however, she had recovered.

Standing in the moonlight by the farm gate, they kissed each other. Anne lay back against the encircling strength of John's arms, one hand round his waist, the other tenderly stroking the thick silky hair at the back of his neck. How long they stood there embracing she did not know, or care. Eventually, dizzy with desire, they moved slightly apart.

"Am I really free of her?" he asked gruffly. "I hardly dare believe it."

"We must wait and see. If I were Isabel, I would be ashamed to show my face again in the neighbourhood. But then, I'm not."

"When I think of Molly…" He buried his face in Anne's hair, unable to continue.

"Hush! Hush!" she whispered. "Try not to think of it."

"Will I see you tomorrow?" asked John, holding her close once more.

"Yes. About eight? On the hill? I'll be able to tell you of my meeting with Mrs Shaw. Goodnight, John."

The farewells were said but it was some time before they could bear to be parted. At last, they separated and John walked away into the darkness with Anne feeling the sense of loss she always experienced when he left her.

A moment later, Ben came out of the farmhouse.

"Was that John? Has he gone?"

"Yes. Why?"

"A pity. I was going to suggest he went home a different way. A dog-fight's been set up. They keep it quiet but some blabbermouth always lets it out. Don't worry. John's got sense to keep out of trouble. Best go inside. It's coming damp."

John reached the summit of Castle Hill without realising it. The shock of what he had learnt that night made him feel quite sick. It would take time before he could absorb it fully and appreciate his fortunate escape from Isabel Blezard.

The night was very dark, with both moon and stars eclipsed by cloud. In front of him, down in the valley basin of Huddersfield, window-shaped lights glowed here and there in houses and taverns huddled at the feet of the mills and factories. The landscape behind him was even darker, the Woodsome valley thickly wooded, the cottages fewer and more scattered.

He listened to the familiar sounds of the night, the cry of an owl, the far-off barking of a dog and as always up here on this high, exposed place, the soughing of the wind. All at once, a different sound, a muttering. Only when he heard a smothered laugh did he realise that there must be men approaching. Too late for the tavern, they had to be climbing the hill for their own, clandestine purposes.

John strained his ears for more clues. Although the sounds were faint, he sensed that men were approaching the summit on all sides, from Farnley and Honley to his left, from Almondbury village to his right, from the Woodsome valley at his back and creeping up from Huddersfield in front of him. A break in the clouds showed him the answer – a black dog padding along the hill path held tight on a short leash, its back and haunches squat and strong, its thick snout heavily muzzled. Close behind its keeper, a group of rough-looking men trod softly, silent apart from the occasional curse and scuffle as they jostled each other in the darkness.

John thought quickly. To leave the summit now meant he would surely meet the spectators coming up. It had also become lighter, with the moon free of clouds. Below him, a grassy ditch curved round the base of the summit, like a narrow, deeply-gouged moat, the remnant of some long-gone fortification. Silently he slipped down into it, some ten feet deep, seeking its shelter until it was safe to leave. He judged that nothing would distract the men once the snarling, bloody encounter flared in the darkness.

He could not know that this ditch had served, in the past, as a hiding-place for the police constables. Nor that three thugs would take it upon themselves to scout out the territory before their sport began. There was a sudden roar as he was grabbed round the shoulders by unseen hands.

"Here's one on 'em!" shouted the stranger, pulling him round violently to face the other two. One of them pushed his face close to John's.

"Let's give 'im a good thumping and throw 'im down t' banking."

"Wait on," said another, familiar voice. The third youth stepped forward, his mouth open in a broken-toothed leer. "Why! It's John Brook! Gives me chance to get mi own back. Just 'old 'im still."

Ned Stott swung his fist at John's face so hard that he fell back, stunned, sharp flashes of light exploding in his head. The blow had come so fast that the two accomplices dropped John to the ground. An instant later, Ned was astride his chest, raining blows to John's head with both fists. Somehow John got his arms and legs up and thrust Ned off him. Free of Ned's grasp, he tried to make a dash for it but the other two caught him and held him fast.

Ned came up close again. Tearing his arms out of the restraint in which they were held, John attacked first, using his longer reach and greater height to advantage. Blow followed blow, punctuated by gasps and grunts. As a well-aimed punch from John sent Ned staggering, another youth threw himself on John's back and brought him down with a thud. A kick in his groin made John curl up in agony, only to feel more pain as heavy clogs thudded into his kidneys. It flashed through his mind that he was going to die and somehow he didn't care.

Suddenly there was more noise and a confusion of thrashing arms and legs. There was no-one laying in to John. Instead there were two more men in the ditch fighting Ned and his fellow thugs. Pulling himself up, John saw Ben Haigh had pinned one of the two youths against the side of the ditch and was hammering blows at him until he sank down, covering his head with his arms and whimpering.

A few feet away, Eli Haigh was fighting two youths at the same time. Gripping Ned Stott round the throat with his left hand and holding him at arm's length, he lashed out with his right arm with such force that it winded the other youth and felled him where he stood. Turning back to Ned Stott, Eli continued to hold him in a vice-like grip until the younger man, eyes bulging, began to choke. With a snort of contempt, Eli suddenly dropped him. Ned lay helpless on the ground, gasping for breath.

"Just what you'd expect from Ned Stott!" growled Eli. "Only brave enough to fight when he comes three to one." He spat and wiped his mouth with the back of his hand. "Let's get off 'ome."

One of the youths was unconscious, the other pretending to be so. Ned Stott lay still, watching. Eli put out an arm to include John and Ben and the three of them began to move away. They plodded along the ditch together and had almost reached the end of it when there was a quick thudding of feet behind them, then a groan from Eli as Ned punched him, very hard, in the back of the neck, followed by the sound of feet running away.

Eli lay still, face down and silent.

"Has he killed him?" asked John, horrified.

"Nay. But he's knocked him out. With that rabbit punch. We'll have to carry him."

Their progress home was slow. Mercifully, they met no-one. The law-abiding were asleep in their beds; those still abroad on Castle Hill were too engrossed in savagery to notice anything else.

Hannah received the group with remarkable calm. Eli, as the most deserving, was laid gently on the settle, his head and neck dabbed with arnica and herbs until he came to. Apart from the blow to his neck, he was unscathed. Although in his fifties, he was the strongest of the three, his body as hard as weathered oak.

Ben had cuts and bruises on his face and hands but had not suffered much else. When Hannah had cleaned him up, she sent him off to bed where Anne and Rachel had gone some time ago. Making John take off his clothes, she sucked in her breath when she saw the red weals. She dabbed them gently with her lotion.

"I fear you'll be in some pain when you wake tomorrow. I'll make a bed up for you here. You're in no state to go out again tonight."

She looked at Eli who was now sitting up but still slightly groggy.

"Eli. You'd best sit up for a bit before you come to bed. I've heard Rachel say you don't let folk fall asleep right away when they've had a head wound. Do you think I should wake her and ask her advice?"

"Nay," said Eli, trying to look as alert as possible. "I'll talk a bit to John and then come up. It wasn't a killer blow, not from that young weasel."

Hannah had put some more coal on and for a while, the two men sat silently, mugs in their hands, watching the flames spurt and then die down. John was thinking that if he was ever to broach the subject of fatherhood to Eli, this was the moment. Trembling slightly, he began.

"Thank you, Eli, for what you and Ben did tonight."

"Nay, think nothing of it, lad."

Another pause, another deep breath.

"My mother, Martha, told me something. After we buried Walter. She said you were my true father."

Their eyes met, dark brown and blue. Eli sighed, as if releasing some tension.

"I had an idea you might be my lad. You were so much at home here. Good with your hands, like all the Haighs. But Martha never spoke of it. So I didn't either."

"She told nobody. Nobody knew, not Walter, not her family. Nobody, except me."

"I did speak about it to one man," said Eli slowly. "But it will have gone no further. I went to a prayer meeting with Hannah once, to please her, and there was something about the preacher that made you want to open up to him. I was that relieved at confessing that I joined t' Methodists, which pleased Hannah even more."

"Does she know? About me?"

"Who can say? I'd not be surprised. She's a woman who seems to understand everything. But has no need to talk about it." The older man looked tired. "I think I'll be off to bed now, John. You make yourself comfortable down here."

Holding onto the side of the settle, he pulled himself to his feet. John stood up too.

"Goodnight – Eli."

He had meant to say "Father" but it would not come out.

"Goodnight, lad."

John knew it was not the custom in Yorkshire for men to display affection for one another but to make no move seemed churlish. Stepping forward, he embraced his father gently, aware of his own bruises and allowing for Eli's. It was over in a moment.

"Goodnight, lad," said Eli again. He turned and made for the door but not before John had seen his eyes fill with tears.

CHAPTER FOURTEEN

Anne slept late the next morning, only waking when Rachel was leaving for work. Putting on her hat and cloak, she came over to Anne's bed.

"Anne. I should prepare you. John is downstairs. He slept here last night. There was some fighting on Castle Hill."

Anne sat up quickly but Rachel put a hand on her arm.

"Don't worry. They're all a bit bruised, Ben and Father as well, but not seriously."

Washing and dressing without delay, Anne was downstairs in time to join Hannah and John at the table. Ben and Eli were already out, despite Hannah's pleas.

"I've told Eli to come back when they've seen to the beasts. Whether he will or not, I don't know. I suppose he knows how he feels."

John was to be taken home in the cart when Ben returned He had spent a poor night, unable to lie comfortably because of his bruises, but made light of it.

"I'll be as right as rain by tomorrow."

Alone in the house with Hannah, Anne thought the moment had come to try and solve the puzzle of her parents' marriage. Better to face the truth, however unpalatable.

"Hannah. Can I ask you about my mother? And my father?" Sitting in the warm farmhouse kitchen, she told Hannah how she had wondered about her mother's reluctance to discuss the matter, the absence of any marriage lines and the accusation, made by both Jack Stott and Isabel Blezard, that she was illegitimate.

Hannah was offended. "Some people have nowt better to do than say nasty things about other folk! Just a minute." She got up and went upstairs, returning with a cardboard box.

"I've got your mother's letters here which she wrote to me when she first went to London. Had she lived, I'm sure she would have told you all this herself."

There they were. Letters written twenty years ago. It felt strange to see her mother's handwriting on the envelopes. She hardly dare touch them.

"Here," said Hannah, taking the letters out. "I've kept them in order. I'll leave you to read them on your own." She left the room, shutting the door quietly.

The first letters were as Anne expected – descriptions of her mother's new life in London. She spoke of the fine houses, the crowds of people, the shops and the park nearby where she took the children to play with their hoops and balls. She also spoke of feeling homesick, of longing for the fresh air, the green landscape and simplicity of life she had left behind in Yorkshire. Then something new.

"Dear Hannah,

I'm sorry I have been so long in answering your last letter. I do hope little Matthew and Joe have recovered from their colds.

You may remember I told you of the delightful afternoons I spend with the children in the park, whenever the weather is fine. I particularly enjoy the concerts at the bandstand. You know I have always loved brass bands. Just lately it was a military band and I couldn't help noticing a most handsome trumpeter who played his solo like an angel. I think he noticed me as well because in the interval, he came down and chatted to me. His name is Arthur Graham and I found him a most pleasant young man. He is stationed not far away and says he hopes to see me again soon."

The next one, dated two months later, was more emotional.

"Dear Hannah,

Thank you for your letter. I know how busy you are at the farm and with your little boys to look after. And you say you have not been well. Do take care.

I have thought of you often, dear Hannah, in the last few weeks because I so wished you could have been here with me to celebrate. Arthur and I were married three weeks ago and I am happier than I thought possible. The Crowthers are not very pleased, which is understandable, but I cannot think they will find it too difficult to find a replacement. Whereas how could I find such another as Arthur, the dearest man I have ever met?

We began to walk out regularly since first meeting in the park. I had heard about love at first sight but never thought that it would happen to me. We had not planned to wed so soon but Arthur heard that his regiment was to be sent abroad before long. You know they keep these things as quiet as possible. So we decided we would be married and have at least a few weeks together as man and wife.

I have written to Father with the news but I fear he has still not forgiven me for leaving and doesn't answer my letters. I shall wait until I can return to Almondbury for a visit when I am sure I shall be able to patch things up."

The next letter was sober in tone but showed the resilience Anne recognised as part of her mother's character. After conventional opening remarks, it continued.

"Oh, Hannah! I have been so lonely since Arthur left. It is not easy to get post through so apart from one brief letter, I have heard nothing. Still, one knows when one marries a soldier, that this is to be expected.

In the meantime, I have been very fortunate in gaining a position as cook-housekeeper to a Mr Pearson, a lawyer who lives in Victoria Park. As he lives alone (he is a widower), he has no need of much else in the way of domestic staff, though I am to engage a maid of all work if I think it necessary. I have neat rooms in the basement which is not as gloomy as it sounds. The windows are above ground level so I can see people from the waist down as they pass by It is interesting how you soon come to recognise people in this way!"

Dated a month later, the next letter continued her mother's story.

"Dear Hannah,

I have heard people say how hard it is to write a letter when you have no news and nothing to say. Believe me, it is even harder when you have so much news you don't know where to begin.

As I think I said in my last letter, I had heard almost nothing from Arthur but did not worry because he told me it would be so. One day I did receive a letter, not from Arthur but from his Commanding Officer.

He informed me, with regret, that Arthur had died of typhus, not in battle because, as a bandsman, he was a non-combatant, but simply waiting in the barracks to be shipped to their next destination. There was an epidemic apparently and scores of men died. The letter went on to say that Arthur's effects would be sent back to a Regimental Office in London where widows could collect them. I never thought to be a widow so young.

Mr Pearson has been very kind. He said he was very pleased with the way I had carried out my duties and hoped I would continue to work for him. I thanked him but felt I had to tell him that I believed I was with child. If this was the case, perhaps he would prefer me to leave. He was somewhat taken aback but said he would have no objection to my staying seeing that he was out all day and the house big enough for us not to disturb him.

At the moment I should like nothing better than to be back home with you, Hannah, telling you my troubles by your fireside. I will write again when I have decided what to do."

It was another two months before Emma Graham wrote again. This time, there was an enclosure with the letter.

"Dear Hannah,

I am writing to tell you that I have decided to stay in London as Mr Pearson's housekeeper and have the baby here.

Yes, it is confirmed and I have made some good friends in the neighbourhood who I know will help me when my time comes.

I wrote to Father to tell him of Arthur's death and the expected child but he has not replied. His silence strengthens my decision to stay here and make a new life for myself and the child in London.

I count myself very fortunate to have such an understanding employer as Mr Pearson. I have seen poor creatures on the streets who have nowhere to go but the workhouse and know how lucky I am, especially after my visit to Arthur's Regimental Office last week.

I had to fill in a form declaring who I was, giving the date and place of our marriage and so on. Then I sat and waited for a long time while an officer went to find Arthur's records and bring me his effects. I was not feeling very well that day, quite faint.

At last the man returned, carrying only a sheet of paper. He said, without showing any feeling of any kind, that another Mrs Graham had already collected Arthur's effects. When I expressed disbelief, he showed me the place on the form where it said 'Date of Marriage'. Oh Hannah! It was not our date but one over three years ago when he had married someone else!

What happened next I'm not sure because I did faint. After that, another man in uniform, a kinder one than the other, helped me into a cab and paid the driver to take me home. How I should have got back without it I do not know.

I have been turning everything over and over in my mind and trying to make sense of it. I can only think that Arthur loved the excitement of falling in love and where I was concerned, knew we had to be married if we were to love each other fully. What he did was very wrong but I do think he loved me and nothing can destroy the memory of the little happiness we shared. And this child of his will never lack love for one moment. I shall see to that.

So you see, Hannah, it is better that I stay here. No-one knows but you of Arthur's bigamy. Will you keep my marriage lines for me? When I look at them, they remind me of my folly and my pain. But somehow I cannot destroy them. Please write back and tell me you understand."

Pushing the correspondence and the tightly folded marriage certificate to one side, Anne put her head down on the table and wept. After a while, she felt Hannah's arm round her shoulders and a token of comfort, a buttered scone, pushed in her direction.

"Now come on, eat this. You need to eat something if you're going to impress that Mrs Shaw."

"Oh Hannah! Thank you for letting me read these! Thank God you kept them!"

"How could I not? She was my dearest friend." Hannah took out a handkerchief and blew her nose. "Now look sharp and get down to the Blezards. Teachers mustn't be late. And keep all these papers. They belong to you more than they do to me."

It was just on eleven o'clock when Anne arrived, pink and breathless, at the Blezards' house and was shown straight in to meet Mrs Shaw in the drawing-room. She was as Anne expected her to be, a dignified, middle-aged woman with a pleasant manner underpinned by an air of authority.

The interview went well. Mrs Shaw had no trouble with the fact that Anne had previously taught only younger children, and seemed impressed by the breadth of her reading and her views on the education of young women. Only at the end of the interview was some doubt expressed. It was clear that Mrs Shaw was embarrassed.

"Miss Graham. I hesitate to mention this but feel I must. One family have told me that they were considering withdrawing their daughter's application for enrolment. They have heard rumours about the dubious background of a young woman known to be applying for the post of my assistant – yourself, in other words. I dismissed the suggestion as idle gossip but should be glad to hear any explanation you may have."

Anne took a deep breath and replied as calmly as she could.

"I think you will find that the rumour was started maliciously by a woman who had occasion to dislike me. Do you want me to give you her name?"

"No, that is not necessary. Although if I receive any similar complaints, perhaps I may ask you for it?"

"Of course. I suppose the dubious background in question means that my parents were not married?"

"I imagine so."

"I think you will find the accusation groundless. I happen to have my mother's marriage lines with me at the moment."

Anne took out the folded piece of paper, aware, as she did so, that its legality was questionable. But when it was written, her mother had believed it to be true. In her heart, Emma Ramsden had married Arthur Graham. That was good enough for Anne.

Mrs Shaw glanced at it briefly before handing it back.

"Thank you, my dear. I am sorry to have mentioned such a delicate matter."

"Not at all, Mrs Shaw."

The older woman smiled pleasantly.

"I shall be most pleased, Miss Graham, if you would take up the post of assistant teacher as planned. Term will begin early next year, assuming that all the necessary work will have been completed by then."

Anne stood up and shook Mrs Shaw's hand warmly.

"Thank you very much, Mrs Shaw. I am most happy to accept. You may contact me at the Haighs' farm or through Charlotte at this address."

In the corridor, Charlotte was hovering with a look of expectancy.

"Did everything go well? Did she engage you?"

"Yes, she did! Where is Isabel?"

"Leaving! Soon! Bag and baggage!"

Anne beamed back at her friend.

"Come up later and tell me all."

Anne covered the steep ground between Wood Lane and the Haighs' farm with surprising ease. In her bag she carried the marriage certificate. Should she tell John about it or not? Perhaps there were always secrets of some kind, even between the happiest of couples.

It all went according to plan - Isabel's plan.

By midnight, the house was silent, the staff all asleep in the servants' quarters. Wearing soft shoes, Isabel stole downstairs, her full skirts brushing against the banister rails, her feet meeting carpet and then the smooth tiles of the hall floor. Moonlight filtered through the engraved glass panels of the front door, casting patterns on the dado, slantwise on the wall.

Parlour, dining-room, library. Isabel glided from one room to another, turning the brass doorknobs of the heavy doors with both hands so as to make no noise. It did not take long; she knew the items she wanted. Gathering them up, she went back upstairs time and time again, her arms full. Finally, the hall itself yielded up its only treasure.

She slept lightly and fitfully that night; she could not afford to do otherwise. As dawn was breaking, she went downstairs again, this time opening the door to the two poorly-dressed men who stood there, packers from Broomfield's factory. Without a word, they followed her upstairs and immediately set to work packing the goods into the tea-chests they had brought with them. They worked fast, with the errorless speed of professionals, bending, wrapping, pushing the items into places which seemed made for them.

It took them no more than twenty minutes to complete the task. When they had finished, they began carrying the goods downstairs, returning for the numerous trunks and valises which the maids had filled with her clothes and personal possessions the day before. A few moments later, the sleepy coachman brought the carriage round to the side door. Again while Isabel watched, the workmen loaded up the carriage. Then they took the coins she proffered and left as silently as they had come.

There was no leave-taking. Wrapped in her warmest clothes, Isabel clambered inside and sank down against the leather upholstery, luggage pressing against her on all sides. It was only just becoming daylight. With the sound of horses' hooves and the crunching of heavy wheels on the gravel, the carriage ground slowly up the drive and out into the road. The four tea-chests were strapped and lashed outside. Each bore a label which read "PROPERTY OF MRS ISABEL BLEZARD."

That evening Anne flew along the lane from the farm and made for the crest of Castle Hill as fast as she could. Up, up she went, up the steep grassy slopes in the twilight, the first lights of Huddersfield twinkling away in the distance down below her, stumbling when her feet met stone poking through the paths and pausing only to catch her breath before she resumed her uphill climb. Would John be there already on the summit? Tonight she would tell him the good news, that Isabel had gone, perhaps for ever.

For a dreadful moment, she could see nothing but the bare outline of the earthworks and then, suddenly, to her great joy, she saw him standing on the rim of the summit, outlined against the sky, his hair flying, his jacket open to the wind. When he saw her coming, he turned and opened his arms wide. She ran towards him, although she could hardly breathe, and threw herself against him. They stood locked together, not needing words, while the wind roared around them. Then they looked at each other in joyous wonder, kissed and then clasped one another tight again as if they could not bear to let the other go. The despair and heartbreak of the past vanished as if it had never been.

How long they stood, their hearts beating as one in their embrace, it was impossible to know. Eventually, over John's shoulder, Anne watched the sun sink to its rest behind the distant hills. Hand in hand, they crossed the summit and began their way back, to a new beginning and a new life.

Printed in the United Kingdom
by Lightning Source UK Ltd.
134878UK00001B/265-291/A